THE DREAM POLICE

Select other works by Randy Blazak

Fiction
The Mission of the Sacred Heart: A Rock Novel (2011, CreateSpace Books)
"Elvis is My Rider" in *A Matter of Words* (2015, Scout Media)
"Ants of Uranus!" in *A Journey of Words* (2016, Scout Media)

Non-fiction
Renegade Kids, Suburban Outlaws, with Wayne S. Wooden (2001, Wadsworth Publishing)
Hate Crime: Issues and Perspectives (2009, Praeger Publishing)

Blog: https://watchingthewheelsdad.net
Twitter: @rblazak

THE DREAM POLICE

A Rock Novel

Randy Blazak

CreateSpace Books

ISBN-13: *978-1536835489*

ISBN-10: *153683548X*

CreateSpace Books

Printed in the USA

Cover painting by: Andrea Barrios

To HR ladies, everywhere.

ACKNOWLEDGEMENTS

This book was written during one of the most challenging periods of my life, as if in a dream. Its predecessor, *The Mission of the Sacred Heart*, was written in my house while on healthy doses of Zoloft. *The Dream Police* was written on lots of coffee in some of my favorite cafés, including Random Order in Portland, Café Mogagua on Isla Mujeres, Mexico and Caffé Dante in Greenwich Village, New York. Every step of the way I was supported by my talented wife, Andi Barrios. The best writing sessions were in our Portland home, The Southern Comfort, while she painted, Cozy slept, and we drained a bottle of Oregon pinot.

The structure of this book was inspired by the 1979 Cheap Trick album, *Dream Police*. I have to thank Robin Zander, Rick Nielsen, Tom Petersson and Bun E. Carlos for writing and recording the music that fueled my imagination when I was 15 years old. A special thanks to Holland Zander Jutras for connecting me to one of the greatest rock bands in the world.

All the dreams in this book are based on real dreams had by real people. Most are mine but I'd like to thank all my friends who submitted their dreams to me on Facebook.

This book has had some great support from folks I truly admire. I appreciate the support of Brian Paone of Scout Media, Andrew Miscoe, Holly Aguirre, and Jessica Baumann for the copyediting and Elizabeth Carlton Chase, who is writing the screenplay for *Mission*.

This book would not exist without the 195 people who contributed to the 2015 Kickstarter project to fund this writing project. A very special thank you to Kathryn West, Heather Dunn, Haynes Brooke, James Barber, Holly Aguirre, Ana Ammann, Katie Paden Sturdivant, Edward Overstreet, Michael Overstreet, Steve Wickham, Robert Peacock (who all got amazing paintings from Andrea); and John Haus, Sally Cersosimo, Delia Rae Saldivar, Rovena Cardiel, Doug DeLoach, Christina Holding, Takako Saito, Shannon Kettering, Peter McDade, A.J. Arriola, Laura John, Shahiyar Smith, Laurie Garner, Eli Allman, Larry Fish, Sonja Taylor, Joelle Davis, Dave Sobel, Elena Lauterbach, Jules Cozine, Tim McEvoy, Maria O'Shea, Gwyn Fletcher,

Barbara Leedom Young, Vivian Alverez, Scott Long, Kara Sanborn, Raechel Packard, Lynn Martineau, Julie Pristach Rosenthale, Chris Elicone, Anna Jensen, Joya Misra, and Kevin Warren. Thank you to all who contributed to making this book possible.

Finally, I would like to thank Cozette, my little daughter, for proving that dreams come true.

Note: There are no page numbers in this book because, in the dreamworld, you never know where you really are.

Table of Contents

"Life's lived least when you don't let go of a memory, of a dream." (Parquet Courts)

Chapter 1: Dream Police

1

Time is bedspring that bends around itself. It pushes itself towards older coils but never actually touches them. Just close enough to feel the magnetic pull of the physical through the conceptual. We try to straighten it out for our own intentions, but as we sleep, it returns to its original form, designed by forces we will never begin to understand.

A crack of white light flashes against a dirty panel of ceramic tiles. His face slams against a post but he keeps his footing. The dim expansive room is knee deep in streaming water, coming in waves from all angles. The steamy air seems opaque but is gashed with velvet red streaks. It isn't a room, it is a subway station. The flickering fluorescent bulbs give fiery glimpses of semi-submerged turnstiles and the yellowish-white tiles that every commuter in New York City sees as the background color of their work week. But this is a subway station at the end of the world.

"Shit! What am I doing here?" thinks Zak. The station is empty and the ceiling is creaking and bowing, like the hull of the Titanic going under the North Atlantic. There is rumbling and muffled screaming but no people. He knows exactly where he is; the station below the World Trade Center.

He had been there once as a kid on a family trip. The Twin Towers were the modern giants from the King Kong movie (the one with Jeff Bridges, not Jack Black or Fay Wray). He and his mom sat on a planter staring up at them, eating donuts and watching all the morning commuters pouring out of the station below. In waves of thousands, as if all the burrowing animals and insects were escaping the earth, they came to the surface world, wearing sneakers and carrying their work shoes in their hands, grabbing coffees off a counter without ever slowing down. Thousands of beehive workers on their way to some office in the giant skyscrapers that King Kong climbed. When the towers fell in 2001, he wondered how many of those people from that morning had returned to dirt.

Suddenly, he's here and the buildings are coming down on him at any minute. Flashes behind his head. His skin burns without feeling heat. A woman in a grey business suit rushes by in the torrential waters that are filling up the station. She is screaming for help. Zak reaches out to her but she is yards away. He closes his eyes after he sees her back break against the turnstile as the water heads for the deeper platforms. There is no exit, only the knowledge of this historical fact, that on this day he will be crushed by one and half million tons of concrete, steel, and human flesh. He lets go.

When he opens his eyes, a ledge has appeared on the upper western wall of the station, like a narrow mountain pass. It is a mountain! In subterranean lower Manhattan! A mountain above the tree line but safe from the waters that are pulling Zak down to the electrified tracks. His feet are knocked out from under him. He's ready to be crushed, drowned or ripped apart by the metal debris filling the station. But there is a figure on the ledge in a white uniform. It's a cop.

"Follow my voice! I'm going to get you out of here! This is not the day you die!" The cop was calm, like he knew that Zak was in Portland and not New York on 9/11. "Push your way towards me!" Zak begins using the debris, that now included mangled body parts, like a ladder, dragging himself towards the ledge. He sees the faces of people that he knew; family members, high school friends, musicians, and Claire, his late wife. He clutches his chest. Then come the babies, some floating face down and others face up, with eyes closed, most with umbilical cords still attached. Their bodies are mixed with children's toys: mangled Barbies, rubber ducks and laughing Elmos. He gasps and inhales what feels like a quart of tasteless oily water. He moans a soulful wail as tears stream out. And then his body lifts out of the water, floating safely above the flotsam.

As the beams crack and the explosions get louder he finds himself on the dirt bank, inches away from the mountain path. Behind him is water and flame and, like a scene from Dante's *Inferno*, bodies floating down to the depths below, some crying, most already dead. In front of him, just before the bend in the path is the cop, with his white uniform. "I told you so," says the cop before walking away.

Hitler's not always funny. In fact, hardly ever. Charlie Chaplin once said that if he knew what Hitler was really up to, he never would have made *The Great Dictator* in 1940, one of the greatest political satires ever filmed. Adenoid Hynkel was hysterical. Adolf Hitler, not so much.

But most guys have a Hitler moment. Not a genocidal maniac with one testicle moment, but a Hitler mustache moment. It comes when it's time to shave off the winter beard or ill-advised handlebar mustache. It's a moment that became even more common with the invention of "Movember," or "No-Shave November" when countless men use a vague cause of "men's health issues" to get lazy with their faces. When December first hits, there is a flurry of weathermen and high school math teachers getting back to the business of manscaping.

There are plenty of ways to shave it all off; top to bottom, right to left, try out a goatee for a minute or side-chops. Then there is the Hitler. It should be the Charlie Chaplin, but that fucker Hitler ruined that little stache forever. "I wonder what I would look like with Hitler mustache," has thought almost every guy ever. (Including Jewish guys. Maybe *especially* Jewish guys.) So for a second or two, they give themselves a touch of evil and imagine commanding Panzer divisions into Poland. And then, before anybody can see this obviously sick fascistic fantasy, quickly scrape it off and go for a clean start.

That's why this morning was funny, but not in a 'ha-ha' sort of way. Okay, maybe 'ha-ha.' Zak had given up shaving after the accident. After his pregnant wife had been killed, his depression came back with a roaring vengeance. It's fairly typical.

He stopped eating right and started drinking wrong, and became a bum. Some of his students had begun calling him the "hobo professor" and his chili peppers on RateMyProfessor.com were replaced by emojis of skunks. The right leg limp added to the effect. So the beard was easy. Professors had beards, so he wore it as a mask to hide his sad, aging face, now asymmetrical from the brain injury. Anyway, beards were as common in Portland as rain and the bulldozing of black neighborhoods, so nobody noticed.

But that sadness was all behind him. Enough time hanging out in bereavement forums on the internet. Enough of seeing Claire's face on every pregnant woman he passed. Enough of barely saying "fine" when anyone (everyone) asked him how he was doing. Enough of closing his eyes and trying to jet back in time. He was ready to move on. The year of mourning was over and there had to be plenty of happiness ahead, right? That was the lesson from before. It was time to shave the beard off. He took his electric razor and went bottom to top, starting with his neck, then his cheeks, then his chin. All that grey and brown sadness fell from his face on to a newspaper he had placed in the bathroom sink. "I wonder what I would look like with a Hitler mustache?" he thought.

He worked his remaining facial hair into a perfect square under his nose and turned the razor off to admire himself at his most politically incorrect. He stomped his foot and gave the Heil Hitler salute, uttering some broken German he remembered from reruns of *Hogan's Heroes*. "Gott im Himmel, mein herr!" His smile (on the side of his face that fully worked) snuck out as he felt ashamed at the rush of authoritarianism. It's just Hitler.

Okay, enough. Time to finish the spring facial cleaning. Here's the funny part. Zak's razor wouldn't turn back on. It was old and chose that moment to drop dead. And there were no straight razors in the house. Not even one of Claire's old Lady Bics. He was already running late to teach the first day of his Public Health Policy class and instead of being Mr. Fresh Start he looked like Der Fuhrer. How could he walk into the classroom like this? The university's Human Resources director would be speed dialed before he could hand out the syllabus.

"What the fuck?" Zak sunk at his seemingly endless bad luck. One step forward, two steps back. He could not get out of the ditch. The only people this look might be appreciated by were the neo-Nazi inmates who were participating in his prison hepatitis study. On top of this, he was supposed to meet a former student for coffee to discuss careers in public health research and she was not a Nazi, she was Asian. Could he just cancel the whole day?

He crumpled up the paper with all his non-Hitler trimmings and threw it in the bathroom trashcan. Since all his maybe helpful neighbors were all gone, he decided to make a mad dash to Walgreens on his way to work for shaving supplies. "Now would be a good time to have tinted windows," he mused, quickly climbing into his car.

At a red light on Northeast Broadway Street, an anarchist on a bike saw the little Hitler in a black Acura and spit on his windshield, screaming something about fucking Nazis. Zak sat there, staring at the spit drip down the window until the car behind him laid on the horn. Then his phone rang. It was Lenny, the one guy who could lighten his mood, calling from Seattle. He put it on speaker and hit the gas.

"Dude, what are you up to?" Lenny sounded close by.

"Looking like Hitler."

"Du fuh?"

"I was shaving my beard off and my razor died before I finished." Zak had to laugh as he said this.

"Oh, you did the Hitler? Dude, that's always the risk you take when you do the Hitler."

"Yeah, thanks. I gotta buy a razor and some shaving cream and shave in the car before I go to class. What's up?"

"Hey, I'm coming down to Portland this weekend to see some bands and wanted to see if you wanted to hook up," said Lenny.

"Yeah, I suppose. Let's hang out. Hey, I had another 9/11 dream last night."

Lenny paused. "Man, I always hate when people talk about their dreams but your dreams are so fucked-up, it's better than Netflix."

Like anybody born before 1990, Lenny had a 9/11 connection. Some people were in planes that were grounded on that day. More people knew people killed in the attacks. Everybody over the age of 20 knew where they were when it happened. Lenny's story was that he was on the 107th floor of the North Tower of the World Trade Center from 4 to 9 pm on September 10, 2001.

His band, Sort Of, was being signed to Interlope Records. It was the great leap forward they had all been working towards. The label had flown the band and their manager, Dax, to New York for the big signing. Lenny brought his wife, Cozy, along so she could see the Metropolitan Opera House, where she hoped to perform someday. The future was wide open. Only good times ahead. Everyone felt it, including the label that saw Sort Of as the perfect band for the new century.

It was agreed the signing should be someplace symbolic of this optimism. Andy, the drummer, wanted it to be at Shea Stadium. "No, on top of a skyscraper," said Lenny. "We are only going to the top!" The A&R woman at Interlope suggested the perfect place, Windows on the World, the restaurant on the 107th floor of the World Trade Center. "That is perfect!" said the band.

So on Monday, the label execs headed down from West 57th Street and met the band who was already sitting at the circular bar, with Dax and Cozy. The Greatest Bar on Earth was its name. Perfect. The stars were aligned. And there, as the late summer dusk fell over Brooklyn, they ate tapas and drank champagne and signed the paperwork, discussed producers and album covers and the infinite possibilities of being the next big thing. Afterwards, on the elevator ride down, Cozy threw up a little bit but caught it in her hand.

The next morning the hang-over dream began. Their hotel in Chelsea jolted, then people began screaming. "We're under attack!" and "They're jumping out of the windows!" Cozy woke up first. Dax was banging on the door. Lenny rolled over to go back to sleep. Zak was calling on the flip phone.

"What the hell? Can't a guy sleep in?"

"Len, wake up! Something is happening. Something really bad," said his wife, her face bluish white like a ghost.

Suddenly they were extras in *Independence Day*, but with no Will Smith to save them. The band congregated in the hotel lobby in front of the TV, and then ran into the streets when the towers fell. The ash of 3,000 souls caking in the corners of their eyes. Cozy fell to her knees and wept and vomited out the dust into the monochrome street. The world as they knew it was ending on a pristine September morning. There would be no waking up.

Lenny was paralyzed by the attacks. He couldn't write songs. The guys in the band couldn't write songs. When they finally went into the studio in Portland, they fell back on their tried-and-true set list, intelligent party songs that sampled the fifty-year history of rock and roll. But they weren't in the mood. When their debut album, *Yeah, No*, was released the following April, it stiffed. America didn't want post-modern pastiche, they wanted war songs. They wanted Nickelback with some J-Lo on the side for the troops.

Sort Of was done for. The label wrote them off as a tax loss. Interlope had lost the enthusiasm for the band, especially after one the young interns had to go back to the World Trade Center to take care of the band's bar tab and was never seen again. The five musicians soldiered on, but the moment was gone. The climate had changed. The new century was going to suck. The bubble bursting killed Zak as well. This was the band that was going to change the face of rock music. He was looking forward to being close to the center of a phenomenon, with dear Cozy, watching it unfold from the inside.

The start of the summer of 2002, Cozy and Lenny had a baby. But Lenny wasn't there for the birth. It was Zak who held her hand. Lenny couldn't give up his rock star ways and dealt with his disappointment by slinking back into the womanizing that ran his life before Cozy. At first, his pregnant wife hoped it was only a post-9/11 phase. But when Lenny slept with Cozy's doula it was over. They were history. Cozy had a little boy named Daniel, moved to Washington DC and got a job working at the

Kennedy Center for the Performing Arts. The divorce was signed by the end of summer, on September 11th.

2

All those years piled up on Zak and Lenny, but they stayed friends. After a few more (better) albums on an indy label, Sort Of broke up. Lenny moved to Seattle and got a job in music licensing where he had a succession of girlfriends, none as talented as his ex-wife. Zak finished his Masters and got a faculty job at the teaching hospital, teaching public health policy and doing research on at-risk populations, first with homeless youth and then with inmates. He finally completed his dissertation and became Dr. Crisp.

That's how he met Claire. She was a counselor at a state prison and was helping Zak to understand the inner workings of correctional institutions, which could be petri dishes of diseases. Zak wanted to begin looking at inmate health behaviors and how they brought things like hepatitis with them when they walked out of the gate to freedom. Claire and Zak bonded over their common romantic dead ends, their love of weird music and strong desire to make the jump out of the endless adolescence of American culture into adulthood. So they got married.

One mad day they drove down to Reno and got married at the Sands Regency Casino. The two hundred dollars they won on the roulette wheel after the ceremony was taken as a sign of good things to come. Claire was pregnant a month later. Everything was coming together. The grey fog was in the distant past, like a forgotten novel that goes eternally unsold at Goodwill.

Professor Crisp looked out at the Portland skyline from his office at the university. It had become a forest of construction cranes covering the city that Zak loved. New towers sprouted like giant mushrooms from the wave of money moving back in after the economy recovered from the crash of 2008. Old dive bars were now condo towers. Old record stores were now office towers. It seemed like the city planners were in as much of a hurry to forget the past as he was. The city of roses had become the city of weeds. Very expensive weeds.

He met his former student, Kiko, for coffee after his last class, without his Hitler mustache. She had been coming to his office hours to discuss career options and share her anime drawings, something Zak was mildly interested in. She was semi-good looking with a petite frame and light brown eyes, but Zak never noticed, lost in the funk of Claire's death. His students saw the funk and were afraid to approach him because of the menacing black cloud over his head. Everyone knew what happened. But Kiko wasn't afraid. She often popped in to his office to talk about classes and banal J-pop culture. He saw her as a friend when every friend he had reminded him of his dead wife.

"Hello, Professor," she said, bobbing into the campus coffee shop.

"Hi, Kiko. You can call me Zak now. You're not my student anymore."

"How are you today, sir? Happy or sad?"

"I think I'm happy today. How about you?"

"Happy to see you!"

They talked a little bit about health research jobs in the city and abroad. Kiko had vague plans to work in Japan. They talked more about monster movies and animation. In his loneliness, he began to think it would be okay to at least invite her out for a bite. Some new thoughts to fill his head. Maybe he could meet up with her in Tokyo some day. His mind began to wander. How had his life lost its game-plan so severely?

"Professor? Are you okay?"

"Yeah, sorry. I tend to drift off. Don't take it personally. I'm planning out my lectures in my head."

"No, you weren't. I know what you need. Sushi!"

Her squeaky little voice lifted Zak out of his drone and he thought it might be a good idea. So the two made a plan to meet at a sushi bar downtown the next night. Kiko promised to show him how to not eat sushi like an American, which meant he would be eating sea urchin instead of California Rolls. It seemed like an appropriate diversion. Not a date. Just sushi. She seemed harmless enough, an ambassador from the child-like land of Hello Kitty.

Kiko Matsugane was not actually Japanese. She was Korean but changed her name in college when she became obsessed with popular culture in Japan, including the bizarre world of Japanese porn. She came to Portland a year prior to study public health, and maybe stay in the US or get a job in Japan. She didn't really have much direction. She was a slight thing, and blew around with the wind like a dandelion seed looking for a place to root down.

Portland, like much of the west coast, had a close relationship with Asia. It was most evident in Vancouver, BC, where the Chinese with money fled after the takeover of Hong Kong at the end of the twentieth century. But all the way down to San Diego there were enclaves of every Asian ethnic group and nationality, from Hmong to Cantonese. Some were the descendants of nineteenth century workers who suffered some of harshest brutality America had to offer. In 1887, more than thirty Chinese workers were murdered and mutilated for their gold in a part of Eastern Oregon that is now known as Chinese Massacre Cove. Just another day on the west coast. Some are the grandchildren of Japanese Internment Camp inmates or Vietnamese boat people. Some are fresh off the plane to attend college or sign up for English immersion courses. All Zak knew was that there were three Thai restaurants within five blocks of his house.

Kiko spent most of her time in Portland inside her stark apartment, living online instead of in her new city. She maintained a number of online social networking sites, was a moderator on several Reddit groups dealing with Japanese animation and erotica, and wrote a blog about her imaginary adventures in America. She existed on her laptop which served to retard her social skills. Like a home schooled kid who "graduates" and enrolls in an online university, she was not sharp with social cues. But she was smart enough to know that Americans had a fetish for Asian females in short skirts who giggled and squeaked. When doors needed to be opened, that usually did the trick.

Zak was holding the copy of the *Oregonian* that had the story about the crash in his hand. It was wrapped around something soft and wet, like a chicken breast. He watched the drips hit the floor in slow motion. The splashes were beautiful, mini Jackson Pollocks. He realized the paper was wrapped around his heart.

In her office, Kelly Claiborne updated her new profile on the university website. "Vice Provost for Professional Development." It sounded quite impressive. Kelly was a social climber who rose through the professorial ranks fairly quickly after giving up the economic dead end of academia. University administration was where the six-figure salaries were and her flirtation with the university president hadn't hurt. At age fifty-five she had finally broken through the glass ceiling to become the top dog of the human resources department. It wasn't that much of a glass ceiling, since most of the people who ranked in HR were older white women, but it seemed like something important. She rocked back in her pleather chair and wove her bony fingers together.

Kelly understood the grab-ass world of office politics. She had smiled through most of it but bore a resentment at the way men advanced up the ladder with less effort (and less hair dye). The old boys network was still firmly entrenched and if women were to get anywhere they were expected to be twice as ruthless as the men. It was the sixties version of feminism that said a woman can do anything a man can, including being a prick or a serial killer. Kelly was going to beat them at their own game.

Her new position was a bit of a hollow victory. She really had no one to share it with, other than her cats. Her husband was long gone. He had connected with a younger woman and split because Kelly was "married to her job" and "no fun anymore." Everywhere she looked she saw men her age with younger women and it made her seethe. Just the feeling of being put out to pasture. Traded in for a newer model. If her life expectancy was 80, she had another 25 years to offer. But men her age were chasing cute young things. In tribal societies, women with age and wisdom were sought out. Not in America, the land of spinsters and old maids. At least President Woodbine paid her some eye service.

He had created the position for her and the rumors flew that there was some hanky panky going on in the Admin Building. It was half true. At last year's holiday party there was some kissing and groping in his office with promise of more to come. Kelly was delighted a man her age even looked at her, especially one who could advance her career so directly. And it was a position that would give her considerable power over all the employees of the university, including those self-important professors. She imagined her desk as the center of a fiefdom that she would rule with an iron fist. On her desk she kept a picture of herself with President Obama, but in her desk she kept a small picture of Joseph Stalin.

Kelly admired the view from her sixth floor window before calling it a day. The highway was jammed with people headed home to their families, some stopping at local bars for a few happy hour cocktails. She thought of the young women who would be targeted by boozy businessmen for impolite propositions before heading back to the wife. For some reason, the image reminded her to pick up cat food and a box of Franzia on the way home.

3

Zak was feeling self-conscious about his non-date with Kiko. Now that the beard was gone, his twisted face was a reminder of what he had lost. He often wished he was the one who had died instead of being put into a blissful coma. He felt like a twenty-first century Elephant Man. "I am not an animal. I am a human being!" The last year had slipped by like a semi-lucid dream. Thank God for good healthcare benefits that covered therapy.

He began attending a grief support group at the Marky Center, but, at first, it was too much. Gradually, it became a comfort to share and have a place to openly cry, even if he said nothing. They were like a little club who knew the true depth of despair. He didn't have to fake it and he could share his gnawing fears without anyone saying, "Oh, it will get better. Time heals." Fuck that noise. His brain injury made him worry he would forget her and the dream of their child. Or that he would remember - but incorrectly. There were times he mixed his memories of Claire up with old episodes of *The West Wing*. Did he ever refer to her as "Madame Secretary"? It's possible. Most of all he worried he would forget what it felt like to be in the room with her.

Zak was ready for a new emotion, even if was fear. The dwelling was a drag into a tape loop. Over and over again. Like B'rer Rabbit punching the tar baby, once he started throwing fists at the past, he was back in a world of hurt. Staring at her pictures on Facebook was self-inflicted torture. Anything was better than slicing open that vein again. Some mindless babble with Kiko over who was the best Japanese monster (Gamera) and some toxic wasabi would be a different vector to explore.

He didn't know what to wear so he stayed in his work clothes, sans tie, and met her in front of Fuko's, a medium-priced sushi bar in Portland's tony Pearl District. Zak liked it because it had a sushi boat going around the bar and nobody really knew how long some of that fish had been circling. It made it like a bacteria-sickness version of Russian Roulette. A little gamble with your sashimi.

"Hello, Professor!" She was skipping down the street. Literally.

"Zak, please call me Zak." He noticed her thigh high stockings that stopped just below her skirt and began to have second thoughts about the whole thing. Kiko had told him that the Japanese anime term for this flash of flesh was zettai ryōiki ("absolute territory") and that fact gave his eyes permission to linger for a split second.

"Okay, Dr. Zak. Let's eat sushi!" She sounded like one of the Powerpuff Girls.

They went in and Kiko began grabbing plates off of the little boats. Zak almost gagged on the uni but covered like he enjoyed it. They discussed the world of Japanese gravure models and which monster was the best (MechaGodzilla) and generally had a fun time floating in the superficial.

"Professor, why do you stay in Portland?"

The question caught him off guard. He didn't have an answer. He had a million answers. Because he liked the music in the city. Because he felt he couldn't get a better job anywhere else. Because he liked the healthcare benefits that covered his therapy. Because of the coffee and record stores. Because of his memories of her. Because he couldn't physically move.

It felt like his seat at the sushi bar grew arms and hands that held him in place. His feet were stuck to spilled soy sauce on the floor. The ginger slid out of the bowl and covered his mouth. There was no leaving this place ever. The hostess locked the door and everyone stared at him like we was a registered sex offender. The uni began to crawl out of his stomach.

"I don't know. I guess I just like it," he said.

"You seem so sad here, sir. You should go someplace happy."

"Where would that be?"

"Tokyo!" she chirped.

The idea of being as far away from this spot had it's appeal. It would be like being on another planet. He could drift away on a rice boat with a bottle of sake under the flashing neon signs and start over.

"Yeah, I'm not sure Japan is the place for me. Maybe Hawaii. I've always wanted to surf in Waikiki."

After dinner he felt he should invite Kiko for a drink since there was a swank lounge across the street. So they dodged a streetcar and went for a nightcap.

Sitting at the bar, he had a scotch & Coke. She had a Lemon Drop and pretended she was tipsy so she could kiss his cheek. It was the side of his face that was numb from the stroke so he didn't feel it, but appreciated the act of kindness anyway.

Kelly was at the Portland Airport. She knew this by the iconic green and blue carpet below her leather boots. In fact, she was all in leather, in a dominatrix outfit. Leather, or rubber, or pleather. She looked like Catwoman, her jet black hair streaming out from under her mask, but no one seemed to notice. There were only men on the concourse. Businessmen. The lights were dimmer than normal and there was familiar music playing. It was Barry Manilow singing, "Looks Like We Made It." Her outfit creaked as she looked for a target. Each man she touched with her crop silently fell to his knees.

That night Zak couldn't get to sleep. There were two forces conspiring to keep him in the waking world. The first was Kiko. What was he doing? He wasn't that interested in her but she was acting interested and seemed to want something physical. He still knew the signs. But it felt like a betrayal to Claire, or to the memory of Claire. People would understand, right? It's just fun. Something light. After a year of crying he could have something light. She was leaving Portland at some point, so it would seem there was little risk of getting stuck in the muck.

The other thing was his dream life. Since the accident, his dreams had become incredibly vivid. Short drops into the alternate universe of grey matter. His dreams felt like they were stitched together with gossamer and Christmas lights and existed before long before he entered the spasmodic scenes. He was lowered into their disjointed realities to spend a few moments believing all was as it should be. He put the surreal excursions down to the brain injury from the accident, which led to the stroke and the thankful release of a short coma. While in that coma, they made their first appearance.

They were usually in white uniforms, three or four figures. There was often no clear gender, but usually appearing as men. They appeared in his dreams as authority figures or guides, like benevolent police officers. He wasn't sure. But not always benevolent. Sometimes they held him down or forced him to look at things. They spied on him during the day and then took him to task for his thoughts at night. Judge and jury all in one.

It was a trade off, because in dreams, she was often there. Claire would visit him in his dreams and remind him that she was close by. The visions were comforting because he missed her so much. They also served to hold him in an inverted daydream. She wasn't really dead, just gone, someday to return. Then those men inside his brain would make him look at the ugliest truth he could imagine; the one he never actually saw with his own eyes.

Zak was smart enough to know that dreams were the subconscious letting loose. Freud was obsessed with the idea that dreams gave the dreamer clues to what was really going on in their brain. But Zak's dreams were starting to fatigue him.

Sometimes he looked forward to the adventure, safe in his bed. But most times he woke up feeling like he had run a marathon and still had to figure out what the hell it all meant. He was missing her even more. It was like a vomit-inducing roller coaster ride that never ended.

There were a lot mornings like that.

But tonight he didn't want to deal with it. He didn't want to think about Kiko or have another run in with his dream police. He just wanted seven hours of dead-to-the-world sleep. Of course that didn't happen.

Lenny was on stage. He was *always* on stage. Sometimes he would forget the words to a song or the audience would ignore him. But he was always on stage and Cozy was always in the audience, looking at him with scorn. "You're a million miles away when you're here," her face read.

Tonight she was leaving with a tall guy. Through the loud music, she looked at Lenny and said, "He's better looking than you and has a better job. I bet his dick is bigger, too." And she walked away. Lenny had to finish the song. That was his job. He knew he should run after her. That's what she wanted. But he had to finish the song and start the next one.

Zak was is some biblical scene. Maybe it was on the Sea of Galilee. He was a fisherman on the shore. He could hear Claire and a crying baby inside the house. Zak was recruiting men to help him fish, because flying dinosaurs ate the last boatload. They were still hovering overhead, so nobody wanted to fish. Four men in white robes were there telling him he had to get men to fish to provide for his family. They were the figures who were always there.

After much begging, three young men agreed to climb in the boat but were immediately lifted into the sky by the dinosaurs. They screamed in agony as Zak looked back at his house with the baby crying. He needed more men.

Lenny drove down early on Saturday to take a break from the office and his steady diet of TV violence to catch up with Zak and cruise some familiar Portland spots. They met at the Carlos Café, a coffee and pie shop, near Zak's house, on Northeast Alberta Street. It was in a neighborhood that was laughingly referred to as "the hood" in the eighties and nineties. That was before the hipsters paved the way for the gentrifiers that Zak liked to pretend he wasn't. "I bought the house from an old German family," he'd tell people. So he was okay. The drug dealers on the corner had been fully replaced by Caucasian parents pushing strollers carrying babies with Misfits onesies bought at the Punk Baby Gap.

Both seemed so much older than when they first met in the late nineties, when they lived in the same downtown apartment building and spent days record shopping and nights seeing bands. Zak's injury and Lenny's divorce gave them some ware on their cheeks. But Lenny still dressed like he was 22, in skinny jeans and tour t-shirts under his black leather jacket. He was like a wormhole that time bent around. Each tattoo he added to his body was an attempt to erase one year of aging, affecting a look that probably scared small children. He performed a public service as a cautionary tale of those who refused to relinquish their childhood. It was clear he longed for the freedom of his youth when more was ahead of him instead of behind him. Raw potential instead of memories and another story of 'back-in-the-day.' There was comfort in the caricature and he had no plans to release it into the void.

Lenny was there for Claire's memorial service. Lenny hoped Cozy would fly in from DC. (She didn't.) He came down from Seattle a few times that year, bringing mix CDs to cheer Zak up. For Lenny, the one thing that had changed the most was Zak's love of music; his obsessive search for the newest new sound or the rediscovery of a lost classic. The guy was a true fanatic. These days Zak just listened to NPR. Lenny wanted to reignite the old spark and bring his friend back into the world of light and sound.

Zak was parked at the café with a cup and a slice of pie. "Hey, Lenster. I got here a bit early so I'm already super caffeinated ."

"No worries, mon frère. It's good to get off I-5 and have a sit," said Lenny, pulling up a chair. "Seriously, people in Oregon are such shitty drivers."

"No, it's people from Washington. They're all methed-out looking for an Insane Clown Posse tribute show. Plus they're all depressed from paying sales tax," said Zak.

"Wrong, as a former Oregonian, I can say this. You guys can't get off your phones even after they fucking outlawed it. And drivers here have to constantly brake for guys with beards on bikes on their way to brunch or a Pokémon meet-up. It's treacherous. But all I gotta say is - Jesus, what happened to this neighborhood? When did it become the Pearl District?" Lenny's leather jacket creaked for effect.

"I know. I blame *Portlandia.* Ever since the show came on this town has been overrun with new money,"

"Wait a second Professor, I remember your big lecture on causation. What's that thing you made me repeat three times?" Maybe Lenny should have repeated it four times.

"Correlation is not causation."

"Yeah, dude. Your assertion is spurious. That's right, right? Alberta was blowing up long before that show came on. Portland is ground zero. You should move to Seattle. It's been totally yesterday's news for years. Anyway, how's it hanging?"

"Fine. Same old, same old. Living the good Portland life. What band are you in town for?"

"Gonna see Parquet Courts at The Palais tonight and then maybe some Portland bands tomorrow."

"Your job is like a paid vacation. Where are you staying tonight?" asked Zak.

"With you!"

Kiko spent the afternoon in her tiny room near campus blogging. She wrote a story about meeting some snowboarders and climbing half-way up Mt. Hood with them, only to run into a bear. It was complete fiction, but the outside world didn't know any better. To them, she was leading the life of Riley. To her, there were thousands of people reading her blog. It was considerably less than that. The peppy J-pop music of Bennie K played out of her laptop. There was no stereo in the apartment, only the tiny speakers on her MacBook.

Because Kiko had been cut off from her family, she was living on student loans that covered her tuition and rent and not much else. She taught a Japanese language night class at the college for money for her internet and phone service and a few nights out each month, but nothing for her apartment. The white walls had only her drawings taped to them and the floor was covered with noodle boxes and dirty laundry. She never had anyone over. Her friends were all in cyber-space.

That evening she began drawing sketches of Zak, making him taller and more muscular than he really was. Next to him, she drew herself, with bigger eyes and larger breasts, fashioning herself as the sidekick to her super-hero. These pictures did not go on the wall but into a manilla folder, and then into a bottom drawer.

Kelly's house seemed empty. Emptier than normal. Life in the suburbs was quiet, but the quiet had been disturbed. Papers were on the floor of the kitchen and things were gone from the living room. Little things. At first she thought she had been burglarized. She had noticed a lot more Mexican kids in the neighborhood lately. "They finally broke in, those little gang bangers."

The usual stuff wasn't gone. Her TV and stereo were still there. It was like someone had tossed the place around to scare her. "Jay!" she yelled as she imagined her ex-husband in their house. Maybe he was looking for something or maybe he was trying to get inside her head. She fell to the living room rug and wondered when the abuse would end.

She had filed a restraining order against him even though he had never actually threatened her. He had left with the other woman and never looked back. The judge granted the order because that's what judges do. Why would a woman scorned lie about a man? If Kelly could find evidence that he had been in the house, she could have him arrested. A footprint or a lock of hair. She had seen it in movies on the Lifetime Channel; there had to be some evidence to punish him.

She looked for a bit but then sank into the couch with a cup of camomile tea and a cat. Lifetime was showing *She's Too Young* again and her Saturday evening was in place.

Zak's house was a hundred year old bungalow in the rapidly changing Northeast section of the city. Things were breaking without any urgency for repair. The garbage disposal, the closet light, the bathroom door handle. There was dust on the picture frames and unread magazines on the end table . The refrigerator was filled with things that you don't actually eat, like salad dressing and expired vitamins. Moss spread out across the roof. The home was being reclaimed by the earth.

He and Claire had been transforming it into a nest for their new stage of life, painting and childproofing. A new playpen in the living room, a hand-me-down stroller in the study. Most of the records and books were boxed up to make room for the nursery.

If this was a movie, that would be the room Zak hadn't gone in since the accident. But he did go into it quite often. Most of the gifts from the baby shower were given to friends with little ones or to Goodwill. But he kept the crib, and the clothes and decorations his mother had saved from his own childhood. There were Berenstein Bears books and Raggedy Andy dolls. Zak like to lay on the floor and listen for Claire's voice in the kitchen. "Zak, have you figured where the dirty diapers are gonna go?"

Mostly he closed his eyes and prayed that he could wake up from this dream.

"You're coming out with me, right?" said Lenny, throwing his duffel bag in Zak's spare room. "It's Saturday night and you're fucking coming out with me." He pushed a stack of papers out of the way and plopped on the bed.

Zak had given up on Saturday nights. They were now reserved for catching up on his Netflix queue, trying to get up to speed on *Orange Is The New Black* and old episodes of *Nurse Jackie*. "I don't know, man. I thought I'd hang out on the couch tonight."

"Dude, I'm about to go apeshit on your ass. You are coming with me to see this band and maybe meet a few ladies.

Life is waiting for you to get back on board. It's not anywhere near your fucking couch. It's out there waiting for Professor Cool." Lenny was pushing his hair back so he could stare right into Zak's eyes.

Zak couldn't argue with the logic. He was sick of sulking, but worried being out would somehow negate the enormity of the loss. He could stay in and analyze inmate interviews with old music playing, but where was the chance of excitement in that?

"Okay, man. Maybe I'll go out for a bit." It was a permission slip to rejoin the world, to be an imperfect human being, floating in the Great Pacific Garbage Patch with the rest of the lost souls.

Lenny and Zak were mirror images of each other. Both had shoulder length hair that was quickly thinning. Lenny's stubble had the touch of grey that Zak had shaved off. Both were backward-looking at what they had lost, not forward-looking at what joy might lay ahead. But at least Lenny had some some silver train momentum. Zak was still trying to get out of the station.

Lenny had seen this boy in quicksand before, a decade and a half earlier, when his fiancé called things off a week before the wedding. It unlocked Zak's severe depression and very nearly sent him over a cliff. His friends had to reel him in and make him put all that crazy drama in the past.

"Zak, brother, no downer shit tonight. Let's cut loose, alright? We both need some reckless abandon. I don't want to hear about dreams or old days or anything. Let's paint a new canvas."

"I appreciate that, man. I'm really trying. I've been dealing with a tsunami of guilt lately. I feel like all this was my fault. The accident. None of this had to happen. I changed everything by my choices that day. If I had stayed home, Claire would be here here with our baby."

"Dude, I can totally relate. I have the same kind of thoughts."

"Len, you slept with your pregnant wife's doula. It's not the same thing."

"At least I didn't sleep with the mid-wife. She was hot in an earth momma kind of way."

Zak had given up on Lenny a long time ago. There weren't enough skirts in the world for him to chase. But he dug out his brown leather jacket and accompanied his friend to the show. He had seen so many bands at The Palais they all ran together. Tonight would be another blur. But he was trying, right? Trying to rejoin the living.

Parquet Courts sounded good, like late Velvet Underground, and made him get his groove back, if only a little bit, but he knew it would be another night lost in the youth culture he no longer had time for. Once the band started he wanted it to be over and climb back in his bed. He got it after the first song. Fortunately it was a short set.

There was the baby. The goddamn baby. She was perfectly intact. No birth defects. Big brown eyes. Completely engaged in the world. She was their Amistad. The culmination of all Zak and Claire's ancestors. The promise of all their futures. There she was on a blanket, in her perfect adoration of the sun and the daylight that embraced her. There she was representing everything that was innocent and good about the world. Her flawless mouth offering the promise of the goddess of peace. "Mama."

The baby was on a blanket at an arts festival in a huge park. Zak looked at her and at their apartment on the edge of the park that they were renting from a famous jeweler. Jeweler that sounded like jewer. More Jewish. But still an artist of jewels. Zak wanted to be jewer if it meant being able to take care of his wife and child. He wanted the stereotype to apply to him. The America song, "Ventura Highway," played from a window or a boom box.

There was his sweet baby on a blanket at this beautiful festival. It was Saturday in the park. It was a Chicago song. But the baby was on the blanket alone. Claire was not there and he was bargaining with artists. He locked eyes with the child who suddenly looked panicked. The baby began gasping for air and he couldn't get to her. She was trying to cry and turning inside out. Suffering. It wasn't fair. What had she ever done to deserve this? Zak deserved to suffer, not this child.

The sky turned black and the men arrived, standing on the edge of a field to end the scene. Then the rain came and all the people melted like the cake in "MacArthur Park." The baby melted as well. She didn't even know her name and she was melting into the grass. "Goddamn, let me at least hold her once," thought Zak. "Goddamn. Don't take her way from me again. Please God, stop this. I'm not a bad man. Let me be free of her cries."

And that's all that was left. Her cries. And they cut him in half.

"Tomorrow's dreams become reality to me." (Black Sabbath)

Chapter 2:
Way of the World

1

Lenny was riding his bike through downtown Seattle on a rare sunny afternoon. Friday at five. He coasted into a parking deck that took up the first two floors of a skyscraper. The middle of the parking deck had collapsed within the last few days and people were removing the cars that hadn't been crushed beneath the concrete and steel.

He sat on his bike looking at the site, dust settling on his neck, and wondering why he hadn't heard about this catastrophe. Was anybody hurt? Was this on the news? "I'm so out of it."

There was another scene down on the marina. One of the ferries that crosses the Puget Sound to Bainbridge Island was suspended, hovering in the air about a hundred feet above the water. Lenny thought it was an odd site so he peddled his bike down the hill toward it.

A small crowd was gathering to see the floating-in-air boat. A young woman approached him. It was actress Mila Kunis.

"What's going on?" asked Lenny.

"Terrorists have hijacked the ferry. But they are exchanging the hostages for better looking hostages," Mila said. Lenny could see the relieved passengers climbing down one rope ladder as people who looked like catalog models were climbing another up to the ferry. "Do you want to come be a hostage with me?"

The offer was tempting but, with little thought, Lenny replied, "No, thanks. I have to get home to my wife and kid."

He looked towards downtown, back at the skyscraper with the collapsed parking decks. From the harbor he could see that all the floors right up to the top had collapsed in the middle and the giant building was titling to the right, like a massive leaning

Tower of Pisa. What would happen to Seattle if that thing fell over?

Lenny had been having a hard time getting ahold of his ex-wife. He wanted to talk to his son, Daniel, who was already in middle-school (man, how time flies), but as usual he really wanted to talk to Cozy. The three-hour time difference always threw him off. Seattle and Washington, DC seemed like distant worlds these days. He was torn between being the care-free over-sexed rocker of his imagination and the grown-up dad who was still connected to his son's mother.

"Hello?" He answered the call on the first ring.

"Hey, Len." Finally. "I saw that you called. Sorry. I've been runnin'."

"It's the way of the world, I guess. How is my Danny Boy?" Lenny used talk of the kid to keep her on the phone so he could bathe in the sound of her voice.

"Really good. He got that mix-CD you sent him. I need to dig out the CD player."

"Jeez! What do you play music on in DC?" Like Zak, Lenny was loyal to the physical format. You needed to be able to hold something in your hands. A complete work of art. He knew her answer.

"I've got some good speakers for my laptop now. Next time just email him a playlist. So what's going on?"

"Nothing. I saw Zak last week. He was less like a zombie. I dragged him out to a show and he didn't die," he said.

"We're you in Portland? How's the professor doing?"

"Yeah, I went down for work. He seems okay. He didn't have that weird stare. And he shaved the lumberjack beard off. There's also a good chance his underwear was clean."

Cozy chuckled a little. "Well, that's encouraging. I can't imagine what he's been through. All that loss. It's too much to imagine. I think his job has been his salvation. He emailed me that he's still doing that study about guys in prison."

Lenny envied Zak's work in prison. He had visited his father in prison when he was a teenager. When you move through a prison, the door in front of you does not open until the door behind you has closed and locked. Lenny wished life worked that way. His world was a collection of partially opened doors. He imagined the door back to Cozy was open wider than it actually was. It wasn't open at all.

"He likes to run with the rough bunch," Lenny joked. "Oh, speaking of, I think he went on a date with a former student. Some Japanese girl who likes monster movies."

"Gawd, that sounds short-lived. Well, I guess it's a start. He needs to get out. He's gotta be the palest man in Portland. And that's saying something. Any other news from the Great Northwest?" She sounded like she missed the rain planet.

"No. I was thinking about you today. Hey, remember when you were in school and I used to follow you home?" He thought a trip down memory lane would warm her up. Remind her.

"Okay, boy. Let's not go there. It's over, remember?" It seemed a bit curt but she caught herself. "Sorry, but Daniel's at a sleep-over and I'm headed out for a drink."

"With your boyfriend?" Cozy had been engaged but never remarried which Lenny took as a sign even though he did nothing to make it happen (like move to DC, or stop being a whore). In his mind he was a great dad but in reality he was just another absentee father who left the weight of parenthood on the mother's shoulders.

"Life goes on and on, Lenny."

When he opened his eyes, and he was in standing in a brightly day lit street in Fallujah. Zak was suddenly struck with panic. He stood out like a sore thumb. He would be immediately dragged off the street and be beheaded by Al Queda in Iraq or ISIL. He could feel everyone's eyes on him. They must think he's CIA, even though he probably hates the CIA as much as they do. Where were the cops in white to help him? He tried to run for a dark doorway but he could only crumble into a fetal ball on the sandy street. He closed his eyes and waited for the prick of steel on his neck.

It was a cold rainy day in Portland, so Zak needed some warm vinyl. He went upstairs and pulled out a copy of Neil

Young's *Decade*. Six-sides. That should keep his head occupied for a while. Old man, take a look at my life. He opened a can of soup and slunk into a soft chair that Claire had bought at Ikea.

"Right, what's the plan?" he thought as Neil crooned about a man needing a maid. When will I see you again?

Maybe he should clean his house. Presently, he never much went much past "picking up," which had come to mean picking up clothes from the floor and putting them on. The malaise had left his living space in a state of chaos that he hadn't quite gotten around to reforming back into something approaching order.

He had thought, since he was past the sadness, that now was the time to get more involved in faculty governance. The university brass had been pushing to reduce the tenure-line faculty in favor of much cheaper adjunct instructors and more online classes. It was the beginning of the end of what a university was supposed to look like, and some of the faculty were organizing to push back. Zak wasn't much of joiner, but he had put his email address down on a sign up sheet and promised himself he wouldn't delete any messages before reading them. His tenure promotion was fresh so he felt a little bulletproof.

For now chicken and rice soup and Neil was enough. Dream up, dream up, let me fill your cup. But his phone buzzed in his pocket and he spilled his soup in his lap. It was a text from Lenny.

Calling Dr Bombay

Hey

Whassup in PDX?

Rain

Duh here 2. Can we talk later?

Sure. Bout what?

Dreams

Fleetwood Mac or Allmans?

Theres my boy Skype ya tonight TTYL

Bye

The office needed a lamp. That's what Kelly thought as she looked up at the fluorescent lights. She was examining her face on her phone, touching up her make-up. The overhead lights made her wrinkles more noticeable. Living in high definition can cripple a mature woman. You are fighting the clock every day and losing. A nice soft lamp would set the mood. Cover the reality. And make her office feel less threatening to the people who would be brought in to be given bad news. Too bad she couldn't have a cat at work.

President Woodbine had given her a pressing task that would be her chance to show her loyalty to the machine. He wanted her to get in front of the grumblings by faculty. The last thing the school needed was a faculty union. The University of Oregon had gone through that and the administration lost considerable control over its most expensive group of workers.

If there was a task she was cut out for, this was it. She had spent several years as a faculty member in the English Department and found her colleagues pompous and full of delusions of grandeur. They felt their work was going to make the world a better place, one inflated grade at a time. This was the case with most professors, in her mind. Over-paid and under-worked. Some only taught two days a week and moaned when they were asked to serve on university committees. There was never a committee that Kelly said no to. Committees opened doors to upward movement. Committees filled CVs with evidence of commitment to the institution.

When she was a professor, she never much liked it. The students were ungrateful grade-grubbers who didn't appreciate the artistry of nineteenth century romance literature. They wanted zombies in their Jane Austen. But she managed to earn her tenure even if she never stood out. She only had one online teacher review (which she had written herself). It was the committee work that got her up the ladder. It's who you know not how you teach.

Kelly was also convinced the professors' over-romanticized vision of themselves extended to their love-lives. Or rather their sex-lives. Because she had experienced this first-hand when she was in college in the seventies, she knew the male professors were treating their undergraduate classes like brothels, trading grades for all manner of perversions. She had read *Fifty Shades of Grey* (twice) and knew how sick modern sex could get. And they could rationalize it by referring to themselves as "mentors" and "life guides."

Sure, occasionally some of these predatory professors married their students, but, to Kelly, the whole thing looked a lot more like high-class sex-trafficking, with a stable of broken young girls left out in the rain each semester. The professor and the young co-ed. So much like what her husband had done to her. It was the college world's dirty little secret and she was finally in a position to do something about it.

"I deserve a nice lamp," she thought.

2

Later that evening, Zak was sitting in front of his computer looking at videos of babies falling over instead of reading a grad student's dissertation. His laptop rang and a box opened up on his screen. It was Lenny beaming in on FaceTime.

"Looking at porn again, Professor?"

"Almost. Funny baby videos."

"Jesus, man," Lenny worried aloud.

"They're funny, okay? I'm procrastinating. What's up?"

"Nada. Going to see this hot local band later called Xiphoid Process. Thought you'd dig the name." Lenny was always going out, never staying home.

"I'm not that kind of doctor. So what's the story?"

"I tried to Skype you earlier, but you weren't picking up. Busy?"

"I think my Skype is broken. I need to update it or something. Anything wrong?" It was another thing on Zak's to-do list.

"I talked to Cozy. She says hello." Lenny's image broke up for a second, like there was more to that statement that wasn't making it through the wi-fi.

"You know, you never mention Daniel. Did you talk to him, too?" Zak wasn't up for hearing Lenny pine away.

Lenny paused. "He was at some sleepover and Cozy was headed out to get drunk with her boyfriend, so we didn't say much. I told her you have a new girlfriend." He saw the look of alarm on Zak's face. "What? Worried she'll think you're taken? Don't worry, bro, I'm just kidding. Hey, I want to ask you about your crazy dreams."

"Yeah, I'm starting a dream journal," said Zak, thinking it was a worthwhile task.

"You said that Claire is in a lot of your dreams, right? Cozy has been popping up in my dreams lately. You're a scientist. What does it mean?" He took a sip on a can of Rainer beer and waited for Zak, who took a moment to answer.

This was a topic that Zak had been thinking a lot about lately. "There really is no science of the meaning of dreams. The conventional wisdom is that when you hit REM sleep, your brain is still thinking even though your eyes are closed, so it gets a lot of self-generated random imagery. Basically, your brain is at rest and a lot of your images and ideas are turned loose in a random scramble of little stories."

"Boring. They have to mean something. Not all of them but if you start getting the same things over and over again."

"Well, that's sort of what Jung called the archetypes of the collective unconscious, themes in all of our minds. But Freud thought they were clues to your subconscious. But he thought everything was. Why? Is it Cozy or something else?"

"No, it's just that my dreams are so short and they always end up the same. She splits and I'm standing there, holding my dick. Not literally. I would love to have some control over them to make them last a little longer. I hooked up with this chick the other night and she said I should get into lucid dreaming, like where people control their dreams and decide to fly and shit."

Lenny gravitated to what Zak called "edge thinking;" conspiracy theories, bad science, ninety percent of what gets posted on Facebook. Chemtrails, 9/11 was an inside job, immunizations cause autism, Obama was a member of the Muslim Brotherhood, Tupac is alive and well and living in Dubai.

"Man, I wish that was real. Just imagine what you could choose to see. The Beatles at Shea Stadium!" The fab four were Zak's go-to fantasy.

"The Stones at Altamont!"

"You could stop that Hell's Angel from stabbing the guy. Hell, it's your dream, you could be *in* the Stones."

Lenny laughed. "I have that dream all the time."

"Yeah, Lenny. I don't know anything about it. You should do some research and let me know if you find anything cool."

"Hold on." Lenny made a few taps on his keyboard and Zak's Instant Messenger feature on Facebook popped up on his screen. Lenny had sent him several website addresses, including one that linked to a *Scientific American* article on the topic and a Reddit discussion group for lucid dreamers. "You should take a look at this shit, man, it's off the hook."

Zak promised to and they talked for another thirty minutes. Lenny asked if Zak was going to see any bands this weekend (no), if he was going to interview anymore Nazi inmates (yes) and whether he was going to go out with Kiko again (maybe).

That night he began to think Lenny was on to something. If he could hold on to Claire and his baby for a bit, long enough to tell them that he was so sorry, even if it was only in a dream, maybe he could have some closure. He had a cup of herbal tea before bed and put on Claire's favorite Joni Mitchell album, *Ladies of the Canyon*, and hoped to conjure her up in tonight's dreamscape.

Zak had been to the Troubadour in LA before so he recognized the stage and tables. "It's so much smaller in real life than it sounds like on that Van Morrison album," he thought. Such a historic center of music. Anything from Southern California had a connection to this little joint. The Eagles met there. When he was last here, he drank four Brandy Alexanders, the drink John Lennon got drunk on when he was bounced out the Troubadour door in 1974 for heckling the Smothers Brothers. The young bartender didn't know the story, how to make Brandy Alexanders or who the Smothers Brothers were.

"John Lennon? That dead guy from the Beatles?"

This time he had a device in his hand instead of a drink. It was like a Geiger Counter, something that might come in handy in the city of angels. But this box measured how attracted a person was to you. Sort of like the one Elvis had in the film, *Live A Little, Love A Little,* but this one was real. It ticked as he walked through the crowd.

He was out of time and place. If someone was viewing the scene they would recognize it as the late sixties by the clothes and the fact that The Stone Ponys were on the bill. That was Linda Ronstadt's folk band. But Zak only thought, "I'm at the Troubadour with this funny box."

The device revved up as he approached a young woman with straight blonde hair, dragging on a cigarette. "Speak now or forever hold your piece," she said with a smokey voice.

He couldn't speak. The woman proceeded to tell him how she had given a child up for adoption and was feeling lost so she came there to drink and listen to the music. "I'm feeling low and I've got no place to go."

Zak couldn't tell if she said it or he did.

Kiko was trying to not be too obvious. She wanted to see Professor Crisp but didn't want to be a pest so she waited for his mid-week office hours to visit him. She wore her schoolgirl skirt and knee socks in hopes that her ensemble would catch his glances. Her classmates talked behind her back about her questionable clothing choices. Not Portland at all. But Kiko was oblivious.

"Hello, Professor." His door was open and he was reading a letter from an inmate. The office was a mess of books and student papers and an outlawed coffee maker under the desk.

"Hi, Kiko." He had given up on asking her to call him Zak. But he admitted he sort of liked being called "sir." It was like that Sydney Pointier movie about the teacher. The English film with the great song. "What are you up to?"

"Just on a break between classes. How are you today, sir? Hungry for more sushi?" It sounded like an invitation.

Zak wanted to say yes. Or no. He could tell she had hot love for sale just by the outfit. But was the time right? Hot love will burn you. He hemmed and hawed as she leaned on the door frame and struck a pose that she has seen the Japanese gravure models on soft porn sites strike.

How could he resist?

That was the exact moment that Kelly walked down the hallway in the Health Science Building, right past Zak's door. It was evidence. Not of students seducing professors, but of professors using their power to make female students think they had to prostitute themselves for grades. Kelly didn't know that Kiko was not in any of Zak's classes. She was just a student in a short skirt who had gotten the memo that this is what female students have to do at this school.

She lurked a few feet away, pretending to read a flyer that was taped to the wall.

"Sure, I guess," said Zak. "I'm always up for sushi. But no drinks, okay? I had a few too many last time." He hadn't, but he was trying to save face from not better responding to the kiss.

"Last time?" thought Kelly. Oh, something was going on here for sure. After Kiko shot her a glance from the doorway, Kelly quickly moved down the hall, shaking her head at how horrible the male professors in this school were. She made a mental note to go back later to see the name on the door.

There was a break in the rain so Zak thought he'd go downtown to a food cart pod for lunch. There was a cluster near campus that had one cart called La Sirena de Boracha that served up burritos the size of your head. He had to walk past Thai carts and Lebanese carts and crepe carts and bratwurst carts to get to it. In front of the brat cart is where he saw a familiar face.

Lucinda was a street kid when he first met her back at the turn of the century. She was a nineteen-year-old homeless mom with a baby who ended up opening the door to his study of Portland's gutterpunk scene. Researching their world would earn Zak his doctorate. But more importantly, she was his roommate for a year, her rent paid for by his previous roommate, Telly. It was an unexpected living arrangement that allowed Zak to bond with her baby daughter, Polly, and that helped mend his own heart. He loved to play records for the toddler and toy with the idea that he might be ready to be a parent one day.

At the end of the year, Lucinda had a job at a Goodwill and moved into a house in the north part of the city. The last time Zak saw her was about five years ago when she married an upwardly mobile guy from Santa Rosa who adored her daughter.

He almost didn't recognize the woman in her thirties with long brown hair. She would always be that dirty kid at the bus stop clutching a baby to him. It looked like she was asking cart diners for spare change, but that couldn't be right.

"Lucinda! Lucinda! Hey, girl! How are you doing?" He was excited to see her.

She tried to turn away but realized it was too late. "Oh, hi Zak. Jeez, it's been a while. You're looking better than I expected." Lucinda had heard about the accident and even tried to visit him in the hospital but went to the wrong one.

"Can I buy you a burrito?" He sensed there was hard luck story coming so they should find a spot to sit and debrief each other. It was clear that neither had lives that kept to straight lines. "How is Polly?" he asked.

"She's in school and doing great. They used to tell me she was retarded when she was a baby and now she's rocking high school. She's a helluva a lot smarter than me." She ordered a chicken molé burrito and Zak ordered a chili relleno burrito and a couple of pops.

"Where's your California man?" We might as well get to the story, thought Zak.

"In prison, of course." The two old roommates sat on the metal gate of the parking lot the food cart pod was in. "Oh, Zak. I really fucked up. I fucked up bad."

There had been times when they were very close. And not because Zak had accidentally put her refrigerated breast milk in his coffee a few times. They had a lot of deep discussions about the nature of love and the need to power through the rainy days of life to get to the bits of sunshine. There was no romance. Just two lost souls in a Portland fish bowl. And a baby that loved eating crackers and Zak's schoolbooks. So Zak put his hand on the back of her head.

"I thought I had it all when I married Zander. I was finally out of the shit, man. We even had a picket fence at our house. It was like a fucking dream. Finally. But it was a huge lie." She began sobbing and handed Zak her burrito so she could cover her face.

"What the hell happened, Lu? Why is Zander in prison?" He had a feeling he knew the answer.

"That piece of shit was photographing Polly and selling the pictures. He was forcing her to do sick shit and she was afraid to tell me for almost a year. I walked in on them one day and almost stabbed him with a knife. I was going to have some of my friends kill him. But I had to prove to my girl that I was there for her and had him arrested. It's wrong what he did. My husband." She paused to catch her breath. "They found naked pictures of her on his phone so he plead guilty and is down in Salem now, locked up with the other perverts."

Zak was stunned. Zander had seemed like the most normal of guys. "Jesus Christ. How is Polly? Is she okay?" He often felt like Polly was his warm-up child, getting his soul ready.

"She's damaged like pretty much every girl in this world. I don't think she really trusts me for bringing him into our lives. She throws herself into her schoolwork, which is better, I guess, than running away from home like I did. But we lost the house. I couldn't pay the mortgage after they arrested him. Polly's living with a friend and I'm in a shelter at the moment." She took the burrito back and took a big bite out of it.

A pang a guilt welled up in Zak, living in his house all alone. It was challenging living with her fifteen years ago but he did owe her in a way and there was now a lot of space. "I still live that house in Northeast. Do you need a place to stay for a while? There's plenty of room."

She sniffed and wiped her nose with her sleeve. "No, thanks, man. I know you've got your own shit to deal with. I decided I'm going out to my mom's house in Seaside. My dad died last year, so I need to go keep her company and get something happening, but I'll let you know if I head back into the city. I'm gonna get on Facebook so I can keep in touch with everyone."

"Fuck. That is so fucked up. He seemed like a really decent guy. I'm so sorry." There was some value in being reminded that his wasn't the only shitty story out there.

"Everything seemed so perfect. My 'great plan.' Like I wished all that fairy tale to happen and then my Prince Charming turned into a monster," said Lucinda. "It's like the people that win the lottery and then get murdered for it. Or welcome to your dream house in Beverly Hills and then an earthquake kills everybody in the neighborhood. Sorry," she said realizing she was getting a bit morbid. "Enough about me. What's going on with you these days?"

"Oh, my wife and child are dead. Other than that, not much."

3

Stan was a big man. He'd gotten bigger in prison because of the starchy food and anti-psychotic medicine they had forced him to take. He was fit when he was a semi-pro wrestler, but now he was heading to three hundred pounds. The swastika tattoo on his chest was showing signs of stretching as his body widened.

He was alone in six by eight cell out in the boondocks of eastern Oregon. He had spent the last fifteen days in Ad Seg, the administrative segregation unit, also known as solitary. He was placed there after a guard caught him performing oral sex on another inmate and separated the two.

He claimed he was being extorted into the act, a common reality behind the gate; that a gang was forcing him to pay a tax for living on that particular unit. The reality was he was lonely and craved some type of human contact that didn't involve fighting. He wanted to let his guard down for a few minutes and fifteen days in the hole was the price.

In a setting full of characters, Stan was not unique. He was in for armed robbery, even though his weapon was a pack of Juicy Fruit in his pocket. He claimed to be part of a skinhead gang that had never heard of him. And he came from a foster family that had given up on him by age sixteen. All common stories in the joint.

Also, like many in prison, he exhibited sociopathic characteristics. "Anti-social Personality Disorder" is what the psych-worker had written on his file. Highly intelligent, he was both psychopathic and psychotic, a winning combination. All this meant he was constantly looking for an angle to boost his trapped delusions of grandeur. At one point it was claiming to be a ranking shot caller in the Peckerwood Syndicate gang.

And now it was cultivating the interest of a college professor.

Zak wanted to carry on his prison research as a way to keep Claire's memory alive. She had thought the project was a really good idea, so he couldn't abandon it because she was gone. He had secured a small grant to survey a random sample of Oregon inmates and parolees about their health behavior, and to do face-to-face interviews with a smaller subsample.

He created a random sample of inmates from the Oregon Department of Corrections website and began sending letters. He figured few inmates would respond to requests from a strange egghead in Portland. What he discovered quickly was that inmates were infinitely bored and craved any connection with the outside world. Soon he was overwhelmed with long letters, written on yellow legal paper, of men wanting to participate.

These letters were soon followed by follow-up letters that said things like, "why haven't you responded to my first letter?" And others that said stuff like, "if you don't respond we will make sure nobody talks to you." So Zak used some of the grant money to hire a graduate student named Heather to respond to the inmates before he started a riot in Cell Block 11. Suddenly this project had gotten a little scary.

He had a hard time focusing on the project though. The focus was on getting better. Work helped, but it was too easy to scroll one more time through the internet. One more swipe through friends' pictures, funny YouTube videos. or the hilarious comments below FoxNews.com stories. He had given up on masturbation because it only ended up making him sad. Surrendering to the glow of his laptop was the new jacking off.

The visions in his dreams pushed him away from work as well. What if he could use his dreams to get to her? What if he could travel back to that moment and change things? He thought about it way too much. But, to be honest, many of his dreams seemed to take place in other times or outside of time. He wanted to stay in that dreamworld without the intrusion of the figures who haunted him.

It didn't seem like he was moving as far forward as he had hoped. Maybe it was time to drop back in to the grief support group at the Marky Center. Nothing to make you feel better like being around other heartbroken people.

The center was on the same side of the river as Zak's house so it felt like an extension of his home. He had spent a lot of time in its cozy meeting room hugging a cushion last year and it hadn't changed much. He felt like a veteran of these meetings now. You could always tell the first-timers. They had that shell-shocked look. "Why did this happen to me?" "Is this a bad dream?" "I just saw him a week ago and he was fine." "Please, God, tell me how I can go back in time."

Kelly wasn't expecting to run into her husband today. Since her hysterectomy she'd been suffering from night terrors and had taken to walks in her neighborhood to calm her nerves and burn off some of the caffeine before bedtime. The street seemed quiet despite her concern over the increase in Latino kids in the neighborhood.

She had practiced what she would say to him if she happened to bump into him at the store or the bank. She would remind him of the restraining order. She would tell him she was doing better without him, with a better position at the university and that he really missed out. She would ask him if his girlfriend's young tits were worth it. She would tell him that she gave all his records to the Salvation Army.

And there he was before her, calm as the night. His eyes were fixed on her as she walked up the sidewalk toward him. He looked particularly good with his salt and pepper hair falling over his forehead and Kelly felt a pang of heartache. But she still had things to say to him. Angry things.

But she would not be able to say them tonight. A gentle breeze blew and his body swung with its shifting direction. The noose around his neck was clearly visible and led up to the branch above the sidewalk. She thought he had done this for her benefit, a last statement of contrition, and she couldn't help but smile.

Even though it was late, people were chugging coffee like it was spring water. "This is probably what it's like at AA meetings," Zak thought. But people needed the liquid courage to talk or not fall asleep during other people's stories. People tend to wander, even when talking about death. Suddenly it's a ham-fisted soliloquy about all the the things they would never get to do.

Coffee in hand, he found his old spot on the couch next to a couple who had pained smiles plastered across their faces. Probably first or second-timers. It's all about face-work when you are first grieving. Don't let anyone know that your glass heart is still shattering into infinitesimally smaller shards, each one cutting into your flesh, and leaving a trail of glass pieces you have to worry about innocent victims injuring themselves on later.

The leader of a group was a middle-aged therapist who surely had heard so many horrific stories she must routinely think about throwing herself in front of a bus. But suicide is a selfish act. That's what you learn in group. So she probably blocked it out and opened another bottle of pinot.

"Hi everybody. I'm really glad you came tonight. Looks like we don't have any new folks here so I will remind everyone of the ground-rules and then we can just get started. I want us to have as much time as possible. Does anyone want to go first?"

The room was dark and inviting. The furniture was meant to look lived in, not clinical. Table lamps and blankets on the backs of sofas. No music but there was a parakeet in a cage that seemed like an odd flourish. Maybe it was meant to represent the soothing sounds of tropical birds in the rainforest.

The couple next to Zak went first. Their daughter had been killed on her bike in downtown Portland, right in front of The Palais. A garbage truck made a right-hand turn while she was waiting for the light to turn green and crushed her against a utility pole. Zak had seen the white "ghost bike" cyclists had put on the spot to remind drivers of the vulnerability of people on bikes.

They spoke with great composure. The father spoke of how proud she was for helping to pay for her classes at Portland Community College. The mother spoke of how she keeps expecting the phone to ring with her girl's number on it. Her husband nodded when she said she felt guilty for hoping that it was all a mistake and it was someone else's daughter who had been killed.

The sniffles in the room became chokes.

"It's all about process," the therapist said. "We are getting through the hurt, so don't feel guilty about any of your thoughts or feelings. Nobody can be truly prepared for how make it through the loss of a child."

More chokes.

Then it was Zak's turn since the room looked at him next.

"Hi, I'm Zak and I'm an alcoholic." An attempt at humor.

"Hi, Zak," said the room, sensing it might be true.

"I guess I'm here because I need a booster shot. It's been a year and I thought things were getting better. But my wife has been showing up in my dreams a lot lately and I feel like I'm right back at that moment. I thought I'd come and talk with people who can relate."

"Zak, do want us to share with the group what happened? That might be a good way to start." She had heard the story before. It was a tough one. But she knew that he needed to tell it.

Zak got a lump in his throat like the first time he went skiing. You're at the top of the ski run, looking down the mountain. You don't know what the hell you're doing but you can't not go. It took too long to get all that gear on. So you're gonna go but you know you are going to slam into a tree or fuck up your back. But if you go through this enough times, you might finally make it to the bottom. To be the Suzie Chapstick of grief. So he dug his poles into the ground and pushed himself forward.

Claire was six-months pregnant with a little girl. Everything was going perfectly. They decided Caroline would be a good name. Zak worried she would always have guys singing her that Neil Diamond song. Ba ba ba baa. Regardless, their dream of normal, drama free middle-class life was coming together perfectly.

So they took off for one last road trip before they doubled down on the nesting duties. One last hurrah as a childless couple who were responsible only to themselves. Claire didn't want to go far in case, well, whatever. So Zak loaded up the car with CDs and they took off for Reno. One last time. One last night at the roulette wheel.

They got in Friday night and spent Saturday afternoon hanging out at the pool. Claire felt self-conscious that her baby bump was now a baby hump. Zak thought it looked amazing but teased her when she floated on her back and all you could see was her stomach. "Nessy!" he shouted as the other women at the pool flashed his wife the sympathy look. That night they gambled at the table and the machines. Zak won $100 at an Iron Man slot machine but Claire lost $200 at a Judge Judy slot machine. That's how Reno works. Mostly they were annoyed by all the old people smoking, turning the casino into a cancer farm so they decided to leave in the morning.

Zak didn't tell the people at the Marky Center about the casino. He started the following day when they made it from Reno up to Crater Lake, in southern Oregon, for a picnic lunch on the edge of the lake. It was a perfect Sunday. The sky and lake were both deep, deep blue. Claire fed part of her sandwich to a chipmunk that then scurried over the ledge, between the rocks.

"Caroline will love this place," they said. "We should get back on the road," they said.

The park was in the middle of the Umpqua National Forest and it was an eighty-seven mile drive to the next town, Roseburg, Oregon. A great spot to get dinner before the next four hours to Portland. But there's pretty much nothing between the lake and

Roseburg. No Starbucks, no gas stations, no creepy inns where horror films take place. Just trees and rocks. And rocks.

Zak explained how they were driving down Highway 138, and talking about the usual things. They needed to go to Ikea and Target to get things for the baby's room. They needed to thank everybody that gave them gifts at the shower. They needed to make sure the mid-wife had all the medical records before the birth. Claire rubbed her belly.

"I can feel her turning over," she said.

Zak smiled in supreme happiness. He took his eyes of the road and the right tires slipped off the pavement.

"Careful, honey. There's three of us now."

"Sorry, I love your glow. My glowworm." He had gotten the Volkswagen back on the pavement and rounded a corner, next to a cliff.

Zak and Claire were grinning, high on the endorphins pumping in their brains when the car was suddenly ripped in half.

This was the part of the story where Zak always stopped. He was suddenly like one of those eighty-year-old World War Two vets, talking about the invasion of Normandy. A million and one things have happened in their lives since June 6, 1944. But, suddenly, they are back there on the beach, climbing over their friends' bodies, trying to not get their faces shot off. They choke back the tears. Time heals nothing. The unfairness of humanity punches them in the gut one more time.

It was the moment where time stopped for Zak. Where the happiness that hid under logs and behind locked doors was handed to him, wrapped in a pink bow, and then snatched away with a cruel laugh od a schoolyard bully. It was the moment when the whole world could burn to the ground and that would be just fine.

"Take your time, Zak," the group leader said, in a hushed tone. "We're all here for you."

The parakeet squawked. "If you don't talk, I will! Squawk!"

He tried to swallow but his throat was blocked. It wasn't a panic attack. Maybe an allergic reaction to the grief itself. Finally, he continued.

The last thing he remembered was the soft smile on Claire's face and her right hand on her stomach. Her left hand was reaching out to hold his. Then nothing. There was a crunching sound and then blackness beset with endless dreams. Dreams of his family in their Portland home. Zak and Claire staring at baby Caroline, watching her try to roll over on the living room carpet.

Two weeks later, Zak came out of a coma in a trauma unit in Portland to learn what had happened. The unholy injustice of what had happened to his family.

Around that bend a large boulder had slipped loose from the cliff above. Apparently the recent rains had eroded the soil around a rock the size of a U-Haul trailer and gravity did the rest. It fell on the passenger side of the car, crushing Claire and sending the car into the ravine on the other side of the highway. A trucker stopped and called for help on his CB radio as there was no cellphone coverage in the forest.

The jaws of life worked for hours to pull them from the twisted wreckage. It was clear to the paramedics that Claire was dead and Zak was very close. When they saw that the woman was pregnant, they raced the two bodies to the hospital in Roseburg to try and save the baby. But the fetus had been crushed by the weight of the rock and the steel roof of the VW. Caroline was pronounced dead at 10:48 pm. Her parents never even got to see her perfect face.

Zak was Lifeflighted to Portland and put on life-support. His colleagues and students came to visit but he was just a very well-educated vegetable. A Portland news station did a story. The university president sent flowers. Cozy came to hold his hand and tell him to wake up for his life. Had he known what news awaited him, he would have preferred to stay in the coma.

He ended the story there. He didn't discuss the brain injury that caused the right side of his body to just quit. He left out the months of physical therapy and how the university supported him in his recovery. It was obvious enough from his Quasimodo features that he should feel lucky to be alive.

"I guess like everybody here (he had been to many meetings like this), I can't get past the unfairness of the whole thing. If I had driven a little bit faster, the boulder would have fallen behind us. Or if we had stayed in Reno, like we planned, my wife and daughter would be alive." He stopped for a breath. "I don't know. I feel like I died on that day too and my ghost is just propping up this body."

"Life is rarely fair, bro," said some young guy who was probably there because his dog died. "It's the way of the world."

4

Lenny came out of a house in a cul-de-sac to get into his black SUV. There was a note on the windshield. "That better not be a parking ticket," he thought. But it wasn't.

The yellow sheet of paper was a change of address form from the post office with handwriting covering it from all directions. Sideways, upside down, girly fourth grade handwriting. There was only one name on it: Jaimie Lynn Spears.

What's up with this chick? She was following him on Twitter and Instagram and had friend-requested him on Facebook. "I'm being stalked by Britney Spears' little sister," he snorted. It didn't dawn on him that she might be a songwriter looking for a publishing deal. Jamie Lynn Spears was trying to ruin his marriage.

Stan Stipich spent most of the day in his cell writing a long letter to Dr. Crisp. He wanted to let him know that he knew all there was to know about the health behaviors at his prison. Not only did he know who was using dirty needles for tattoos, but he also knew which nurses were handing out extra meds for the kickbacks. And if Crisp could get him the hell out of there, he was ready to talk.

In the world of the prison there is a very clear hierarchy. It's not the sex offenders or pedophiles at the bottom of the human shit pile. It's the snitches. And snitches get it from both sides. If they snitch on the underground inmate culture, they could easily end up with a shiv in their carotid artery and bleed out on the shower floor. But they can also snitch on correctional officers who are doing a little dealing on the side and then they'll wish they were dead.

Stan had done both and he needed to get out.

So he wrote this letter, his hand shaking from the meds.

Dear Professor,

 I hope this letter finds you well. As you know from my previous letter, I am incarcerated at TRCI until June 2020. In my two years here I have become very connected to the health care staff and knowledgable about the types of inmate behaviors you are interested in. You are correct in that inmates often do not take their health issues seriously. Last week we had another inmate in my unit hospitalized with Hepatitis B and who is now on dialysis. There are also inmates with AIDS, cancer, and other serious diseases.

 I believe that this is because the state does not want to pay for education programs for inmates. The cost of the treatment ends up being much greater. That's why I believe your research project is important and that I think I can help you a good deal.

 I offer my services as a project assistant free of charge. My only request is that you contact Superintendent Reese and ask that they transfer me to another facility so I can be closer to Portland. This would make it easier for you as we could meet in person. I would not feel comfortable sending you this important information through the mail. If I was housed at CRCI, we could meet on a regular basis and I can provide you with the data you seek.

 Please tell Mr. Reese that this is a significant project to protect the health of both inmates and prison employees. If you could let me know what you hear soon, I can make plans for my transfer.

  Respectfully yours,
  Stan Stipich

The real reason that Stan wanted the transfer was that the Insane Peckerwood skinheads and the Northwest Hammer skinheads were both punking him out for being a rat and a poser and his life was hell, 24-7. He'd been attacked in his bunk, on the toilet, and in the shower. Word was out that he was a snitch and there was no recovery from that rap. An Aryan shot-caller was forcing him to pilfer psych meds from the infirmary. The threat if he didn't was to hand him over to the Black Gangster Disciples on the top deck for a "let's gang-bang a Nazi" party. That drug supply couldn't last forever. At some point he'd be fucked.

If he could get into Columbia River Correctional Institution, he'd have it made. CRCI was a minimum security prison with trees and visiting college students, according to the inmate chat line. The cons there were all close to the gate, with less than two years to go on their time. Everybody there was on their best behavior. Nobody's gonna let an old gang feud or prison yard beef get in the way of walking out of the door. Not when they are so close to freedom. Once Stan could move there he could sleep with both eyes closed and then start working the professor to push for an early release. It was all set, in his head.

With all the doom and gloom going around, Zak thought it would be a good idea to accept Kiko's invitation for another night out. His brain wasn't settled enough to develop and organized dating strategy and she had made herself available. There was a Japanese film based on a manga comic book playing at the International Film Festival, and she thought he'd like it. So they messaged each other on Facebook and agreed to meet in front of the theater at 7 pm.

The film was about a ninja named Naruto who was fighting a bunch of aliens hell-bent on crashing the moon into the Earth. It reminded Zak of Speed Racer, Astroboy, and Pokemon; basically all the Japanese animation he grew up with, full of wide-eyed kids taking on the world.

Kiko giggled at the translations. During the sad parts, she put her head on his shoulder. Zak took it as permission to at least think about something that Americans and Japanese people can surely agree on; that you have to start with first base. Baseball metaphors were lost on the French, but they held true in the land of the rising sun. "Hottu doggu!"

After the film ended, Zak noticed he wasn't the only white guy with an Asian date. Oh, the pain of realizing you are a walking cliche. They followed the crowd of international film fest-types out onto the park blocks. The night was cooler than normal and Kiko held Zak's hand.

That he was conflicted would be stating the obvious. He figured that his first post-'my wife and unborn child were crushed to death' date should be with someone more significant. Someone who could empathize with his story. Someone with their own baggage. But his story might be too much for *them*. This was the transitionary phase and such flights of fancy could be excused.

Besides, she had given him more green lights than a presidential motorcade.

"Buy a girl a drink, sir?" She studied the come-hither look and perfected it in selfies that she posted on Flickr. To Zak, she looked like the girls in the manga comics, complete with white knee socks. So they slipped off to a bar down the block. Nothing too fancy.

In a dark corner booth, with the excuse of a beer, he kissed her. It was his first kiss since he kissed Claire while standing on the rim of Crater Lake. Her tongue sent a blast of electricity through his crippled body and, for a second, he forgot all the pain.

She kissed like a high school girl on crack, like she was trying to eat his face off. So Zak pulled away. But Kiko threw her left leg over his lap, exposing her white panties as she tried to climb on him. After only one beer. Granted, it was a huge Sapporo, but things were moving too fast.

Suddenly Zak was back in the VW, with the domed roof caving in. Glass was shattering and he could hear the sound of Claire's bones breaking under the weight of the boulder. The music playing was by the band Modest Mouse, but it was drowned out by the sound of the tires dragging sideways across the pavement and into the ravine. He could faintly make out the sound of Caroline crying out, "Daddy, save us!"

"Hey, Kiko, do you think we could call it a night? It's been a long day and I still have exams to grade."

Kiko fell back into her seat and hrumphed like a disappointed child. "Oh, Professor. You got sad again. Let's be happy tonight, okay?"

But it was too late. Zak's head was in the past and it was going to be there for a while.

Lenny didn't like getting older. He dreamed of a magic potion that would bring his hairline back to the 2001 boundary. He wanted the crow's feet to stop becoming ruts, and then canyons on his face. Most of all, he wanted to be able to drink beer without it going straight to his paunch.

He stared at his face in the bathroom mirror and pushed his skin off his cheeks. Maybe some Botox. Everyone was doing it. He looked at his teeth, yellow from endless coffee and dark beer. They looked like goblin teeth. And they felt even worse. When was the last time he had gone to the dentist?

He put his fingers on one tooth that caught his eye and gave it a little push. It was loose! He pushed it again and it fell out, into the sink. "Crap!" he thought. "I need that tooth!"

For the sake of symmetry he pushed on the tooth on the opposite side of his mouth and it jumped right off the gums. Better, he thought.

Suddenly, the bottom front teeth were wobbling and, with a push from his tongue, were out as well. "Shit! I'm too young to need dentures already!" he thought. He tried to save the loose teeth, but some of them had already gone down the drain. He could feel his gums loosening to expel what was left in his mouth.

"Wait a second! This is a dream!" (He heard his voice say that in his head.) "I've had this dream before. Lots of times! I'm in a dream and I know I'm in a dream!"

Lenny didn't know what to do next. Should he jump out of the bathroom window and see if he could fly? Should he create some scene from sacred rock history? (The cover of the 1977 Kiss album *Love Gun* crossed his mind.) He rubbed is tongue across his empty gums and tasted what must be blood.

He rubbed is tongue again but there were his teeth. All of them, perfectly secure. He opened his eyes and saw the skylight above his bed.

It was three in the morning when Zak's phone rang. It was charging in the living room so he had to find it. At this hour it must be important. He stumbled over his dirty clothes in the dark, nearly wrenching his ankle on a shoe. The house was a mess so he'd have to follow the sound.

Shit, it was Lenny.

"Hello?"

"Dude, you up? I think I just did it!" Lenny sounded excited.

"Killed a guy?" asked Zak.

"I think I had a lucid dream!"

"Lenny, Christ. Could this have waited?" Zak knew that if he didn't write his dreams down right after he awoke, they would be gone forever, so he got the urgency, but still.

"No, man, I had to tell you about it. I think all that stuff is real. I was having a dream that my teeth were falling out, but, get this, I knew that it was a dream. So I made my teeth come back and then woke up! How cool is that?"

Zak was not as enthusiastic. "That's a pretty common dream, Lenny. I've had it before, too. It's supposed to mean that you have anxiety about becoming an adult. It's your subconscious memory of losing your baby teeth, one of the first physical transitions in life. That's all it means. You're Peter Pan and you don't want to grow up."

"Okay, Dr. Freud, you're all talk. That's all true but the point is that I knew that I was dreaming and I did something about it. Do you realize what this means?"

"What does it mean, Lenny?"

"I don't know what it means. But if it happens again, I'm going to try to fly or play at Coachella or something!"

"Or see Cozy?"

"Oh, yeah, you think you know everything. One guess where you would go in your dream." Lenny knew Zak well enough.

Zak was quiet. Seeing Claire in his dreams had become a drug he was not ready to kick.

"Anyway, I gotta come back to Portland on Thursday so we should talk. I think I'm on to something," Lenny continued.

"Don't come down on my account. I'm behind at work."

"No, there's a hot new band called The Falsies. All chicks. They write really catchy songs so we're going to sign them to a publishing deal. Their stuff would be great in a Target commercial or something."

"Fuck. Does anybody remember rock and roll? When did you become the devil?" Zak forgot that music has a long history of being exploited for some purpose.

"Shut it, Zak. You know ads are the only way to get your music heard any more. Blame MTV, not me." He had a point. "So, how did the date go with your Fukiyama mama? Come on, come on, spill."

"It's late. I'll tell you all about it on Thursday." Zak clicked Lenny off, like on TV, when people hang up without saying goodbye, because it's; a) fast and b) cool. But if he thought he was going to fall right back asleep, he was sadly mistaken.

His mind bounced around the last year of his life. He tried to calculate how old Caroline would be now. (Around 9 months old, out as long as she should have been in the womb.) And he thought about what he should have told people about at the group meeting; that after he awoke from the coma he regularly thought about suicide. Or at least moving to a mountain top somewhere down in Australia. Now he only craved escape.

As he drifted in and out, he heard Lenny's question. "You know what this means?"

Zak and Claire were at the Target in Jantzen Beach, almost to the Washington border. There was always baby stuff to get and those gift cards were coming in handy. Diapers, breast pump accessories, and endless socks (one was always missing). It was a hot summer day and they checked their list.

"Did you remember the gift card?" she asked.

He nodded yes, lost in her big brown eyes. They seemed to be calling his name. Zak, wake up. Pay attention.

"Honey, where's the baby?" Her big eyes turned to panic.

Zak calmly pointed to the red Target shopping cart. The car seat with the baby asleep was placed inside it. It was in the middle of the parking lot slowly rolling across the hot pavement.

"Caroline! Zak get her! She's rolling away! She's gonna melt in this heat or get hit! Why aren't you doing anything?"

He didn't understand why she was so upset. The men in white were watching. Everything would be fine. The world goes round and life goes on and on and on. He stood there watching his baby roll farther away from the Target store until she disappeared into the Home Depot on the other side of the parking lot. "She'll be safe there," he thought.

"You dream too much. It's going to end bad." (Richard Thompson)

Chapter 3:
This House Is Rockin'

1

Stan watched the stream of blood and shit flow past his face, across the bleached floor. It circled the drain endlessly. He lay there denying what had just happened. He had become a pawn between two skinhead gangs. It wasn't the Black Gangster Disciples that jumped him, it was three Aryans. They weren't even that big, but one wrapped a towel around his neck from behind and choked him out. That's what you get for letting your guard down in the joint.

His legs quivered as the now cold shower water ran over them, but he stayed put. He'd have to get up soon before someone saw him laying there and the news spread across the entire prison. He needed a minute and watched the brown and red swirls in front of him. They had their own serene beauty.

He rolled over and looked into the ceiling light. It had a throbbing rainbow halo around it. The yellow glow of his birth mother was faintly visible. Mother Mary. He thought he might be able to escape through it. But then he heard the sound of Spanish-speaking men coming into the bathroom. He found his towel and pulled himself up to his feet. "I got to get out of here," he thought.

Some of the faculty were meeting in a classroom at 5 pm to discuss their issues with the administration. Zak got an email and thought he'd stop by for a bit before seeing Kiko. He wasn't much of a rabble rouser, but he shared some of the concerns about the direction the school was headed. Tenured faculty were disappearing and being replaced by online courses and outsourced research projects. Higher education was becoming McDonaldized, and Zak worried about his future in it. Would the university become an artifact of the second millennium?

The room was a quarter full. Professors are solo actors, for the most part, happy to be locked in their offices with a stack of papers. They typically don't see themselves as "workers." They are the intellectual elite that have opinions about workers. But word had been going around that President Woodbine would be bringing the hammer down on anybody who flew the union flag. That meant cancelled promotions and shitty committee assignments. Oh, you think you have earned tenure? Well, we need you to chair this curriculum evaluation committee. Wrists slit.

Zak recognized Robin Nielsen, an education professor who had been putting up flyers for the meeting and had been talking to the media about the plight of the twenty-first century academic. Robin was a 40-something white woman who was fond of Mr. Rogers sweaters and skinny jeans. She looked more like a bookstore employee than a professor.

"Hi, Robin. Is this the meeting? I was expecting more people."

Robin looked around the room. "Yeah. Woodbine and his henchmen have put the fear of God into people. I'm going to start having screenings of *Norma Rae* just to piss them off. Word is he's got Claiborne spying on us." She fidgeted when she realized that seemed a bit paranoid.

"Who's that?" asked Zak.

"The new vice-provost. She's a real social climber and fucking hates professors. So this is going to be a tough fight. These people could care less about the students or the faculty. They only care about their little fiefdom in administration. If we don't push back now, we're going to lose this place to the management class. Anyways, we better get this meeting started before they send their goons in to bust it up."

Robin pulled the ragtag group together and talked briefly about the growing tension on campus. She presented some data on tenure-line faculty that had left for better paying positions at other schools. There was data on how faculty pay was falling behind the cost of living, but administrator pay was increasing, averaging over $200,000. Then she introduced an organizer from the

American Federation of Teachers to talk about the process of unionization.

Zak noticed an older woman with dyed black hair lurking outside the classroom door. He had a bad feeling about her in the pit of his stomach. So he grabbed his stack of data sheets and slipped out the door on the opposite side of the room. Sorry, Robin.

In the hallway he ran into Heather, his young graduate assistant. She was normally bubbly, her brown curly hair bouncing off her jean jacket, but today her hair was pulled back revealing a brow, wrinkled with concern.

"Professor Crisp. I was looking for you. Do you have a minute?"

"Hi Heather. Yeah, what's up?" With his life it could literally be anything.

"It's one of the inmates who has been writing you. This guy Stan Stipich out in eastern Oregon."

"Yeah, is that the guy that wants to be my RA?" Heather had briefed him on his first letter.

"That's the guy. I got to three more of his letters. They're pretty intense. Like, scary intense. He thinks you are blowing him off and purposely trying to get him killed. I think you need to respond to this guy personally. He saw my form letter as an insult. I'm kinda worried about this one."

"What's he in for?" Part of Heather's job was to take the inmates' State ID Numbers and use the Department of Corrections website to see what they were locked up for.

"Armed robbery, but I checked and he has some assault charges on his record. No gang affiliation but I emailed you his picture. He looks pretty scary."

All inmates look scary in their prison pictures. Only celebrities and politicians smile when they get arrested. Cons have to look as mean as possible. "Okay, let me take a look at them tonight. Maybe I should meet with this guy and diffuse the situation."

Heather pulled the letters out of her backpack and handed them to Zak with a look that said, 'I'm glad these are out of my hands now.'

Kiko was sitting on the floor with a half-eaten box of lo mein next to her. She was wearing a t-shirt of a band from before her birth that she had never actually listened to, The Clash. Her Converse sneakers were untied as she typed away on her laptop. As was the norm for the ADD generation, she had three tabs open and was participating in three worlds simultaneously.

On one screen she was moderating a discussion on a Reddit board about Hentai, a form of Japanese anime porn that strays into the bizarre. The topic was the presence of eels as rapist spirit animals in Japan. Kiko was arguing for the beauty and symmetry of eels as wish fulfillment of teenage sexuality. On a second screen, she was having a conversation with some of her American pupils on their class Blackboard website about Japanese verb conjugation. And on the third screen, she was creating a story on her LiveJournal blog about meeting an old man in Portland and cooking dinner for him and his cats.

She flowed between the three worlds as if they were one; pornographic, educational, and imaginary. Nobody on Reddit had their verb usage corrected. Nobody on the class website was told that sex with eels was acceptable in Japan. And the little old man had the best lo mein ever served in Portland.

She was about to go to YouTube to add a fourth screen when her phone rang. Her favorite professor's name flashed up on the screen.

"Hello, Professor. How are you? Do you want me to come down?"

"Hi Kiko. How's it going? Hey, something came up."

"Sir, you have to eat. We have to keep your strength up." Kiko was starting to feel used, like she was a placeholder in his emotional ping pong. "It's okay if you are sad."

"No, it's nothing like that. My graduate student handed me a stack of letters today from an inmate who is going off the deep end. I need to read them tonight and write a response. It's gonna take some focus. I promise we will catch up later in the week."

Kiko was crestfallen. Again. Her plan was not going very well. She could penetrate the wall of sadness. But the wall of work was a bigger challenge. It always seemed so important. She looked at the screens in front of her and saw her evening.

"Okay, sir. I don't want you to get murdered, so be careful. Can I send you some pictures later tonight?"

"Yeah, that would be great. Okay, I better get home and get this little project started. Goodnight."

"Goodnight, Professor."

Kiko took a break from her screens and watched some TV, masturbated three times, and took some pictures of herself striking provocative poses, pulling her T-shirt up to reveal her pink bra. She was going to email them to Zak but chickened out right before she hit the return button to send them. Instead she sent files of anime girls from various cartoons so she could later figure out kind of female he liked best.

It was the next day and Kiko was on campus for a zombie-themed art show. The university gallery was filled with giant canvases of people being eaten alive by the undead. The students really made the most of their red paint supply. There were a few sculptures of mangled body parts, and some low, eerie music playing.

She was in charge of the show and was meant to open the event by introducing a zombie dance number that the students had prepared. The crowd was waiting but the zombie dancers were nowhere to be found. Her mother was doing the make-up and must have been running late.

One of her Nursing Department professors approached her. "This looks great, Kiko. Is it starting soon? I have to get to class in a few minutes."

Kiko thought about how her mother was always screwing up her plans. The zombies could be on their way, or the dancers could be still standing in the parking lot, wondering where the make-up lady was. People were getting restless and her big event was about to go down into flames.

She didn't know what to say to her professor so she fell to her knees and bit into the woman's left thigh. Blood sprayed across her face as she made a growling sound. Kiko ripped large chunks of flesh away but the professor just looked at her with pity.

There were two drifters at the door. Zak saw them come in the gate through the front window. Two scruffy white guys in their late fifties, one with a grey hood over his head. They didn't look like canvassers, the twenty-something kids who came around selling environmental salvation, hoping to make their quota so they could cover rent.

Zak immediately had a bad feeling.

They could be tree-trimmers, looking to cut down the towering fir in the backyard. Or garden variety con-artists who occasionally knocked on his door. But he suspected that these two had something to do with one of the racist inmates he had somehow pissed off.

"Go into the bedroom and call 911," he told Claire. "And take the baby."

"What? Why?" She took Caroline up into her arms, trying to see what her husband was looking at.

"Just do it. It's probably nothing. A few homeless guys on the porch. But I'm going to go around back. I don't want to open the front door."

Claire had a look on her face like, "this better not be the last time I see you." Zak, thought for a moment that there was something he needed to say to her in case it was, but couldn't remember. Mother and child were fused together and his only impulse was to protect them. So he headed out the back door, grabbing a baseball bat along the way.

Circling around the north side of the house he saw the two men knocking on his front door. "Can I help you?" Zak asked with his face.

When they saw the baseball bat in his hand, the men pushed their way through his front door. Zak watched. To his left he saw the police in white walking down the sidewalk and tried to call out to them but no sound came out of his mouth. One looked over his shoulder at him as they walked away.

In the morning, Zak took one last look at the letter he wrote to the anxious inmate before he put it in the outgoing mail with the bills.

Dear Mr. Stipich,

Thank you for your letters. I'm sorry I haven't been able to respond to you personally until now. As you might have guessed, we've received an overwhelming response to the requests for participants in this study. Heather has been a huge help responding to people. It's great news, as the more folks we can interview, the stronger our findings will be and the more weight they will carry when it's time for policy recommendations. So your enthusiasm is much appreciated.

Heather gave me the visitor application form you sent me. I will send it in today and perhaps be cleared to come out and visit you in a week or so. I'm anxious to have a long conversation with you about the health issues of inmates. After reading your letters, it's obvious you know a great deal about it and will be of great help to this project.

Since I don't work for the Department of Corrections, I don't know how much sway I would have in getting you transferred to CRCI, but I will ask if it's possible. You're right in that it would be much more convenient. But until we can figure that out let's plan on meeting soon.

It sounds like you have a good relationship with other inmates. It would be helpful if you could ask around and get a sense of how many people you know had left a particular correctional facility with some illness, even the flu. Thanks again and hopefully we we talk in person soon.
Sincerely,
Dr. Zachary Crisp
Department of Health Studies

After reading Stipich's letters, Zak could tell that he was highly intelligent. Even though he was associated with white supremacists, he reminded Zak of a character in *The Autobiography of Malcolm X*. West Indian Archie was one of the criminals Malcolm ran with in his early days. After he became a black nationalist, Malcolm realized that many of those "thugs" were just as smart as the white guys on Wall Street and, given the same chances of life (meaning without the racism and classicism), would be down on Wall Street beating them at their own game. Given another set of circumstances, Zak could be discussing this project with Professor Stipich.

But Zak also remembered Claire's warning; be careful with inmates, they can be users. Once they get their hooks into somebody outside of the wall, they can play on your heart strings. Soon you are putting money on their commissary books, writing letters to the parole board, and delivering drugs to their old lady. He felt uneasy sending Stipich a visitation form with his driver's license number on it. He imagined an Aryan Brotherhood identity theft ring operating in the prison laundry room. To be safe, he sent the form directly to the prison supervisor.

Because he didn't have to be on campus that day, Zak decided to work from home. And since putting that letter in the mail was the only pressing requirement on his "work" list, he spent the next hour on his laptop entering online contests for trips to anywhere. London, Hawaii, Ireland, Los Angeles to see a Disney movie premiere, Nashville to see the CMA awards. Anywhere was better than here. He could take Lenny or give the extra ticket to charity, or have his own contest. Win a free trip to Orlando, Florida with a widower! There surely would be stiff competition for that prize.

He made a pot of coffee and splashed some Scotch in his mug. It was after noon somewhere. He switched on Oregon Public Radio and plopped back down on the couch with the laptop. There was time to plow through some emails before *Who Wants To Be A Millionaire?* came on. He ignored the ones from Robin Nielsen and anything that looked spammy. (This included messages from the American Federation of Teachers. Robin must've shared her email list with them.) There was an email from Lenny and another from Kiko. Both came in late last night. He hesitated and weighed the pros and cons of opening either. He chose Lenny's first.

Hey bro! Looking forward to meeting up Thursday. I think I'm on to something with this dream thing. Been having some good ones. Last night I was at an AC/DC concert, Highway To Hell era and Angus was like 500 feet tall!

Much to discuss. You're going to see the Falsies with me on Friday and there's a house party Thursday. Let's party like it's 1979.

Zak thought about pretending the email from Kiko never made it though the internet, but his curiosity got the better of him. It was attached to a large Zip drive, so he poured a cup of Scotch-coffee before opening it up. He had a feeling there would be a quiz on the contents later.

The file had about a hundred pictures of cartoon girls, not Betty and Veronica, but Japanese anime girls in seductive poses. They had names like Black Henekawa, Isuzu, Obvi Illya and Holo the Wise-Wolf. Some had cat ears, some had tails. All looked looked like over-sexualized twelve-year-olds. Kiko had included a note in the email.

Here are some J-girls for you, sir. I hope they make you smile. Please tell me which one is your favorite.

Tucked in the file, pictures 77 and 78, were two non-animated jpgs. They were selfies of Kiko, on her futon staring seductively into the camera. Her shirt was unbuttoned, showing her bra and her right knee was up, lifting her plaid skirt above the crotch. Consenting adults, okay, go.

The whole thing made him feel a bit dirty so he thought he'd do some yard work; more specifically, clean out the garbage can. Portland garbage collection was only bi-weekly; a sad attempt to get people to recycle and compost more. Besides the fact that much trash was now thrown in blue recycle bins, the green garbage bins, with two weeks of trash housed in them, created a new and horrible stench that floated across the Rose City on hot days. The sun was out, so without more pressing matters, Zak decided to grab a garden hose and spray his bin out.

The chores of a homeowner, a simple task with a beginning and an end. He had never done this before, which meant some of the funk was festering from before the accident. Whatever foulness was in there may have been started by a leaky garbage bag that his pregnant wife had tossed in one Monday night. He set the can on its side in his front yard and turned the water up all the way to blast the past out of the bottom.

What came out was a black goo. God knows what it was. Like squid ink stuck to bits of tissue paper and plastic. The more water he sprayed into the bin, the blacker it got, pouring onto the grass and then seeping onto the sidewalk. There it pooled into a puddle like a black hole. People walking their dogs and kids on tricycles would have to go around it, because that's who lived in the hood these days. Zak tried to wash it away but it just got blacker.

Stan grew increasingly impatient with the lack of response from the Portland professor, not knowing a reply was already in the mail. "I will not be used," he muttered under his breath.

"What's that, fat boy?" It was Kennedy, the prime shot caller of the Peckerwood skinhead gang. Stan was sitting on a bench that was the part of the prison yard that they had claimed as their territory. "You know, you're not supposed to be sitting here, bitch." Kennedy was a big fella. He had come up as a runner in the Irish Mafia and got sentenced on an illegal weapons charge. Inside the joint he saw a vacuum and filled it with a new chapter of the Insane Peckerwoods. Now he had full run of the yard and the house and was not a motherfucker to be trifled with.

"Hey, Kennedy. Sorry, I was a little tired and needed to sit a minute." Stan made no eye contact as a sign of respect.

"No doubt, punk. I've heard you've had a rough week. I shouldn't be seen even talking to you. But since you're here, let's have a little parley." Kennedy got uncomfortably close. Stan looked at the ground. "According to the niggers, there's a new box of Oxy in the infirmary. I want you to get it for us. It's not locked up yet."

"How the hell am I supposed to do that?"

"You think I give a fuck, snitch? You're supposed to be the little brown nose in the clinic. Figure it out. I've already told all the tribes that you're going to procure this shipment for us, so if you don't, it's gonna be bad. Real bad."

Stan nodded like he had it all under control and walked away. Things just went from bad to worse.

The dark Portland night washed into her office window. Kelly was working late. She worried about her cats getting hungry but she had an important task. She had access to the university server and therefore all the emails that passed through to and from *.edu* addresses assigned to the school. She started with Robin Nielsen's email announcement of the organizing meeting and logged everyone who replied, even those who said they couldn't come. She looked up each person on the department websites to see who she could recognize from the meeting to create a second list, labeled "Core Agitators."

Zak had sent one of those emails. *I have another meeting but will stop by if I can get out of it.* She looked him up and immediately recognized the professor trying to lure the female student into his sex web. "That guy" she whispered and put an asterisk next to his name.

She had taken down many of the meeting flyers herself and had a student worker from the provost's office collect the rest. (He said he did, but actually he helped take flyers down that were covering the meeting flyers.)

Kelly made a spreadsheet. Who was tenured and who was up for promotion. Who had big external grants and who brought no money into the university coffers. She used Facebook accounts to try to find out who was married (not that that meant anything). What did spouses do? Did any work in unionized jobs? Most telling, she put the men at the top of the list and the women at the bottom.

The Excel sheet quickly filled up with columns and rows of useful data. But the task was coming at the end of a long day and Kelly was beginning to crash. The sugar from her venti Caramel Frappuccino had long washed away any effect of the caffeine and the vice provost felt her eyelids sink together as the screen blurred out.

She was finally walking across campus when she noticed something strange. There were two cars parked on an empty grassy lot. One car was empty but two people were in the other car, talking. It seemed like a scene in a mobster movie. When the two got out, she immediately recognized them: Professors Nielsen and Crisp.

She silently glided behind them to see what they were up to. They entered a campus building she had never noticed before. Through the window she could see them join other faculty members in a large room. Retired Professor Toth was playing bongos. This must be a union meeting. Then her view faded to black.

3

It was a potential minefield. Even if it went his way, Zak could end up with a complaint or a shitty review on RateMyProfessor. He was free and clear; Kiko was not his student anymore. But she was young and foreign and it could look bad. He once taught himself that when in doubt the best course of action was to do absolutely nothing.

He didn't listen to himself.

It seemed like the time. She had basically thrown herself at him and seemed upset every time he rejected her. But where would this end? That question didn't get as much attention as it should have. So he called her to make up for the missed sushi date and maybe push himself out of his slump.

She seemed excited on the phone and agreed to take a bus and meet him in a karaoke bar on his side of the river. Karaoke, roughly translated from the Japanese words "empty" and "orchestra," was a bit of an empty institution in Portland. Portland, where everyone was a rock star when the beer and shots were flowing. According to Yelp there were over a hundred bars in the city with karaoke. On any given night there was some drunk doing an ungodly version of "Bohemian Rhapsody" or a caucasian douchebag thinking he's being clever by rapping "Baby's Got Back." Then some chick blasts a reverential version of an Aretha classic before it's back to the dorky couple doing "Summer Nights" from *Grease*.

So when Kiko walked in in a white t-shirt and a plaid skirt, Zak could only guess what she would sing.

"Hello, sir!" She seemed elated to finally be asked out. "I like this place. Are you going to sing?" The bar was called The

Fish Tale and had a tiki vibe right out of 1958. The KJ wore a Hawaiian shirt and handed out leis to singers, good or bad.

Zak sat with the song book in front of him and a bottle of beer. "I'm thinking about it. But only if you sing. Can I order you a drink?"

"I'll have a Lemon Drop, sir!" Someone was doing a fair version of "Don't Stop Believing" as Kiko sat next to Zak, not across from him, at the table.

"Okay, then, we're going to sing. Better get your song in. Looks like there are a couple of groups here," he said.

Since she had already thought about it, she wrote her song on a little slip of paper and handed it to the KJ. Zak followed suit with his slip and a dollar. A fat tip to tell the master of ceremonies to move them up on the queue.

But, for a Wednesday night, it took forever. There was another version of "Don't Stop Believing," two versions of "Sweet Caroline" (each making Zak want to vomit) and what seemed to be a bridal party/interpretive dance version of "Love Shack." Zak ordered another beer and a giant plate of nachos to share. Kiko ordered a second Lemon Drop and waited patiently for her song.

After a drunk guy fell off a table doing an over-acted version of "Born to Run," the KJ announced, "Alright folks, next up at The Fish Tale is Miss Kiko Kitty doing another classic from the seventies."

She leapt up and took the microphone. Looking like she had practiced it in front of the mirror twenty times, she took off into her rendition of "I Want You To Want Me" that was, at best, uncomfortable. It wasn't that she was horribly off-key (that's expected in karaoke), but that she sang it directly to Zak in a sexual manner that directly contrasted her juvenile outfit. Surely registered sex offenders all over Portland were getting texts that read, "Get down The Fish Tale right now!" Zak smiled nervously and very quickly regretted the whole thing. The routine made him look like a major creepazoid. He wanted to crawl under the nacho cheese.

The song seemed to go on for an entirety. Longer than a Meatloaf song. The erratic dancing made the number more like an elementary school Ritalin meltdown. Zak quickly scanned the room to make sure no one he knew was there. Suddenly he was paranoid that his students were in the bar.

Polite brief applause. Kiko wasn't singing to the room so she didn't care. "Did you like that, sir? That song is old as you." She laughed and blamed it on the Lemon Drops.

Before Zak could answer, the KJ called up the next singer. "This should be good. Next up we have a singer called The Professor with his rendition of 'I Am Woman.'"

Karaoke song choices are a big deal. If you actually have chops, you can get away with an Adele number, but most people screech over-the-top versions of Journey and Madonna songs. A drunk dude doing a Judas Priest song or a nerdy girl doing Ariana Grande might be entertaining, but it's always the same. The song books have thousands of songs, but people sing the same thirty songs over and over again. KJs must have a high suicide rate.

Zak wanted his choice to be clever and meaningful, not for Kiko but for the universe (and the poor KJ). So he chose Helen Reddy's 1972 hit, "I Am Woman." Zak fancied himself as a feminist but the fact that he was a he singing a she song would make it a hit with the drunkards. Plus, the song was in a lower key, so it was actually perfect for a dude to sing. Yes, I am wise, but it's wisdom born of pain.

Unlike Kiko, Zak sang to the room and they responded in kind, with the fellas joining in on the chorus. I am strong! Women came up and put their leis around his neck. It was a great moment in his mind. So much better than another Bon Jovi song.

Kiko was confused. She didn't understand why he chose that song (Was he secretly transgender?) and why he didn't sing a song to her. But she kept up appearances. "That was wonderful! You can really sing!" All said with a beaming smile.

The next singer launched into the Johnny Cash version of "Hurt," bringing the vibe in the bar down to self harm-level and Zak decided to use his momentum to take a chance. "Hey, do you want to get out of here? I'm kind over this scene."

Finally. Kiko took a last sip of her drink, grabbed her sweater and hopped up. "I'm ready! Let's go!"

They climbed into Zak's Acura without much of a plan, both glad to be out of the noisy bar, but for different reasons. Zak was glad because his hearing was shot after years of shows and music turned up to 11. In noisy bars he could no longer make out what people were saying to him and blankly nodding had gotten him into trouble in the past. Kiko was happy because this was the next step of her fantasy adventure and would at least provide material for her next blog post.

"Well, where to next?" asked Zak, turning over the reins to his young companion.

"I think we should watch monster movies. Do you have any?" It was a not-too-subtle I'm inviting myself to your place question, but Zak didn't mind.

"Jeez, no but we could pick one up at the video store. You can choose." So they zipped off to the late night video store on Northeast Alberta and spent a half hour inspecting the weirdly obsessive collection of classic Japanese monster movies. After much thought, Kiko decided Zak needed to see the 1966 film, *Gamera vs. Barugon.*

Upon entering the house, the butterflies were back bouncing around Zak's belly. What was he doing? He didn't exactly prepare the house for guests, let alone a potential lover. Customarily he would have begged pardon of the messy living room but instead nervously excused himself to the kitchen to nuke some popcorn while Kiko settled on to the couch. She noted the books and stacks of student papers on the table. "So this is where the professor lives," she thought. "I like it."

About thirty minutes into the film, around the time Barugon starts smashing Osaka like a city made out of cardboard models, Kiko put her hand on Zak's and gave him a look that said, "So? What are you waiting for?" So he gave in to the opening and kissed her.

Kiko launched into the moment. Hands and legs were a blur of motion. Zak let go and melted into the slobberfest as thousand foot tall monsters screamed in the background. It felt good not to care, to connect to another person while Osaka burned. His shoulders unclenched as he ran his hands up her back under her shirt.

Still interested in the outcome of Gamera and Barugon's little conflict, he used the film to slow things down, to take a break from the necking. She had deemed it important for him to see this particular flick, right? So they kissed and watched and watched and kissed. Kiko smiled and Zak saw Barugon destroyed by his own rainbow beams. Then it was time for the "What now?"

Lenny was back in New York on an elevated subway platform somewhere outside of Manhattan. Fortunately it was enclosed because there was a pretty heavy snowstorm in the city and station was warm. While he waited for the train, he gazed out the giant arched windows at the scene below. The street was completely white with snow. There was no traffic at all, just a handful of people in the middle of the road throwing snowballs. The storm had shut everything down and people were enjoying the disruption from the normal noisy grey by soaking in the silent white.

Suddenly, the playful people hit the ground, all facing the end of the street. Lenny spun left to see what had made them all take such a drastic action. It was a giant wave of snow blowing their way, maybe three hundred feet high. It reminded him of the giant sandstorms that were becoming more common in the Southwest as climate change turned Arizona into the Sahara. Haboobs, that's what they're called.

The snow tsunami made a massive roar that beat against the station windows. He wanted to see if the people survived, but his train was pulling in to the station, its roar as loud as the snow. He turned away from the window and towards his train. Through the train windows, on the opposite platform, he saw Cozy walking away. What was she doing in New York? Maybe an opera thing. The Brooklyn Academy of Music might be near.

He thought he'd jump through the train to her platform and surprise her. But the doors on his side of the train didn't open. He tried to follow her through the crowd of commuters but as the train pulled out of the station she disappeared and he stood there. Suddenly the whole thing seemed wrong, like it had never happened. He wasn't in New York.

By the time the film was done, Zak still had some options. It was 2 am and he could have offered to drive her home. But he remembered the game. "It's pretty late. Do you want to stay over?" he asked. There were still options at this point. He could sleep on the couch, or on the floor of the nursery.

"I think that's a very good idea, sir." Kiko's face was beaming. Enough with this first base business, it seemed to say.

The train was pulling out of the station. Or about to pull in the station, if you're a Freudian. Whatever it was, Zak decided to ride. So he showed her his bedroom, clearing away a mess of books and boxes from the grocery store that were used to hold the last of Claire's things until he could find them a suitable home. Kiko looked at the framed rock posters on the wall. The Replacements, Madonna, and ELO. It was smaller than she imagined and, for some reason, it smelled like peppermint.

"It's kind of a wreck in here. Sorry. I'm going to brush my teeth. There's a new toothbrush if you want to use it." But she didn't. She wanted to get undressed and climb under the comforter in the professor's bedroom, which is exactly what she did while Zak was in the adjacent bathroom.

His face still looked lopsided in the mirror. Maybe not as lopsided as usual. Maybe his good luck had healed his deformity a little. At least he wasn't horrified by what he saw. He tried to focus on that instead of the looming question - Was he about to do something stupid?

When he returned, breath fresher, he first noticed Kiko's white shoulders above the comforter that Claire had bought at Macy's. C'mon, train, carry me home. Forward, forward. She was still smiling.

"Get under the covers, sir. It's cold in here!"

He slipped off his jeans and climbed into the bed. When he ran his hands over her hips, he could tell she was naked. She reached up to turn off the lamp on her side of the bed and his eyes focused on the acne on her back. As the lights went out, she turned to lay her naked body on top of his.

"Don't you want to take all your clothes off?"

So he did, nervously. But then he let go. He had put on a Death Cab For Cutie CD in the living room and let the music carry him away. His arms wrapped around her and he kissed her neck. She smelled like hand soap but moaned like she was not quite clean.

"Sir, I have something to tell you." Okay, this is where the adolescent "I love you," speech comes on, or the VD disclosure. Zak braced himself. She put her lips to his ear, "I've never done this before."

4

One of the things that had turned Zak's neighborhood from a low rent inner-city red zone to a gentrifying destination spot for tourists and young professionals was Last Thursday. Last Thursday was an art-walk meant to contrast the monthly First Thursday event in the upscale Pearl District, where people who dress like magazine models looked at over-priced paintings in swank galleries while sipping wine and talking about who was having kids. Last Thursday was the low-rent cousin who hawked her watercolor art on the sidewalk.

Like every bohemia before it, the bourgeois tourists flocked in and ruined Alberta Street. They ruined the Latin Quarter in Paris in the 1850s and North Beach in San Francisco in the 1950s and they ruined NE Alberta's Last Thursday. Instead of people coming to patronize up-and-coming artists, they came to stand in the middle of Alberta and text their friends the following message;

Dude, I'm standing in the middle of Alberta. This scene is off the chain. I'm so much cooler than you.

And they'd never buy any art before heading, drunk, back to Beaverton or whatever suburban shithole they drove in from. Sometimes before retreating they would stop to pee or puke in Zak's front yard. The art walk had become everything that was bad about Mardis Gras and it happened every month.

Zak was standing on his porch and there was a couple in flagrante delicto in his front yard. He'd seen a lot but he'd never seen a naked couple having sex under his Azalea bush. He was about to yell at them but then he stopped. It wasn't Thursday, let alone Last Thursday.

He looked at the woman, his eyes moving down her back, and a black tar was seeping out of her vagina, on to the grass. It definitely wasn't blood. It was black as pitch. He recognized it. It was the black goo that he had just washed out of his dumpster. Holy shit! This was a dream!

A feeling of euphoria filled him as he realized that he was lucid in his own dream. He instinctually started swimming up in the air. The excitement overcame him as he realized he was levitating, about five feet up. He looked back down to see if it was really happening.

Below him he saw Kiko, asleep in his bed with her head on his shoulder. He was there asleep, having the dream where he was above looking at himself. The elation turned to sadness at Kiko's intrusion into the scene.

Why can't I share this with Claire? And then it ended.

Kelly stood outside of Professor Crisp's Thursday morning Public Health Policy class. She was looking for clues. How radical was this guy? Was he openly critical of the administration in front of sixty impressionable undergraduates? More importantly, was he currying favors from the female students? She might be able to figure out if she could get access to his gradebook. Who was his teaching assistant? On one hand, this skulking was below her pay grade. But a big win against the faculty would surely put her in line for the provost's position, if it ever opened up.

Listening to Crisp drone on about "perceived socio-economic disadvantages among health care professionals" seemed lefty enough, but it also took her back a long, long, long time ago. She was a professor once. She could hold a room full of students in the palm of her hand. But where was the real reward than that? It was a pompous illusion. Oh, I got these kids to think about Louisa May Alcott differently today. And then one asks, "Hey, is this gonna be on the test?"

Zak was oblivious to the administrative spy taking notes in the hallway. He barely even noticed the several students who walked in after the lecture began. He was half there. Maybe only a quarter there. Another quarter thinking about his brief moment of lucidity, a third quarter excited that Lenny was coming down to pow wow about dreams and a big fat quarter processing his sexcapade with Kiko.

He felt like a school girl who had reluctantly lost her virginity. It was less special than he had hoped but he was glad it was out of the way. He felt unclean. He certainly acted shamefaced as he dropped her off at her campus apartment on his way to work and told her he'd call her (no kiss). He really was barely present for this class at all.

Fortunately all his lectures were now on PowerPoint slides. Since the accident knocked out his right side, his handwriting had become illegible. As much as he loved the sound of chalk clacking against the board, no student could be held responsible for the scrawl that would cover the board now. So he relied on the crutch of too many teachers. Throw the slide up and watch the little doggies start to drool. It's like you're not even in the room. So while they copied whatever was on the screen, he juggled his thoughts.

As a new slide went up he glanced down at the syllabus on the podium. It was his and the students' guide to the ten week class, planned out to the day. Next Tuesday's lecture topic will be... Have Chapter 3 read by... The mid-term is on... It was a perfect plan that never happened. In all his years of teaching he never made it to the material listed for Week 10. Some news event or prolonged discussion or film that ran long or snow day always got in the way and upset the orderly procession. While the students scribbled the bullet points on the slides in their notebooks, Zak wondered how his personal drama would fuck up his pretty syllabus this quarter.

If Kelly knew what Zak was thinking, she would have been much more interested. She even tried to see if the Asian girl from his office was in this class. But the lecture bored her and she had other names from her spreadsheet to poke her head in on. For now Zak was safe.

Stan's morning was not so boring. His job at the prison clinic was only Sunday through Tuesday. He had to find excuse to be there on a Thursday. He told the guard that he was covering another inmate's shift and when the guard couldn't get the nurse on the phone he wrote Stan a pass to go and head on over. It was one crack in a very tightly sealed door.

"Hi, Stipich. You're not working today. You sick?" The staff only ever used inmates last names. It was a step up from referring to them by their inmate number, but it was still meant to remind them of who was in charge. Only human beings have first names. This nurse would have had to look at some paperwork to know that Stan's name was Stan.

"Oh, I left a book in here the other day and it's due back in the library. Can I grab it?" He was nervous. There was no book, only a box of OxyContin that was too big to shove up his ass. His only plan was that the clinic would be empty and he'd grab the box and walk out with it. Maybe stashing it in a trash can until he could get it to one of the Peckerwoods. He forgot that in the joint you always need three or four plans.

The nurse wasn't buying it. The cons always had a con going, especially when there were meds around. She folded her arms around her blue smock. "What's the name of it?"

"Um, it's called *Paradise Lost*. I think I left it in the storeroom. Okay if I go back there and look for it?" Maybe he could stick it in an air vent or in the recycling.

"You know I can't let you back there today. It'll probably be there on Sunday. You can look then. Have a good day, friend." And she shooed him out the door. Some friend.

The claustrophobic walls in the hallway got a lot closer. The yellow painted cinderblocks felt like an overly lit tomb and he was not climbing out. Kennedy's sergeants would be looking for him to deliver and he was a cat on life number nine. His best bet was to just keep moving in the shadows. Stairwells and psych meetings. Not the yard and definitely not his cell.

"Every time I come down this street it's completely fucking different." Lenny was meeting Zak back at Café Carlos.

(Zak had a weakness for their Oregon Cherry pie.) "Are we even still in Portland?"

"Yeah, the crack house around the corner is now an artisan sushi bar." It was a line that Zak had been using for years now.

Complaining about gentrification was something of a pastime in Portland. Everyone loved the city the way it was five minutes ago, before "they" invaded. When Zak moved here from Alabama in the 1990s everyone was complaining about Californians. People were getting bumper stickers that read, "Native Oregonian since 1958," like anyone who came after 1958 was a total poser and Mr. Came-In-1958 was the authentic deal. It was the same with bands. "I saw Sleater-Kinney at LaLuna in '96. All these new fans are posers!" Everyone claims authenticity.

Gentrification was the newest status hierarchy for hipsters. "I lived in this neighborhood before the Yuppies (Is that even a thing anymore?) moved in!" Of course, the hipsters were the first wave of gentrifiers, pushing the long-time black residents out of the inner-city "wilderness," making the land safe for white settlers. It was an old story. But the complaining never got old.

"It's only a matter of time before this coffee shop gets turned into a Starbucks," moaned Zak. "So tell me about this band, The Falsehoods."

"Falsies, Jack. But The Falsehoods makes for a good name as well. I'm gonna hold on to that." Lenny pushed his hair back and took a noisy slurp from his latte. "They're really good, all young chicks, four piece, power pop, lots of hooks. You can tell they got their mom and dad's Kiss records out and studied every lick."

"So you think you can sell them to Madison Avenue?" Zak asked with a disgusted look on his face, like 1958 Oregonians looking at a bunch of 1995 Californians moving into the neighborhood.

"Dude, you know how it is now. MTV is dead. Radio is a bunch of preprogrammed animals and geographic features. The Wolf, The Mountain, The Eagle."

"The River," said Zak

"The Lamprey," replied Lenny.

"The Sinkhole," said Zak, picking up on the absurdist game.

Lenny, in is best fake FM DJ voice, "Rock 107.7, The Sinkhole. We're going to take you down to the bottom."

Zak was on board. "Yeah, I know. College radio is gone and whatever's on the air now plays the same 100 songs over and over. You know what? I used to really love 'Black Water' by the Doobie Brothers. Now if I ever hear that song again, I'm going to throw a puppy off a bridge."

"Harsh, Holmes. Maybe a kid but not a puppy."

"But commercials aren't any better. Remember when The Who mattered? Now they are the background noise in a shoe commercial," said Zak.

"Well, don't judge me but I tried to get 'Squeeze Box' sold for an ad." Lenny looked down.

"What the fuck? An ad for what? Charmin?"

"Playtex tampons. I didn't go over very well. Anyway, it's the world we live in. It's the best bet for a new band these days. They get a song into a car commercial and they can make a shitload of money."

"And forever be known as that band in the car commercial." Zak still had hope for rock and roll authenticity, as mythical as it might be. Lenny had the same hope, to return to a golden age when the music mattered to the kids, but, for now, the song harvesting business paid the bills.

"Hey, we're being up, remember?" reminded Lenny. "Good times ahead. Some Falsies will be at this party tonight. You should bring your new girlfriend. How's it going with her, anyway? How was karaoke?"

Zak paused. Should he tell him about last night's crossing of the Rubicon or would it be too much like bros bragging about a hook up? Lenny leaned in, sensing there was some news.

"She's not my girlfriend," said Zak, digging into his Brandied Peach pie.

"But…" C'mon, Zak, you're among friends. Pretty much your only friend these days.

"Well, um, she spent the night last night and I'm not a virgin widower any more." It felt good to say it.

"That's stellar. It's about time. I get the sadness, but it's been a year. And don't worry about it. It's just a thing. You broke the seal. Now you can date like a normal human. You should invite her to this party tonight." Lenny was trying to be a pal.

More hesitation. "No, I don't think so. I think I gotta do the cooling off period. Besides, I think she likes me too much."

"What, is she like sixteen? No worries. Lots of cool ladies await tonight. Who wouldn't want to meet a hip… what is it that you do again?"

"Health science," muttered Zak.

"Yeah, who wouldn't want to meet a health scientist?"

Zak stuck his face in his coffee cup as Lenny eyed a young woman coming into the café. Before Lenny could play matchmaker, Zak asked, "So what's up with your dreams these days. I've been anxious to talk about it."

"Me too, Professor. But I think we're gonna need a few jars of beer in us first. I'll lay it all out tonight."

"Thursday night rockin' house party. Oh boy, you don't get more Portland than that," said Zak with a sigh.

Stan was standing outside his house in outer Southeast Portland. The snobs in the Pearl called the area Felony Flats. It probably deserved the name. His house looked more run down than normal. The sky blue paint was peeling and the screens on the window were torn. He heard a crash of a lamp against the wall and the sound of his girlfriend and a man screaming. It was probably her smack dealer. Heavy troubles.

This wasn't a rare occurrence. The two fought all the time. Usually, he went into the backyard for a smoke and waited for it to resolve with her getting some heroin and Mr. Dealer getting something Stan didn't want to know about. This time it sounded like the end of the world. He stood there and his feet were glued to the driveway.

She had been trying to quit and maybe get her kids back. Her dealer had bought a gun. Stan couldn't explain what he couldn't see but he knew something was wrong. He had to get inside. But he couldn't move or speak. He just stood there and watched the house rock.

Chapter 4:
Gonna Raise Hell

1

She had assembled a group of Japanese females for him to have sex with. There were older women in traditional geisha costumes, teenage girls with enormous breasts, punk girls and professional women of his age. The line went out the bedroom door. Kiko wanted to see which type excited him the most so she could adjust herself accordingly.

She stood beside the bed and translated Zak's comments or wishes into Japanese and their replies into English. An entire night seemed to take place in a moment. As hard as it was to watch him make love to other women, she knew it had to be done. She was hoping the underage schoolgirls would do the trick. She could pull that one off. That he responded to the thirty-something woman who slowly slid out of her business suit and talked more than giggled worried her. That would be more of a challenge.

But the line was long so there was still a possibility that he could be aroused by someone that was closer to who she was willing to be.

Zak and Lenny got to the house party late. Zak had a few errands to run including a trip to the grocery store. If he was going to be hosting guests again he needed a few things in the fridge. Beer and salsa and maybe eggs for breakfast. Lenny wanted to tag along. "There's always hot mamas at the grocery store," he said. There are also "hot office girls" working at the bank. And "hot yoga girls" at the gym. Lenny seemed to base his interaction with the business world based on the likelihood of running into hot chicks. That's probably why he joined a rock band.

"Don't you ever quit?" was Zak's only reply.

"Why? It's my engine," he said. Zak didn't know if Lenny's skirt chasing masked sadness over losing Cozy or if Cozy was a manifestation of his lust for all women. Well, almost all.

So after dinner, a trip to Fred Meyer to buy beer and lottery tickets, and a couple hours watching Lou Reed videos on YouTube, they finally got to the party around ten, which is late-ish for a Thursday. It was in a large house in Southeast Portland in the Hawthorne neighborhood, one of the few residences in the district that hadn't yet been flipped by prospectors yet. It was Portland pre-*Grimm*, pre-*Portlandia*, pre-Voodoo Donuts.

Lenny was in his usual attire, including a vintage Stones shirt under his black leather jacket that was not bought at Urban Outfitters. It was Zak's first party in a while so he kept it simple: jeans, a red Gang-of-Four T-shirt (reunion tour) and a black Dickie jacket, his eyes down at the ground. They walked in to a Fugazi song from the early nineties playing on a downstairs sound system, a signifier of coolness. The crowd was certainly younger than the duo but Zak guessed that Lenny didn't notice.

"Geez, I haven't been to a party in ages," lamented Zak.

"There were a lot more parties before Facebook took over," replied Lenny. "Okay, we're in. Let's get our red cup on and see if any of the Falsies are here." Lenny was anxious to have the dream talk and Zak was beginning to feel like being at a lame party was the price to hear it.

"Lenny T. Rockstar!" A young woman with straight brown hair and tattoos on her bare arms came out of the crowd. This was Kathy East, the bass player of The Falsies and acting manager. An aspiring filmmaker, she picked up the guitar after seeing Sleater-Kinney play an all ages show when she was thirteen, but switched to bass because her left hand refused to make bar chords. "I was hoping you'd make it. Do you want a beer?"

"I'll get 'em," said Zak hoping to excuse himself from any business and/or pick-up action he wasn't part of.

"Hold on, man. I want you to meet Kathy. She's in this band I was telling you about. She's a great songwriter. This is my friend Zak. He's a boring professor but has one of the best record collections you ever saw."

"Nice to meet you. How did you meet up with Lenny? This guy is the high priest of rhythmic noise." Ah, there's the rock star adulation Lenny craved.

"We fell into the same tar pit during the Triassic Period." Confused look.

"Don't mind him, he's a braniac," Lenny said to Kathy. "We used to live in the same apartment building. You know the Eldorado on Burnside?"

"Yeah, I can't believe they haven't turned that corner into condos yet. We're super-glad you came down for the show. We've got a bunch of new songs."

"I like you, kid," joked Lenny. "You've got real ambition."

Kathy laughed. "Ambition? Ha! Hey, let's not talk business tonight. Hang out and there is beer in the fridge and booze on the counter. I need to go put some music on from this century. Let's catch up in a little bit. The other girls from the band should be here soon. They went on a vision quest for cheap wine." And Kathy disappeared into the crowd to get a new playlist queued up on the iPod.

"A little cutie, huh? Those tats are sweet. I could tell she's covered." Lenny being Lenny.

"Lenny, don't you ever quit?" Zak definitely thought Kathy was good looking but didn't want Lenny's game to get in the way of the business at hand.   "Hey, I'm just a singer in a choir. I was talking about you. I bet she'd go for you. A hundred bucks says she secretly listens to Joni Mitchell and cries in her Veganaise. Totally your speed." Zak rolled his eyes and looked for an exit. "Okay, okay, let's grab a few beers and talk about our trip to the dream world."

Kiko woke up and rolled off her futon. Her face hit a half-empty food container and she was reminded that she was in her bed and not Zak's. Where was he? Was he thinking of her? Was he talking to some woman more sophisticated than her? Was he lost in his research? What could she do to entice him further? She checked her phone. No messages. It was almost the weekend, there should be plans, right? Isn't that the protocol after sex? Her mind bounced around like a fly caught between a window and a screen looking for a hole big enough to squeeze through.

She replayed her night with him in her head for the hundredth time. It went pretty well by her account. She was a good lover. She didn't do much of what she had seen in American porn. Maybe that was the problem. But she had thought he had wanted submission, yeah. She could have used a hint or a clue. It was the first time so it would have been a little weird to pull out a bucket of eels. Playing the virgin schoolgirl was supposed to be a favorite, according to the Reddit discussion.

It was no use going back to sleep so she went on the "relationships" board on Reddit and asked for guidance. Pretty much everyone said to chill the fuck out.

A couple of hipsters vacated the old couch in the front room so Lenny and Zak claimed the spot, beers in hand. Jay-Z's *Black Album* was playing and a couple of party-goers faux-danced, their asses shaking too close to our boys faces. Scooting back and settling in, it was time for the proverbial deep party convo.

"Okay, Lenny. What have you got?"

"I think you already know what I'm going to say." Lenny spoke in hushed tones, like he knew the secret of where that Malaysian plane went. "This lucid dreaming shit is for real. It's totally possible, which means anything is possible. Literally."

"I don't think you mean literally literally." One of Zak's peeves.

"Oh, but I do, old sport. Literally, literally, literally. Three literals. If you can dream it, it can be real. I've been reading how to do it and it's starting to happen. Like you can make it with any girl in history. Like if you wanted to get busy with eighties Madonna, she's there."

"I'm more *Ray of Light* era. She was a bit more zen. What about Sally Field? Could I make it with her?"

"Like as the *Flying Nun*. Zak, that's hot."

"No, I'm thinking more *Spiderman 2*." This was his head game to play.

"Oh, barf. Okay, granted a way hot Aunt May, but still, at least go *Smokey & the Bandit.* Look it doesn't have to be sex. It can be superpowers. I've had dreams where I can move things with my mind. You could be all four of the Fantastic Four if you want."

"I don't know if that would make sense. What would the point of an invisible Human Torch be? So this is what you're doing with your dreams? Having superpowers?"

"That's not the point. The point is that it's your dream so you can control it. I was having this dream that I was in this deep pit and about to be attacked by two monsters. One was a giant mummy and the other was like a robot with all these razorblades coming out of him. I was scared shitless, like how the hell am I going to get the fuck out of this? Then there was a this voice that said, 'this is not real,' and I was immediately relieved. I was like, 'fuck this,' and I flew up into the air and used my telekinesis to smash them against the walls of the pit. And then I woke up."

Zak took a sip of beer and looked at the skinny jean asses that were swaying inches from him. "Lenny, that sounds like a dream you would have. I thought you were going to tell me about seeing Cozy or Daniel in your dreams. Or at least Hendrix."

"Okay, Cozy is in a lot of my dreams, but they're never lucid. I feel like I'm almost about to know it's a dream when I see her, but I never do. I'd love to have some time with her. And Danny, of course. But it's totally possible. I've been studying it. Did you read any that stuff I sent you."

The hip hop brought more people into the front room to faux-dance and Zak was getting frustrated. "Dude, if you want to see your wife and child, you can just get on a plane. I don't have that option. You want to see them the way *you* want to see them. Like some fantasy version. Go deal with the reality."

The kids ironically twerking had killed the gravity Lenny thought this conversation deserved. "Let's get more beer and go out back. I have an idea." As they lifted off the couch, two twenty-somethings plopped down in their spot and pretended to make out.

The buzzing next to her bed woke Kelly up. Her phone was receiving a text. She still hadn't figured how to turn the damn thing off. It peeped and piddled at odd times. Without turning on the light, she felt for her glasses and grabbed the phone off of the night stand. It was a message from President Woodbine. Walter. What was so important at this hour?

Kelly thanks for your efforts on the faculty issue. We should strategize. Available for dinner tomorrow?

Dinner? She knew what that meant. This would be more than work-related. But should she reply now? That would mean that she was up. And eager. She knew the rules of the game and decided to reply in the morning.

The second cup of beer got things back on track. The backyard had red Christmas lights strung from the trees and it created a dreamy feel under the grey Portland clouds. Suitable perhaps. Lenny put his hand on Zak's shoulder. Time to get to the conferral.

"So what if you could use this dreaming thing to see Claire again? Would you?" Lenny had figured that lucid dreaming could be a lot of fun but maybe also help his friend. The comment struck a chord in Zak and his pulse sped up. It wasn't because Lenny made him think of his dead wife but because he had been having the same thought a lot lately. A whole lot.

"Okay, dude, don't freak out by this. First of all, Claire is in my dreams all the time. I know, big surprise, right?" Lenny gave a sympathetic nod, forgetting that his wife was actually alive and well. "And secondly, I had a fucking lucid dream and it was insane."

"Holy shit. No way. Tell me what happened. Was Claire in it?" Lenny had his fellow traveler. He wasn't one to undertake something so epic on his own.

"No. It was really short. It was last night. After the Kiko thing. I saw these people having sex in my front yard and the woman had like this black tar coming out her vagina and I was, 'this must be a dream,' so I swam up into the air."

"Then what?"

"Then I fought a giant mummy with my mind beam. No, that was it. But I was so excited. Like in the dream I was excited and then I woke up excited, but kind of bummed because I still had to deal with this girl in my bed."

"Oh, poor you. Look you can do it again. I've been studying this a lot."

"You mean Googling," snorted Zak.

"Dude, I bought a fucking book, okay? I told you I am starting to do it. Look, there are some tricks. Like this thing called reality checks. Just get in the habit of asking during the day, 'Is this a dream?' The idea is that if you do it when you're awake, you'll start doing it in your dream and then you'll be like, 'fuck, this *is* a dream,' and then you can do whatever you want."

"That's sort of what happened with the tar vagina thing. I knew it couldn't be real," said Zak.

"Exactly. Sick, but exactly what I'm talking about. Those are called dream signs. Like a clock that runs backwards. The easiest one is asking how you got there. If you're on a boat and you don't know how you got there, you're probably in a dream. Or blackout drunk. But if you know it's dream then you can do whatever, fly, time travel, have sex with Aunt May."

"So how do you stay in the dream? I wanted it to go on longer. It's like my brain only sort of knows it's a dream." Zak was facing the classic lucid dream roadblock.

"Yeah, that's my problem. I start to realize it's a dream and I get excited and then I start to fade out of it. That's called stability. I think it takes a lot of practice. Some people say you should spin around three times or say the word stability." Lenny had actually been reading an actual book about the subject.

"That sounds pretty goofy. But you know I'm interested in this shit," said Zak quite honestly. "The dream journal has really helped. I remember a lot more of my dreams now. Like there is more detail each time I write one down." Suddenly these two old friends were right in tune with each other. They had a new secret club that bonded them, the desire to transcend this particular plane and find some control in the chaos.

"That's what this book says. The more you talk about dreams, and write about them, and think about them, the more the dream world and the real world intersect, and the better chances you'll have of getting lucid." Lenny was actually so excited to be discussing this with Zak that he was oblivious to the fact that the rest of The Falsies were standing in the yard next to them.

Zak wasn't ready to reveal that there was a constant theme of police in his head. It probably didn't mean anything. "Well, we do talk about our dreams a lot. I used to think hearing about people's dreams was the most boring thing in the world. What does it have to do with anything other than random shit inside your brain? But now I think it's a whole world to explore."

"Are you guys talking about dreams?" It was Mollie Saldano, the slight singer of The Falsies. "I had a crazy one last night." Her strawberry blonde hair was cut in an A-line and brushed against her freckled cheek. Zak noticed that. Lenny noticed her short polka dot dress and the Guns N' Roses rose tattoo on her left thigh.

"Is this a dream?" asked Lenny and then walked away.

2

Kiko had made a note of the band Zak's friend was coming to see so she looked The Falsies up the internet. They didn't have a webpage so they couldn't have been very big. In her world, to not have a web presence is not to exist. She found a brief write-up in the online version of the *Portland Mercury* with a picture. Cutsie white girls with tattoos. Maybe she should get a tattoo. But of what?

The article took her to a blog by the bass player that had a few sound files by the band. She put on her headphones and listened to the tracks, imagining herself at the show with her professor. Then she imagined writing about it in her blog, with a link to the bass player's blog. She was about to become a part of the Portland music scene.

She put her head back on her pillow, stared at the ceiling and went over her tattoo choices.

Zak could feel Mollie staring at the asymmetry in his face. It happened. People noticed and then pretended not to notice. He usually didn't notice them noticing, but he always noticed them pretending to not notice. "My dad was Igor," he said as Mollie was thinking of something to say.

"What's that?" She worried she was supposed to know.

"Igor. The guy that's always the mad scientist's the assistant. That's my dad. That's why my face looks like this. My brother got the hunchback."

She paused. "Oh, you're making a joke, right? Honestly, I didn't notice. I think you have a nice face." She was trying if only because he didn't seem like the other guys at the party who seemed to be trying. "So, do you live here in Portland?"

"Yeah, I've been here since the grunge era. It was a car wreck actually. That's what happened to my face." He wasn't going to go into it, especially not the Claire part. But he had to put the Igor rumor to rest. "Lenny says you guys have really great songs. What are your influences?" It was a junior journalism question but it would turn the conversation over to her.

"I like old metal: Faster Pussycat, Tesla, Guns N' Roses, obviously." She brushed her left hand over the tattoo on her thigh. Zak let his eyes hang there for a moment and drew in a deep breath.

"Yeah, obviously." Those bands weren't "old metal" to him. Old metal was Black Sabbath and Hawkwind, not bands from the Gulf War-era. But that thigh negated the need for a history lesson. He was going to look for a picture on his phone in a Facebook folder of him trying to look like Axel Rose in 1993, with a backwards baseball cap but thought it would drop him in the file marked "vintage."

"So are you coming to the show tomorrow? It's gonna be tight. I bought a new dress for it and everything."

"Yeah, I'm planning on it. I wanna see you guys before Lenny makes you do a hamburger commercial." Zak actually winked after that line.

The line loosened Mollie up and they fell into a discussion about the disappearance of record stores in Portland. Not just the chains, like Tower and Sam Goody, but the local shops that clustered downtown. At least All Day Music was still there and open all night. Mollie dropped some vinyl references that fired Zak's attention. Despite her riot grrrl smirk, she had a weakness for jammy seventies head music that wasn't the Grateful Dead. She quite eloquently made the case that Spirit's 1975 album, *The Spirit of '76*, represented the official closing of the 1960s, clearing the way for punk and metal to ascend. Zak felt gobsmacked, not because this singer was in praise of obscure seventies album rock, but because he'd never heard this piece of vinyl and that used to mean something. Suddenly Mollie was a lot more interesting.

Kelly had to fly a lot for work. Somehow, on this flight, she was seated in first class. "Seems right," she thought. She stretched her legs out mid-flight and realized the person in the seat next to her was none other than Cher. Gypsies, tramps and thieves Cher. Kelly had been a fan since the Sonny & Cher days, not of the music, but of the persona. She liked her strong woman stance and how she would berate her dinky husband. But Cher was on her phone, texting. On a flight. Kelly immediately envisioned the plane going down in flames.

"Excuse me, Cher? My name's Kelly and I've admired you for years, but you know you can't use a cell phone on a plane."

Cher looked over her reading glass at Kelly and pushed her straight, dyed (obviously at seventy-ish) black hair (like Kelly!) away from her face. "It's okay, honey. I'm just checking on my dogs to see if they are alright." She went back to texting.

Kelly's heart rate began to race. Rules exist for a reason. "Um, I'm really sorry, but you can't do that. It interferes with the plane's electronic systems. You could crash this plane."

Cher took her glasses off. "Oh, that's a myth. Besides these are my dogs. Cher's dogs. I have to check up on them, okay? Calm down."

What was happening? Cher was not listening to reason. Who cares about her dogs? There were 150 people on this plane. Kelly pushed the flight attendant call button and a tall, thin blonde came to her seat.

"Can I help you, Miss?"

"Yes, would you please tell this woman that she can't use her cell phone on the plane?"

"I'm sorry, but that's Cher. She's just checking on her dogs."

Kelly couldn't believe it. She looked out the window and saw the engine below the wing on fire, and then the lights flickered out. In the dark, Kelly heard the unmistakable voice of Cher. "God dammit!"

"So was it bad?" asked Mollie, leaving the rock talk for a moment.

"Was what bad?" asked Zak. But he knew.

"The car wreck. Was it very bad?" She seemed to want to cut through the chit chat which was refreshing.

"Yeah, it was really bad. People died. People I loved. It was only a year ago so I'm still kind of in a state of shock." His right hand trembled a bit. "But it's not really party talk."

"I know. I'm really sorry. But I'm glad you're here. I want you to see my band." The corners of her mouth turned up in the kind of smile that says, 'life sucks but it could be worse.' Zak made note of the freckles inside one dimple.

"Hello kiddies!" Lenny burst in, probably from surveying the female landscape at the party. "What's the buzz over in this corner of Portlandia? Discussing who has a better seven-inch collection?"

"Hey, Len. Yeah, we're talking about seventies space rock. Did you get your business done with Kathy?" Zak was anxious to get away from the doom and gloom. But he thought Mollie might be somebody to know.

"We did little bit of shop talk. But it's a party. All that can wait until after the show. Hey, I don't want to be a party pooper but I know it's after the professor's bedtime. He get's grumpy after midnight and starts to look like a hideously misshapen monster." Lenny pulled a juvenile cripple pose and made some gurgling noise.

Zak thought it was a kind gesture to state that, at the moment, he wasn't a hideously misshapen monster, which he was. He was also a little surprised that Lenny was ready to call it a night. This was the guy who wanted to hang out at the all night Hot Cake Hideaway after the bars closed, waiting for them to open back up again. But then he figured Lenny was anxious to push this little dream experiment to the next yardline and he needed his compatriot. "Yeah, it's true. I've got a committee meeting in the morning. It was really cool talking to you, Mollie. I'm going to track that Spirit album down."

"I'm going to see you at the show tomorrow, right?" As Zak nodded, she gave him a little hug and touched the side of his face. She didn't seem to be doubled over in revulsion. Maybe she appreciated its imperfection in a scene where truths are hidden behind layers of posturing.

On the way back to the car, Lenny whispered, "Dude, I'm supposed to be the lady-killer."

"Nobody is killing any ladies, you misogynist. We had a good talk about records. She's cool but it's just records."

"And the world goes round, like a record," said Lenny, spinning his finger in the air.

"The world streams, like Spotify, with annoying commercials for itself," Zak responded.

"Hey, don't bite the hand that feeds me, bro."

It was a dark and stormy night. Actually it was just wet. This part of Seattle always stunk when the rain stirred up the garbage. Stan was hanging out with his street gang in Pioneer Square near the football stadium. The old Seattle. It wasn't a gang of racist skinheads. He never really could keep up with those guys. It was the gutterpunks; the street kids who hit up shoppers and sports fans for spare change. They called him Nazi Stan because that's what he wanted to be called.

"Nazi Stan! What's wrong with you?" Six homeless punks were playing hacky sack and throwing garbage at tourists. Stan just sat there. He thought he saw his mother in the crowd and didn't know if he should hide or run after her. Her heart would be broken seeing him on the street. So he sat there, peeing in his pants. He heard himself crying out for her but it was just in his head.

"Dude, you are so gross! Go pee on a fucking tree or something. This is our bench," said a white kid with matted dreadlocks and a dingy jeans jacket. When the other kids saw Stan was peeing they started laughing and yelling at him.

"Crazy motherfucker!"

"You stupid Nazi!"

"I told you he was a retard!"

Silently, Stan stood up and grabbed the punk in a headlock. Then he twisted the head off of each kid and kicked their skulls into the gutter. Pedestrians looked on in horror, but there were no police present. He raised a bloody fist and screamed, "Gonna raise hell!"

The never-used Pioneer Square PA began to play music. It was a heavy bass and drum beat. And out of the dark corners came a dozen tattooed skinheads, whose muscular bodies stood in contrast to Stan's dumpy frame. He didn't care. These were his people. On cue, Stan and the skinheads began performing a dance number, like a more macabre version of the "Thriller" video. The skinheads had blood on their hands as well. One of the shocked crowd watching thought it might have been homoerotic, or a riot, or a homoerotic riot, but Stan pumped his fist and matched the steps. The pee was gone from his pants and his tribe was having a war dance, knees locked and jaws jutting out to reveal razor teeth. Gonna raise hell.

3

Lenny was settled in the guest room and Zak was climbing into bed. In the car on the way home, Lenny had explained the best technique he knew to have a lucid dream. "There's only two things you've got to do," he said. Intention. It was all about intention. Lenny had told him to think about the dream before he went to sleep. "Say to yourself - I'm going to be awake in my dream tonight," he said. "I'm going to dream I'm on a mountain top with eighties Rebecca De Mornay." The second thing was to be mindful of that time when you are drifting off, between wake and sleep. The twilight. Stay focused on the goal through that. There was some science behind it so it wasn't just another of Lenny's crazy theories. Zak thought it was entirely possible.

"Sweet dreams, sonny!" Lenny called out from the other room.

"You, too, Mom! Say hi to the giant robots for me!"

But Zak wasn't ready for sleep. He was stuck in the ritual of the scroll. He rubbed his thumb over his phone and pushed his way into the past. Pictures of pregnant Claire. Crater Lake, Reno, decorating the nursery, the baby shower, holding a picture of the sonogram. Going backwards in time, watching her belly shrink until Caroline disappeared. He stopped at a picture of Claire in a tanktop on a sunny Portland day before she was pregnant. With every atom in his body he wanted to travel back to that moment and live it all over again, with one small difference, one route adjustment or one more hour at the lake. He stared at her eyes like she was in the room with him and he had something to tell her. This was his dream.

It was really too dark to see much. The long red fluorescent lights made Lenny feel like he was in a submarine, but it was a club. The tables were full of hipsters from any time, but heavy mascara and glittery headbands put him in the early seventies. There was a screen print of a Campbell soup can on the wall.

"Holy, shit. I'm at Max's Kansas City," said Lenny, out loud. Max's was Mickey Ruskin's club on the lower east side of Manhattan, by Union Square, where all the scene was seen. And Lenny was there in the back room, looking at Andy Warhol sitting at a corner table surrounded by glamorous transexuals. He recognized the faces if not the names. They were all characters from a Lou Reed song. Should've seen them go, go, go. There was Patti Smith and Robert Maplethorpe and Candy Darling with an bottle of Pernod. Someone put his hand on his ass and Lenny spun around. It was poet Allen Ginsberg. Lenny thought he might go home with him tonight. That was the dream sign.

"Wait, I'm not gay," Lenny thought. "This must be a fucking dream!"

He looked around the room carefully. The first thing he noticed was that absolutely nobody was on their phone. And that was definitely Andy Warhol. Lenny got so excited he worried he was going to ruin it, so he took a seat at the bar. The bartender was a blonde boy in a black and red striped shirt and red rouge on his cheeks. "What'll ya have, honey?"

"Um, what's good?" Lenny was trying to be cool and not spin himself out of this scene.

"How about a Milk 'n' Cookies? It's milk and brandy but you look like you could use some Vitamin D."

Lenny saw himself in the bar mirror and realized the look of this bar had been incorporated into his own style since he was 20, but he now looked much older and/or more worn out than the people he ripped it off from. "Sure. Hey, what's the date"?

"It's Sunday, sugar. You got somewhere to go?"

"No the date. What's the date?"

"God, who knows?" He turned around and looked at the calendar next to the cash register. "The twenty-third." And then he grabbed a beer for Ginsberg, who was now belly up to the bar. Lenny focused his excited eyes on the pin-up calendar. August. 1970.

"Fuck. Hey, where's the stage?" He was trying hard not to lose his shit.

"Upstairs. Two bucks for the milk." Lenny had a feeling they didn't take debit cards, but he reached for his wallet anyway and pulled out a five. As he stared at it, it changed. The color went monochrome and the Lincoln's picture shrunk. He looked at the date on the bill. 1968.

"Keep the change." And with that, he found the narrow staircase and pushed his way to the top. He knew what he was going to see. He was willing it to happen even though he knew the significance of the date. He could hear the clang of guitars, playing "White Light/White Heat." You know it fills me up with surprise. The fact that everyone was smoking, reminded him he was not in his reality.

At the top of the stairs, he pushed his way through the crowd, but no one seemed to mind. On the small stage four guys in black bashed out what so many people now called indy rock. But Lenny knew what he was looking at, The Velvet Underground. More specifically, Lou Reed's last show with the Velvets. Even more specifically, the show that would be recorded by one of Warhol's flunkies and be released as a live album a few years later.

"I'm really here," said Lenny to nobody.

"Well, if you ain't here, you're nowhere," said a drag queen to his left. To his right he saw a woman with a cassette tape recorder. Next to her a tall skinny guy talking too close to the mike she was holding. That had to be poet Jim Carroll. He was still eight years away from publishing *The Basketball Diaries*, the memoir that would put him on the literary radar of countless "alternative" teenagers and mainstream junkies.

Lenny focused on the stage. John Cale was already out of the band. That was Doug Yule on bass. And that was Doug's little brother sitting in on drums for Mo Tucker, who was off having a baby, if Lenny remembered his rock history right. He's pretty good, Lenny thought, imagining a pregnant Mo playing at that pace, as the song ended.

"This is a slow song," said Reed, as the band tuned. Lenny tried to hear but the chatter was too loud. Didn't people realize they were seeing history? The Velvet Underground at Max's Kansas City! Half of his generation of rockers would kill to have seen this show! But to these people, it was just another Sunday night gig. As the band started "I'm Set Free," he looked around the room and saw one of the most influential rock groups of all time as the background music for another self-absorbed youth scene. This could be any time. It could be tonight.

Somehow, his drink had disappeared so he headed over to the bar for a beer. There was just one guy leaning on the bar, being too cool. Lenny didn't want to claim to be from the future, fearing that would unravel the experience. "This is it. Lou Reed's last show with the Velvets. Fucking historic. Literally," he said.

"How do you know he's leaving the band, man?" asked the guy, pulling his sunglasses off.

"It's in all the books." He paused. "I mean, I heard that it was. That he was going solo and make commercials for Honda scooters."

"Yeah, I doubt it." He put his glasses back on. "What's your name, man? I like your vibe."

"Lenny. From Seattle." He held out his hand.

"Lenny, from Washington Heights. New York." It was Lenny Kaye, Patti Smith's guitarist.

"Holy shit," said Lenny from Seattle. "Dude, I'd love to tell you all the great records you're going to make but just trust me." He tried to talk over the Velvets. "I have to tell you something." He wasn't sure if Lenny Kaye was listening. There was something about the near future he needed to hear. "Lenny! In three years a guy from New Jersey is gonna play here named Bruce Springsteen. You need to be here. And do not miss the opening band. They're called Bob Marley and the Wailers. Seriously!" Lenny realized he could probably beam himself to that show.

But he didn't. He sipped on a beer that appeared in his hand and watched The Velvet Underground play "Sweet Jane." They looked so young, he thought. He knew what Lou would look like at the end of his life and tried to connect the dots. The set sounded so much better than the album, but still had a tinny quality. Sound systems had come a long way. This was like a set up you'd expect a garage band to have, which was fitting, because there were a million bands that started out trying to sound like The Velvet Underground.

Lenny looked around again. "Man, this scene is exactly the same," he thought. Bodies swaying. Girls up front watching the guitarist. Disinterested older cats towards the back. The connection made the room flash for a second. It was a Seattle club from Lenny's time. For second he saw a small crowd in front of a band in black. The difference was the staging and the fact that half of the audience were holding up smartphones to record the show. The image only lasted a second. "No!" Lenny screamed in his head and view switched back to Max's.

"Man, just watch this show. And you can fly away later," he said out loud.

"Hey, do you have any Seconal?" asked Jim Carroll.

Zak was on his own time trip. Portland a hundred years ago. Chinatown, or what's now known as downtown. He didn't have the delayed reaction that Lenny did. Once he got his bearings, he knew he was in dreamland. He was standing on the corner of the Southwest 3rd and Stark in front of the Golden Dragon restaurant. It's a strip bar now but it was a restaurant once. Zak knew this because he had lectured about how this part of the city was the original Chinatown, filled with immigrants who came to work the railroad and become hop farmers.

North of Burnside Avenue is what is now called Chinatown, but that was originally Nihonmachi. Japantown. After the Pearl Harbor attack in 1941, all the Japanese and Japanese-Americans were rounded up one night and thrown into internment (don't say concentration) camps. Portland became known as the first "Jap free city" in America. The Chinese were being pushed out of downtown because of floods and rising property values, and moved into the vacated Japantown in an act of displacement that would be imitated by generations of victims of gentrification to come.

But Zak was in the original Chinatown and he knew it. There was Huber's Café but no Voodoo Donuts. There were Shanghai tunnels where unwilling sailors were drugged and sent on slow boats to China. The tunnels weren't just a historical footnote, they were under his feet. He looked at men, hunched over, carrying vegetables on long poles over their shoulders, heading off to market. There were horses and buggies and a streetcar. Portland as a gritty frontier town, absent idle hipsters.

"Huh," he thought. "I wonder why I'm dreaming about this." It seemed very real, including the smell of manure and strange spices. Then he remembered his lecture on the topic and thought that must have been the trigger for this dream. He was calm, standing on the corner, taking in the chance to see images from old black and white photos in living color.

He was trying to figure out what to do since he could do pretty much anything. Then he saw a woman on the opposite sidewalk in a yellow dress stained by the dirt it dragged across. She had a broad-brimmed yellow bonnet but he saw the edge of her face. It was Claire. That's why he was here. Out of his time, they could talk. He ran off the wooden sidewalk into the street toward her and almost collided with a man on a horse. The black horse jostled for position on the street and Zak let him pass, but she was getting farther away.

"This is my dream," he thought. "I can catch up to her if I want." Within seconds he was feet away from her, but she stepped behind a wall that further obscured her face. "Claire, it's me." His voice sounded crystal clear, like the first time he heard a digital recording. She stopped, but was only partially visible through the wooden slats. Why couldn't he see her? He wanted to look at her face before he forgot what that felt like.   "Claire, talk to me. I miss you so much. I conjured you up so we could talk. I need it. Please."

He felt the emotion well up like every damn time he looked at her picture. The wooden slats seemed to be moving closer together. He could only see her jawline. That jawline that he saw in Caroline's ultrasound.

Suddenly he felt an arm around his neck and he was jerked backwards into the street. Away from his wife. His face hit the dirt, scraping his cheek. Actual pain. A wicked trolly wheel. A Chinese girl pointing. A measure of control and then not. Zak turned to see no Claire, but a Keystone cop in white with a menacing grin and a billy club slapping his palm. The wall was now gone. The cop drew his right leg back and kicked Zak in the gut and he saw blood. And then he saw nothing.

Zak was pissing on a rubber duck. He didn't realize it until it was too late to do anything about it. Lenny must've put it in the toilet sometime during the night, thinking it was cute. It was one of the baby presents that Zak had held on to. Lots of people have rubber ducks. But he was contemplating throwing it out. It was a reminder of the pain. Another layer stacked on another layer. But the pain was something that linked him to the past. What would happen when the pain was gone? So he held on to the rubber duck and savored the jab each time he looked at it.

But now he was peeing on it. The yellow duck floated in the yellow pee water. Funny. After he was finished he reached down and threw it into the sink, washing his hands over it. Lenny was such a child. But he still kept the duck, like a hoarder with some master plan for all the stuff in the world that meant something or other to somebody at sometime. Zak looked in the mirror at his lopsided face, wondering if Claire had seen it in his dream. Maybe she didn't recognize him. "Is this a dream?" he asked himself, splashing water on his face.

"Probably," said Lenny from the living room. He was already up, sitting on the couch, holding a cup of microwaved coffee. He didn't know how old it was. "How was your night? Did you get any cool dream action?" For once, Lenny was waiting to tell his story.

"Shit, man. Maybe there was something in that beer." He paused as he was still processing. "Of course I had a dream about Claire, but I never could see her whole face. It was obscured the whole time. Like by a hat and then a wall. I was trying to talk to her and I couldn't."

"Fuck, you should be able to figure that out. Maybe her face got messed up in the accident." By the time Zak was out of his coma, Claire had been cremated. Fortunately, he didn't have to identify the body. The police did that. "Or it's about your face. Like, you didn't want her to see your face. So, were you lucid? Did you know you were dreaming?" The burning question.

"Yeah, I think so. So get this. I was in Chinatown. But not Chinatown with all the clubbing douchebags. I was in Chinatown from a hundred years ago when it was on the other side of Burnside, where the X-Ray Café was."

"Chinatown was on the other side of Burnside?" Lenny didn't know the history of displacement that was Portland's grand narrative.

"Yeah, Chinatown used to be Japantown. Anyway, I was right there. Like I traveled in time. Right downtown. And I knew I was in a different time. But now that I think about it, everyone looked really well dressed. Was J. Crew around a hundred years ago?"

"I'd have to Wiki that," quipped Lenny. "But that's how dreams are, man. Like almost everything is right, but enough is wrong to tell you it's not real. Sounds like you picked up on that. So what happened then?" Lenny was anxious to hear about the part with mummies or maybe Jim Morrison.

"Nothing really. This cop threw me into the street and that was it. There are a lot of cops in my dreams. Is there any more coffee?" Zak was now comfortable on the couch.

"The cops are because you're neurotic. You always think you're gonna get caught for something. Probably something you did as a kid." Lenny read that once in an issue of *Psychology Today* that he leafed through in a doctor's office when he needed treatment for HPV. "Sorry, this is the last of the bad coffee. You should make a new pot."

"Yeah, I have a committee meeting later this morning." He began to get up.

"Wait. Aren't you going to ask me about my dream? Typical."

"Sorry. Have any good dreams last night, Lenny?"

"I only saw the Velvet Underground at Max's." Lenny proceeded to tell Zak how he had been transported to the New York club in 1970 and everyone was there; Warhol, Ginsberg, Jim Carroll. He told him how he managed not to freak out and stay in the dream, at least through three perfectly clear songs. And that Lou Reed looked like a baby.

Zak put on another pot of coffee and jumped into the shower while Lenny checked his messages on his phone. It felt good to have Lenny in the house, a nod to simpler times before marriage, pregnancy and complete emotional investment in someone other than himself. If he could only get back to that moment, he could figure out what to change about the trajectory. He watched the water go down the drain and thought about when, around age seven, he switched from baths to showers. Maybe he should go back to that moment.

He got dressed and rejoined Lenny on the couch, both with fresh cups of the good stuff. "So, I guess we're dream travelers now," said Zak, letting the dark roast creep into his sinuses.

"It's all a dream, man." Lenny was being Lenny. "How do you know this is not a dream?"

"Because I know I have a fucking graduate committee meeting to go to, and then tomorrow I have to drive 200 miles to talk to a psychotic inmate. Shit, maybe it is a bad dream." Zak was about to give up on the significance of the distinction.

"Seriously, think about it. How do you know the difference between your memories of what's real and what you just imagined or dreamed? Did you read Keith Richards' book? He says, 'Memory is fiction.' Think about that."

Zak pretended to think about it. "Well, I'm sure for him it is. How is he even still alive?"

"No, seriously. How do you know your memories aren't just fantasies, made up in your imagination?" Lenny was feeling the caffeine.

"Because I was fucking there," said Zak.

"Quick, tell me something about your high school graduation that's not in a photo of it. What was your mom wearing?"

"I don't know, I think a red dress." It was a long time ago and but he was fairly certain she was there.

"See, you don't know, but your imagination put her in a red dress. It's a fantasy. It's like when they colorize a photograph from a hundred years ago. They're only guessing but we accept it as reality. Look, I could climb Mt. Everest and remember it or I could just imagine that I climbed it. At this point, in my mind both are exactly the same. I've told so many bullshit stories over the years that I now believe most of them."

"Like what?" Zak thought there might be something here. A window.

"Remember that story I used to tell about seeing Bob Dylan go through a drive-thru at a KFC in Anaheim? He was by himself but bought like a sixteen-piece bucket and sat in the parking lot eating it. But it was just some guy that sorta looked like Dylan. I was trying to impress this chick at a show so I turned him into Dylan."

"God, you asshole. I loved that story!"

"The point is, after telling it a hundred times, now when I hear Dylan I think to myself, I saw that guy at a KFC eating a whole bucket of chicken. The lie is real and the real is a lie. You don't have a computer brain, so you imagination fills up most of your memory."

"So, what you're sayings is that Keith Richards is a genius."

"Exactly."

Kelly was sitting at her neat desk deleting spam emails when President Woodbine wrapped on her open door. He was a stout man who carried himself like the labor lawyer he was in a former life. He had made his mark as the first African-American Chancellor of the state higher education board. Charismatic and charming, Walt Woodbine usually got his way and thought a few years at the helm of a state university would give him some legacy points. Kelly admired his swagger and was ready to follow.

"What'cha working on?" he asked halfway through the door.

"Oh, Walt." He had given her permission to call him by his name after their brief semi-intimate encounter. "Going over some HR forms. I think there might be a few positions we can eliminate in the fall." She was the model of bogus efficiency.

"Nice. Hey, thanks for sending me copies of those spreadsheets. Are we still on for dinner tonight? Mona is going to join us to talk about next steps." Mona was Mona Sanders, the provost, and the addition of a third wheel make Kelly's heart sink.

She was of two minds. Some quality alone time with Woodbine and a glass of Chablis could better position her for advancement and maybe some much needed ego stroking from the male sex. On the other hand, the university president was really an overpaid ceremonial position. The provost had the real power and Sanders had an even bigger hard-on to reduce faculty lines. Her vision of the university was to eliminate as many tenure-track professors as possible and offer more online classes to internet-addicted millennials. They could get a college degree without ever looking up from their smartphones. So if there was a coattail to ride, it was Mona's.

"Yeah, sure. I'll bring my notes. What time?" She kept her professional demeanor but batted her eyelashes ever so slightly, mentally telling him that it was still a date.

"How about Harvest at 6:00? I'll reserve a table in a corner so we can talk." He looked like he wanted to say more after that but stumbled on his thoughts. "Okay Kelly, see you then." And he tapped his ring twice on the metal door frame as he headed out into the hall.

Kelly didn't even say goodbye, she just grinned. Then she felt self-conscious, then she felt stupid. So she quickly went back to her computer, pulling her glasses down on her face. She gave herself two minutes to imagine a romantic moment at the swank Harvest, but quickly returned to deleting emails. "No, I don't want a free Lasik evaluation." Delete. "Want a Sex Affair?" She didn't delete that one.

4

He was sitting at his desk but not doing any work. Zak's mind was still on the previous night's dream. Was he really lucid? It was hard to tell. It certainly didn't go the way he planned. He liked the time travel element, which he didn't actually ask for. Maybe if he wandered around that part of Portland something would catch his eye. Something that would suggest why Claire wouldn't talk to him.

"Wake up, old man!" It was Sammy Sullivan, a colleague from his department who studied the epidemiology of obesity. He was also the chair of the graduate committee that had a meeting in ten minutes. "Can you grab any new files that have come in since the last batch of applicants? We need to divide them up."

"Yeah, sure. Sorry, making a list in my head of what gets done today." Zak was always covering for his daydreaming.

"No worries. Hey, I wanted to share this one letter that came from a kid at Gonzaga. Ready?" Sammy pulled a stapled two sheet letter out of a manila folder and began reading. "I am applying to this department specifically to work with Dr. Crisp. His 2008 article, 'Scabs and Salve: Understanding the Gutterpunk Subculture as a Crisis of Community Health,' changed my life. I read it in a community college class I enrolled in while living in a homeless shelter. It encouraged me to continue my education and one day attain a masters in Public Health." He looked as Zak with a smile. "You saved this kid's life, Zak. I don't get letters like this."

Zak wasn't very good at taking compliments. He should have appreciated that his work impacted people's lives in various ways. Instead, he deflected it by grumbling something about the kid needing some serious help. It wasn't the first time someone had said that, either. He wasn't sure if that should be a motive to do his research, to get kudos from former street kids.

Sammy was about to encourage him to take the file to read it but he noticed someone waiting to talk to Zak and excused himself. It was Kiko, who slid into the doorway and leaned against it like she was doing an imitation of James Dean in *Rebel Without a Cause*. "Is she trying to be sexual?" Zak asked himself with a snicker. He felt guilty for not fully responding to her texts after their hook-up so now he had to deal with it. She was wearing her plaid skirt and fake private school blazer, so he let a little smile creep out.

"Are you happy to see me, Professor?" She leaned her head back with a tilt. She seemed like a cartoon character who was struggling to be a real girl; a cross between a Japanese line drawing and pony in estrus. Zak was pulled in as much as he wanted to push back.

"Hey! Hi, Kiko. I was hoping I'd run into you today." Maybe that was true. Or maybe not. "How are you doing?"

"How was your party last night? Did you meet any pretty girls?" Well, that didn't sound like a set up to a bad horror film.

"Oh, um, no. It was just Lenny and I. We've been talking lot about dreams lately. So that was it, really." The thought of Mollie's freckled neck had crossed his mind. He was in the zone where he had to create space with her but not come off as a dick. The "We're just messing around, right?" zone.

"That's nice. Are you still going to see The Falsies tonight? Because I'd like to do something with you this weekend. I think they're a cool band, by the way. Have you read their blog?"

Zak wasn't sure what to make of this, but he thought he could invite Kiko to the show and it would be safe because Lenny would be there and if he got any weird vibes he could plead a responsibility to his house guest. Plus, maybe the first night together was a lot of nerves on both sides. Something light, remember? So he took the bait. "No, I haven't. I didn't even know they had a blog. Hey, if you like them, you should come out with us. I think it's gonna be a good show."

"Oh, sir. That sounds like fun but I don't want to be any bother." She looked down at the floor. Her mission, yes.

"Don't be silly. It will be cool. You can meet my old friend Lenny. He's a real riot." He was about to make the plan firm when Sammy called to him from the meeting room. "Oh, shit, I'm late for a meeting. I'll text you the information later." He gave her a friendly hug as he pulled his office door shut behind them and that's all that there was.

It had been a block of bad days for Stan. And it didn't take much to have a good day in prison; a compliment from a CO, a cup of no-strings-attached pruno from a cellie, cake for desert that wasn't a month old. So the hide-and-seek game with the skinheads was wearing him down. The word was out that Kennedy was looking for him. He had failed to procure the box of Oxy after he had made it sound like a done deal and now his ass was grass. Or something much worse. He had one last play.

"I think I hurt myself lifting weights." He was talking to his counselor who had kept him on anti-psychotic medication since he walked into the facility. Maybe she could score some painkillers. She was a softie. "I've been getting too fat and I'm really trying to be better about staying healthy. I got teased a lot as a kid for being fat." Heart strings.

"You should go to the infirmary and have them check you out." She'd heard this line before.

Stan noticed Kennedy out through the window. He was talking to two other Peckerwoods in the yard. He was sure they were talking about him. He felt his pulse race. "I was thinking you might be able to save me the trouble and write me a script for some painkillers. I'm trying to stay away from that place. There's a guy there who thinks he has a beef with me." Sounded good.

"Sorry, Stan. You know I can't do that. I'm strictly psych meds. They won't even let me give you a Tylenol." And then she tried to steer the conversation to his relations with fellow inmates but Stan stared out the window and wondered if it would come as a fist or a dirty dull knife.

Harvest was one of those faux bourgeois restaurants that poor people went to on anniversaries and rich people went to when they wanted to go slumming. The waiters wore black and long white aprons and never had tattoos or nose piercings. Specials were $22 a plate and sturgeon was always on the menu. Several of the six-figure university administrators were regulars at the bar.

Kelly was a bit early, even though she had locked herself in her office to freshen up first (reapplying her make-up and changing into a dress that showed a glimpse of clavicle). "Right this way, Miss." She appreciated the "Miss" but wished she would have waited instead of looking like the eager beaver. Better to look like you were busy and got away for a few moments, looking fabulous. Now she was early and waiting for the *couple*.

She hadn't had more than one sip of her Pear Martini when she saw Walt Woodbine and Mona Sanders walk in through the side door. They must have walked from campus together. There couldn't be anything going on there. She was married so put it out of your mind. But Mona was laughing.

"Hi Kelly. Thanks for getting us a table." Walt's grin was so broad it made his eyes close. "Us." What did that mean? Nevermind. "Mona was telling me you've really hit the ground running. I guess I appointed the right person." Okay, better.

There was the usual small talk about the weather, the volleyball team, and who was zoomin' whom in the HR office. Walt ordered for everyone and said don't worry, the university was paying. A needed expense. Then the talk got serious. Walt took his glasses off and lowered his head. Kelly thought he was about to pray.

"We've got a serious issue here, ladies. Kelly has told me about the AFT unionizer on campus. Mona was telling me that the deans are reporting that most department chairs are siding with the faculty. And I spoke to the president at Oregon. He told me that their faculty union has tied his office up in bargaining demands and unfair labor practice suits. We have to nip this thing in the bud. You two are my closest allies in this with connections to faculty. So I thought maybe we could brainstorm for ideas." He looked to Mona first.

She seemed ready. "Well, we could lobby for Oregon to become a Right-to-Work state. No collective bargaining. No unions. That would pull the rug right out from under them."

"No. Not with a Democratic governor. And even if we could win that long campaign, they'd be fully vested in union-negotiated contracts. Too chancy. Kelly, any ideas?"

She was glad to see Mona shot down so quickly, especially since she had been thinking of a real solution to the problem. Not just thinking but dreaming. "Yeah, Walt. I know exactly what to do." Walt put his glasses back on and Mona wished she had glasses. She leaned in anyway. "The problem isn't the faculty in general. Most are happy to teach their classes and write their little papers and hide in their offices. It's a few troublemakers that are stirring the pot. We need to remove them and win the hearts of everyone else. We're supposed to be one big happy family here. It's the radicals that are trying to turn it into us versus them."

Woodbine rubbed is chin and then clasped his hands. "I think you're on to something. But how do we do that without looking like the Gestapo. They have a right to their opinion." He knew she had more to add.

Kelly now controlled the conversation. "Think of it as a two-part strategy. The first is winning the hearts and minds of the rank and file. What is it that professors love the most about their jobs?"

"Summers off," said Mona, trying to get back in.

"That's a big one. But what is it that makes the job different from being a school teacher? That adds a little excitement into the school year."

"Going to conferences," said Walt.

"Exactly, going to conferences. Especially if it's in someplace warm. The Social Work professors had a conference in San Diego last year and they were all begging for travel funds for it. So the first step is to free up some travel money for faculty."

"Buy them off. Brilliant. What's step two?" Walt was close to frothing at the mouth.

"Eliminate the agitators." Kelly turned to Mona to invite her into her secret with the president. "Mona, I shared a document with Walt based on my monitoring of faculty emails. I've ranked the faculty activists in terms of their commitment to unionization and their contractual weakness. I'd like to propose that we target them for termination."

"How the hell do we do that?" asked Walt, fully on board but unsure of the legality of such a purge.

Kelly took her glasses off and placed them on the table for dramatic pause. "By any means necessary. If they mis-cited a source in an article. If they have negative reviews on RateMyProfessor.com that say they are biased in any way. If they have dated a student. We agree not to think twice. If there is a hint of a contract violation, they are outta here."

Walt and Mona nodded. It was evil but it was good evil. They'd feel dirty now but forget it like yesterday's celebrity scandal. The fix was in.

5

Zak ended up bringing Kiko the Falsies show. Lenny thought she was cute, in a comic book sort of way. The gig was in a basement club below a trendy bar called The Lonesome Pine. It was a good slot for a Friday night, even though they were only opening for a singer best known as somebody who killed zombies on TV and then was eaten by said zombies. But it ensured a bigger crowd of folks who would probably hear the women play for the first time. Zak, Kiko, and Lenny made an odd trio and Kiko positioned herself between the two men. Her mission.

"Everybody's here!" said Lenny, happy to see the audience arrive in time to see "his" band. "I can't wait for everybody to hear these songs. You have to tell me what you think, Kiko, okay?"

"Okay. Are you going to use them for laxative commercials? That's what Sir said." She looked at Zak who grimaced.

"Sir? Sir Zachary?" Lenny laughed.

It was funny in private when she said it. Okay, maybe a little hot. "Yeah, that's a little joke of hers. I told her you place songs with advertisers."

"You said laxatives. I remember. Laxatives." Kiko remembered correctly. She sipped the strawberry daiquiri Zak had bought her.

Zak was about to justify his comment when the four women walked on stage and picked up their instruments. The crowd of about fifty or so twenty-somethings (with a few older zombie fans) moved forward. Mollie, dressed in a sun dress died grey, smiled at the crowd and saw Zak and Lenny halfway back. She winked at Zak, an act that did not go unnoticed by Kiko.

"Hello there ladies and gentlemen. We're really glad to be here tonight. We hope you like our set. We're The Falsies from Portland, Oregon and this is a new song is called, 'You're Quite Interesting.'" The drummer counted to three and then Kathy came in with a fast bass lick. The band crashed into a song about crushing on a boy. When they got to the chorus, Mollie looked right at Zak.

You're quite interesting
You've really got a lot to say
I find you not at all boring
We should hang out some day

Lenny shot Zak a look and, out of respect for Kiko, Zak ignored it. But it was obvious to him what was going on. But the song could have been about anyone. Or no one. The crowd moved to it and that's all that mattered. Definitely not a laxative commercial jingle. (Although the next song, "I'm Pushing You Out," had potential.)

After the initial awkwardness, Kiko began to enjoy the show. She liked The Falsies quirky rhythms, guitar hooks and cute haircuts. While she danced, she noticed other men checking her out in her short skirt and ever-present knee socks. This included Lenny, who was split between making notes on his phone, scanning the crowd and sneaking peaks of the back of Kiko's thighs when she spun in a way that raised her skirt. Zak was busy thinking about what bands The Falsies sounded like. That's the good old Zak.

Throughout the show Zak grew to appreciated Lenny's attraction to this band. The four women had mastered short hooky pop-rock songs. Great harmonies, positive energy and songs about losing your ATM card, road trips in hybrids, and mending a broken heart with some retail therapy. "By the time I checked out, I forgot all about you." There was a heavy moment when the band channeled some Riot Grrrl fury on a song about domestic violence called, "Do You Give?" Instead of her upper register, Mollie used her guttural man voice.

Face in the floor
My arm on your neck
Do you give?
I never lose, bitch
Do you give?

Being the opening act, there was no time for an encore if the audience wanted one. (They surely would have.) So they finished the set with a 1977 song by The Runaways called "Neon Angles on the Road to Ruin." The song tore through the club as the women leaped around. Most of the audience had never heard the song before but Zak and Lenny had. And Zak loved the version he had on the original vinyl and he loved this version. And suddenly he thought he could love Mollie.

"Good night, Tokyo!" screamed Mollie. "That's the end of the show!"

Based on the energy in the room, you would have thought they were the headline act. The fact that they quickly came back on stage to break down their equipment while the house PA played was a reminder that the night was still young. But Lenny was buzzing. The combination of a tight band that knew there way around the stage and the chance for a big payday had him feeling full.

"That's the sound of my soul!" exclaimed Lenny.

"Okay, Spandau Ballet. They were pretty good, I'll give you that," replied Zak trying to not let on that he more than a little loved it.

"When does Zombie Girl come on?" asked Kiko, wanting to move the boys off their post-Falsies high.

"Hey, these people are going to brag about how they saw this band open for Zombie Girl. It's fate. So, let's go backstage in a few minutes," said Lenny.

Kiko perked up at her first chance to go "backstage with the band" and it served to assuage the weird vibe between Zak and the singer. She asked Zak for another drink but Lenny told her there would be free booze in the dressing room.

The Aryan inmates always showered in the morning. They had some kind of fake working class ethic that said you had to start the day clean and ready. White people didn't spend all day stinking up the place. So Stan thought he'd slip in before lights out for a quick hose down. His cellie sold him a big hunk of soap that was a bunch of small soap bars melted together and dried. It looked like shit but inside a sock could make a good weapon. There were still a few Mexican Mafia guys in bathroom and there was only a few more minutes of shower time.

"Hey ese, you gotta wait your turn. No Nazis in the shower," said one of the vatos, with tattoos all the way up his neck.

"I'm not a Peckerwood." In the joint it was good be to allied with somebody, but Stan was bad medicine. The only people who would clique up with him were the pedos or the chimos, or maybe the Christians. He was on his own.

"Yeah, I heard. The Nazis don't like you. Los jodiste. You're gonna get a torpedo. You better watch your back, pendejo." Stan was a bit perturbed that these supposed white supremacists would talk to the Mexicans before talking to him. "You can have the shower, 'holmes.' It might be your last one." And the men left, laughing a sick kind of laugh.

Stan put his head under the shower and closed his eyes, letting the now cold water run over the back of his neck. How did his life get so fucked up? How was he going to avoid this confrontation? And where was this professor who was going to be his ticket out? That's when he heard footsteps. Then he felt his giant wad of soap inside his sock slam against his back. Then nothing. Nothing but dreams of his mother.

The backstage for bill openers at the Lonesome Pine was essentially a closet. The room for the headliners wasn't much better, but at least it had a fire exit. The four band members had guests (including the drummer's dad) when Lenny ushered Zak and Kiko into the room.

"Great show, ladies! You guys really owned that stage. Love the new songs. We got lots to talk about." They all said hello, but Lenny still had the limelight. "You remember my pointy-headed friend, Zak, right? And this his little friend, Kiko, all the way from Japan." More hellos and Zak looked at Mollie looking at Kiko while Kiko wanted Zak to look at her looking at Mollie. Just a little tension. And besides there were several people, a cooler full of beer, and two guitars between Zak and Mollie, so there would be a safe buffer.

"Thanks, man," said Kathy. "Glad you dug it. Have a beer. That gallon jug has vodka and orange juice in it." She pulled Lenny aside to get him a drink and make a plan to talk rock.

Zak went to grab beers but Kiko got stopped by the guitarist who was a fan of Japanese pop culture. Kiko was flattered to be a momentary expert on the topic but was trying to keep close to Zak. Fail on that score.

"Hey, did you like the set?" Mollie had made it to the beer cooler, too.

"Yeah, you guys have your power-pop chops. Rolling numbers, like hearing my favorite records sung by chicks." His eyes met hers as he handed her a bottle of Sessions Ale.

"All my favorite records *are* by chicks," she said with a raised eyebrow. "Who's your little friend? You've been trolling for mail order brides?" Kiko was 10 feet way explaining the pornographic nature of Japanese comic books. Mollie took Zak's bottle and opened it for him, since he looked like he was having trouble.

"She's just a student. Not my student. I mean she was last year. She found you guys on the internet and asked to come along." Zak was not navigating this well. Last time he was in this situation was when he was in college. Come to the party with one girl but meet another girl there and have to step carefully.

"Are you guys dating?" Mollie asked.

Zak wondered what this pretty future rockstar with a Guns N' Roses tattoo on her thigh wanted with him. Maybe she thought she could fix his twisted body, make him whole.

"No. Definitely not. Just hanging out a little now and then. You know."

"She's cute. I'd go out with her. I like her crazy style. How'd you like the first song?" She batted her eyes and tugged on a wisp of hair that hung in front of her left ear. It all seemed to be in slow motion for Zak. He forgot where he was. He forgot Lenny and Kiko and the beer in his hand. And, for a brief, brief moment, he forgot about Claire and Caroline.

"Man, I loved it so much. Really raw. Just a raw punk rock love song. The world needs more songs like that." He was being honest, even though the song was probably not for him.

"Yeah, it was for you. I wrote it after the party and we worked it out at soundcheck. I don't know, I guess I felt inspired." She took in a moment to drink in his body language. Would it say, "Check, please!" or "Yes, sir, may I have another?" He didn't run so that was a good sign.

"Well, I'm glad you found me interesting." He felt his lopsided mouth as he said it. "I would really like to hang out sometime. Maybe we could meet at All Day Music and do some record shopping or something." It was a bold move. She was the singer, after all.

Kiko sussed out what was going on from across the room and through all the chatter and made a bee-line for her date. Her heart beat like drums in her ears, moving her through the obstacles. "Did you get me a beer, honey?" she asked. It was a line out of the blue and Zak didn't know what to do with his eyes.

"Oh, yeah, let me grab you one. Mollie this is Kiko. We were talking about, um…"

"Records. We were talking about records. Hi, Kiko, nice to meet you. Did you like the show? I love your outfit." Mollie already knew what was up. Kiko didn't have to clutch Zak's arm (which she did) to declare she'd staked a claim on the professor.

"You are very good. I liked your last song the best." Zak cringed a little bit. It could mean that she liked it when the show was over or that she didn't know it was a cover.

"Yeah, that's a Runaways song. Lita Ford wrote it." Eyes back to Zak.

"*Queens of Noise* album, 1977, Mercury Records," he said, right on cue.

"That's my boy," said Mollie.

"Okay, sir, can we go now? I want to see the zombie girl sing." Kiko had to cock block this hussy. Mollie pulled off the perfect eye-roll and wink, that gave Zak a lifeline.

"You guys go enjoy the show. I heard her earlier. She's really good. And Zak, yes to record shopping." Mollie moved away to join another conversation. People always wanted to talk to the singer. To Zak she looked like the balloon he accidentally let go of at the fair. There it goes.

Zak almost fell back as Kiko pulled him towards the door and back out into the club. "C'mon, Professor. We don't want to miss it." She was seething underneath. How could she compete with this rock singer? More importantly, how dare Zak humiliate her like that in public. He was sleeping with her. She was his girlfriend. Boyfriends don't ditch their girlfriends to drool all over some rocker skank. The more she thought about it, the angrier she got. She didn't even notice that the headliner and her band were playing. And she was a fan of the zombie show. She looked at her shoes and thought, "I am going to raise hell," over and over again.

"Then I fall asleep to dream my dreams of you." (Roy Orbison)

Chapter 5:
I'll Be With You Tonight

1

     Zak was woken by some random screaming. It's so annoying to be woken by street noise, especially when your are in the middle of a good dream, but that's the way the neighborhood's been lately. Always somebody bringing in the drama. Zak climbed over the bed to look out the bedroom window to see what the commotion was. When he looked down he saw a bearded homeless man screaming up at him. Forgetting he cared about homelessness he thought, "Fuck, the hobos are attacking." The man started throwing garbage at the house as he babbled in a fury. Zak flung open the window.

     "Hey, hobo! Get the fuck out of my yard. Shoo! Go away!"

     But the hobo didn't go away. He hollered and threw more trash that hit Zak in the face. Not surprisingly this pissed Zak off and he reached down to grab the old man by the arm and yell for reinforcements. "Claire, call the police! There's a rabid hobo in our side yard!"

     Claire did not call the police. She was not there. She was dead. Zak got tired of holding the guy and Claire not answering so he let the old buzzard go and walked into the kitchen to look for his wife. It suddenly dawned on Zak that she had been gone a long time and he must be confused or dreaming.

     "Is this a dream?" he asked himself. He reached his right arm out and put it through the kitchen wall as if it were a merely a projection of his kitchen wall. He smiled and whispered to himself, "Alright, let's try this."

     As before, his first impulse was to fly up into the air. It took a bit more will power, but gradually he lifted up through the ceiling and was hovering over his house on a clear star-filled night in his bathrobe, like the Big Lebowski. He'd been on this roof before, to put up Christmas lights and kick off the moss, so he knew it was his house. An excitement overwhelmed him. He could do anything, but what?

It seemed like he should start simple and be around people in his dreamscape. So his house disappeared and a green lawn with hundreds of people appeared in its place. He lowered himself to the ground to take in his first conjuring. He recognized it immediately as the backyard of the White House in Washington. He had been looking at a friend's Facebook pictures from DC, so this made sense. It was a grand nighttime picnic at the White House. It must have been the 4th of July.

He studied the faces of the people moving around him. They were so crisp but unfamiliar. They weren't the faces of friends or students or people from TV. Were they created from forgotten memories, or the actual faces of people he'd never seen before this moment? They didn't seem to notice him but he briefly analyzed each one that passed. When he got bored with that question, he thought he'd test his powers.

"If this is really the 4th of July," he said to a guy next to him, "you all need some fireworks." And with a wave of his arm he made the most spectacular fireworks appear in a giant arc across the yard, from the White House to Constitution Avenue. They didn't look like *Love American Style* fireworks either, more like giant Chihuly colored glassworks that filled the sky with every hue. The crowd oohed and awed and Zak became even more excited.

"Holy shit, this really works. Okay, stay cool, boy. What's next? Should I have sex with Marilyn Monroe or Halle Berry?" Halle Berry would have won that choice but he didn't want to waste this experience on something so pedestrian. So Lenny. He knew he had a whole dream wish list of times and places and people, but his excitement caused them all to leave his head. The same thing happened whenever he entered a record store. (This is why God invented list-making.) He was holding stable in this lucid dream, so he better decide quick. "I know, Liverpool, 1962."

As a Beatle fan, he'd always imagined seeing the Fab Four right before they broke big. The ultimate "I saw them when…"

claim. So that's where he went. There was no whooshing sound, no time tunnel to slide through, no misty portal. He just transported himself with the blink of an eye.

Zak, in his street clothes, was standing on High Park Street in a poor part of Liverpool called the Dingle. Based on the sideburns and the women's shin length dresses, he guessed he'd zipped back in time more than fifty years. He'd hadn't given much thought to where he should exactly land, but he knew this spot well. In front him was a tall monolithic pub called The Empress. Most people know it from Ringo Starr's first solo album, *Sentimental Journey*. And true fans know, just past it is Admiral Grove, the street where the Beatle drummer was born. Maybe Ringo was home.

"I did it!" Zak shouted. He'd never been this excited in his life. Every cell in his body was telling him he'd done the impossible. "I did it! I'm going to see the fucking Beatles!"

Then he woke up. He knew instantly that his excitement had blasted him out of his lucid state and wrecked his little adventure. "Damnit," he said, looking at his ceiling.

He looked out the window to see if there as any evidence of the hobo but his side yard was clean. No hurled trash. Zak saw his neighbor, Rose Jackson, working on her yard and was so excited about his dream he had to tell her, so he opened the window. "Rose, I had a lucid dream! I was at the White House!" Rose was an older African-American woman who had lived in the neighborhood a long time. She'd heard a lot of stories but probably never one like this.

"What's that?" The look on her face said she was interested but confused.

"Yeah, I was at the White House and made the fireworks appear and then made the decision to go to Liverpool in 1962 and see the Beatles!" In his enthusiasm, he hadn't noticed that, somehow, Rose had gone from working in her yard to sitting on the end of his bed."

"That's quite a feat! I remember when they came to Portland. Did you see them?"

"No, I got too excited and woke up. But I'm going back. Hey, how did you get in here?" Zak opened his eyes and saw the fan on his ceiling not spinning, but very real.

"Damnit!"

"Remember Saturday morning cartoons?" Lenny was sitting on the couch flicking through the hundreds of channels on Zak's TV. "Man, what I would give for a bowl full of Apple Jacks and thirty minutes of Scooby Doo."

"How about a jalapeño bagel and an hour-long Proactive infomercial? Will that cut it?" Zak was in his pajama bottoms and a Café Tacuba shirt he got at a show he went to with Claire. The sleep was still crusted in his eyes.

"Fuck, no. Saturday morning TV sucks. How many damn channels do you have. They're all in Spanish. When does Shark Week start?" Lenny seemed agitated.

"So I take it you didn't have any good dreams," said Zak.

"Hell no. I had a dream that I was choking on a piece of cake. That's it. And my dad was there laughing at me. I wasn't even lucid enough to tell him to fuck off. You?"

With dramatic pause that included turning off the TV, Zak proceeded to tell Lenny about the dream within a dream that included him going to the White House and 1962 Liverpool. He made great emphasis of the fact that he was quite lucid and in control of most of the experience, including the Chihuly fireworks. Lenny was impressed, to say the least.

"That's some *Inception*-level shit," he said, pulling his legs up on to the couch.

"Yeah, I know," said Zak. "I had to write it down as soon as I woke up. I feel like I made a breakthrough in this thing."

"Dude, you chose to time travel and you teleported to that time. Do you know what that means?" Lenny seemed even more excited than Zak.

"No, what?" asked Zak.

"I don't know."

"Lenny!"

"I mean I do know. It means you can time travel at will even to times in your own life. Like Reno. So what was the last thing you were thinking about before you went bed?" There had to be a clue.

"I was bopping around on my laptop. I was looking at a friend's pictures on Facebook. He's on a job in Washington so I think that's where the DC thing came from. I read a music blog."

"What else? Did you look at any pictures of Claire?"

"No. I usually do. Maybe that's why she wasn't there. I went on to a Beatles discussion board and griped about how shitty it is that Paul McCartney has never called Pete Best up to say, 'hello and how are the grandkids?'"

"Fuck McCartney. What a douche. Give Pete a call, will ya?"

"Well, that's why I had Liverpool 1962 in my head." Zak was making the connections. I wonder where those cops were, he thought. Then he realized they might have been there at the capitol or Bobbies in Liverpool but he was too distracted to notice. He wasn't even looking for them. He was looking for Pete Best's band.

"This is so cool. Dude, you have a method now. Focus on some images. Maybe using your laptop is the key. If you want to go to Paris, put an picture of the Eiffel Tower on you desktop and stare at it before you to sleep."

"I'd go to The Paris for the storming of the Bastille. That's a hundred years before the Eiffel Tower."

"Stop being a fucking intellectual," chuffed Lenny.

"What are you guys talking about?" Kiko came out of Zak's bedroom wearing one of his T-shirts, her hair askew in the way that said, A. "I just woke up" and B. "Yes, I had sex."

Zak hadn't told Lenny about the increasingly sexual emails he and Kiko had been sending. The last week she had been sending images of hentai anime. They were bizarre pictures of which women having sex with eels was the most vanilla. Zak reciprocated by sending equally bizarre images from American porn. It wasn't stuff he found particularly erotic. Some of it was just gross. It was more a game of out-shocking the other. She would send a cartoon of a woman having sex with a seahorse and he would reply with an image of a woman having sex with an actual horse. It built up the sexual tension between the two, so, in

Zak's mind (and surely in Kiko's), it seemed their second night together would be more exciting than the first one.

It wasn't.

After The Falsies show, the trio went to the Hot Cake Hideaway for eggs and coffee and Kiko made baby doe eyes. Zak invited her over and Lenny tried to fade into the background, the invisible houseguest. But once in bed, like before, Kiko laid there and waited to be taken. Zak was still thinking about Mollie and essentially masturbated to a fantasy of her using Kiko's body as a stand-in. There were moments when he hoped that Kiko would join the party and make it about their shared wade into the pool of perversity, but she seemed absent. Maybe she sensed what was on his mind. Maybe this the way that she was; Just Lay There Girl. It ended more awkwardly than the first time. "Goodnight, Professor," she said. But he was lost on his laptop.

The 200 mile drive to the prison gave Zak plenty of time to think about all the things that were suddenly filling his brain. The supervisor at the facility had expedited his visitation request, and Zak used a free Saturday to drop in and finally meet Stan Stipich. He hoped he wouldn't mind the unannounced visit. With Lenny on his way back to Seattle and Kiko back in her apartment probably looking for more weird shit to email, he turned his attention eastward on I-84 and towards the Columbia Gorge.

The Columbia Gorge is a massive cavern of beauty, eighty miles long, that divides Oregon from Washington. It was largely formed by the Missoula Floods at the end of the last Ice Age. Over about a two thousand year period, starting around 15,000 years ago, massive waves of water and earth crashed their way towards the Pacific, leaving a scar that local humans would later define as sacred. In 1805, two other humans named Lewis and Clark, and their motley crew, rode the current of the Columbia River, through the Gorge, happy to finally have the wind at their backs. They marveled at the spectacular cliffs but totally missed out on the delicious salmon the locals offered them. Stupid white people.

Zak wasn't thinking about any of that. He probably should have focused on his evolving situation with Kiko, but he was still ruminating on the dream, the fully lucid dream. Where was Claire in this dream? Or the dream police? Would he have seen them if he had kept it going? The problem was that he was so excited to be lucid, he lost his focus. When ultimate reality is open to you, it's hard to check your to-do list. Should I have a beer with Karl Marx or walk on the surface of Mars? Shit! I can't decide! (And beer with Marx on Mars is a possible third option.)

He needed a dream plan.

Kelly cherished her Saturday mornings. It was a moment not to be on-point in the climb up the ladder. She could let her defenses down. Sundays were all about preparing the battle plan for Monday, but Saturday at eleven am, she was sunk deep into her couch with a cup of mint tea, thinking about her win at dinner last night, but also letting herself gaze out the window. Portland was so beautiful when the rain stopped.

The grey tinge of the sky contrasted with the lush green of the trees in her neighbors' yards. It seemed to have some symbolism that she could only guess at. Young versus old? Nature verses bureaucracy? She would leave that to the philosophy professors to discuss while they seduced coeds into their (probably) grey sheets. For now it was enough to stare out and let her brain recharge. The cats rubbing against her were enough kinetic energy for the moment. The dragons could wait to be slain. Maybe there was something good on the Lifetime Channel. Click. Ah.

Portland grey turned into Oregon blue as Zak moved into the high walls of the Gorge. Past the towering Multnomah Falls and towards the mythical Bridge of the Gods, an alleged ancient land bridge over the Columbia, that indigenous people, like the Chinook indians, believe existed before the great floods that carved the Gorge. The majesty of the canyon always impressed Zak, who often wondered what Lewis and Clark really thought about it as they floated towards the sea. His thoughts bounced between the cliffs, still not thinking about Kiko.

"So, do you think Mollie really likes me?" he asked himself. She seemed kind of perfect. He should at least explore it.

They could see some shows together. He missed going out to shows. He missed standing in front of a band and letting the music and dancing crowd embrace him like a giant sea anemone. Maybe he should wait to start his adventure with her until he'd followed this dream experiment to its natural conclusion. He already felt he was living in two worlds. And his research wasn't just in the back seat, baby it had been put in the corner. Forget relationships, he was barely ready to interview this inmate. It was more an exploratory visit. After the coma, people gave him a break for not being on top of his game, the sick role. But he really needed to get his shit together. Maybe this interview should wait. But he had gone too far to turn around. He was already at the Bridge of the Gods.

Past the Bonneville Dam and the wind surfers in Hood River and then the Dalles Dam, where the Gorge begins to spread out into a flat high desert, Zak fretted about his state. Was he ready for anything new? Was it too soon? Stopping for gas along the way he saw a Mexican woman holding a new baby with pierced ears. When would he have let Caroline pierce her ears, or would he even have been in on the decision? Everything took him back to that moment. Even talking to inmates. What if the accident had been no accident? What if someone had pushed the boulder? A kid or a psychopath. It wasn't likely given the size of the thing but it would give him someone to blame. What was he doing talking to inmates? Maybe he should be researching post-natal care for new mothers. No, that would be too much.

Finally he arrived at the prison, located next to a chemical weapons dump on a plain overlooking the Columbia. It looked desolated and isolated as Zak approached. He was there forty-five minutes before visiting time started so he went into town for a bite at the Subway shop. It was located inside a gas station convenience store. The only other building on the block was a strip bar across the street. "What a God-awful outpost of humanity," he thought. The edge of reality. Hopefully this landscape wouldn't reappear in any dreams, but it was probably inevitable.

Lenny was crashed out on the couch in his apartment in the Ballard section of Seattle. The drive from Portland always took it out of him. He'd justify the trip as a time to listen to new music for potential licensing deals. But his mind tended to wander, to Cozy and Daniel and what he was missing by being so far away. He'd play over in his head the deal with Interlope and what he could've done differently to keep the band's momentum going. He really had it all and then watched it slip through his fingers.

The Discovery Channel played in the background as he veged-out, staring at the ceiling. Would he ever get back to that place? His walls were covered with posters from Sort Of shows and other peers of his "new rock" generation. Reminders of the rush of the stage. He melted into the throw pillow and imagined it was then.

The ceiling glistened with light blue ripples about forty feet overhead. The sunlight made a grid of soothing, meditative patterns. It startled Lenny to realize that he was under the sea. He opened his eyes and he was swimming deep in the Caribbean, in full scuba gear. It was his first time scuba diving, but he felt quite calm. He took deep breaths of air in through his regulator and the tank air tasted sweet. His mask was slightly fogged so he let in a bit of water in to wash it out and then pushed it out by blowing air out of his nose.

With his mask crystal clear he could see thousands of fish of every shape and color. He was alone along a reef. The first rule of diving is to breathe, but the second one is to never swim alone. Always have a buddy. Too many things can go wrong. Lenny couldn't remember any training, but he knew that. He took a deep breath and moved along the reef. A blue and yellow angelfish swam along side him and a big parrotfish swam up to his mask and seemed to be telling Lenny to change directions.

The water was warm and there was something peaceful about the pressure of the entire sea holding him in place and carrying him in its current. Sea fans came up from the coral and gently waved back and forth. His bubbles drifted up to bump into several snorkelers at the surface. A sea turtle nibbled at the reef, took a moment to make sure Lenny wasn't a predator and then went right back to lunch. A grouper seemed to be watching him like a wise old matron.

Time for a reality check. He was tempted to take the regulator out of his mouth and see if he could breathe underwater like Aquaman, but if he was wrong, that would be a bad ending. His body might not ever be found and then what would Daniel say about his deadbeat dad? He tried to put his hand through a fish but it just swam away. He couldn't think of a good reality check and if it wasn't a dream he would run out of air at some point. He checked the gauge: 2000 PSIs. All he knew was that he had time.

So he kept moving, trying to stay above the sea floor. There might be stingrays under the sand and he didn't want to end up like the Crocodile Hunter who wasn't done in by a crocodile. It's the things just below the surface that will get you. There was a massive school of yellow butterfly fish to his right and Lenny kicked his way into their midst, saying, "Let me join you here!" As he swam up through the top of their pod he saw another scuba diver coming over the top of the reef.

Of course it was Cozy. He immediately recognized her sparkling eyes through her mask and her long, slender frame extended by the flippers. He loved sharing experiences with her so of course he conjured her up to take all this underwater beauty in with him. She floated in her black and pink wet suit and the tiny tropical fish swam around her like an underwater version of Disney's Snow White. Even the fish loved Cozy. It reminded him of the time they went to Petco high on mushrooms and wandered through the aisles of fishtanks. She was so beautiful, her long brown hair floating around her mask while she stared into his eyes. Could they talk here?

Suddenly she jerked back. Her face registered a confused look. Lenny was about to tell her that everything would be okay, but she was moving away. He swam up the reef to grab her hand and then he saw it. A large bull shark had grabbed her right ankle and had begun to shake her violently. Blood spilled out in an expanding cloud. Cozy's regulator fell out of her mouth and he could hear her scream, "Lenny, save yourself!" through the bubbles. And as quickly as she appeared, she was gone. It was completely quiet except for the bubbles of his exhale.

"It's just a dream. It's just a dream," he said, without removing the regulator from his mouth. It's not exactly what he wanted to be happen, but Cozy had to be safe in DC, not devoured alive. Just then the large sea turtle swam up and positioned himself in front of Lenny.

"You really should listen to her," said the turtle, in a slow pokey voice.

Lenny, took the regulator out of his mouth. "Yeah, I know," he said.

The parking lot of the prison reminded Zak of every main street in every Western he'd ever watched. There was even a tumbleweed blowing up against a green SUV. It was arid and stark, with multiple tan brown structures and yard to one side where a half-a-dozen inmates in blue denim played basketball. Visitors had to park behind staff and Zak picked the farthest spot to give himself time to collect his thoughts.

The entrance for visitors was a small building the size of a 7-ll. The people moving toward it seemed barely alive. A collection of parents, wives, children and friends preparing themselves for the hard walk; that transition from the depression of knowing your loved one was locked in a place like this to the happy face, "Hi son, it's so good to see you!" act.

He took note of the license plates in the parking lot. Some had come from California and Colorado. Some with Oregon plates were rental cars so they may have come from even farther away. Since Oregon had built more prisons as crime rates dropped, it had picked up a healthy side business of renting prison beds out to states whose facilities were overcrowded. Oregon got sent the worst of the worst from hellish places like Pelican Bay and San Quentin, and put the money back into the Department of Corrections coffers.

At the door, the electronic surveillance gave him the once over and he heard the heavy metal bolt unlock and let him in. There were visitors who had been through this ritual many times before and one waved him in. "Is this you first time visiting?" asked a short old white woman who looked like a refugee from the dustbowl.

"Yeah, how could you tell?" he asked.

"You look a little confused. It's okay. The guards here are really nice. They'll tell you want you need to do. A lot nicer than the guards at Snake River."

He thanked her as she directed him to the guard desk where Zak was asked to show his ID. He told them who he was visiting and had Stipch's State ID Number on his phone. The guard gave him a plastic bag and a locker key. The locker key was to lock up his wallet, phone and anything that might be considered contraband (including his pen), and the plastic bag was for quarters from the change machine. He could bring up to three dollars into the visitation room for sodas and snacks. Zak put two dollars worth of quarters into the bag.

From the moment the steel door opened he felt he was the one who was being incarcerated. That he was the guilty one. The guards looked at the visitors with distrust and at the handful of small children like charity cases. Future offenders. If you know somebody in prison, you must be a criminal too. Or maybe the reason they became criminals. Zak wanted to announce that he was a PhD, a researcher who did important work that helped people, a teacher whose lessons gave people alternatives to crime. A card-carrying member of the ACLU. But he kept his mouth closed and prepared himself to enter lock up.

One by one the visitors' names were called out to march through the metal detector. One kid had jeans on and was told he couldn't enter the prison as inmates wore denim. (The kid would probably be thrown in with the arsonists.) One woman had an underwire bra and had to leave. (Could be used as a shank.) Zak waited to set the thing off, forgetting if he had any metal plates in his head from the accident. (He made it through.) The next step was getting a black light stamp on his left had that would be the pass back out.

The visitors made small talk. They talked about the weather and the Blazers. They didn't mention who they were visiting or what they were in for. Purely surface. Zak tried to cut through it by engaging a guard instead of the rag tag hand-stamped pseudo convicts. "So do you live in this town?" He was curious if there was any life here aside from the Subway and the strip bar.

"Sorry, sir. We don't talk about personal matters," said the guard, stoically. It made sense, Zak thought, personal information could be used to extort correctional officers. "I know where you live" kind of shit. "Get me some weed or I'll have someone set your house on fire." "I'd keep my mouth shut, too," he thought. But Zak just smiled and looked at the next steel door.

Once the last visitor made it through the screening process, the correctional officer by the door gave everybody a stern look and opened the next door. They were led to a holding area outside, and once everybody was in that area the gate opened. Then the sad group was walked across the yard to the next door. It was a series of doors, really, each one holding the world out and the nightmare in. Like a hermetically sealed Bio Dome, a little gap here and there to whisk family members in for a gulp of institutional air. When Zak was finally in the visitation room, it seemed like a sterile no-man's land where little personal business could get done. It was a dumping ground of souls.

About the size of a middle school lunchroom, the visitation center had rows of plastic chairs and little tables. In the corner there was a stack of board games, a carpeted area for small children to crawl around on, a few vending machines, and a single guard in a booth to oversee the whole thing. Zak wondered if there was an initiation. Did you have to get beat down before you got to see your inmate? But the little old lady had done this before. "They'll tell you where to sit," she explained. "They gotta get us situated first."

One by one the visitors' names were called out and assigned a seat facing the same side of the room. "Crisp? There in the center." And one by one inmates came through a single door to meet their guests. There were some tears and brief hugs. Kisses on daughters' cheeks and a mother tousling her son's hair. Brave faces all around. Everybody is doing fine. Zak only had Stipich's picture from the ODOC website but recognized him as he came through the door. He was a hulking figure by any measure. But this version had two black eyes and a split lip. Taken back a bit, Zak still had the presence to smile and wave him over.

"Mr. Stipich? It's a pleasure to finally meet you. Please sit down."

"Hi, Professor. You can call me Stan. I'm really glad you're here." Stan studied Zak's body frame and made sure that he kept a few inches from his guest.

Not wanting to waste time, Zak asked, "Is it okay if I ask what happened to you? Are you alright?"

"This?" He motioned to his fucked-up face. "This is because I'm talking to you."

2

Kiko was creating a new photo file on her Facebook page. It was the *My Sweet Life with Zak* folder. There wasn't much to put in it. She had taken some pictures at The Falsies show, including a selfie she took with the doorman. She took a picture of the drawings she made of Zak. There was a picture of her legs in his bed she had snapped. This was meant to be the beginning of something big, something that would show her mother that she could get it right. That she could land a big fish.

She rearranged the pictures a few times, including a stock photo of a Lemon Drop to signify their first night together. She laid back on her futon and imagined all the photos that would fill the file; trips to Las Vegas, pics with his parents, poses with cool bands, snaps at faculty parties. She thought about Zak's stoic demeanor with her and apprised it as a classic American "strong but silent" archetype. It was something to celebrate, not fret about.

Her room seemed especially stark to her. Not stark, blank. She was an empty canvass. She was ready to move into her professor's world of color and sound. It was time for things to start.

Lenny puttered around his apartment for a while. He needed to write up a report of his trip to Portland to see The Falsies and make an expense report, but he was procrastinating. He was trying to get into early Genesis, when Peter Gabriel was still in the band, so he put on a second CD of the *The Lamb Lies*

Down on Broadway from 1974. He still didn't get it. It sounded like a lot of pompous wanking to him. Where was the backbeat?

There was a picture of Daniel on the bookshelf that his mom had taken of him at the base of the Martin Luther King, Jr. memorial on the Mall. He struck a serious pose. So grown up. So many years going by. He hoped his son didn't like Genesis either. He really should call him. He hit the "Favorites" button on his phone.

"Hi Cozy." Before she could lay any attitude down, he continued, "Hey, is Daniel around? I just wanted to have a little convo. We haven't talked in a while. Wondering what's on the boy's mind these days."

"That's sweet, Len. I know he'd appreciate that. No, Brian (ugh the boyfriend) took him to the Smithsonian Air and Space Museum today. They wanted to look at drones." Her voice sounded kind even though she basically just said they were going to look at robots that wiped villages off the face of the earth.

"Nice. Yeah, you mean the drones that 19-year-old video game junkies in Nevada slam into families like ours in Afghanistan? Nice Saturday lesson for our boy."

"Dial it back, Lenny. There is no 'family like ours.' Besides, Brian is a total lefty. He's probably saying the exact same thing to Daniel right now. Daniel wanted to see the exhibit." There had been a lot of these moments that should be father and son moments but were some other dude and son moments because Lenny had screwed things up so bad. "I'll tell him you called. Try a bit later tonight. He'll be in. How are you doing? How's Seattle?"

"It's good. I've been down in Portland. There's a band there I want to sign for a publishing deal. It's been fun staying with the professor."

"How's he doing? Still dating that student?" Cozy always took a keen interest in Zak's well-being. It was her mothering gene.

"Well, he's sleeping with her, but I don't think he's that into her. He floats along waiting for something real." Lenny didn't want to psychoanalyze the infinite sadness of his friend, just help move him through it.

"Waiting for closure, I suppose. Not that he's ever gonna have it. Poor boy. Hey, if you get a chance, can you send me that link you saw about jobs at the Seattle Opera? I've got a friend who wants to move to the Northwest." Lenny's heart jumped at that thought that she might be the friend.

"Yeah, sure. I'll send it today."

Stan was trying to be menacing and it was working. He sat with his elbows on his knees and stared into Zak's face. He spoke in a low tone that Zak could barely hear. Between the background noise of reuniting families and the damage done by years of loud rock shows, his ears were shit and he could only make out a few words, but nodded like he heard every one.

"Listen," Stan said, "I'm catching serious hell for talking to a researcher about people's fucking health behavior." It was a lie. He was catching serious hell for writing a check to the skinheads his ass couldn't cash. But he saw an opportunity to use his bruises to manipulate a naive outsider. "I've been getting the information you asked for and this is what it cost me. They jumped me because they think I'm ratting on them to the prison officials. You need to get me out of here, right away."

Zak heard most of that. Especially the last part. He had never established a formal working relationship with this inmate so he wasn't quite sure how culpable he was. He hadn't even gone through the Internal Review Board on research with human subjects yet. He was only trying to put the feelers out to see if inmates would talk to him about these issues. Stipich was one of dozens of men he had reached out to and now it was all this, black eyes and blue bruises.

"Mr. Stipich, I mean, Stan, I had no idea this would happen to you for talking to me. I think I made it really clear in the first letter that I sent out that nobody who corresponds with me should take any kind of risk with their safety. I was only asking for very general information. So I feel really bad about this. I'm glad you're so eager to help, but you kind of went beyond the bounds of what I asked for. Before I can even get this research started in earnest, I have to get human subjects approval from the university. There's a ton of regulations when studying inmates." Zak was trying to maintain his professionalism in the face of this man who looked like he wanted to rip his head off. "I really don't have the power to get you out of here, but maybe there's someone I can talk to that can make sure you're safe until we can clear all this up."

Stan was steaming. How dare this skinny little pinhead not respond to his demand. "Look, I've put myself out on a limb to help you and you're telling me I'm being used for your curiosity? I don't think you understand how much weight I pull around here. I'm connected to cons in every facility in this state. I can get your project shut down in a fucking heartbeat. I'll a send a kite out and nobody will talk to you ever again." Zak could smell his breath. It was rotten wet cardboard. The heat came off him like an oven someone forgot to turn off.

"Okay, well, there's really no need for all that." He had pretty much lost all interest in this project since Claire's passing, so it was an empty threat. Shut it down. But there was some pressure to at least get one article out of the research question. Even a conference presentation would justify the half-hearted effort. "What can I do to make things right here so we can have some good conversations about your take on this stuff? I think this issue is important to folks both inside and outside of this prison."

"I told you, get me moved to Columbia River. You're a goddamn PhD, figure it out. Okay, here's a name you can contact. Talk to Ms. Padilla , she's the head psych nurse here. She'll tell you what's going on and what you need to do to file the forms to get me moved." It was a gamble because she might actually tell the professor the truth. "Or call Reese, like I told you to. I can get you all the 'data' you need. Just do this, okay?"

Zak could see the veins pounding in Stan's forehead. He seemed unhinged. He was torn between trying to help him, holding on to a motivated research contact and getting up and asking to be escorted to his car, forgetting the whole idea. He could always go back to studying homeless youth. Pregnant teens were a hot topic again. Even old people with open wounds would take him into less psychotic territory than this topic. But Zak liked the edge. He felt at home with society's misfits, even ones as unbalanced as Stipich. He rocked back on his white plastic chair to give himself some space. To the left was a young inmate with a ponytail playing cards with his grandparents. To his right was a black inmate about his age listening to his wife talk about their son. He squinted his eyes like he had a plan, which he didn't.

"Let me make some calls to see what I can find out. It would definitely be better if you were in Portland instead of way out here in East Bumfuck."

"You can't imagine what a shithole this place is."

Stipich seemed to be placated by Zak's offer. Zak used his quarters to buy him a Mountain Dew and a bag of Doritos, and they spent the rest of the time talking about the health care facilities at the prison and how inmates got meds that they needed. Zak tried to remember as much as he could so he could regurgitate the details into his phone when visitation was up, since he wasn't allowed to bring in his notebook and a pen. The rest of the conversation was more upbeat, with Stan cracking a few jokes about prison guards and sex offenders that Zak didn't really get. Zak made a few prison movie references and hoped his subject wouldn't feel like such a subject.

At the end of the two hours, Zak noticed something interesting. All these men who had been so gentle with their children and wives and parents pulled away for one last hug and one last assurance that everything was fine. And then they were called to pass through the door, out of the visitation room and back into the belly of the prison. Zak saw their body language change. The soft slouch became the rigid back. The tearful smile became the menacing glare. The open hand became the clenched fist. They were arming themselves for the return to the coliseum. Zak shook Stan's hand and Stan gave him a look that said, "Don't you fuck me over again." And he disappeared behind the door with the other gladiators.

As Zak was ferried back out in the reverse order that he was brought in, the old woman asked, "Did you have a good visit? It always takes a little chunk out of my heart to have to leave my boy in here each time. He's a good boy, really." Zak nodded and gave that smile that doesn't involve actually opening your mouth; the Bill Clinton "I feel your pain" smile. The air outside the iron gate seemed dry but full of direction as compared to the stale recycled air in the prison that had passed through God knows how many nightmares and ugly scenarios of men at their worst. The tumbleweed was free. The breath of the inmate just ended up inside another inmate for all infinity.

Once in his car he took a moment to check his messages but there was no cell service in East Bumfuck, so he spent twenty minutes in the parking lot reporting the highlights of the conversation into his voice recorder app while Stan's words were still fresh in his ears. And then another ten minutes recording his impressions of the setting and what, if any, value it would be to a larger research project. Later he would transcribe the recording, his least favorite part of being a qualitative researcher. Writing down his own spoken words was a level of torture he should probably foist off on his assistant, Heather.

When the return drive took him back through Hood River, he decided to stop. His phone started popping and pinging as a backlog of messages, updates and "Likes," busted through the cloud of data that hovered over civilized areas. He pulled along the river to take a moment to watch kite boarders and wind-surfers bring their walls of colored fabric to the dark green water. Up in the air, against the current, diving and swooping. What would Lewis and Clark have thought?

There were several emails and texts from Kiko, a couple of Facebook comments from Lenny (probably clips of vintage rock performances) and an instant message from Mollie. Guess which one he opened.

Hey, Zak. I looked up your funky name but I am not a stalker. I prefer to be referred to as an interested party. Anyhoo, some of us are going to see a Janis Joplin tribute act in your hipster neighborhood later this week and wanted to invite you to come along for some cosmic blues. Ciao.

That message was enough to keep his mind busy for the remainder of the drive home. Thoughts of Mollie's possibilities warmed the Acura's compartment as he headed back to damp Portland.

Kelly thought it would be nice to spend some quality time at Vowel's, the huge bookstore in downtown Portland. While Borders and other book chains came and went, Vowel's managed to remain an outpost of independently owned bookstores and book lovers treated it like their own personal Mecca. The block-sized store smelled of old paper and coffee cups, and since Portland was a city that lived to read, the store was usually packed with locals and tourists alike. You could find your section, plop down for a few hours and block out the demands of the material world. Zak was fond of the rock biography section and the oversized photography section (Subsection: Canyons), but Kelly was at home in Contemporary Romance.

She liked to wander the isles, letting the walls of book spines surround her, hoping something would catch her eye; an escape she could read on Sunday under her down comforter. The new E.L. James novel was top on her list but she was open to anything. She was weened on Barbara Cartland novels, like *Open Wings* and *No Heart is Free*, so she wasn't averse to some fanciful bodice ripping. She had mixed feelings about how sexual the genre had become. The left side of her brain found it liberating to read what was once called "smut." But the right side of her brain was disgusted that women would let themselves be taken in that matter. She had read enough nineteenth century literature to know this was nothing new, but still.

There was a calmness about the store even though it was packed on Saturday afternoon. People were respectful, like visiting a church they've been a member of since childhood. All those pages and words, all that wisdom. Kelly figured there were probably billions of thoughts in a store that big. Some ignored, some over-analyzed and some gulped down on vacation, beside the pool. She was looking for a cover or a title or a recommend read that spoke to her at that moment. And that particular moment was split between the desire to fly away like a seagull and dive into a deep tome that explained her anger at the world, attributing it to some great fault in the world itself.

Lost in thought and facing the end of the isle she saw a student walk by. It was Kiko who was headed to the anime section to look at manga comic books. "That's the girl from Crisp's office!" she registered. Suddenly, she forgot about bodice-ripping fluff and thought she had an opportunity to at least learn more. Was he meeting her in the coffee shop for a rendezvous? There had to be some salacious tidbit that she could use. So she took off in Kiko's direction, glancing down the isles, past the pale faced kids in Science Fiction until she spotted her in the manga section of the "Gold Room."

Kelly thought she had stepped right out of a 1960s children's book. Kiko was wearing a sailor top with a short gingham skirt, white socks and Mary Janes. Her youthful flash made Kelly's grey and black jacket over a grey shirt buttoned up to her neck and black knee length skirt seem that much more matronly. She wasn't dressed right to win over this woman-child but she didn't have any real options so she approached Kiko who was thumbing through the thick Japanese comic books.

"Excuse me, hi! You're a student at the university, right? I've seen you in the Health Science department." Kelly didn't have much of a plan. Just get her talking.

Kiko cocked an eyebrow. Who was this woman interrupting her mission to find the perfect gift for her new paramour? She took a step back but kept her thumb on a page of a particularly erotic image that she thought Zak might respond to.

"Um, yeah. I go there," she said, sheepishly, her Korean accent slipping out at the end.

"I don't mean to bother you. I'm book shopping. Trying to find something for a Saturday. What are you looking at?" It seemed like a good entré.

Since Kiko was in the market to shock, she opened the manga comic to the page she had her thumb on. It was of two seemingly naked young girls. They had breasts but big puppy eyes and no pubic hair. One girl was going down on the other, while a trio of monkeys watched. She remained silent waiting for a reaction from the lady in grey and black. A smile curled up around the edge of her lips when she saw her face go blue-white.

"Oh, my. What is that?" Kelly noted her proximity to a few tweens browsing the same isle.

"It's called manga. It's a Japanese art form. You've never heard of it?"

"No, I haven't. They sell that here? It looks pornographic. Are those children?" Kelly didn't know how to process this university student dressed as a child holding open what could easily be viewed as child porn by most Southern judges.

"I guess one person's art is another person's porno," said Kiko with a smirk. "I like it. A lot."

The book was still being held opened but Kelly desperately wanted to move to another subject.

"Don't you know Professor Crisp? I think I saw you at his office one day. Do you have a class with him?" She was fishing.

"I did last year." Recognizing there might have been a more delicate English translation of their current situation, Kiko decided to go for the basic but blunt description. "Now we are lovers. I'm shopping for a gift for him today."

The pale hue in Kelly's face turned to purple, from the top of her forehead to the bottom of her chin. She knew it. She knew he was one of those. He had it written all over him. Predator.

"Oh, well, alright. And he likes this kind of stuff?" This was too perfect.

"Oh, yes, he's a big anime fan. We share all kinds of things like this. He's very worldly. We're both adults so nobody should have a problem, right?" It was a valid question. "Vowel's has a whole aisle of books like this. Maybe it's what you need for your Saturday."

"Maybe," said Kelly, thinking that she might actually need it for court evidence. "But I'm going to keep looking. Can I ask your name?"

"Kiko Matsugane, what's yours?" Kiko knew she should be more respectful of the older woman, but this was America, where you were allowed to stand your ground.

"I'm Vice Provost Claiborne." It sounded even more authoritarian saying it to a girl in a sailor shirt. But Kelly wanted to exit with her morsel. "Enjoy your manga books. I might see you around campus." And with that she backed out of the aisle, her mouth dripping from the new intel. "Oh, Walt is going to love this," she thought.

When Zak got home, his house had a nice ray of late afternoon sunshine coming in through the kitchen window. It was only one beam but it seemed to warm up the place. A little ray of hope after the grim prison encounter. Something about Stan had bugged him the whole way home. The guy seemed like a walking time bomb. He needed to purge it from his head and since he couldn't find the TV remote he plopped on the couch to deal with his messages, still putting off responding to Kiko and waiting to craft an answer to Mollie. There were a couple of new texts from his colleague Robin that seemed urgent.

Zak, got some info W is playing dirty. We need to talk.

You around this afternoon? I'll buy you a beer.

Gotta talk before Monday.

He regretted responding to that first email from Nielsen. Now he was being pulled into a labor battle when he was just trying to get things on track. He'd respond but first some mindless scrolling and email and maybe a few online contests. The messages (emails, texts, Facebook PMs) from Kiko all said she had a gift for him. He could only imagine. There was an email from Lenny detailing his latest dream (with Cozy, of course), lots of spam and political posts complaining about Mexican immigrants from his right-wing friends from Alabama and a reminder to renew his membership in the American Public Health Association. He responded to Robin first, via text.

Hi, sorry, was out on a prison interview. Yeah, let's talk.

Headed to a local bar on Alberta called Jinks in about an hour. Could use that beer.

He responded to Kiko that the gift sounded interesting. He had some work to do transcribing the inmate interview and maybe tomorrow would be good. On all the right-wing Facebook posts about immigrants he was too tired to argue so he posted a picture of a face-palming Jesus on each one to make the point. Then to the Facebook message from Mollie.

Hey Mollie, that sounds cool. Glad to know Janis Joplin is alive and well in my neighborhood. There's a bar across the street called Jinks. I'll be hanging out there playing the jukebox. Thanks for the invite.

He thought he'd keep it cool and not act too over-excited, which his stomach was telling him he was. He didn't have much time to process the merit of the message after hitting the Return button when his laptop blooped.

Good boy.

Just know I will fully judge you by what songs you play on the J.B..

Fucking A. How many times had he said you can't judge people by their race or religion but their record collection was fair game? Things seemed to be looking up, even in a new friend kinda way. Time for a beer.

Jinks was one of the first bars in the neighborhood to open before the wave of gentrification exploded. Even though there were bars that were closer or "nicer," Zak was loyal to this one as it was home to the folks who existed between Alberta being a black neighborhood and a white neighborhood. There were old timers, and Curtis Mayfield was on the jukebox, and occasionally obnoxious fratboys with backwards baseball caps were cut off and told to go get drunk in the Pearl. In other words, it had character.

It was a seven block walk to the bar, and since it was that moment that the afternoon gives way to the extended Portland twilight, Zak took the scenic route. Instead of walking down Alberta, past the lines of out-of-towners waiting to get in the latest hotspot restaurant or artisan ice cream shop, he walked past the homes of his neighbors, to creep on their normal lives; washing cars in the driveway, kids toys scattered in the yard. But then he stopped.

About four blocks from his house there was a vacant lot. It wasn't there last time he walked by. There was a home there but it had just vanished. There was a growing trend of developers buying homes in his "hot" neighborhood, tearing down the old house and building something bigger and more modern. Granted, most of the hundred year old homes didn't have enough electrical outlets for modern living, but slowly the old neighborhood was being erased and re-created with mini-McMansions. So much for "bohemia."

But it wasn't the decimation of his neighborhood by money-hungry developers that stopped Zak in his tracks. It was that he couldn't remember what the house had looked like. He had walked passed it a million times on his way to Jinks. He should know what it looked like. It had housed families for probably a century and now it was gone. All the stories the that lived under its roof, births and deaths, heartaches and parties. He should at least remember what it looked like but he couldn't even conjure up the shape. One story or two? Did it have a front porch? What color was it? A house like that deserved to be remembered but now it was as if it had never existed. How can that be? Was this a dream?

"Hey, Prickich! Who was that guy you were talking to today?"

"Who? Nobody," said Stan, head down.

"In visitation. I heard you had a guest."

Word travels quickly in the joint, and Derek Stemphill was up in Stan's face about it.

"Really, Derek. It wasn't anybody. Just talking about my case." Stan's eyes were to the floor but he could see Stemphill's forearms flexing, expanding the Nazi tattoos that covered both.

"That's not what I heard. I heard he's a doctor or something. Is he going to get you the stuff? You're in deep to Kennedy now and if you've got a line on a product, you better let us know." Stemphill opened his right hand and Stan, eyes still down, could see a razor blade in it.

"Look, he's not that kind of doctor. He's a college professor. He's just helping me with my case, okay? I'll come through on the meds." Stan was skirting the truth as usual. Stemphill was Kennedy's errand boy but his weapon was his reputation as a crazy-ass mother-fucker. He'd add time to his bid by slicing somebody if it added credit to his swagger. One of the scores of cons you don't want to piss off.

"You better be straight with me, you faggot, or I'll lob your ear off in your sleep." The sweat glistened off the 88 tattoo on his neck; 88, code for Heil Hitler. "You made a promise. Time to fucking deliver, fat boy."

"Yeah, I got the message last time," Stan said, motioning to the bruises on is face. "I'm good on it, Derek."

And with that, Stemphill pushed Stan out of the way, muttered something that Stan couldn't make out and headed down the hall for chow. Stan decided to skip dinner and quietly walked back to his cell, eyes never lifting above navel level. "It never ends," he thought.

Jinks was not a big place. Big enough for a bar, a pool table, a few dark corners to hide in and one of the last jukeboxes in Portland not connected to the Internet. Albums ranged from Otis Redding to D'Angelo, The Who to The War on Drugs. Something for all the cool kids, young and old. The bartenders were all also engaged in some other artistic endeavors: dress makers, potters, nude models. It was an oasis of stability while change washed up and down the street like the tide, remaking the landscape every few months. Jinks stayed as constant as the elbows of the regulars on the bar.

Zak walked into the bar with "Day Tripper" playing and it felt good, like he had a good reason. It had been a while and he worried about losing his status as a familiar face. It was the pre-Saturday night crowd, so there was room at the bar. Three hours from now the place would be slammed with slumming suburbanites and bros, laying heavy on the jukebox's one Notorious B.I.G. CD. But, for the moment, there a was stool with his name on it.

Jinks was the proverbial "third space," some place between work and home where you went to find your community. For some it was the coffee house (Bob Dylan), or the beer hall (Adolf Hitler) or the diner (Steve Guttenberg), but for most it was their local pub. It's where people went to watch the game or the debates and not feel alone. You could still have conversations in a bar. Even with half the patrons staring down at their phones, you could still talk to someone, especially the bartenders. "You wanna go where people know people are all the same."

"Hey, Professor! Where ya' been?" asked Lola, the slim, short bartender who was also a jewelry designer. Her tattooed arm wiped down the bar in front of Zak. "You want your regular? Rum and Coke?"

"Oh, you know. Getting my act together. I know I need to get out more. Um, no. I think I need a stout. Whatever you have on draft." I was nice to have his belly up to the bar. The guy on his left was scrolling through his phone and the guy on his right was watching the Blazers game. No Dr. Robin yet.

"Getting all heavy on us. I don't remember you ever ordering a dark beer." Lola prided herself on knowing the potions of the locals.

There was a reason to go to the black water, as the Irish are fond of saying. "I'll tell you why, Lola. It's for my dreams."

"You have dreams about drinking stout?" Lola grabbed a clean pint glass and headed for the tap.

Raising his voice over The Beatles, Zak said, "No, you have better dreams when you drink dark beer. It has more iron in it, you see." The last sentence got the attention of the guy on his phone. Iron in it! Zak brought his voice down as Lola got closer. "Anyway, that's what this English guy told me. He said people who drink Guinness have more vivid dreams because of all the iron in it." He watched his beer slowly flowing into the glass like Vermont maple syrup.

"Did he work for Guinness?" As a bartender, Lola thought she should have heard this little tidbit. It would at least explain some of the weird behavior of some of the old timers who came in and babbled about the big one coming.

"No, and I don't even know if there's any science to back it up. I'm doing this lucid dreaming thing." Lola motioned for him to hold on a second while she grabbed his beer and then she pulled in like their was nobody else in the bar. "Yeah, so I'm trying to have a specific dream tonight and if a few pints of stout help, who am I to argue?"

"I've read about this. That's where you can control your dreams, right? Can you actually do that?"

"Yeah, I've done it a few times. But I think I've got it figured out, like, you know, the strategy. So I'm going to try it out tonight and see if it works."

"Shit, that's so wild. So what's the dream gonna be?" Lola wanted a vicarious ride.

Zak was embarrassed to say that he wanted to go back in time just a little bit. But most of the people in Jinks knew Claire and what happened, including Lola, who figured that's why his attendance had been spotty, ranging from drinking binges that lasted a week to dropping of the face of the earth for twice as long. But it was written all over his face.

"Oh, dude," said Lola. "Well, of course you want to see her again. Nobody is gonna fault you for that. Just don't get lost in a dream, you know? I need you to come in here and play good music. If I hear 'Uptown Funk' one more time, I'm going all Columbine on this joint."

"Careful. Nancy Grace will come after you if you say that too loud. Why don't you let me replace that CD in the jukebox so when they play that song, they'll get 'Revolution #9' or some Tibetan monk throat chanting. That would be great on a Saturday night. I have a disc of hog calls from the Ozarks that might be fun."

Lola was laughing and the Claire thing was left in the dust. "Zak, if anybody in Portland has a CD of hog calls, it's you. Enjoy your beer and your dream." And she moved on to the guy and his basketball game. Zak was about to make a break for the jukebox and shove a couple of crisp bills in but there was a young couple loading up something surely disappointing. That's when Robin came in, looking more Mr. Rogers than usual.

"Hey, Zak! I got your message. I was over on MLK and thought I'd try to catch you. Can we grab a table?" She always seemed intense but it was ramped up to a level that made Zak want to bolt for the door.

"Sure. Can I get you a drink?" he said, getting off his stool.

"Can I get a 7 and 7?" she yelled to Lola, like she was getting an order into a short order cook. "Next beer's on me, remember?" she said to Zak, as she sat down at an open table. Led Zeppelin's "Rain Song" came on and Zak took it as an omen that bad news was coming.

"Zak, I'm really glad you agreed to meet." Robin's eyes squinted and Zak wondered if she had forgotten about her drink. "Look, we wanted to take this unionization effort slowly, build a consensus, but Woodbine and his slimy gang are going to play dirty pool to derail the whole thing, Some shit went down on Friday that's like something from an episode of *House of Cards*." It sounded over-dramatic. Where was that drink? Maybe some chit chat first? Fuck.

"Shit, what's going on? Does this have anything with Claiborne lurking around the halls outside classes?" Zak asked.

"You've noticed that, too? She's not too subtle. In our department, whenever she's wandering by our secretary yells out, 'Where are my gompers?'"

"Oh, that's clever," said Zak, getting the reference to labor leader Sam Gompers.

Lola brought Robin a drink and gave Zak a look that said, "I'm only bringing this drink all the way over here because she's with you."

"Yeah, that's exactly what it's about. One of the students that works in her office told a faculty member that she's making a list of everyone who is coming to the meetings and responding to my emails. She's reading our fucking emails!"

Zak's stomach started to sink.

"And that's not all. On Friday, two full professors got called into Human Resources. One because he had porn on his office computer and the other was having some weird three way sex thing with a student and her husband. Guess what they had in common." Pause.

"Poor impulse control?" said Zak. It was that or some David Duchovny-level sex addiction.

"No, damnit. They were both on my union listserve. The porn guy never even made it to a meeting. They're trolling our communications to find something to go after us on. It's classic intimidation tactics. These types of proceedings are supposed to be confidential, but they let it leak out to humiliate these people and scare everybody else."

Zak's stomach sank even farther and his heart was pounding like a drum. He thought about the emails that he'd been whipping around the last few weeks. He got a sour taste in his mouth that even the darkest of beers couldn't wash away. Robin stared at him with red in her eyes until Zak let out a gasp.

"Holy fuck," said Zak. "So it's Claiborne doing this?" She seemed like a harmless older woman who only needed a good fashion makeover.

"I think they're working off of her list. I'm sure Provost Sanders is part of it, too. She wants to get rid of faculty and put all our classes online so some kid in India can run them, turn the whole place into a University of Phoenix." She took a big gulp of her drink for effect.

"Why would she want to do that?" It seemed alarmist but Zak had already heard the theory and seen the evidence that other schools were moving in that direction. They were called MOOCs, Massive Open Online Classes. Stanford already had MOOCs up and running that had 200,000 students enrolled in a single class at a time. That's a different animal than a senior level research class with fifteen students sitting in the same room, discussing the finer details.

"Obviously money. What's the biggest budget line these days?" No pause this time. "Us! Faculty salaries. Even bigger if we get collective bargaining rights. Think about how much they could raise their pay if they got rid of us and ran classes online. I used to think my job was safe from out-sourcing but it's happening as we're sitting here."

Zak's mind wandered for some reason to Sally Field in *Gidget* and then Sally Field in *Spiderman 2*. Then he found a place in the middle; Sally Field in *Norma Rae*. Could Robin be their Norma Rae, standing on a table in the faculty lounge with a sign that had "Union" scrawled on it and her nipples clearly visible under her sweater?

Robin continued. "It's a lot cheaper to set up one department with one professor and have all the classes run by a few techies on the other side of the planet. It's all packaged and ready to go. The provost has said that it's the future of the university and this is how it's happening. Unless we fight back." Very Norma Rae, toward the end of the movie.

Zak was loyal to the brick and mortar idea of the university. He was sure it had at least another century to go. "Do you really think they're trying to create a university with no professors or classrooms? We've been doing it this way for centuries."

"Look around this bar, Zak. People are in love with their technology. They're drugged by it." Zak noticed that the third place of the bar looked a lot more like a place to have a beer in while you checked your Facebook activity. "Besides, these administrators don't have any loyalty to the university. They're like corporate raiders. Most of them will be working somewhere else in five years. They're like Haliburton. They come to fuck everything up and make as much money from the chaos before they move to some new field to devour." That was at least three mixed metaphors in one allusion.

Zak stared in his drink, not sure what to say. He'd worked so hard to get to this point.

She went on. "I'm surprised they haven't come after me, yet. I'm dreading going in on Monday and opening my email. You don't have any skeletons in your closet, do you?" she said with a half smile. "I'm sure you're safe after what you went through last year." With that comment her face relaxed a bit and she went from Dr. Intense Eyes to Dr. Sympathetic Eyes.

"I hope not. I don't know. Um, what are we going to do?" Seemed like it was time to shit or get off the pot on the union issue.

"There's an emergency meeting Monday at a faculty member's home. We can't meet on campus anymore and I can't say where until the last minute. Woodbine has moles feeding him info, mostly department chairs because they all think they're going to be deans one day. I don't know how this is going to end up. It's such a long shot. Part of me wants to chuck it and let them have their shitty online university." The drink was having its effect. Lola probably poured it with a heavy hand. Robin sat back in her chair.

"Yeah, but you've got tenure. What would you give that up for?" asked Zak. Robin was just a few years ahead of Zak on the ladder, sort of a future version of himself.

"I've been doing some writing on the side. I took a screenplay writing class last summer. I've been working on some scripts. I've been thinking about telling the dean to fuck off and move to Hollywood." Suddenly this conversation got less dire and more interesting. Zak waved at Lola for another round.

"Hollywood? Really? That's a pretty competitive gig, I bet. What are you working on?" asked Zak, suddenly wishing he had a Plan B.

"I've got several scripts that are started. Some of it is heavy stuff, related to my work on education and the sex trafficking of immigrants. But I'm working on a comedy that I think will be the one that sells."

Zak laughed a bit, mainly because the thought of this super intense academic writing a comedy seemed like a basis for a *Saturday Night Live* skit. "A comedy? Really? About what?"

Robin took her glasses off and looked around like there was another screenwriter in the bar waiting to steal her idea.

"It's a film version of that TV show *Charles In Charge*. I picked the lamest eighties TV show that hadn't been made into a movie yet. But get this. It will be an all obese cast. If there's one stereotype that Hollywood refuses to get rid of it's that fat people are hilarious, right?" Zak didn't answer but he started making a list of fat actresses in his head. "So the joke will be that Charles and Buddy keep meeting girls but they always die of diabetes-related illnesses. Then at the end of the movie, they both have heart attacks."

"That doesn't really sound that funny." Zak was starting to thinking Robin was a bit mental.

"It's a dark comedy. It will be a commentary on America's obesity epidemic wrapped in a redux of a crappy TV show. Besides, Hollywood loves bad ideas. Look at two-thirds of Eddie Murphy's movies. I think this could be my ticket out of the academic ghetto." It was such a bad idea, it just might work. "Anyway, just something I'm working on in case we all get shit-canned."

"Well, I'd go see your movie. *Charles, Large and In Charge.*"

"Oh, that's good. Mind if I use it?"

The second round of drinks came and Zak and Robin chitted and chatted, the small talk that usually goes at the start of a few drinks. The bar began to fill up with the Saturday evening crowd and somebody played "Uptown Funk" which led Lola to shoot Zak a glance that said,"Get on the fucking jukebox ASAP."

4

Kiko was standing on a street corner downtown wondering where the usual rush of traffic was on a Saturday evening. She seemed to have all the city to herself. She tightened the red bow around her collar and slowly crossed the street. She knew her one job was to find the legendary silver crystal. If she could find it she could seal her enemies in the Moon Kingdom and have Zak all to herself. No research demands, and no rock band girls.

She noticed a reddish cloud in the grey Portland sky and flew up to the roof of the Heathman Hotel to get a better look, her long pigtails bounced off her bare legs as she sailed through the air. From ten stories up the city looked like an old map. The trees on the Park Blocks hid homeless kids and trusting lovers. Under a big maple she thought she saw him, Zak, but he was with another woman. In anger she soared into the red cloud.

"Let's see if that dark beer was worth it," Zak thought, looking at his belly. He never had a six pack, but now it was more like a stack of pancakes. He could've stayed at Jinks and rode out the Saturday night crowd, maybe hijacking the jukebox and playing the one Miles Davis disc all night, but he was anxious to get the experiment under way. It had been in his mind all day, even while he was at the prison. When Stan's berating blurred into the background noise, he'd drift off to visions of Claire. On the drive home she was beside him, even when he took mental exit ramps to think of Mollie. There was a need for resolution.

She had him doing crazy things. He had been planning his bedtime ritual like an OCD outpatient. He had his laptop queued up to old photo albums and the stereo cued up to play a Paul Simon album she loved. Her red spring dress was out of the closet and hanging on the back of chair in the bedroom, like she had taken it off after a night on the town. He had envisioned this setting before he even reached the prison.

Before climbing into bed he drank a glass of ice water to freshen his mouth. The coldness numbed the back of his throat to the point of pain. Maybe it would be the last sensation from the waking world. He leaned against the kitchen counter and felt angry he had to go to such bizarre lengths to see his wife and child. He noticed a chip on the surface where she had dropped his power drill. He was fixing a shelf in the cabinet and she let it slip, gouging the counter top. There were a lot of dents like that.

With *So Beautiful or So What* playing, he turned off the house lights, looking at the living room couch. When she was pregnant she liked to stay up some nights and read baby books while Zak hit the hay. Books about baby cognitive development and books about how not to turn your kid into a self-centered prick. Often that Paul Simon album would be playing. He'd kiss her on the forehead and tell her to make sure the front door was locked before she came to bed.

Zak slid his legs under the covers, reached into the nightstand to find his wedding band and started looking at pictures of his dead wife on his laptop. He had a folder on his desktop of their drive through Death Valley. There was a picture they took of themselves in front of a sand dune and Claire was pouring a bottle of water on his head. You could see the wicked grin on her face. It was so hot that he didn't mind. "Why'd you have to be right for me?" he asked himself.

He realized he hadn't taken as many pictures of her as he should have. Lots of pictures of high cliffs for some reason. He wished he had more candid pictures of her in unguarded moments. That's when her real light shined through. But he focused on the pictures he did have, hoping that would jump start a lucid dream with her and he could hold her for as long as the Dream Gods would allow him. He didn't let in any other thoughts as he let the beer have its way with him. He whispered to himself, "I'll be with you tonight."

There was the drift. One foot on the shore and one foot being carried out to sea. Paul Simon's voice was in his ears and then not and then back again. "Love is the eternal sacred light, free from the shackles of time." He knew he was stepping off the cliff into slumber. "Mind the gap," he thought. This is where the door opens. Arms and legs fall away and you are in Wonderland.

But the music stopped and there was just blackness. Time ceased to move. He was stuck in the void. There wasn't even thought. No lucidity, just the grave of sleep.

"Do you think he's ready?"

"No. Look at him laying there."

"But he really wants to go."

"I know what he wants. Look at that boner."

"I think that's his phone."

"Next position please."

"Oh, let's take him."

"What the fuck?" Zak opened his eyes to four men standing at the end of his bed, dressed in white police uniforms. "What the hell are you doing here?" But he knew. He had seen these guys before.

"Oh, I think you know why we're here," said one with blonde hair. "The question is do you know why you're here?"

"Shit, are you guys my dream guides?" He had read about dream guides in one of the articles that Lenny had sent him. "Can you take me to Claire?" He sat up like a kid on Christmas morning.

"Yeah, he's definitely not ready," said one of the cops.

There was a a cop with sunglasses and a cigarette hanging out of his mouth. He farted and the others looked at him.

"Right, I guess that means we're going somewhere," said another.

Zak was going to get out of bed but there was no bed. Tonight was all he really wanted.

"Nice dream, if you think that you're strong enough." (Radiohead)

Chapter 6:
Voices

1

There was not really any 'here' there. A void made up of the year without her and the sound of their child. It pulled at the walls of his heart as he kept his eyes shut. Of course the void was black. What else would it be? When he opened his eyes there was no difference. Black black matte, not even a refection off the blackness. He didn't even know if he a had a body at that point. He felt like that soldier in *Johnny Got His Gun*, his face blown off and no way to communicate with the world.

"Hello?"

The four large faces of the policemen appeared in a circle around him. They definitely did not have bodies that he could see. Was this a trial? Their voices had a distinct warm reverb, like an old Phil Spector record.

"There's our boy," said one.

"He looks like a lost cat," said another.

"Let's just give him a taste, shall we?" said the blonde. And the guy with the mustache said nothing.

Zak was starting to get his bearings. If he hadn't been trying to have a lucid dream he might have thought this was a trip to Closetland. But it was his dream and that meant he could control it. That's what he thought alright.

"Okay, this is my show. You guys are going to help me get back, right?" he said, looking up at the four faces.

"Why do they always think they're in charge of these things?" asked the blonde.

"Back where, Zachary?" said one with a long boyish face.

"Do I have to say it?" All four heads nodded. He tried to remember to not get lost in thoughts of The Beatles or seeing what his neighborhood looked like fifty years ago. "I need to see Claire."

"And why do you need to see her, Professor?"

Zak wasn't really ready for the question. This was his wish fulfillment. He fumbled through all the things he wanted to say to her. That there were moments when he couldn't breathe. There were moments when he thought he would survive, maybe even meet someone new. There were a thousand times when he thought he saw his wife on the street or at the grocery store only to realize it was only a look-a-like. There were times when the sight of a baby would bend him over in pain. Well, that one was still a constant. He tried to keep his focus so not to spin out like he did in Liverpool. He could hear his jaw creak as he opened his mouth.

"I want to tell her that I'm sorry. That I want to go back and change that moment."

"Oh, that's all. Why didn't you say so in the first place?"

And with that their faces disappeared and stars appeared over Zak's head. He looked up and gazed at the band of stars that was the thick part of the Milky Way his planet was in. That band represented about 25,000 light years full of alternative solar systems before one reached the true void of space. Now that's some blackness.

Looking down was another matter. Zak was above a city, alight from electric signs that illuminated the desert that surrounded it. It was clearly Reno, with the mountains to the west and Interstate 80 running latterly through the city.

"Okay, let's go," he said to no one. But he didn't appear at the roulette wheel with Claire or zoom down to their hotel room on the fourth floor of the Sands. He didn't go anywhere. It seemed he was encased in some kind of wet concrete, like had he been dunked in a tank of rocky goo, all the way up to his face. His only motion was to slowly climb down into it. The bright lights of a Reno were now a dim red glow but it served to guide him to the city.

After what seemed like hours, he fell through a trap door into a room in a building with a clear view of Reno out of the window. It was like being shat out the asshole of space onto terra firma. Lying on the floor in the clothes he had on before he changed for bed, he was not covered in space shit. He was clean. It was an old building. This definitely wasn't a room at Circus Circus. It was devoid of furniture or light aside from what came in from the brightly lit city. He was alone but for one man covered in sweat and grease. His broad shoulder muscles pushed out from under his dirty white tank top. He worked a large lever that held a giant gear in place. When he made eye contact with Zak, Zak thought this might be the next step in what was shaping up to be a hero's journey.

His voice was low with a deep Southern accent. "Come pull this lever." There seemed to be a glow coming from his mouth that illuminated jagged, shark-like teeth. "Come pull this lever," he said again, but louder.

Zak climbed to his feet and walked to the gear, his limp slowing him. He looked at it rising out of the floor and through the gap saw the floor of a casino, filled with gamblers and drinkers and soon to be three time losers. It seemed like a generic casino but it might have been the Sands. Zak was confused about what was happening.

"Why do you want me to pull the lever?" It was his dream but he wasn't sure how these things worked. It looked like pulling the lever would release the gear wheel allowing something to happen.

"Every action has a price," the man said. "You want to see her you have to pull the lever." His sweat dripped to the floor and then fell through the gap.

A panic welled up inside Zak. He worried that pulling the lever might cause his world to unravel, like pulling a thread on an old sweater. This was getting to be too much like an episode of *The Twilight Zone*. He could see his favorite roulette table. He recognized the Asian woman who was the dealer as she waved her hand over the chips and said, "No more bets." There was a noisy ringing in his ears that suddenly stopped. He saw Claire and his lungs constricted. She was in the black and white dress she had on their last night in Reno. He could see her big belly pressed against the table. Sitting next to her was a man, dressed in Zak's brown leather jacket. But he had a thin mustache. What was this? Zak could feel his pituitary glands secreting hormones into his brain as he began to slip out of phase.

"Pull the lever." The voice was louder. But what did it mean?

Between the floor and the ceiling of the casino there was a small crawl space he could see in the crack. There was a small man, a midget, also sweaty, working a smaller gear that was connected to the larger gear. He looked up at Zak through the space between the wheels and shook his head. He saw one of the cops on the casino floor, the one who didn't speak. The other three were standing behind him.

"I told you he wasn't ready."

Lenny was on an old couch having sex with Debbie Harry, the singer of Blondie (circa 1977), and a young woman that worked in his bank (circa a few days ago). They were taking turns kissing him with their hands darting in his pants. The bank teller's top was off and Debbie's torn Creem Magazine t-shirt was barely on. She pushed the teller back and said, "Hands off this one, sweetie. It's my turn."

"This is fucking awesome," said Lenny, taking a swig from a can of Budweiser. He was backstage at any club in the Western world in the late twentieth century. It could have been CBGBs, since the sound of The Ramones was coming from behind the Magic Marker-covered walls. It didn't really matter.

Lenny began to pull Debbie's hot pants off and the teller took the cue and slid her own underwear off and threw her black leather booted leg over Lenny's lap. The music got louder and Lenny noticed the box of cheese pizza on the table in front of him. "Shit, I love this song." The Ramones were playing, "Teenage Lobotomy." The teller didn't recognize the song and it irked Lenny. He looked at Debbie for some assurance but she was grabbing a slice.

Kelly woke up out of a dream about Walt Woodbine. All she could remember was seeing his milk chocolate brown fingers on her bare hips and his voice from behind her, whispering something in her ear. She didn't know what, but she felt damp under the sheets in a way she hadn't for a while. It had basically been a wind swept desert down there, complete with a coyote howling at the moon. She immediately regretted throwing away her vibrator. In one of their last fights, upon hearing about the other (younger) woman, she threw it at her husband. It bounced off his head and landed in the cats' litterbox. So it had to go, but it would've come in handy this morning.

She let her head sink into her pillow as the sun snuck in through the window. Pulling the 1500 thread count sheets up around her chin, she contemplated spending the day in bed and writing a romance novel in her head, one that ended with Walt proposing to her in her office, the provost's office. But Sundays were pre-Mondays so she unplugged her phone from its charger and looked at her to-do list.

As if she had slipped back into her dream, she saw there was a text from Walt. It must have come in after she went to sleep.

Looking for an excuse to try a new brunch place. Want to meet in the Pearl around 11?

"Holy cow, he wants to go on a brunch date," she thought. "That only gives me two and half hours to get ready." She leapt out of her bed to race to the bathroom and tripped over a cat. Not a great start to what could be a significant day in her life. But don't count any chickens yet. She considered laying on the floor and going back to sleep to see how this dream would play out.

2

Zak woke up in a state of confusion. He felt hung over and wrung out, like his veins were full of sand. He'd had a series of dreams but only remembered the one where he saw Claire through the crack in the floor. Thinking about it made his face hurt, but at least he could feel the pain and know it was a marker of his place in reality. He wrote down as much of it as he could piece together in his dream log. "I was so close to her but she wasn't with me," he wrote. "Was any of this real?"

He pulled himself out of bed to make coffee and put on some music. Sunday morning selections are important. It's one of the moments during the week that has a specific musical feel, like Friday at 5 pm or Saturday at midnight. If it's raining, you have to play jazz, but the sun was out over Portland so he selected some seventies vinyl, 10cc's *How Dare You!* He needed to hear the song, "Art for Art's Sake" in his bohemian bungalow.

As he ground the coffee, the images of Claire at the roulette wheel swirled around his kitchen. He felt a warmness whenever she appeared, but the fact that she was with another man made him slightly sick. Maybe coffee wasn't the best choice. Maybe he should start drinking vodka. He remembered how much he hated the world in that instance. But the moment the aroma of the brewed coffee touched the end of his nose, he thought things might be manageable. That sense of well-being only grew as the smell merged with the hot liquid on his lips. Ahhhh. The sand began to get flushed as the caffeine roto-rooter pushed through his bloodstream.

He melted into the couch with his cup and the Sunday paper. The first order of business was to see how his lottery ticket did. Shit, he only had one of the seven numbers, 62. Funny. Like Liverpool 1962. Maybe he should only play Beatle-themed numbers. Eight days a week. When I'm 64. There were surely other things in the paper to peruse but he wasn't motivated. Losing that Lotto meant he couldn't escape Portland in a hastily purchased first class ticket to New York or to some ghost town in upper Kazakhstan. He was stuck where he was.

Maybe a check of the inbox, so he flipped open his laptop. There was an email from Robin with the subject line all in caps. Ignore. There was the usual glut from Kiko with God knows what kind of perversion attached. He was hoping for a dream update from Lenny so they could compare notes but that guy wouldn't be awake for hours. So he ignored anything work related and read a few Facebook posts and watched some YouTube videos of babies hitting kittens. Why did he even have a subscription to the newspaper anyway? Oh, that's right; because it mattered.

There was a cat in the window that wasn't his. A peeping tom cat, he guessed. Nothing to see here. Come back a year ago, before the anger and paralysis took their toll. The paralysis looked physical; his asymmetrical jawline, how the fingers on his right hand were askew, the slight droopiness of one eye. But it masked the paralysis of his mind. He was unable to leave that moment. He spent most of his time on Highway 138, slowing the car down or telling her one last time she was the one who made his life make sense. There were a million ways to tweak that afternoon. Fifty years ago, when TV stations went to static at 2 am, there was the sound of nothingness. That was Zak's brain. When there wasn't a pressing thought, like boiling water or a student with her hand up, his head went to Highway 138.

The doorbell ringing shook him out of it. Ding dong present time frame. Sundays were usually off limits to canvassers who typically hit the neighborhood between five and seven on weekdays, in time to interrupt dinner with an opportunity to save the owls. Zak was a pushover and usually wrote a check. There are few jobs harder then knocking on doors and asking people to put money where their mouth was, especially when their mouth was full of tuna casserole. Well, this was Portland so it was probably salmon casserole. But not on a Sunday.

It was Kiko, with a neatly wrapped package under her arm. She had a green jacket on that might have belonged to one of the lesser Kennedys in 1963. Zak hesitated before opening the door. What if someone (Mollie) had spent the night?

"Hi Professor! It's me again." she squeaked. "I wanted to see if you wanted to get brunch in your neighborhood." It was the best line she could come up with and not look suspicious.

"Kiko, hello. How did you get here?" Zak thought he should be better dressed than boxers and a t-shirt, but he had slept with this woman. "Come in!"

"I took two busses." She walked in the front door and sniffed the air to see if another female was lurking in the shadows. "I brought you a present and I didn't want to wait for Monday to give it to you." She held out her gift, wrapped in colorful paper with Astro Boy on it, wrapping paper that Zak has seen in a stationary store on trendy Northwest Twenty-third Avenue. Her eyes were wide and childlike, like Astro Boy's. She wanted to see him every day.

"Thanks, Kiko. You didn't have to come all the way out here." Zak could feel an ulterior motive in the gesture, like some low-level stalking. "Yeah, we can get brunch. Let me get dressed."

He seemed disappointed. She thought he would he happier to see his girlfriend. Sweep her up. Smother her. "Aren't you going to open it?" she asked.

Feeling rude, he sat down on the couch and pulled off the paper. It was the manga book she had bought at Vowel's. He was both intrigued and a bit scared by the explicit sexual images in the comic. Penetration of all sorts including, child-like lovers and animals.

"It's one of my favorite mangas. It's got everything in it, including some great incest stories." She acted like it was a coffee-table book of tourist pictures.

"Um, thanks. We've talked about these books, but I've never actually seen one." If Zak's head was confused his dick was completely bewildered. Was this erotica?

"Oh, don't look so shocked, sir. People in Japan read these on the subway. They sell them at Vowel's, you know." He looked at the back and noticed the Vowel's price sticker and was relieved that this was legal paper. "I thought you would really like it," she said and when he smiled she sat down on the couch next to him and kissed his neck.

Since Zak hadn't resolved the situation yet in his mind, he just went with it. Why not? No one would judge him after what he'd been through.

So a little a bit of tonsil hockey ensued with the prog rock playing in the background. Kiko could taste the coffee in his mouth and pulled him towards her. "You're the world's greatest lover and you're mine," she thought to herself. Going just as planned. She straddled his bum leg and began to hump it, making little squeaks with each thrust.

Zak felt like he was being sexually assaulted by one of those eels. If he put the brakes on, he risked sending her into a crying spell but if he continued the friends with benefits thing without some clarification, there would be the inevitable drama of "I really like you, but." It was a touchy, touchy thing. So here we go.

"Hey, Kiko, I think we should talk." She felt her spine jerk backwards, towards the wall. "I'm really glad you came over this morning, but you probably should have texted me first. I might not have even been here."

She wasn't even trying to kiss him at this point. "Where would you have been?" Really, what were the options on a Sunday morning?

"Well, I could have been out on a run." (Not likely.) "Or shopping." (For what?) "Or maybe I was out all night and crashed somewhere else." (Bingo.) Her head pulled down into her shoulders at the very idea that this distinguished professor would "crash" at some slut's disgusting apartment.

"Why would you do that?" she asked, like she had a right.

"I don't know. I used to do it all the time. Like when you go to show and get too drunk to drive, or…"

"Or meet someone?" She had been waiting for evidence that he was all fake.

"Yeah, that could happen, sure. I mean, it didn't, but it could." He sensed her shrinking, like he was letting the air out of her schoolgirl crush. All of a sudden the power balance of two consenting adults became a growing chasm of adult and child. He had to be careful here. "That's what we need to talk about. You know what I've been through. I'm still grieving. I'm not ready for a relationship right now. I really like you, Kiko but…"

She didn't hear anything after that point. Her ears filled with the sound of waves that you hear in seashells. It was also the sound of rage. This was not how this morning was supposed to go. She was being dumped or strung along or sexually exploited. It was all the same to her. She was supposed to be stepping into his life. He gave all the signals that he wanted her full time. In her mind they were on their way to every Sunday morning, from here on out. It's gonna really end. She began to cry.

Zak sensed she took it too hard. "Kiko, don't cry. I'm not saying I don't want to hang out with you. I just want to clarify where we stand."

"Oh, where we stand. It's all up to you, I guess." Snot coming out of her nose.

"Okay, where I stand. I didn't want to lead you on. We've just been getting to know each other." For five thousand years this has been a shitty no-win conversation.

"Yeah you, you broke my heart. I remember every word you said to me. I gave you my virginity and everything! You can't do this, please, sir! You belong to me!" The words didn't come out right. "I hope you understand my meaning."

She was beside herself for no good reason. Later she would realize that she could've handled it much better, played it cool, said she wanted to be casual as well. She could've hung back, sown the seeds of love. But instead she was in full grilled cheese meltdown, making a sticky mess on her man's couch. Well, not her man it seemed. "I'm just gonna go," she finally said after blowing her nose on her shirt.

"Don't you want to go get some brunch?" Zak thought the clouds might break around her and the afternoon could be saved by watching a movie and some maybe better "we're officially just hanging out" sex, but she kept moving towards the door. She wanted to go to brunch, more than anything. She wanted to make cute faces while they waited an hour for a table, their hands around matching coffee mugs. But she had her dignity, so she closed his front door behind her and wondered how long it would be before the next bus came. Would it be long enough to dry her eyes?

The clock had officially run out on Stan. He had no more time left with Kennedy and his goons. If the professor was going to be able to swing anything, the word wouldn't come down until tomorrow when Superintendent Reese got in, so he was jammed up hard. Usually on Sundays he went to the blot, the weekly gathering by the Odinist pagans worshiping their Viking gods, but that would be a hotbed of Aryans today. They pretended to be all spiritual and down for the pagan ancestry worship, but it was a cover for a lot of white power talk. Freedom of religion, they claimed. If the Muslim inmates could have it, white guys should too.

The options were limited. He could go to the Christian service with his cellie, but that group was mostly child molesters and black ex-gang bangers. They'd know he was only there to hide out. It was a bit late for an eleventh hour come to Jesus moment. He'd stick out like a fat thumb and word would get out. He could really use that prison transfer but he might as well stay put. If they came for him in his cell it would be quick.

So he decided to stay on his bunk and read the Prose Edda, a thirteenth century chronicle of Norse gods and giants that Stan believed was important. He rested his mind in the story of AEgir, a giant who threw elaborate parties for Thor and the gods, brewing massive barrels of beer for the lords of Asgard. Stan imagined himself in a beautiful Viking hall with the gods, endless food and beer and safe from the demons of the underworld. Each page turned was a passage into safety, or a marking of a one moment closer to death.

Just then Stan's cell door swung open and banged against the wall, causing the muscles in his shoulder to clench and his breath to stop in is mouth.

"Hey, man. Didn't mean to scare ya. I forgot my Bible. Sure you don't want to come?"

It was Val, his cellmate. Breathe out. Val was in for statutory rape of his girlfriend. He was 18 and she was 16, so under Oregon's Measure 11 sentencing guidelines that was an automatic eight years and four months of hard lock-up, no questions asked or answered. He'd served two and was using Christianity to pass the time and keep his mother from worrying too much. Val was a skinny boy, not old enough to drink, so he was punked out by the older cons. The only upside was that the staff kept him loaded on anti-depressants so he didn't hang himself with a bed sheet. The result was a painfully cheerful boy two seconds from self-immolation.

"Next time don't give me a fucking heart attack," barked Stan. He didn't know if Val knew how high his shit had risen and that he barely had an inch to breath. "I'm good, Val. Thanks. Tell zombie Jesus I said, 'Hi.'" It was a ongoing point between the two cellmates. Not only did Stan not believe Jesus Christ ever existed, he believed the Jesus myth was the invention of a Roman magistrate to justify the persecution of the locals. He had books on his small shelf that proved it. The Odinists believed the creation of the Jesus story was a Jewish plot to turn warrior Europeans into cheek-turning wimps. They had books, too.

"You may not love the Lord but he loves you." Val was ever patient. "There's always space for you when you're ready to accept him."

Stan was about to lay into him about his Jesus shit, but then a lightbulb flashed over his head. "Hey, Val, I've got a question for you. How many happy pills is the shrink giving you each week?"

"I take two Effexor a day and one Remeron. Why?"

"And do you always take them?" Stan stood to approach Val who was next to his desk.

"No, not always. The Effexor gives me really weird dreams and the Remeron makes me constipated sometimes, so I puke them out in the john, but don't say nothin'. It's too much stuff in my system sometimes." He had a guilty puppy look on his face, like he was letting down the psych nurse who was only trying to keep him from a pine box.

"I think I might be able to help you out with those jokers who are giving you a hard time 24-7." He paused for effect. "If you start palming your extras on the med line, I'll send a kite to some of my boys that you're off limits now." Stan liked to pretend that he had more juice than he actually did. He had no juice.

Val sat on his bunk and took a deep breath. "You'd do that for me?" He seemed stunned that Stan might suddenly save him from his daily hell. "Hold on a second."

Val opened up his Bible to reveal a small space carved into the Old Testament with a sandwich bag tucked in it. He pulled it out revealing a stash of a dozen red capsules. "I was saving these if I ever wanted out of this place fast. You know how it is. I don't read the Old Testament anyway."

Stan knew he had bought a little bit of time.

3

Zak was on his couch, laptop on lap, entering a contest for free wooden flooring when his FaceTime feature rang in. Lenny was beaming in from the emerald city, so he minimized the contest entry page and brought up the Facebook page.

"Herr Doctor?" Lenny was still in his bed, his hair the perfect Keith Richards mess that he would try to prop up for the rest of the day. "Lazy Sunday afternoon?"

"Hey, Lenny." Zak took if for granted that most of his close relationships were all experienced through the tiny pinhole camera lens on laptops these days. "Just hanging out. About to grade some writing assignments. How's Seattle? Go see any good bands last night?"

"Yeah, a little four piece called Led Zeppelin. Heard of them?" He watched Zak's face for a reaction.

"One of these tribute bands? I saw an all female one called Lez Zeppelin once. Pretty good." The music scene was full of tribute bands for people who came of age in the wrong century. Every classic band had a junior version making the rounds. Missed Pink Floyd? Go see The Machine. Always wanted to see the Kinks? Tickets for the Kinx are super cheap. Wanna know what Radiohead was like back in its heyday? Check out Green Plastic. It was only a matter time before Mumford & Sons and Imagine Dragons had tribute bands for the next generation of missers and cheap daters.

"Nope. The real deal." Led Zeppelin broke up in 1980 after the death of drummer John Bonham. There was a show in 2007 with Bonzo's son on the kit but in the 2010s they were a non-entity.

Zak wasn't thinking "dream" yet. He was a little slow to catch on. "Are you high? What are you talking about?"

"LA Forum, 1975. I was there. Dude, I was dreaming and I decided to go. I had pretty good seats, too. I decided to experience the whole show. It went on for hours it felt like."

"That's pretty cool, Lenny. That was definitely their peak. How was it? Could you see Robert Plant's bulge?"

"I forgot what it was like where everything at a show was not projected on to a giant screen. I've gotten used to watching TV when I go to big concerts now, so I had to squint. And man, the pot. So much better back then. But no, it was kind of boring. Too many fucking solos. I think Bonzo's drum solo during 'Moby Dick' was like half an hour. I almost fell asleep."

"Well, that's why Jesus invented punk rock. Too much bloated beating off going on at the Forum in those days. And you were asleep by the way." It was cool but just a dream.

"Yeah, but it felt really real. Like really real. But after 'Stairway to Heaven,' I decided to split and bang Debbie Harry backstage at CBGBs."

"What the fuck, Len, you're kidding me, right?" It was classic Lenny so…

"Serious, my man. It was her and this hot chick that works at a bank here in Seattle, like from now. We were getting busy, all three of us, and the Ramones were playing. It was pretty hot." Lenny didn't mention that there was some coitus interruptus thanks to pizza.

"That sounds like you. I guess you don't have to worry about crabs in dream sex," laughed Zak.

"Nope."

"Alright. I had a weird one last night but I don't know how lucid it was. I knew it was a dream but it went kind of sideways. I've been waiting to get your take on it."

So Zak relayed the whole thing; hovering over Reno, the man with the lever, seeing Claire on the casino floor with some guy who was not him, and the four police who had been recurring figures.

"Those are dream guides. I told you about them. I wish I had one and you've got four! Dude, you know what that means."

"They didn't do a very good job guiding me. More like abusing me." It was all still crystal clear in his mind, like he got home from this surreal scenario and put on his Mr. Rogers slippers.

"Or testing you." Lenny pushed his hair back and lit a cigarette, a guilty pleasure he saved for Sundays. "Okay, I've got this theory and I want you to hear me out."

God, here comes another one of Lenny's crazy theories. If he spent as much time focusing on work as he did chasing dragons he'd be a rich man. But Zak was open now, probably more than he'd been in years.

"So here it goes. Space is infinite, right? It goes on forever." Lenny was stating a generally agreed upon truth.

"Yeah, I guess so." Zak had no evidence to the contrary.

"There were probably universes before the Big Bang and our universe is full of an uncountable number of stars and planets. Every time they focus the Hubble telescope into a dark patch of sky, they find a billion more galaxies. And we have no idea how many more universes exist. It's fucking infinite." Lenny's cigarette was making it's own Milky Way as his hand waved around.

"Billions and billions. I get it. So what?"

"More than billions, Professor. A fuck ton more. So if it is infinite, that means any possibility we can imagine exists somewhere in it. Somewhere there is a planet that is exactly like Earth, but my band became bigger than the Beatles. Somewhere there is a planet where it is our 1975 and Led Zeppelin is on tour. And somewhere there is a planet like ours but Claire and Caroline are alive and Cozy and I are together."

Zak didn't take the emotional bait. "So you are trying to tell me that you went to another planet to see a thirty minute drum solo by John Bonham." Listening to Lenny was better than late night TV any day.

"Yeah, I mean not in a spaceship. What if dreaming is a way to travel to these other worlds? Like going through a wormhole or something. And the reason we can't stay there is that we don't realize we are actually on a different planet, so we let ourselves get sucked back to our Earth. You know it's impossible to go back in time like in *Back to the Future*, the whole Grandfather Paradox thing."

"Right, if you could go back and kill your own grandfather then you wouldn't ever be born and you wouldn't be around to kill your grandfather." Zak grew up on the same sci-fi stories.

"So what I'm saying is it's not like a parallel universe thing. There is no Grandfather Paradox because it's a separate timeline. It's all about getting to the right planet. There's a zillion worlds out there. There's one where I'm the singer of U2 and there's one where Al Roker is the singer of U2."

"Ooh, let's go to that one," said Zak. His mind pinged to various theories of the construction of reality. Lenny's idea of distant planets wasn't dissimilar to the Druid notion of the

Otherworld, a neighboring realm that our human senses are unable to detect. Zak was about to link it to theories of quantum physics but Lenny was on a roll.

"And you can totally alter the timeline if you want. But it's how we can see your weird dream. It wasn't a dream. You were on a planet where, right now Claire exists, but she's in Reno with some dude who is not you. What you want to do is get to the world where everything is the exact same but it's before the accident. Of course, you might go to the world that feels the exact same but not quite."

"What do you mean, Lenny?"

"It could be any crazy shit, like there are talking purple dinosaurs in Portland, or Donald Trump is president, or that you are left-handed. Infinite possibilities means it all exists somewhere."

"Christ. Legal pot has really fucked with your head." There was a certain logic to it. It certainly felt like he was in a real world that was not his.

"Shut up. Speaking of, next time I come down we're going to that weed shop on Alberta Street. They have this hybrid called Gorilla Glue that will make you dream John Lennon dreams. Anyway, think about it, man. Maybe these dream guides can explain it to you. It's a possibility."

"One of infinite possibilities, I guess. Maybe I should stick to going to concerts like you. I might end up on a planet where Claire is pregnant with Kanye West's baby. So anything happening in the real world?" Talk about unreal meetings with his dead pregnant wife made him feel a little sick.

Lenny took another drag. "Nada. Got to write up some contracts for The Falsies to look over. You gonna hook of up with Mollie any time soon?" Get back on the horse, man.

"Well, I'm gonna see her this week, but I think a beer is as far as it's gonna go. Oh, I had a visitor this morning." He suddenly remembered the development.

"Your period?"

"That and Kiko. She just showed up on my doorstep. I could tell she was looking to see who was here. But I sat her down and had the talk. The let's-just-be-friends-talk. It got weird."

"Fuck. What happened?" Lenny thought Kiko might be a path out of the morass for his friend.

"Just a lot of crying. I felt really bad but I never said I was her boyfriend. We were just hanging out," said Zak.

"Yeah, something struck me about that chick, like she was borderline cuckoo. Man, I'd be careful. She was kind of a stalker, right?"

Zak was cautious not to stigmatize her with that label but there might be sufficient evidence. "Well, she used to come by my office all the time and then coming over here freaked me out a little. And she threw the virginity thing in my face. And she sent me a lot of fucked up emails." The more he talked about it the more the bits and pieces came together in an unpleasant way.

"You might want to delete some of those emails. I saw some shit like this on a episode of *Cheaters*. If she goes ballistic, your little fling could be splattered all over the internet."

"Great. I was trying to be honest with her."

"That was your first mistake, man. You can't be honest with women. They want their little fantasies. Reality gets in the way of it every time." Lenny wasn't exactly a feminist.

Zak felt even more sick. "It'll be okay. She needs a little time to digest it. She probably has plenty of boys to obsess over. I'm not worried. She's a big girl." He looked at the clock on his laptop. It was 11:11 and he made a wish that there would be no more drama.

Kelly and Walt's brunch date ran well into the afternoon. It took a while to get a table at the trendy Tasty & Glison Café, even after Walt handed the host his card that very clearly stated he was a university president. This was the Pearl District after all. Get in line, superstar. The mimosas and chit chat slowed it down and all this was fine with Kelly who hoped the brunch would never end.

Sure, they talked about the faculty thing. And they gossiped about some administrators and their proclivities. Woodbine seemed to have a peculiar fascination about which members of his administration were closeted homosexuals, probably vastly overestimating the issue. This included a list of clues that his chief of staff, Abigail Williams, was secretly an angry lesbian, causing Kelly to laugh.

"I hate to break it to you, Walt, but that genie's been out of the bottle for a while. I don't think it's much of a secret anymore. Maybe she's trying to keep her personal life private." Kelly had no truck with lesbians. She totally got it, especially after what she'd been through.

"Hmmm." Walt took off his glasses and pretended to be thinking about it. "Well, at least I don't have to wonder what team you play on." And he placed his hand on Kelly's. Her hand resting on the table next to her plate of Eggs Florentine seemed like an overt invitation to make contact.

Her first impulse was to pull away but then she remembered that this was what she wanted. This was what she had dreamt about, both awake and asleep. If she was unsure of his flirtatiousness before. ("Oh, that's how he is with everybody!") she could be confident he was making a pass now and she didn't want to fumble his ball.

"Oh, Walt. I've been out the game so long. I probably have more in common with Abby than I care to admit." She was being coy, something that always worked in romance novels.

Walt laughed, letting go of her hand and placing it on his belly. "Oh, you're being silly. I think you just need a little warming up." This was tricky territory and he was a lawyer so he should have stopped right there. "Hey, I have an idea. Do you play golf?" It seemed like something that colleagues do. And is there any sport less sexy than golf?

"Sure. I mean, it's been a while, but I know my way around a green." Kelly's mind flashed back to her husband teaching her to putt, with his arms around her, helping her to hold the club just right. She placed Walt in the memory in place of her husband. Was there any sport more sexy than golf?

"Let's do a few holes next weekend if it's not raining. Up for it?" The way he said it, with a head cocked, right eye a bit closer to her than the left, made her think it was a romantic invitation. He sipped his coffee and let the ball hang in the air.

"That sounds nice. I do need to get out a bit more. This brunch has been really nice. Sundays are usually work days so I appreciate you giving me a reason to be out of the house." She glanced around at the other tables full of much younger couples, many of whom surely had met the night before and were having their first post-sex conversations. She required more courting. "I'll find my clubs this week and dust them off."

Walt's eyes squinted with a big smile. "Good, then it's a date."

4

Kiko was covered in blood. Her schoolgirl uniform was soaked in crimson. A fellow student named Noriko Nakagawa lay at her feet, her head almost completely cut off. Kiko tightened her grip on the hatchet in her hand and muttered, "Watashi wa subete no anata o korosushimas." I will kill you all.

There was a human ear on a large stone wall next to her and the ear had a female mouth in the middle of it. The ear told her, "Slaughter them with extreme prejudice. Do it, Kiko. Do not hesitate." She had heard this voice before. And then the ear disappeared into the stone as a flock of black crows flew out of the forest behind it. "I know what I'm looking for," she thought to herself.

She could feel the rage coursing through her thin arms. Her teeth ground together as she looked down the hill. She could wipe out her main enemies and then focus on the rest of the females on the island. Her plan was to appear as a weak victim, allowing them to drop their defenses and then quickly split their skulls open.

Kiko pulled out her smartphone to take a picture of her face before she continued her quest for vengeance. She didn't recognize herself. Her brow seemed distended. She panned the camera down to her chest, which had grown with the beating of her heart. Pulling her shirt collar back she saw a tattoo of Zak's face on her clavicle. He had black X's over his eyes.

There was a comfort to being in the office on Monday mornings. The ritual of the habitual. Everyone in the department gave a brief summation of their weekend. "Went camping." "Saw that Amy Schumer movie." "Went to my kid's Little League game." And then everyone would settle in for the next five days of paper moving and email avoiding. And teaching a few things to the folks who pay the bills. That sound of the computer starting up, that bongggg, meant the flow-chart was in place until Friday at 5.

There was an exam this week and Zak wanted to prepare a review sheet for the students, so he came downtown instead of working from home. He was about to slash and burn the weekend's emails from his inbox when one caught his eye. It was from the National Coalition for the Homeless and it didn't look like spam. Some of those fundraising emails can trick you. *Hi Zak, we hope you've had a chance to approve this.* But this email was not an appeal to save the kids with a debit card, it was an invitation to speak at a conference in Washington, DC.

Zak was being given an award for his research on street youth. *For your contribution to understanding the root causes of juvenile homelessness and your ongoing advocacy for policies that address these issues,* the email said. Did they have the right guy? After meeting Claire he'd left his mantle of "gutterpunk scholar" for the more fundable world of prison research, so it seemed like a former version of himself was getting the email. Without a doubt it was a huge honor but he'd have to go back in time. Still, not a bad way to start a Monday morning.

He thought he should use the positive energy to get on the phone to the prison to see if he could parlay it into some help for Stan. He tried to call Superintendent Reese but was told he was at a meeting in Salem, so Zak forgot about it and went back to formatting his review sheet. His door was open and Heather, his research assistant, poked her head in.

"You're in early on a Monday," she said, arms full of books.

"Yeah, I've got some coursework to get together so I thought I'd do it here. Hey, I saw that inmate, Stipich, this weekend. You were right, he's one intense guy."

"Yikes. What happened? Was he threatening like in his letters?" Heather read Stipich's letters like they were episodes of *Lock Up*.

Zak didn't want to admit that he was intimidated by the inmate's unstable manner. "Well, he thinks we've put him in jeopardy because of this project. It's nothing really but I'm going to try and smooth things out, maybe get him moved to Columbia River. I think he wants to get out of that facility. It's got a pretty bad gang problem from what I hear."

"Be careful. The psychologist in me says this guy has an explosive violent streak. I might just stick to the letters. I don't want to hear you got shivved in the yard."

Zak laughed at her attempt to sound like she'd done hard time. "Okay, killer. If I do I'll leave you my inmate hit list. Right, now go read those books." And she scooted away.

There wasn't a moment to get back to the tasks at hand when his colleague Sammy Sullivan poked his head in the door. "Good morning, old friend. Nice to see you here on a Monday. How's life?" They had been closer before the accident, occasional beers after work.

"Hey! Yeah, trying to get in front of the quarter. There's only so much you can get done at home." Especially when you are staring at old pictures on your laptop. "Hey, I found out I'm being given some sort of award in Washington, DC. I'm going to have to arrange some travel time." It was a subtle way to brag. Nearly every college professor suffers from an inferiority complex (even the workaholics). There were never enough accomplishments on the CV. Not enough awards or publications in top shelf journals.

"That's awesome, man! Making us look good. Maybe Woodbine will send you a gift-card for a Starbucks. Oh, there was a student waiting for you when they opened up the office this morning. A little Asian girl. I told her you didn't usually come in on Mondays and she tore off. Thought I'd let you know."

Zak felt like he had suddenly walked into a snare in the middle of the wilderness.

"Oh, right. Yeah, she's a student here but not currently one of mine. I'm sure I'll run into her on campus. Thanks." He tried to turn back to his computer.

"Okay, chief. She looked a little desperate so let me know if you need any backup. Congrats on your award." As he left Zak got a flash that Kiko was moving into the stalking phase of their relationship. He didn't know she had been there for a while.

Kiko was sitting at a lunch table in the student center with her face in her hands. She didn't have class for almost three hours and not even her phone could distract her from her woes. "I'm a fool again," she thought. "He doesn't know what he's looking for," she thought. "I can be whatever he wants," she thought. And so the rumination went. She'd invested so much dream time in him and was not expecting the door to be slammed in her face.

Kelly was getting her morning carmel macchiato at the coffee counter when she noticed Kiko sitting by herself in the middle of a table. She thought she looked out of place, not just because of her attire. All the students around her were chatting or getting presentations ready for classes or franticly cramming for quizzes. The girl looked shell-shocked so Kelly decided to approach her.

"Excuse me. Hi. Remember me from the bookstore?" Kelly was in a smart navy blue pantsuit, complete with a university pin on her lapel.

Kiko looked up, her hair over her face covering the fact that her hands had left an indentation on her forehead. She squinted to make out the face. She got the feeling she was in trouble. Maybe somebody was going to tell her to stop pretending to be Japanese. Or maybe it was another woman Zak was involved with. Suddenly, the fog cleared.

"Oh, yeah, you're that administration lady. I'm just sitting here, which I assume is okay." She was still in a snippy mood.

Uninvited, Kelly sat down across from her. "Of course it is. I just wanted to say hello and see how you're doing." She tried to put on a cheery face.

"Wonderful. It's all wonderful here. How about you?" Why did this old lady care?

"I'm good. You seemed a little sad so I thought I'd check in. How are your classes going?"

"Fine," she said.

"How are things with Professor Crisp?"

Ah, the real question.

"Fine."

There was enough a hesitation there to give Kelly a clue that she might be the latest casualty of an unchecked faculty.

"Did he like the book you gave him? That, what's it called?"

"Hentai. I don't know. I gave it to him yesterday. Why don't you ask him yourself?"

She was sour, not the sassy bibity bop that Kelly met at Vowell's. Sour like a Monday morning, which it was, so it could just be that. But she sensed that it was more. Kelly took a sip of her sweet coffee drink and studied Kiko's glare, like she was watching her from behind a two-way mirror.

"Okay, well, if you need anything, even if it's just someone to talk to, I'm going to give you my card." Kelly pulled out one of her new business cards and slid it across the table in front of Kiko like a piece of bait. "Before I was the Vice Provost, I was something of an expert on romance, so that's always a good topic to chat about." She was unsure how to proceed as Kiko just stared at her. "I guess I better get to work. Nice seeing you again. I hope your day gets better."

After she walked away, Kiko studied the card. It was embossed. She admired the font but hated the pretentiousness of it. "Vice Provost for Professional Development." What the hell was that? She was going to throw it in the trash but thought better. It might come in handy later. She unzipped her Hello Kitty backpack and slipped it in.

It only took a split second to get to his destination. The dream started out in some Appalachian trailer park that was supposed to be lower Manhattan but Zak knew the Hudson River was wider than a creek, so without wasting any time in this alternative Tribeca, he decided to try again for Liverpool.

In the blink of an eye he was standing on Matthew Street in the British seaport town. There was a giant line of kids dressed in varying shades of grey and blue trembling with excitement. This was it. He had brought himself to the fabled Cavern Club, which began its history as a traditional jazz cellar bar. With the help of some scruffy kids from Merseyside who had made a name for themselves playing strip clubs in Hamburg, it had become the hottest music spot in the north of England, and soon the world.

Zak could smell the sea air rolling in from the North Atlantic. Seagulls over his head mimicked the cries of the girls in the line. Based on the size of the crowd and the names on the poster next to the door, he guessed it was the summer of 1962, right before the moment The Beatles were to launch from their cellar full of noise into the global consciousness. This was the dream gig.

Across the street there was a pub called The Grapes with a white van parked in front. He thought about going in for a quick pint but didn't want to miss a second of the show. If he had gone in he would have met four young lads at the bar who would provide the musical touchstone as well as soundtrack of his entire life.

"Can I get in?" he asked the large bespectacled bouncer at the door. It was his dream so he should have a V.I.P. pass.

"You? What business 'ave you down there? Leave it to the kids, squire," the man said with a thick Scouse accent. He and the kids didn't seem likely to let this strangely dressed American break in the queue.

"Oh, yeah, um, I'm a talent scout from Capital Records, an American record company. EMI in London flew me in to see the band. I heard they're quite good." And with that he was walking down the stairs into a dense fog of cigarette smoke and sweat. He took off his Columbia jacket and gave it to the coat check girl to keep. She thought it was rather marvelous.

There was a DJ spinning American R&B records and a group of girls chanting "Pete forever! Ringo never!" Zak guessed that this was soon after their drummer for two very formative years, Pete Best, had been sacked and never to be spoken to again. He was a bit disappointed to be not seeing the band with Best because legend has it that that was The Beatles at their most punk rock.

He asked a young man with a neck tie holding his blazer if he knew the date. "Nineteenth, isn't it?" August 19, 1962. This was Ringo's very first show as a Beatle. (Well, actually the second. They'd played with him at a horticultural society dance the night before, but that doesn't sound as cool.) This was the nexus moment that would change the face so much more than music. Zak was jostled by the much shorter teenagers as they moved up to the stage. History's first mosh pit.

Then the DJ announced, "Ladies and gents, the Beatles," and the four young men in their shirts and ties and waistcoats launched into the song, "Some Other Guy." And there they were, a little club band elevated a few feet above the crush of their young fans. They looked so childlike. Ringo looked nervous and George had a black eye and seemed more interested in Ringo than the fans. But Paul and John were right up front, as close to the edge of the stage as possible; Paul beaming and John smirking like a madman. And so young. George Harrison was only 19 at this point. The girls screaming about poor Pete gave in and danced wildly, there bouffant hair bobbing in front of the spotlight.

Zak soaked it all in: the sweaty teenyboppers whose condensated perspiration dripped from the stone ceiling, the tiny amplifiers that made the band sound like they were playing through a radio, and the exuberance of four kids with a sneaking suspicion that the world was about to go from black and white to technicolor. Nothing about it seemed unreal. Nobody had two heads, there wasn't a basement window looking out over a Martian landscape. This was it. He was here and he didn't want it to end.

It didn't actually end. It just sort of faded out. Around the fifth song (Paul singing, "Kansas City"), his mind began to wander. He wished that Claire could have been there with him or Lenny, or anybody from his century. He wished he could tell Caroline someday that he saw The Beatles in the Cavern. All this thinking made the scene fade to the murk of slumber.

"In a life of dream am I when I'm with you." (Patti Smith)

Chapter 7:
Writing on the Wall

1

Lenny was having lunch with Cozy in a restaurant in Seattle's Pike Place Market. It was a rare blue sky day so they took a table on the patio facing the Puget Sound. Lenny was fixated on the sun reflecting on his ex-wife's shoulders, which poked out between her white sleeveless top and her open sweatshirt that was falling off her skinny frame. Cozy seemed more focused on the boats bobbing around out on the water.

They had been talking for hours about old friends and about the music scenes in Portland, Seattle and DC. Lenny never asked her if she was wanted to move back to the Northwest and give it another try. He enjoyed the fact that her voice was reaching him from her mouth instead of from a computer or a phone. The actual molecules of her words were settling on his eardrums.

"In my mind Seattle is under this perpetual raincloud. I forget how beautiful it can be when it's a nice day," she said, her eyes on a flock of seagulls swooping around the docks.

"Yeah, maybe someday I'll take up jogging or something so I can run around in the sunshine when it shows up." Lenny had tried running about ten years ago but gave up because he thought running shoes were uncool and the first three minutes always kicked his ass.

"I don't think that's gonna happen anytime soon, Len." Her voice was like velvet, even when she was chiding him.

He had gotten so lost in sharing this familiar space with her that he had completely forgotten to ask about their son. It happened sometimes with Lenny, who loved his son, but sometimes saw him as essentially a lifeline that connected him to Cozy. "So how is Daniel? Why didn't he come out with you?"

"Who is Daniel?" She sipped her coffee like it was nothing.

He laughed. Of course she was going to give him shit for only mentioning their kid now, like it was an obligation to ask. "Daniel, our son. Is he staying with Brian?"

"Brian who? Lenny, what are you talking about? We don't have a son. We had a daughter and she died, so I don't know who this Daniel is supposed to be." Her sunny demeanor was gone in a flash.

Lenny should have been sad or confused, but he only had a flash of that guy in the Edvard Munch painting. "Fuck," he said without opening his mouth. He kept calm and did not spin. Seattle seemed so perfect.

"Cozy, can I ask you a question? What is the name of this planet?"

"What's up with all these weird questions? Ixchel to Lenny. Um, come back to Planet Ixchel." She seemed annoyed.

"Ixchel? Really? And who is the president? Please don't say Donald Trump." He was ready for anything.

"Who? Well, as you know, I never thought Bill Cosby would become president. It's like some weird dream." She rolled her eyes at the strange reality she found herself in.

"Yeah, something like that."

Lenny released himself to the idea that he was either in a slightly tweaked dream or visiting Planet Ixchel during the Cosby Administration. He laid off the questions and enjoyed the afternoon with his charming ex. After a few drinks, he suggested they get a room on the waterfront and Cozy, with a bashful grin, agreed. In their seventh floor room at the Four Seasons (Lenny was spending Cosby dollars) they made love like when they were two starving artists in Portland all those years ago. Afterwards, she fell asleep in his arms but he stayed awake as long as he could to take the evening in and delay his return to Planet Earth.

That Stan's plan to deliver Val's anti-depressants to Kennedy instead of the agreed upon Oxycontin shipment would work reflected his psychotic delusions. That he thought it wouldn't end up getting Val in deep shit was his psychopathy. If needed, Val would go right under the bus. But there was Derek Stemphill hanging out in the commons area so it was time to move this stop-gap plan forward.

"Derek, I've got something for you." Stan was a bit more puffed up than last time.

"What's up, punk? What do you have for me? It better be what I think it is." Derek was also puffed up, two roosters circling each other.

Stan moved Derek towards the alcove of the door, out of the line of sight of the guard and pulled the plastic bag of pills that Val had given him from the front of his pants. Derek looked at the bag like he already knew it was counterfeit goods.

"What the fuck is this shit? This ain't Ox."

"It's better. Snort one and you'll see. Tell Kennedy that there's plenty more where that came from. I said I'd deliver. I'm good on my word." Stan was putting on a brave face like he was handing over a secret high that would make them forget their hillbilly heroin.

Derek seemed placated for the moment and pushed Stan out of the way with a grunt. Stan had either bought some time or sealed his death warrant. In the meantime he had to get more Effexors and Remerons from his cellmate.

Zak was walking across campus to his Tuesday afternoon class when Robin Nielsen called out to him. "Hey, Zak! Hold up! I've got some news." Once she reached Zak, her voice dropped and suddenly everything got very cloak and dagger. "Want to let you know there's gonna be a vote."

"A vote?" Zak had been a little distracted from the whole unionization thing. He probably missed an email.

"Well, not really a vote. We're doing a card check this week. Basically, faculty members are going to fill out these cards that say they want to unionize and then we send them to the National Labor Relations Board with a petition that we want to form a union. The cool thing about it is that the university cannot legally fire anybody that is involved in the campaign. They can't even threaten to. So it might cool these witch hunts coming from Woodbine's crew."

Zak was impressed that so much had happened so quickly. This was exciting. The campus suddenly seemed abuzz with energy as students hurried between buildings to classes or to beat the parking enforcement officers to their cars. Amid the hustle, he noticed Kelly Claiborne a block away watching him and Robin. "Don't look now, but your favorite troll is lurking. Nine o'clock."

Robin pretended to be pointing at a building and saw Kelly facing them, her black overcoat making her look like the Grim Reaper. Kelly quickly looked down at the ground and then at her phone. The effect on Zak and Robin was chilling, like all the paranoia was justified. After the vice-provost walked into a building, they continued their conversation.

"Fuck. Can you believe that? And she used to be a professor. Unbelievable." Robin pushed her glasses back up her face. "This is why we have to get these cards done quickly so they can't do this shit anymore. The writing is on the wall. There's a meeting tonight at Bob Leedom's house and then we gotta get the cards out to people as quickly as possible. Can I count on you to help out?" Apparently, it was now or never.

"Yeah, let me at least get them to folks in my department. I don't teach tomorrow so I can try to get as many signed by the end of the day." It was the least he could do. He might have to hand people a pen and beg a little, but it seemed like the hammer was about to fall.

Robin thanked him and ran off to the next battle and Zak headed to class, forgetting what today's lecture was. Thank God for PowerPoint.

Kelly was back in her office making notes of her campus walkabout as had become custom, when Walt nocked on her doorframe.

"Hey, pretty lady. I haven't heard from you today. Any news from the front?" His grinning face was a welcome sight on a damp day. She had thought of their brunch and his overtures frequently but was going by the rules in not acting overly eager. It's better to be pursued, according to the magazines.

"Hi, Walt. Hi, yeah. There are a bunch of flyers calling for unionization up at the nursing school." She handed him a red flyer that read, in bold letters, *Faculty! Take a stand for yourselves and your future! Know your rights!* Walt took it and glanced at it as if he had already seen it. She continued. "And I saw Nielsen talking to Zak Crisp. They looked like they were plotting a revolution." It was an over-dramatization but, in relative terms, it was true. Things were changing.

"Crisp? From Public Health? I got an email from his chair that he's getting some big award in Washington for his research. He seems like a nice guy. He's had a rough year. You think he's one of the troublemakers?" Walt had surveyed Kelly's spreadsheet but Zak seemed like background noise, someone who was in the email loop but not building barricades.

Kelly didn't want to reveal that her issues with Professor Crisp went beyond the unionization campaign to the profile she was building of him as a predator of young co-eds. That might hurt the romantic profile she was building of herself with her boss. Though their age gap was much less, the power dynamic between them might be viewed as more damaging. He was the president after all, although she certainly was no Monica Lewinsky.

"He's been talking to Nielsen a lot. He was at the first meeting and has a union sticker on his office door. He's popular with the students so I think he may try to rally their support against us. I'm keeping an eye on him." It sounded very NSA. If she could spy on him through his laptop she would, but right now she only wanted to know what fuel Kiko might add to the fire.

Walt put on a serious face for her. "Okay, Dr. Claiborne, you do that. Hey, you still up for a round of golf?" He saw her face go from NSA to high school cheerleader. "Let me look at the weather forecast for this weekend and see if I can get us a reservation at Westmoreland on Saturday."

"That would be great, Walt. I found my clubs but you have to give me a big handicap, it's been a while." The clubs had to have her ex-husband's smell wiped off them before they left the garage so she had considered running them through a car wash. "I'm really looking forward to it." Not too enthusiastic, she thought.

"Wonderful. Maybe we could meet for tea before we tee off. Tea with brandy." Oh, he was just flirting now.

"A man after my own heart," she said and waved him off like she had a pile of work to do, which she didn't.

Kelly busied herself with responding to emails and dropping into a *Fifty Shades of Grey* discussion group to make a case for more sexual humiliation of men instead of women in erotica. Her glasses obstructed her peripheral vision but she thought she saw a young face in her doorway, the face of Kiko. She looked up but no one was there. She got up hoping it was her coming to unload the inside story, but it was quiet outside her door. She walked into the administrative lobby and asked the receptionist if anybody had come to see her.

"There was a student. A young Asian girl. She was waiting for you to finish up with President Woodbine but then she left." No name.

2

Zak decided to walk downtown for a happy hour drink before heading home. He had to contemplate going to the meeting tonight but he'd rather get back to the house and try for another dream adventure. The whole thing was kind of hit and miss at this point. As he left the edge of campus he walked by the student housing building where Kiko lived. He looked up and saw her looking out the window of an apartment on the third floor. He quickly looked away so their eyes would not meet, but it may have been too late. He didn't know what to do so he quickened his pace and hoped she hadn't seen him.

He was headed to the Florida Café, one of the oldest bars in Portland. Along the way he stopped at a new steel and glass office building that was about to open. It had been erected so quickly, Zak was startled by its very existence. It hadn't been that long since he'd taken this route to the bar. Starring up in disbelief, he thought, "Where did this thing come from?" It was a symptom of all the money coming into Portland. Buildings could just appear like that. What bothered him even more than missing the construction of a new tower was the fact that he couldn't remember what was on that plot of land before it appeared. He searched his memory - but nothing. He'd passed it more times than he could remember but it was suddenly as if this new building had always been there. History erased yet again. Unreal.

Once he got to the tavern and let his eyes adjust to the dark, he pulled a stool up to the bar and ordered a whiskey. Sometimes it all felt like a movie with no end. Maybe more like a Netflix series with no hope of cancellation. One more episode. He could feel the backwards slide into the man he was. The man he was hoping to be was out of steam. He saw his face in the bar mirror and it seemed as disfigured as it was a year ago. "If that face could talk," he thought.

The best action is no action. That was what he tried to remind himself after a fuck up. Maybe he should have never responded to Kiko's advances. Maybe he should have begged off helping Robin with the union campaign. Maybe he should have left his dreams alone. Now he was deep in the mud with all three. Stuck like a stick stuck in the mud. The whisky was his only salvation. Drink and make it all go away.

"Hey, Professor. Whatcha drinkin'?" It was Mollie who was working as a waitress at the Florida. Her tattooed arms fit in the place so it made sense, but Zak had a moment of alarm, thinking that he looked like he might be there for her, which he wasn't. But if he'd known she worked there, he might have been.

"A shot of nose paint. Hey, I didn't know you worked here." It was true.

Mollie smiled like she believed him. Everybody comes to the Florida Café at some point. It was a landmark that had resisted bulldozers for decades. "Yeah, just sometimes. Bob, the owner, lets me pick up some shifts when I'm in town. You want a happy hour menu?"

Suddenly he felt like staying for a while. Fried cheese sticks could be rationalized later. "Sure. What's up with the band?" Here was another mud puddle that he could easily get stuck in.

"We're practicing tonight. We're still on for Thursday, right?" Her freckles seemed to twinkle.

"Sure. Sure. Looking forward to Janis ripping my heart out."

"Atta boy. But just a piece. That's all she needs. I gotta go seat these losers." And she went back to work.

Zak ordered another whiskey and let the bourbon swirl across his tongue and into his sponge brain. He felt glued to the stool but his head was headed towards the ceiling. He wondered where he was in his grieving process. He was trying to move on like people say you're supposed to, but every step forward was met with a hurricane of guilt. Even the jolt of running into Mollie at the bar made him feel like shit. How dare he? He didn't want to let go of Claire and Caroline, or even the dream of them. The backward gaze was comforting and eviscerating at the same time. How could he step into the light when he felt content in the dark? But it's right in front of your face, man.

He chatted with Mollie a few more times and they firmed up their plans to meet at Jinks on Thursday. He decided to go across the street to the library to sober up with the other bums before driving home and fell asleep at a table, reading the latest issue of *The Nation*.

Zak, Claire and baby Caroline were floating in a small raft about three hundred yards from the shore. There was a statue sticking out of the water so people could tell if the tide was coming in or going out. It was like an underwater Statue of Liberty with only the torch above the waterline. The sky was a perfect blue but the sea was rocking as if there was a large storm coming ashore. Claire was frantic about the waves because there wasn't a lifejacket for the baby. Zak waved at the shore for help but there was nobody there.

Suddenly a large wave hit the raft at an angle and flipped it over, tossing all three into the water. Claire screamed for the baby. Zak dove, searching for his daughter. She wasn't on the surface or below. He inhaled salt water, going deep as he could as Claire held on to the torch, wailing for her child. Just gone. In the vast sea, the tiny baby was gone.

A bigger wave struck the two and carried them to the edge of the shore. Zak tried to comfort Claire who was sobbing uncontrollably. He laid his body on top of hers in the sand and tried to envelop her sadness. When he opened his eyes he saw a trail of ants marching over his right arm. His eyes followed the trail to more ants next to them. They had formed an outline on the beach in the shape of their baby daughter.

Kiko was the descendent of a race of warriors. They did not create a lineage that would end with a frail flower who would be cast aside with the dinner scraps. She paced between the white walls of her small apartment. Seeing Zak ignore her in the window was the final straw. It was like a switch clicked in her head. It was her mother who denied her. It was her country who disappointed her. It was her classmates who snickered at her. It was Zak who rejected her. She suddenly felt so small, like a single drop of nitroglycerin.

She pulled one of her drawings of Zak out of the drawer and stared at it for a long time. It was a dream that would not come true. He refused to see how special she was and now he must pay. She placed it on the burner of the electric stove in her small kitchen and turned it on. Slowly, Zak's face turned to brown and then burst into flames.

As the smoke alarm rang out she pulled Kelly Claiborne's business card out of her backpack and smiled. Things would be righted very soon.

On Monday, Lenny had gotten a rare call from his father. They didn't talk much these days. Well, ever, really. When Lenny was in his early thirties, his father was locked up for a hit and run incident that left a mother of two in a wheelchair for life. It was the breaking point for Lenny, giving him an excuse to let his rolling stone of a dad roll right out of his world.

The call came from an assisted living facility in Hillsboro, twenty miles west of Portland. His father was recovering from some kind of operation and was rehabbing in an old folks home. He told Lenny that seeing him would speed up his mending. Lenny sat on the information for a few days not really knowing what to do. He told him he had pressing work to do but he'd think about it, which is what he did.

At some point, maybe around his fortieth birthday, Lenny realized he could very well turn into his father. He clearly inherited his eyes and he seemed to have also inherited their ability to wander. Dear old dad never had a stable long-term relationship with a woman. He didn't even really know how to talk to a woman. He'd talk about himself and his ideas and when he ran out of things to say, he'd just move on to the next one. When they tried to share their own views about life, liberty and the pursuit of happiness, he'd tune it out and move up his exit date. He'd often talk about how everyone loved him, but, really, he was merely entertaining and every movie has an ending.

Prison should have humanized him but it only added a new meanness to his narcissism. He still had all the answers but he added a new level of hatred into is repertoire of dysfunctional emotions. If it wasn't the Mexicans, it was the Muslims or the homosexuals. They were all out to take away his country. And don't get him started on the feminists.

By Wednesday, Lenny thought he should make a decision. He called Zak for a little guidance. When the smartphone rang, Zak was sitting at his living room table, reading student essays and jonesing for an excuse not to be.

"Hey, Lenny. What's up?" He put the phone on speaker so he could pretend (to himself) to still grade papers.

"Sensei!" They made some small talk and then Lenny asked. "I'm coming to you for advice, good doctor. You remember what a hard case my old man is right?"

"Yeah, is he okay?" Zak flashed back to how Lenny dealt with his father's incarceration by excommunicating him from his life.

"He's the same wreck of a man. But he's in some nursing home in Hillsboro laid up from an operation or something and he wants me to come see him. Besides the fact it's fucking Hillsboro, I'm trying to decide if I want to see him. You think I should go?"

"Shit man, I don't know. I mean maybe he called because he had some realization about what a bad dad he was and wants to apologize."

Lenny literally laughed out loud with a huge guffaw. "He's a three time loser. Daddy should've stayed in high school. That guy ain't never gonna change. He's like a tele-marketer who won't stop calling, only he's selling himself. "

Zak resisted the urge to say that that sounded familiar. Instead he responded more like a therapist than a dick. "Well, what's your fear about visiting him."

"I don't know! Maybe that it's that he'll look really old. Or maybe he wants some money. Or…"

"Or that he's dying?"

"Fuck, I hadn't thought about that. Should I be sad? I mean I can be sad if I'm supposed to be."

Zak picked up the phone and turned off the speaker feature. "If he is, you're going to be sorry that you didn't go to fucking Hillsboro. It might be kind of important. I vote go and then come hang out with me and get some beers and tell me how the old buzzard's doing."

Lenny said that sounded like a good idea and he'd let Zak know when he was going to come down to Oregon. Zak appreciated being the "wise friend" even though he felt like a complete train wreck himself. They hung up and Zak considered texting Mollie as a way to stall his grading duties, but instead opened his laptop and spent an hour watching *Saturday Night Live* videos from the seventies. "Cheeseburger, cheeseburger."

Stan thought that by Wednesday he surely would have heard something, either from Superintendent Reese or from the professor himself. But nothing. No call from processing to pack up his shit. No letter from Portland saying the move was in the works. Nothing. And it felt like a betrayal. His better angels said he should wait; these things take time. But fuck those angels. They have no hold on a battlefield like this. Fuck 'em.

His anger paralleled Kiko's, unrooted in reality but real in the marrow of the bone. A man can only be disrespected so much. Crisp said he was on it. He was a professor with clout. But Stan realized he was only the good doctor's subject, like he thought all along. The swelling rage gave him mental space away from the looming fear that he was about to be crushed by the full weight of the Peckerwoods. Time was up, but the agenda was to deflect it on to Zachary Crisp, PhD.

While things were quiet, he thought he'd leave his cell. Maybe a cold shower would cool him down before he did something stupid. But as soon as he stepped out of the door, there were Kennedy, Derek and two other thick necked Aryans pushing him back in the door like a bulldozer pushing a pile of leaves.

"Yo, punk. Get the fuck out of here," Stemphill barked to Val, who grabbed his Bible, looked at the floor and slithered out the door, glad they weren't there for him. One of the skinheads closed the cell door after him.

Kennedy moved in on Stan and put is forearm against Stan's neck. The black Nazi tattoos stood in stark contrast to Stan's pale white face. The other three Aryans took positions so Stan could not escape.

"You motherfucker. I knew you were up to something. You think you can kill me? Really, you piece of shit? Your life is fucking over." Stan could see the tendons in his jaw. He was a drawing of the Incredible Hulk, about to bite down on his face. He felt like he was about to be devoured by a Rottweiler.

He knew what the story was, but it was better to play dumb. "What happened, man? I'm not trying to kill you. I promise!"

"Those pills you gave me. I snorted a rail and had a fucking seizure. I've been having seizures all day. The nurse said my kidneys are fucked now because of that shit. I'm peeing blood but you're gonna get it so much worse." The saliva was pouring out of his mouth.

"Kill him, boss!" Derek grunted. "Snap his fucking neck!"

"I should, but I believe in choices. I'm pro-choice, motherfucker! So we're gonna let fatboy here decide. You ready for a choice, fatboy?"

Stan was grateful that he didn't already have a shiv in his belly. "What?" he squeaked out as it got harder to breath.

"I owe the Latin Kings a little debt and you're gonna pay it for me. They've been doing some good work for us and I want to let them know how much I appreciate it. So you are gonna march over to their unit and give them your fat ass whenever they ask." Rape was the stink that hung from every prison wall.

"Fuck you!" Stan managed to push out in a too late attempt to stand up for himself.

Kennedy held out his hand and one of the skinheads gently placed a screwdriver in it. "Well, it's either that or all four of us are going to take turns seeing how far this screwdriver can go into those big titties you got." Stan's eyes looked at the length of the long screwdriver. "Like I said, holmes, I'm pro choice. It's up to you."

There was a gasp and a ringing exhale. It was the last bit of humanity escaping from Stan Stipich. "Okay," he said with a whimper. "Okay."

Kennedy pulled his arm away and Stan collapsed on his bed and then fell to the floor.

"Your choice, fuckwad. Now get up and go over there and beg them to corn-hole you until the sun comes up. I'll check with them to make sure that you did. Don't make me look like a liar." And he walked away. "Pro-choice!" he shouted.

Derek Stemphill gave Stan a quick kick in the stomach and said, "You better fucking do it, corn-holer," and followed Kennedy and the other two skins out into the hall.

Stan didn't move. All he could think was, "fuck that professor. Fuck him beyond all recognition."

3

Zak woke up on Thursday morning after an evening of failed attempts to dream about Claire. He thought he had the setting all set, but there were only random images from TV shows and colleagues. At one point he was a on a cruise ship and a young couple was standing on the deck. They were professing their love for each other. As they went over the side Zak noticed both legs of each were in casts. What did that mean? Regardless, at no point did he realize he was dreaming and go see The Beatles. Lenny was probably at Woodstock but he was floating around in surreality.

In the bathroom, he stared at his bent face and wondered what it would take to escape this time continuum. At least he had his not-a-date with Mollie tonight to look forward to. He gave himself a pep talk in the mirror. "Stay cool tonight. Hang back. It's just a show." Then he dragged the razor across his cheek and nicked himself. The trickle of blood assured him he was in the physical world.

Kelly had opened up the program that allowed her to read faculty emails. Most were quite boring: witty retorts to students who wanted extensions, Doodle polls for committee meetings, messages to spouses to pick up some Gardenburgers on the way home. No clear union activities leading her to think Nielsen had told faculty not to use their school email addresses, which she had.

She thought she'd check in on one of her high profile targets, Zak Crisp. It was the usual academic spam but she noticed one message from Kiko from yesterday.

Sir, I need to talk to you soon. I don't want to live.

Zak replied a few hours later:

You'll be okay, I promise. Please use my Gmail addy. TTYL

What was this all about? Had his abuse driven her to suicidal thoughts? Should she act now or let it blow up into something perfectly delicious?

She decided to go down to the room where he was holding class in a few minutes and listen in. Maybe she could garner some clues. Maybe Kiko would be there. Maybe he would be busy grooming his next victim. "Oh, this is getting good," she thought.

But when she got to his classroom she was let down. He was droning on about the difference between mortality rates and morbidity rates and the students were dutifully writing down notes and studying the PowerPoint slides. None of the young women in the front row seemed particularly taken with this professor who seemed like a cross between Indiana Jones and Quasimodo. Maybe she was wasting her time hoping he would be the weak link.

She bought a Diet Pepsi from the vending machine in the hall. The can falling down the chute caused Zak to look out the classroom door and he saw Kelly. Their eyes met and it was not a comfortable moment for either.

It was a poorly kept secret that before gentrification bleached Portland's black neighborhoods there was urban renewal, or as the city's leaders had called it, "negro removal." The vibrant Albina neighborhood that stretched from the Steel Bridge northward up to Killingsworth Street was alive with jazz clubs that hosted everybody from Ellington to Monk. What was now the Rose Quarter was all housing stock, mostly black housing. It was the area of housing that the Portland Realtor Board had pushed war-time black workers into and they made the most of it. But urban renewal gradually erased it bit by bit. Every time the city had a project, more black homes and businesses were bulldozed. (Whites had the clout to say, "Oh hell no.") First the Memorial Coliseum in 1959, then they ran I-5 right through the middle of the neighborhood. Then Emanuel Hospital displaced more homes and business, and in the seventies there was a plan to expand the hospital and another 300 homes in Albina were demolished. They never built the expansion but the neighborhood was gutted. It's just black people after all. Then gentrification quietly pushed out whatever black families were left, replacing them with young hipsters with seed money. The massive Moda Center arena stood as a tombstone for the black neighborhood, and underneath it white suburbanites came to watch black basketball players run their A game.

Zak was headed home from work, stuck in traffic in the Rose Quarter, east of the Broadway Bridge. The rain on his windshield turned the tail lights ahead of him into a prism of primary colors with the yellow from the traffic signal and the blue bouncing off of the Portland Memorial Coliseum to his left. He was lost in his head and not on the road. A CD of Bob Dylan outtakes played to move his brain to a small, intimate corner. It was "Farewell Angelina," and young Bob sang, "There's nothing to prove. Everything's the same."

Why couldn't he go back in time to that moment? He would sell his soul for one tiny do-over. "King Kong, little elves on rooftops they dance Valentino-type tangos." Zak looked at the roof of his Acura and imagined it being ripped in two by a razor sharp boulder. Maybe if he had this car instead of the VW, Claire and Caroline would be here now. "The sky is erupting. I must go where it is quiet."

His hands gripped the steering wheel at 11 and 1 o'clock like he was racing around a curve instead of stuck in rush hour gridlock. He stared at his left hand and at his wedding ring, still there. Still married. Still in that moment. Zak slowly rotated his two hands forward over the top of the steering wheel and watched the ring disappear over the horizon of his knuckles. That's what the future looked like. His world vanishes with a minor flex of his wrist.

"You should do that more often," said Claire who was seated next to him wearing the Columbia windbreaker she had on the day of the crash.

"Jesus Christ!" shouted Zak, not expecting to see his dead wife next to him on a rainy Thursday night. She was still pregnant, but calm in a way that confused him.

"At some point you're going to have to take off the ring. I'm sure Mollie wouldn't mind." She had a sideways grin that was as real as the rain.

"Oh, are you here because you're jealous of the Mollie thing? She's just a friend," he said to his wife's ghost.

"Yeah, right. I know you like those rock girls. I was too normal for you. You had to explain all that hipster music to me. I still don't like Guided By Robots."

"Guided By Voices. Voices. They're important and…" He stopped himself. Is there Guided By Voices music in heaven? He hoped so. More importantly he thought he better ask the pressing question. "Hey, Claire, are we in a dream right now?"

"Well you are, I'm just trying to get down Broadway." She looked out the window at the Moda Center. "Remember when I made you go to the Madonna concert there? Now that's an important artist."

He looked at her face. It seemed so flawless in the streetlight. The wisp of hair in front of her ears was right where it should be. That jawline he missed so much. You could cut cold butter with it. His eyes drifted down to her plump belly and he was comforted by the thought that Caroline was there with them. Was she dreaming as well? What was her life like inside of her mother's womb in this parallel reality? Maybe he could communicate with her as well. Tell her how much he looked forward to being her father.

"So if this is my dream, I can control it, right?"

Claire shrugged her shoulders.

He closed his eyes and tried not to get too excited about his luck. He wanted to have the conversation with her away from the car. He could smell her next to him. She smelled like hand lotion and straw. He could feel the pressure of the air her body displaced by its arrival. She was with him. If there was one perfect moment to go back to it would be Crater Lake. That day the sky was so blue, the complete opposite of the wet black cloud hanging over Portland this evening. "Take me to Crater Lake," he said, as if praying.

When he opened his eyes he was, in fact, at the ledge of Crater Lake, sitting on a bench facing the water. "Right on!" he shouted. He looked at the parking lot behind him, half expecting to see the Volkswagon. The day felt exactly the same. But there was no VW, and no wife. "Claire!" he called out, hoping she would appear, but she did not. He was alone in front of the massive crater without his chance to tell her.

A loud horn from a truck startled him and he realized he was back in rush hour on Northeast Broadway. The traffic had moved on but he hadn't and a large moving van wanted him to close the gap. He looked in his rearview mirror to make the apology face. For a second the driver behind him looked like one of the dream police but it was only a guy in white. He was solidly in the non-dream world.

Once he got home he thought it was time for a soft but familiar voice, so he decided to call Cozy in DC. It was three hours later there so she should be in.

"Hi, Zachary! You sure take your time calling a girl back." It had been a while since they spoke on the phone but Cozy sounded like she was still one flight up in the old apartment.

"Hey, Coze, yeah sorry. You know, life. Hey, I wanted to let you know I'm coming to DC in a few months. I have a conference there. Let's grab dinner or something. Can you get us a table at the White House yet?"

"Funny. And I know you're coming to get an award. Lenny told me. No White House, but I can take you to the Russia House on Dupont Circle and get you blotto on vodka." She was always familiar with the best places to be seen and/or drunk in, so he trusted her choices.

"Sounds perfect. How's Danny doing?" The short Facebook messages between the two never gave enough detail so he got the updates on her son's school, video game obsessions and lack of any interaction with the girls in his grade.

"He's fine. And by the way, that's usually the last thing that Lenny asks about so ten points to you." Awkward pause. "What is going on with your love life, boy? I'm getting conflicting information here in the nation's capital." There was the maternal tone that Zak missed. "Are you still dating that student?"

"I don't think I was ever dating her. We hung out some but she got kinda crazy so I had to back out. She'll be fine as soon as she finds some new dude to obsess over. I'm sure Lenny told you about Mollie, the singer. I'm supposed to meet up with her and her friends tonight to see a show."

"Sounds promising. What's she like?" There was a glint of glee in her voice. He had been in the trough a long time.

"I think she's about the coolest rock chick on the block but I'm really not sure I'm ready for this yet. I'm still seeing Claire in my dreams. Her stuff is all over the house. I can't bring myself to do anything with it." He started to get a lump in his throat so he thought he'd change the subject, maybe Lenny's dad or the weather or the Washington Nationals.

"You need to box that shit up, Mr. Zak. You are right at the crossroads, just go. I know it's not easy. You have your group. You have me if you need to talk. But you have to get on with the business of living. Push yourself forward."

"I know, I know." It was all part of the grieving process stages, the secret pathway through misery. It looked good as a flowchart but sucked balls as a lifestyle.

"Here's what I want you to do," she said, like a coach. "Meet this girl tonight and have a good time. Think about stuff in the future, not in the past. But don't hook up with her yet. Spend this weekend getting your house ready for company. It shouldn't look like a guy who is obsessed with his dead wife. Sorry, I know that sounds harsh, but you've got to at least give the appearance that you're ready for a new chapter and then once you start that chapter it will all fall into place. This isn't Tosca. You're gonna be okay."

"God, I miss your opera references. None of my graduate students reference Puccini. Ariana Grande, yes. Right, I'm on it. This house needs a good cleaning anyway." She was usually right about such matters of the heart.

"Put on The Beatles *White Album* really loud and be sure to clean your bathroom floor. I know how boys are."

They chatted a bit more about the DC opera season, how much Portland had transformed since she moved away and about binge-watching multiple seasons of *The Good Wife*. She let Zak know he could stay with her and Danny when he got to Washington. It would be good to catch up in person and see his funny face.

Lenny thought he should go to the gym to clear his head. He was paying for a monthly membership but rarely ever went. He wrote it off as a sin tax. Sometimes the sight of his paunch got the better of him and guilt would motivate him to wait for a parking place so he didn't have to walk too far to the front door to check in. And then twenty minutes on the elliptical felt like an eternity. It was as if the cardio machines could slow time down. Civilizations rose and fell in the time it took to do an hour workout on the Stairmaster.

So a yoga class seemed low impact. At least there would be some women his age who still took care of themselves to look at while he did his warrior poses. Namaste, motherfuckers. In his gym shorts, flip flops and Dandy Warhols t-shirt he stood in bold contrast to the hardcore gym rats.

He was distracted on his way to the class by none other than elder rock goddess Patti Smith. One of the trainers was giving her a tour of the gym, explaining all the workout stations and classes for older members.

"I don't really see the point of it," she told the trainer, clutching a notepad under her arm. "I'd rather sit with a coffee and read poetry."

"You can add years to your life to do that," said the kid who looked like he pumped some iron a minute ago.

"What about just walking around Seattle, up and down the hills?" Patti Smith was not an easy sell.

Lenny stared at her. There was no way this was real. There was no way that Patti Smith was in a 24 Hour Fitness in Seattle walking around with a notebook in a black suit. This had to be a dream. That was his cue to take control. So he jogged up to her.

"Hi, Patti! What say you and I go to CBGB's in 1975 and catch some shows. Maybe yours." He reached out for her hand.

She was caught off guard. This wasn't the usual gym encounter, she figured. "Yeah, well, I've already done that. But thanks." Her face, framed by her long grey hair, recognized in Lenny a fellow traveler who might be crossing a line.

"Seriously, Patti, grab my hand. Let's go see the Modern Lovers. We'll go to 1975." Lenny was feeling confident in his ability to maneuver in the dream world.

"Sir, please step back from this lady." The trainer had a chance to use a little muscle and stepped between the two rockers.

"No, let's go," said Lenny. "1975. The Bowery." And he blinked his eyes like *I Dream of Jeanie* but nothing.

"Is this guy a regular?" asked Patti.

"I've never seen him before."

Lenny suddenly realized he had made a grave error. It certainly felt like a dream. He didn't remember at that moment how he had gotten to the gym or even why he was in a gym. But he knew he was frightening one of his rock gods in that gym and it was time to back away slowly.

"Oh, shit. Um, sorry, Patti. I really thought this was a dream. I'm really sorry." Reality, meet Ton of Bricks.

"Not a problem," said Patti. "It's the dream of life."

Zak got to Jinks painfully early. He thought a spot at the bar and a fiver in the jukebox would give him the advantage when Mollie showed up. He thought he was Humphrey Bogart with a thing for Yo La Tengo, claiming the mood of the joint with his selections. Yo La Tengo, Linda Ronstadt, B.B. King, Heart, Derek & the Dominoes. It sounded so sweet, like the way radio used to.

That's when she came in, to "Bell Bottom Blues." She was dressed to see Janis Joplin in 1967 San Francisco so it was perfect. That's what Zak thought. Perfect. But he was a little drunk. Jinks had created a special drink for him made out of Rumchata and Fireball whiskey. They called it "The Professor" and it snuck up on you like a good lecture. So, yeah, Zak was leaning to one side. "Give me one more day, please."

She gave him a sly look and slipped on to the stool next to him. "I'll have what he's having," she said to Lola the bartender. "Well, Dr. Crisp, you look like you have a head-start on me. That's not fair, now is it?"

"Mollie, what do you see in an old fool like me?" Zak was letting the Rumchata do the talking but it was a valid question. He was a busted up academic who had surrendered his street cred to a dream of middle class civility. "You know that scene in every western where the good guy falls in the quicksand? I'm the quicksand." He took another slurp of his drink as Mollie's doppleganger cocktail magically appeared.

"Slow down, cowboy." She was charmed that he had figured out that she was interested in him as more than a friend but a bit miffed that he was already putting the kibosh on things. "You've got a good face. I'm allowed to like a good face, aren't I?" Her freckles seemed to sparkle in Jinks dim lighting. "We're gonna go hear some Janis tonight, okay? It's just a starting point. Let's enjoy some sweet gut-wrenching blues. Ain't no big thing." Her eyes lingered on his face which seemed to fit the music notation.

"I like you, Mollie, that's why I'm telling you to run away." Zak thought his face was drooping more than it was. He immediately regretted saying it after Eric Clapton sang, "I don't want to fade way." But he couldn't shake that he had just seen Claire sitting next to him in the car. He couldn't shake the feeling that he was the one in the quicksand.

Fortunately, she wrote it all off to the drinks and told him to pay his tab so they could go across the street and enter the time machine. Mollie's friends seemed to like Zak and gave he and Mollie a little space once the show started. The band had the late-60s barrelhouse blues of Janis Joplin down. For a brief moment Zak thought he might be lost in a dream with Mollie and Big Brother and the Holding Company in the same space.

In the middle of the song, "Get It While You Can," Mollie placed her hand inside Zak's. He grinned but kept his focus on the band. When the music backed away from the vocals, creating a quiet space, Mollie leaned over to Zak's ear and said, "We could let our hearts go on a road trip and see what happens." And then the music got loud again.

Kiko looked down at her feet and they were white. Like white person white. And her toenails were painted with red and yellow stripes. Was she losing her Asian-ness? It was the only thing that gave her an ounce of uniqueness. If she was a white girl, she would be invisible. Added to this, all ten of her toes were fused together.

She squinted and saw that her socks were still on her feet.

As she pulled them off the leg inside was not flesh but sand, which spread across her futon. Kiko looked at the twin sand piles in the spot where her legs and feet should be and said, "Well, damn. This is not a problem at all. Not a problem at all."

The small-framed young woman leaned up. As her body moved forward each layer of her turned to sand and added to the mounds on the futon. The transformation of body to sand proceeded until it reached Kiko's neck. The end product was a four-foot sandpile with Kiko's grimacing head the top.

"Now it's my turn," she grunted. Her sand-body shook violently as she roared. It formed itself into a red brick-like structure; a masonry bulldozer. The structure sat on reclined legs, like a sleeping cat. But with what sounded like the starting of a steam engine the legs began moving Kiko forward, first off the futon, and then crashing through the wall of her apartment.

The three foot high, five foot long structure (with Kiko's head on top) walked into the street causing cars in the late night traffic to careen out the way. Kiko collided with a hipster on a fixed-gear bike. He rolled to his side and looked up at the wall that hit him.

"You're slowing me down, asshole!" Kiko said. And then she lifted up one of her brick front legs and smashed the hipster's head into the pavement. It didn't take much effort on her part as he wasn't wearing a helmet.

She looked down past the city center, and over the bridges to her destination. She had to get to that neighborhood and smash that house where that man lived. Kiko had to destroy everything around him, including his past, present, and especially his future. She got as far as the Willamette River, leaving a trail of crushed bodies and smashed brew pubs behind her. But the water of the river did something to her front feet. It made them soft and pliable. It slowed down her spin. She needed to be a war machine right now. Not a victim, a destroyer.

There had to be another way. She let her bricks dry up and blow into the gutter. And her head rolled into a nearby soccer match.

On Friday mornings, Zak liked to get his ducks in a row so there wasn't too much work to drag home over the weekend. Weekends were for catching up on shows, moving boxes around and figuring out what in the fridge made a good mixer with Jim Beam. So this morning he was entering some grades into the spreadsheet that Heather had created for one of his classes.

Zak was still resting in the glow of the night before. He took a chance and, after the show, walked Mollie to her car. He kissed her and felt like he was falling into her universe of stars. But of course he couldn't take that leap. It felt too much like a bungee jump. So he extracted himself and escaped into the night.

But he kissed her and she definitely kissed him back. Suffice it to say, the spreadsheet was not keeping his attention.

Matthew Brant, the chair of his department stuck his head in and pulled Zak out of his daydream. "Zak, got a minute?" Zak felt startled, like his hand was caught in the pot cookie jar. "Can you come down to my office? Thanks." And he walked away.

The sinking feeling returned. It was a concern that the chairs of the departments were now lining up against the unionization effort. They were technically management even though almost all of them had been recruited from the faculty. The chairs all had dreams of becoming deans and then maybe making it further on up the university food chain. But Matthew was more "of the people," a true progressive, so the rank and file all hoped he would side with them when the chips were down. Anyway, it wasn't as if Zak was a leader in the movement, just a meeting goer and water cooler chatter.

"Close the door." Matthew's office was twice as big as Zak's but the tone made it seem immense. Zak sat down in the chair in front of the desk but before he could chit chat a few howdy-dos, his chair said, "We have a situation to deal with. Or rather you have a situation to deal with." Ugh.

"Look, Matthew, you know faculty just want decent salaries and some clear promotion guidelines. Who thinks we shouldn't have job security, I mean besides Woodbine?"

His chair stopped him. "It's not that, Zak. I wish it was. I just got an email from the provost's office. You have to go to a meeting with her and the dean."

"What? Why?" His mind bounced around for something sticky. Was there a labor law he violated? Did he screw up some budget form on his grant application? Or was he being moved over to another academic department?

"There's been a complaint from a student of yours that you had a relationship with."

Huh? He hadn't had anything other than friendly relationships with his students. Some liked the same bands or bars and they'd meet out for beers but he always monitored the boundaries. Besides, for the past few years he had been completely off the market and everyone knew it. Oh. Wait a minute.

"Zak, you're being accused of rape by a student named Kiko Matsugane. I know there's more to the story but you have to meet with HR this afternoon. I would suggest that you bring a lawyer if you know one." He looked into Zak's eyes as if to say this better be some big misunderstanding, I don't need this on my plate right now.

The bile crept up Zak's throat and spilled over the back of his tongue. He thought he was going to vomit on his boss's desk but he caught it in time. He knew she was mental, but nothing like this. This was over the top. Surely he could explain it away. How bad could it really be?

"Okay, Matthew." He really didn't know what to say. "I guess I'll wait for an email telling me what to do next." He was deflated. Things seemed to be turning a corner for him. What the holy fuck?

Outside of the chair's office he got out his phone and pulled up Kiko's number to send her a text, feeling betrayed.

WTF, Kiko. Rape, really? U r bat shit crazy!

He returned to his office feeling like he was being viewed from a fish eye lens, distorted and grotesque. Matthew stuck his head in one more time to add to the reality of it all.

"Um, I'm supposed to tell you not to contact this girl. They have a whole process for these things," he said in a hushed voice. A whole process.

"Not a problem," said Zak. He'd wished he never talked to her in the first place. He wished he'd jumped off that cliff when he had the chance.

The chotskies that were usually on Kelly's desk were strewn across the floor. She tried not to think about them and focused on her hands gripping the edge of the desk. They looked particularly old in the daylight stealing in through her office window.

"Who's your daddy?" Walt said, his mouth a few inches from her left ear.

"You are, Daddy. You are!" She tried to keep her voice down but his belly pushing against her back, as she flattened against the desk, squeezed the air out her lungs. She was helpless under him. "Please, Daddy, give it to me. I want it." And she did. She wanted him inside her and then to stay inside her while they had coffee and read the *New York Times* and plotted world domination.

Walt's sweat was dripping off his brow on to the back of Kelly's neck. She felt it land on the clasp of her pearl neckless and follow the chain to the pearls underneath her, clacking against the desktop in rhythm with his thrusts.

"You're my girl, right?" His voice was labored under the exertion.

Kelly was right where she wanted to be. She looked out the window at Portland. Her soul was safe six stories above the commoners and all that mattered was the surface of her skin.

"Yes, I'm your little girl."

"Did I have a dream? Or did the dream have me?" (Rush)

Chapter 8:
I Know What I Want

1

After sweating in his office for two hours, Zak headed toward the Human Resources office in the administration building. Surely he could explain this situation. Surely this had to have happened before. Surely they had to have actual hard evidence before they accused someone of such a damning crime; a career ruining offense. He asked himself if it was a dream and tried to push the fingers through the palm of his hand. It wasn't.

What he should have done is called Robin Nielsen who would have told him to turn around. You don't talk to these fuckers without a lawyer and another faculty member present. She would have told him that this was part of the great purge to remove faculty like yesterday's beer bottles, especially "agitators," which by the broadest of broad definitions included Zachary Crisp.

"Come on in, Zak." It was the dean, Julie Margolis. They'd always been friendly in the past. She pushed his hire through on the weight of his outreach work with homeless youth. "Have a seat."

It was a stark conference room with a window looking out over downtown. Sitting at the table was another middle-aged woman and not the provost, but the vice-provost who had been watching him, Kelly Claiborne. Suddenly this felt like a lynching party. But he was still hopeful he could explain events.

"Dr. Crisp, we haven't had a chance to meet yet. I'm Vice Provost Kelly Claiborne, this is Debbie Werman from the Office of Human Resources and of course you know Dean Margolis. We have some questions we are hoping you can answer for us." Her face was pinched and stern. "Would you mind if we record this?"

She had already pushed the button on the digital recorder.

"Of course. I'm actually glad to have the opportunity to talk about this situation. I'm hoping you can advise me." The best defense is an offense. Get out in front of it.

"What can you tell us about a student of yours named Kiko Matsugane?"

Now this is the part where you say that you don't feel comfortable discussing this issue without appropriate representation. Every accused criminal has the right to remain silent, to invoke the Fifth Amendment. Of course they never do. In the back of the police car they'll tell the cop exactly why they punched that asshole or robbed that liquor store or how they didn't commit that crime because they were busy somewhere else committing a different crime. Accusations make people nervous and nervous people gush. The real bad guys keep their fucking mouths shut. But Zak wasn't one of those types. He was a gusher.

So Zak explained how he and Kiko became friends and that she had been romantically pursuing him but he resisted because he was still grieving the death of his pregnant wife. The three women made sad faces and he should have stopped right there. He went on to explain that after the class was over he gave in to her advances and the relationship turned physical.

"Would you describe it as romantic, amorous or sexual at that point?" asked Kelly.

"Well, it was one of those," Zak tried to joke. Romantic and amorous are the same thing and their relationship certainly was neither.

All three women made a "Hmmm" sound and wrote things down on their notepads.

"Did you have sex with her after consuming alcohol?" asked the woman from HR, looking over the top of her glasses.

"Well, we had gone out to a karaoke bar, had some nachos and a couple of drinks and then went and watched a movie before calling it a night. It was late and I invited her to stay over. She took her clothes off and jumped in my bed. She could've slept on the couch if she wanted to."

"But she had drinks before sleeping with you." Oh, it was clear where this was going. The women wrote more.

"Yeah, but that was hours before we went to bed. She wasn't drunk if that's what you're implying. We went to a video store and watched an entire movie." Zak began to sweat.

Kelly jumped in. "Professor, have you ever sent this student any pornographic material?" Fuck. Kelly opened a folder with pages of printouts of emails. Kiko must have turned everything over to them.

"Wow." He wasn't sure how to respond. But honesty seemed like the best policy. "We're both fans of Japanese anime and that can get a little weird at times, so yeah. But look, we are both consenting adults. I feel I need to say that. And this really doesn't have anything to do with the university." Zak's lawyer brain was thinking these women were overstepping their jurisdiction.

"And did you ever send this student a link to a video of a woman having sex with a horse?" Kelly did not look up after asking that question.

"Look, it was a joke. She sent me a picture of a woman having a sex with an eel and I sent her that link back. It was like a game of out-shocking each other. Did I mention that we are consenting adults?" Zak was struggling for an emotional position to take. Should he scream at their intrusion or break down in tears and beg for mercy?

They kept up the pressure. "Professor Crisp, have you ever sent this student child pornography."

"Oh hell no, absolutely not!" What had Kiko told them?

Kelly reached into her folder and pulled out an anime image of a girl having sex with a robot with a huge penis. "Did you send her this image?"

"That's hentai, a form a anime, not child pornography. I found it on Google. It's a drawing and it's certainly not a child. Look at her breasts!" The big doe eyes and the hairless crotch didn't help. Or the fact that the girl was crying. "There are more obscene images on Guns 'n' Roses album covers. I really don't think I should continue with this." Zak almost made his move for the door.

"We have a few more questions, Zak," said the dean, who did not look sympathetic.

Kelly continued her inquisition. "While you conducted your romantic, amorous and sexual relationship with this student…"

"'Or,'" Zak interjected. "'Or' not 'and.'"

"Yes. Did you require her to call you 'Sir' or 'Professor' while you were together?"

"What the? Certainly not. She did it on her own. I gave up asking her to stop. I told you she's cuckoo for Cocoa Puffs. In fact, that's when I tried to end it. When I realized she had a screw loose. Then she started to say she was going to kill herself! She's conning you ladies to lash out at me!"

"Zak, did you follow the protocol for a student who is expressing suicidal ideation?" asked the dean.

There was a workshop about ten years ago that faculty had to take. Zak was there with bells on after having survived his own trip to the cliff years ago.

"I've struggled with the issue of suicide much of my life. It's very important to me. I know what real suicidal ideation looks like and this wasn't it. This was a school girl with a broken heart." Poor choice of words, Crisp.

"Professor Crisp, how many of your students have you slept with?" Claiborne was circling in for the kill.

"I told you, Kiko was a former student."

"Other than Miss Matsugane, how many students have you slept with?"

"None. Before I got married, I dated a few former students but I take my role as a teacher very seriously. I would never compromise my relationship with my students that way." The university didn't even have a policy prohibiting such behavior, and some faculty had not only dated but married students. This included a female biology prof who married her grad student.

Kelly reached into her magic manila folder and pulled out another slice of evidence.

"How would you respond to this?"

It was a print out from the RateMyProfessor.com website. It was a place were students who loved/hated their teachers went to vent their praise/spleen. It was always the extreme opinions that went up, like a Yelp of academics. Zak generally had good ratings and students had been perhaps overly complimentary since the accident. This review had been posted on Wednesday and it gave Professor Zachary Crisp one out five stars. Zak read the review.

Crisp acts like a big feminist but everyone knows if you are blonde and have big tits, you can get an A. I was struggling in his class and I went to his office hours for help and he said he would change the grade on my midterm if I gave him a blowjob. I wasn't shocked because I've heard other female students say that is how they got through the course. This man should not be teaching in a college.

"Is this a dream?" Zak out loud. "This cannot be happening." He again tried to push his fingers through his hands in hopes they would go through this time.

"Calm down, sir," said the HR lady.

"Obviously, Kiko wrote it! It was posted right after I told her that we should just be friends. Look at the date! Please tell me that you see this is a set up. I can't be the only one that's been falsely accused like this. C'mon." He was the verge of losing it.

"You know, I think that's enough for today," said the dean, suddenly sounding like a mediator. "Let's finish up and let you go. Zak, can we contact you if we have more questions?"

"Yeah, of course," he barely said as he got up to exit the room, leaving the cabal to salivate over their juicy morsels.

Zak wanted to get out of the building as fast as he could. When the elevator door opened to take him down to the lobby, Robin stepped out.

"There you are," she said. "I heard you got called up here and I tried to call you ASAP."

"I had my phone off," he said feeling like it was all over and he should head straight for a bridge.

Robin pulled him into the elevator and the doors closed behind them. She hit the button for the first floor and asked him, "How did it go? What did they ask you? Did Claiborne dig up some bogus shit on you? Fuck."

"I think I need a lawyer."

"Fuck. I wish you would have called me first. Yeah, I've got a lawyer. She's great. If we get the union, she's going to be our employment lawyer. Her name is Nevada Standish. I'll text you her number." The door to the lobby opened. "Let's go grab a beer. You can tell me what the hell happened."

"No," said Zak in a low voice. "I need some time." And he walked out through the big glass doors and just kept walking.

Kiko's fantasy to imbed herself in the heart of Portland wasn't going so well. Her income from her night class was about to run out at the end of the term and she hadn't been asked to teach Japanese next term. Something about her not showing up a for several sessions. Other than her "case" with the university, she didn't seem to have much to look forward to. She thought she could could try to monetize her blog, but she was already loosing readers and didn't want to scare off the remainder with ads between her stories.

She perused the weekly going ons in the *Portland Mercury*, looking at the announcements for all the shows she now wouldn't be going to with Zak. Had she ruined it forever? Maybe he would reach out to her. Maybe the "bat-shit crazy" comment was the way overworked professors vented. Maybe she could find a job in the Mercury that would win his respect. But the only jobs were in the back pages for sex workers; strippers, erotic massagers and escorts. Those are jobs for women who hate men, she thought.

"Who is shooting off firecrackers?" That was Zak's first thought when he heard the popping sound outside his office. Then he heard the screams. Students and faculty ran out into the hall to see the commotion and then some came back ghostly white. There was Sammy Sullivan in the department doorway.

"There's a man with a gun shooting everyone!" he screamed.

Zak thought about the students waiting for him to start class, across the hall. He had to get to them. Matthew Brant burst out of his office.

"We've got an active shooter situation. Everybody needs to lock themselves inside their office!" he instructed.

Zak could see the students running down the hall, falling over the bodies of those who had already been shot. His teaching assistant Heather was on the ground, and there was Ronda, the department administrator. It looked like she had been shot in the chest.

"I've got to get to my class!" shouted Zak, pushing Matthew out of the way. His adrenaline was banging inside his ears, louder than the gunshots.

In the hall he saw the gunman, dressed in black tactical gear, including a helmet, with an assault rifle spraying bullets down the hall. He was a white man with a nauseating grin, looking like he had rehearsed this attack many times. Zak bolted across the hall into an alcove and was one doorway away from his students who must have been terrified at the sounds.

Under the pile of bodies he saw her playing dead, which is what you were supposed to do in these situations. It was Claire. She must have been coming to visit him at work.

Suddenly there was crossfire. The police had arrived and were firing on the gunman, but he was heavily armored and armed. They were no match for this killing machine. Zak watched a few rounds rip through the white pant leg of one of the officers and red blood soak into the uniform. White. Oh.

He crouched down and pulled Claire into the alcove as the bullets buzzed back and forth, and more people hit the floor, dead or otherwise. His face was inches from hers and she looked terrified and frozen.

"Zak, we've got to get out of here! I don't want to die!" She pushed him against the door as the shooter got closer.

At that moment, one of the cops, the one with long blonde hair, dove into the alcove and pressed himself against them. "You kids have two minutes. Try to beat the clock. It never stops." Then he opened the door behind them, and Zak and Claire fell into the safety of a small university office.

"Claire! Are you alright? Where's Caroline?" He began to calm down as he got his footing in this plane of existence.

"She's with my mom. Zak, how are we going to get out of here?"

"It's okay, I promise. I have to talk to you. I have to tell you something." He tried to hold her face with his hands but she was in a full state of panic. "I need to tell you how sorry I am about the crash. It was my fault. I should have slowed down or sped up or something."

Her face contorted into an even greater distortion. "What crash? What are you talking about? Zak, there is a gunman out there killing everybody! We're trapped in here! Hold me please. We have to be quiet."

So that's what he did. He held his wife for the first time in over a year. Her heart pounded loudly in her chest, jump-starting Zak's pressed against it. He kissed her forehead and rubbed his face in her hair. He breathed in every atom of her that had left him on that day. This was her and he was going to hold on for as long as he could.

The shooting stopped and he thought the coast might be clear. He unwrapped his left arm from Claire's shaking body and reached for the door.

"Zak, don't. You could get killed!"

"You can't die in a dream, Claire. Everybody knows that," he said calmly.

He cracked open the door and looked across the bodies down the hall. A good dozen casualties. Across the hall he looked into his department. All the office doors were closed tight except his. There was a face looking out exactly like he was doing. The face looked like his own, like his twin. The twin version saw the bodies in the hall and then retreated back into his (and Zak's) office. The next office door opened and the person who emerged was his old roommate, Telly Max. Telly was an odd, skinny guy who had briefly lived with him years ago and then disappeared, leaving a wad of cash so Lucinda and her baby could move in. He had had a wiseness about him that was cosmic, to say the least. Telly looked across the hall and shook his head, as if to say, you shouldn't be here.

Excited to see Telly, Zak stepped out the door as the gunman came around the corner. He raised his rifle and fired four shots into Zak's chest, knocking him to the floor. Claire screamed and the scream distracted the gunman long enough for one of the cops in white to get a shot off into the shooters face, instantly killing him. Then he ran over to Zak and grabbed the white police mike off his shoulder.

"Code Six. We've got a situation here." He looked at Claire and said, "Dreamers' lives matter."

Claire cradled Zak's head in her lap and wept. He could taste the blood in his mouth. "Strange," he thought. "Sorry," he said.

Zak woke up to the phone ringing by his bed.

"Professor Crisp, this is Nevada Standish. Sorry if I'm waking you. I got your message yesterday and also heard from Robin Nielsen. Sorry I'm just getting back to you now. I was out of town." She sounded very professional.

"Oh, hi, yeah. I guess I need some help with this situation. It's gone off the rails really quickly."

"Whatever happened we have to move fast. Employers like the element of surprise. They get all their guns loaded and before you can get off the floor they've got you out the door. I need you to do a few things for me today. Email me a copy of your contract and the university's conduct code for faculty. Don't use your university email account. They're probably monitoring it. And create a folder that you can download every single email to and from this woman. And send me her phone number so I can get her call log." Oh, very professional.

"Sure. Can we meet soon?" Zak felt assured by her focus but it all seemed like it was spinning away from him.

"Monday morning, first thing. Try not to worry. I've dealt with things like this before." And she hung up. Zak wanted to close his eyes and go back to bleeding out on the hallway floor. They'd probably all say nice things about him if he was dead.

After a piss he did manage to go back to sleep. He had a dream about losing his way in a Toys-R-Us. Aisles of bath toys with no end. Where were the rag dolls?

When Stan didn't show up at his job at the clinic the nurse had a CO go check on him. The guard found him in his cell, bruised with a bloody pile of clothing on the floor. He was rushed to the infirmary and he kept his mouth shut as much as he wanted to scream out who had done this to him. His reputation as a snitch was deep enough as it was. But he didn't have to snitch. It was clear his body had been raffled off and then used as a punching bag.

His counselor suggested he be put in protective custody for now, so he was to move his things out of his current residence and set up in a cell on the other side of the prison. There would be no cellmate, no yard time, no chow hall and lots of surveillance. It was both punishment and rescue. He would be isolated but hopefully safe. He thought he'd be okay with his religion books. He didn't need anybody else. His bones needed to mend and his soul, well, that was long gone in a blaze of rage and muffled cries.

2

So much for sleeping in. There was a persistent banging on Zak's door so he put on some pants to go answer it. It was Lenny, looking a bit more dressed up than normal in an Oxford shirt and blazer instead of his usual black t-shirt and leather jacket.

"Lenny! You didn't tell me you were coming down. Are you going to see your dad?" He pretended to rub the sleep out of his eyes even though it was almost noon.

"Dude," said Lenny, bringing a travel bag into the house. "I've been calling and texting and emailing. Yeah, I told you I was coming down for a few days. You didn't get my messages?"

The weight of the bomb flashed in his face again. Not a dream. "Sorry, there was some serious shit going down yesterday. I had to deal with a fucking nightmare."

"Uh oh. Girl troubles?" he said with a wink.

"Sort of. Let me put on some coffee."

How shallow is the soul, consumed with the weight of the moment. If anything carries over from childhood it is buried by concerns of making it through the next block of days. Make it to turn the page on the calendar. Zak told his old friend the allegations being made against him by university officials who had become the vehicle for Kiko's nihilism. Lenny, coffee in hand, uttered these words no less than ten times, "That bitch!"

"It's a good thing you got a lawyer. Hell hath no fury, bro. No fucking fury. Well, I might be able to lighten the mood. I stopped by the pot shop on Alberta before I came over and picked up some weed for us. This is serious conversation time." Lenny pulled a small canister out of his pocket and set it on the kitchen counter.

"Shit, Lenny. You know I don't really smoke. It doesn't do anything for me. I'd rather guzzle Jim Beam." Zak made fun of the stoners in high school who got wasted and played air guitar to Rush songs.

"No, this is the good stuff. It's a strain called Girl Scout Cookies. It's Snoop Dogg's favorite. I read that. You really need it right now, believe me."

So the two men in their forties took their coffee and their weed into the living room. Zak put a John Coltrane CD on the stereo (*Impressions*, 1961) and Lenny rolled a rather fat joint on the coffee table. The old friends plopped down on the couch and let the music and smoke settle on their skin.

"What time are you going to see your dad?"

"When I'm fucked up enough to deal with him."

"Had any good dreams lately?" Zak was anxious not to talk about the university drama.

Lenny took a big drag and let the smoke drip out of his nostrils. "This lucid dreaming thing is a lot harder than I thought. You really have to fucking focus on it all the time. Most of the time I wake up and I can't even remember if even had a dream."

"I told you, you need a dream journal. Discipline. Just like everything."

"I had a really great dream that I was hanging out with Cozy in Seattle. We had a great day together. Daniel, like, was never born, which was weird, but we had pretty awesome sex, so mission accomplished. Oh, and Bill Cosby was the president."

Zak coughed on his toke. "Maybe it was your parallel universe thing." He was willing to entertain Lenny's space travel theory which suddenly was sounding more reasonable. "I had an intense dream last night. There was a school shooting in my building but Claire was there, so I knew I was in a dream. I tried to talk to her but everything was fucked up with all the shooting. Telly was there and those weird cops. And get this, I saw myself."

"What, like in a mirror?" asked Lenny, letting the smoke hang in front of his mouth.

"No, I saw myself looking out of my office. Then I got shot in the chest by the gunman. I think I died in the dream."

"Whoa. Dude, do you know what that means?"

"Okay, Lenny. Let's hear it." Zak's brain was starting to feel like a marshmallow. The Girl Scout Cookies had reached his medulla oblongata.

"You were not on Earth. You were on another fucking planet just like Earth but Claire is alive and so are you. There were two Zaks there at the same time. That's totally what happened!"

The walls of Zak's living room all moved back about 500 feet from the couch. There was a clarity of thought and a clear understanding between the two.

"Fuck," said Zak. "No, man, it was a dream. I didn't pass through a wormhole or anything. I think I'd know if I would have passed through a wormhole."

"Perhaps, but perhaps not. Do you even know what a fucking wormhole looks like? If that is a real place that means you can get back there and sniff around."

The two were quiet for a bit while Coltrane's bending saxophone notes circled their heads, amplifying their transcendental thoughts.

"Holy fuck, I'm hungry," said Lenny rather softly.

"I think there's half a burrito in the fridge. I was gonna go to the store today. I need a Powerball ticket for tonight."

"You are never going to win that thing, man. Why do you waste your money?" This coming from a guy who believed there were dream doors to alternative planets where The Beatles never broke up.

"I know. It was a thing Claire and I used to do. 'Dollar for a dream,' we called it. We'd talk about all the places we'd go if we won. And the house we'd build for all the kids we were gonna have. Now I'd spend it on a really good hit man to kill these fuckers that are trying to fuck up my life." The mood got seriously serious as Coltrane dropped into a minor key.

"Is that off the record? Man, those old ladies aren't worth the trouble. And Kiko is a classic psycho. In five seconds she'll be obsessing about some new asshole and you'll be off the hook. Believe me, I've got some experience in this area." Lenny did.

"I was trying to be like you. Go with the chick flow. Suck some face instead of staring at the wall for another night. Look where that got me."

"The chick flow is like Russian roulette. Usually it works out fine, but every once in a while you end up with someone with daddy issues and you've got a good season you want to forget. But look at the thing with Mollie. That looks promising. No red flags on her sweet ass." Oh, Lenny.

"We'll see. What about you, man? When are you going to get a real girlfriend?"

"Me? Settle down? But I want to see the tits on every girl," coughed Lenny.

"What happened to that southern girl you were hanging out with? I liked her. She really had a way with words."

"Katie?"

"No, the other one."

"Sonja?"

"No, the other one. With short hair."

"You mean Maddy! Dude, she wasn't Southern. She had head injury and that's just how she talked. I think she moved to New York to become a shoe salesman."

"Well, I liked her. You should call her up," said Zak.

"Maybe *you* should call her up."

And the conversation devolved from there as the jazz and pot served to liberate them from any form of linearity. They briefly lamented that there was no true magic in the world outside of dreams and the occasional lottery win. No three wishes or fairy godfathers. Then Zak became worried that the entire university administration was out to get him and anyone else involved in the unionization effort. It sounded paranoid to Lenny but it was probably closer to the truth than either of them could guess. Then it just got silly.

"Does this dope give you the farts?" asked Zak, giggling.

"It frees you to fart without concern for social mores, my brother."

"One time I was in a men's room at an airport and I was standing at the urinal and this old guy farted and then everyone standing there farted. It was like a quintet of bad tuba players. I was still laughing when I got on the plane." And Zak and Lenny were laughing now.

"That man was truly free," cried Lenny. "Every guy wants to fart when he pees but society tells us to hold it in, to restrict our little buttholes. But he was old and told the butthole police, 'Screw you! I've paid my dues! Besides, I'm never seeing any of these men again. I'm letting this air biscuit go!' And in doing so, he freed the rest of you to follow him to anal liberation. That old man deserved your thanks!" And with that Lenny let out a high pitched fart followed by a long low rumble from Zak. Both laughed so hard they almost choked.

"Shit, I guess I should go see my old man," said Lenny, catching his breath and pretending to sit up.

"You okay to drive?"

"Yeah, it's only Hillsboro. I didn't want to do this straight anyway. Can I throw my shit in your guest room? We can go grab some beers later. I'll give you the whole story."

"I'm going to turn that room into an Airbnb and start charging your employed ass." Zak thought that was funny. "If I lose my job, I'm gonna need the income." That didn't seem as funny.

"You're going to be fine, old man. Everybody loves you. You're Mr. Feminist-save-the-world."

"Inmate! Get up! You got your shit?" The CO was waking Stan up from a nap to escort him to the Protective Custody Unit. "C'mon, it's moving day."

Val sat on the edge of his bunk watching his cellmate. He still believed Stan, now battered and bruised, would serve as his protector. "I hate to see you go, brother. Why don't you take this.

It will keep you company." Val held out his Bible for Stan but the hulking man just knocked it out of his hand as he slowly walked to the door.

"Keep your damn book."

Two correctional officers walked with Stan down the maze of halls. He held a small box of personal belongings and kept his eyes to the floor. In no way did he want to remember this place so there was no need for one last look. He was descending into the bowels of the prison to spend his time in isolation, away from the monsters who would not let him think.

The PC unit was just a long hall, really. The doors to the cell were solid with a small window and closed twenty-three and a half hours a day. Inmates were locked in a safe, like rare gems that no one really cared about. They were safe from others, but not from themselves. If Stan was not insane already, he soon would be. He should've taken that Bible.

His first night in solitary confinement was like an endless seizure. Sleep came in bits punctuated by night sweats and hallucinations. Somehow this was worse than the looming fear of gang rape, to be locked in a closet and forgotten.

At one point he attempted to sit up in his dark cell, the only light coming through the cracks in the closed window in his door. The attempt failed because all his arms and legs had become separated from his torso. His only mobility was his head and neck. His limbs had been neatly sliced off.

As morning approached his mother appeared at the foot of his bed. "Remember when you tore the lace on my curtains?" she asked in a soft voice. "You never were any good, Stanley. You are damaged. I shouldn't have smoked so much when I was carrying you. You're not going to make it." And then she stood silent, with a pitiful look on her face.

Stan could only curse her under his breath.

Kiko decided to spend the afternoon exploring her employment options. Being Portland, her first stop was the Devil House, a vegan strip bar. She had never been inside a strip bar, so after getting off at a nearby bus stop she stood in the nearly empty parking lot, trying to get her courage up. But then she realized that standing in a strip club parking lot probably made her look like a prostitute so she went in the front door.

Even though it was a dim day in the rose city, it took a minute for her eyes to adjust to the dark club with its black walls. A stripper in a bra and panties with a tattoo of Bob Dylan on her arm approached her. Kiko noticed the tattoos, her heavy mascara and the diamond Tiffany ring on her left hand. Here we go.

"Hi, honey. Do you want to sit at a table?" the stripper asked politely.

She certainly wasn't a customer but maybe she should check this place out first. Or not. "Oh, I was wondering if you guys are hiring. And what it's like to work here."

"It's great! All the tempeh sandwiches you can eat. Hi, I'm Ashley. You need to talk to Delia, the manager. She's behind the bar right now. I'm sure she'd like you. We could use a little Asian hottie in here. Just go talk to her."

And there it was. Her yellow card, exotic capital and the assumption she was men's ultimate passive fantasy doll. "Would you like me to walk on your back, sir? Tee-hee."

She took a seat at the bar and noticed an African-American woman dancing nude on the stage to the Kelis song, "Milkshake." There was one man sitting in front of her with a beer and stack of one dollar bills. She works hard for her money. The orange-haired manager was stocking liquor bottles with her back to Kiko.

"Oh, hi, honey. Do you need a drink?"

"I wanted to see about working here."

"Sure, we like the younger girls. You at least 18?" She used the question as an excuse to look her up and down.

"Of course I am. But I don't have any experience doing this," admitted Kiko.

"You're a female right?" Kiko nodded. "Then you have experience doing this," Delia said.

3

Zak spent most of the day sitting in the nursery, letting the effects of the pot slowly wear off. He'd think about packing some more things up and then think, I can't make it alone, and lay on the floor. A few minutes seemed to stretch on for hours. Each song playing on his stereo seemed to last forever. "Oh, this is why stoners loved Rush," he thought.

The weight of the tsunami of bullshit coming his way glued him to the baby's rug. How do you prove you are not something? Where was the presumption of innocence? Was he guilty of the charge but too arrogant to see it? There must be a way to turn back time, just a little. There were enough theories that pointed to the possibility of it. Remember when Superman flew around the earth in the opposite direction of its spin to undue Lois Lane falling into that earthquake crevice? If laws were meant to be be broken, that must include the laws of physics, right? Damn, this ELO song was long.

He heard the front door open. It was Lenny already back from Hillsboro. Zak's ears followed his footsteps around the house, like an old dog looking for her dinner bowl. He finally sniffed his way into the nursery. That should have been the first place he looked.

"Oh, ho!" Lenny grinned. "Look who's still wasted. You need to smoke more, kiddo. Get your tolerance up."

"Sage advice from your neighborhood white Rastafarian. I'm listening to music. So, how did it go? Was there some big reveal?" Zak sat up and Lenny joined him on the nursery floor.

"You were right. He's got colorectal cancer. He's in pretty bad shape. We talked about it and his time in prison. About how he hated missing so much of my life growing up. I couldn't handle it so I split. But I think I'll go back tomorrow." Lenny suddenly seemed vulnerable. He was a boy again without the decades of the cool act ingrained into his habitus.

After a breath he continued. "He was pretty doped up on pain meds, kinda in and out. I think he probably thought he was the one lucid dreaming."

"I'm sure it meant a lot to him that you were there, Len. He probably has a lot he wants to say to you." Zak appreciated the privilege of being able to have a conversation with someone before they died, instead of being left with only regret at the things you wished you would have said.

Lenny picked up a rag doll from an open box. "I read once that the first three months of our lives, when we're babies, we think everything is a dream. When we wake up, it's just a continuation of the dream we were having. I have a feeling my dad's last three months are going to be like that."

It seemed like a profound thing to say as the two men sat on the floor of a nursery built for a baby who died before she was born. So profound that Zak laid back down on the rug and closed his eyes hoping to hear Claire's voice from the kitchen. "Zak! Have you finished the crib, yet?"

The rest of the day Zak and Lenny tried to keep the discussion on music, their go-to safe place. This included linking songs on The Falsie's demo CD to possible ad campaigns and exploration of whatever happened to Alanis Morissette. That led to an internet search that dropped by the website of Zak's new lawyer, Nevanda Standish.

"She's tight," exclaimed Lenny.

Standish was a beautiful woman. Younger than she sounded on the phone, thirty maybe. "Her long red hair must be a weapon to distract juries," Zak thought. He hoped she's was good as Robin said. Her credentials listed on the website seemed to say so. Emory Law School. The Innocence Project.

"She's a talented girl," said Zak, keeping his eyes on the text.

"You better hope so, bub. Do you think you might need me as a witness? I want to meet her."

"Well, since you met Kiko, I'd say there is a good chance of it. You can testify that I wasn't holding her here against her will," said Zak, feeling the weight of it all.

"Oh, she was all into your little sex party. It was written all over her dirty, dirty face."

"Yeah, Lenny, maybe you could find a different way of saying that on the stand."

Nothing much got done this particular Saturday. Zak emailed the documents that Standish had asked for and drank a several beers with Lenny at the neighborhood brewpub where Lenny eye-fucked the waitress. Then they smoked more pot and made a list of all the cool Portland clubs, bars and party houses that had been magically removed by gentrification. Remember RJ's?

Zak had intended to do some really focused dreaming to try to get back to Claire. He'd planned to incubate thoughts of her in Reno before drifting off to meet her in the dreamscape. The beer and pot had other plans so he fell asleep on the couch instead. Lenny let himself out to go to a show with Kathy of The Falsies and talk a little business.

Instead of Claire, Zak dreamed he was inside a burning car and his one year-old daughter was in the back, strapped into her car seat. He got out and opened the rear door to free her from the flames but the heat had melted the seat buckle into a glob of plastic. The baby was screaming and he could feel his hair and arms burning as he tried to extricate her from the safety seat. She was stuck and the heat was intensifying. Her socks were on fire and he pulled them off. There was no way he was going to let her die like this. The flames ripped the flesh from his back as he tried to shield her. Suddenly, she looked him in the eyes, stopped crying and turned to black ash in his hands. "I'm sorry, baby. I'm sorry."

Kelly's Saturday was focused on getting ready for Sunday's golf date with Walt. She had outfits to pick out and clubs to polish. Maybe some practice putting in the back yard and a YouTube video on what club to use when. She thought of Jay, her ex, and all the professors with their ditzy young coeds. The man that wanted her was the president.

By the time Sunday rolled around, Kelly was a kid on Christmas morning. First was brunch with Walt at the Salty Dog on the Columbia River, which meant bottomless mimosas. Then, with a break in the clouds and feeling no pain, they went to Westmoreland golf course where Walt wrapped his arms around her to show her the proper putting techniques. There, on the green grass of the river flood plain, their hips moved back and forth together. Kelly didn't care who saw it. She was in the grips of power and she felt it's tingle enter her from behind and crawl up her backbone, resting in her jaw.

Walt duffed a few balls into the water, giving his new parter a fighting chance. She took it as his submission to her. The top rung of the ladder was just on the next fairway.

Lenny spent a good part of Sunday reconnecting with his father in Hillsboro. It was a semi-private room but the man in the bed next to him was barely conscious. A nurse would poke her head in every once in a while to see if everybody's heart monitor was still beeping.

They talked about the rain and Daniel. They talked about sports, about how Portland and Seattle were the same city when it came to football and basketball (the Seahawks and the Trailblazers) but were bitter rivals when it came to soccer (the Sounders and the Timbers). They talked about cancer survivors they knew and traffic and pretty much everything two men could talk about instead of their real feelings.

They danced around for hours, avoiding it like it was a hairball floating in a swimming pool. Finally, Lenny's dad pushed through.

"I guess I'm not going to be around long enough to make up for never being around."

"Shut up, Pops. You're going to live forever. You're that kind of SOB."

"Well, if I don't, I want to say that I'm sorry and my dying wish is that I don't want you to do to Daniel what I did to you."

That got Lenny. Fucking cat's in the cradle. He could feel his father's hand on his shoulder as he began to cry.

The university was moving fast against Zak. Before he could even get dressed for his morning meeting with Nevada Standish an email pinged into his inbox. Kelly had sent it and it said there would be a "hearing" tomorrow afternoon. The university would present the case against him and he or his representative could respond. The matter would be decided by Woodbine's chief of staff, Abigail Williams.

After reading this, Zak's first impulse was to jump off a bridge and deny them the satisfaction of destroying him.

"When's your meeting with Alicia Florrick?" Lenny was already up with a microwaved cup of yesterday's coffee.

"In an hour. This really is a witch hunt. I think it's gonna get ugly fast." Zak stared at the screen.

"Dude, you're ten feet tall and bulletproof. Oh, and besides, I'm supposed to tell you to call Mollie. So there's that."

Nevada Standish's office was in a remodeled home in the southeastern part of the city. She shared the office with three other attorneys who were not the corporate type, but more the public defender type. As a labor lawyer, she wasn't going to be in any swank downtown office unless she landed the AFL-CIO as a client. The secretary was on a coffee run so she met Zak in the lobby.

"Dr. Crisp, I'm very pleased to meet you."

She was tall and her long red hair was pinned up. Her glasses made her look like a librarian who had walked off the runway. Zak was struck by her Chinese business dress. It added to the post-modern collision that was Portland.

"Hi. You can call me Zak. I have a feeling you're going to know me well enough by the time this thing is done." He was older than her, but they were both professionals, after all.

"Come in to my office. I want you to know that I talked to Robin about the overall situation and read the materials that you sent me." She motioned for him to sit down at the chair across from her desk. She had a kind smile that helped him relax a bit. "We're going to have to have a serious talk, but I think I can help you."

"Did you hear that they want a hearing tomorrow? Can we be ready?" He felt small in the chair. Or she seemed big. He was getting used to feeling small sitting across from women. Maybe it was some karma from his misspent youth.

"I think we can move that back a few days. So this consultation is free but if you decide to hire me, it's a two thousand retainer up front to cover the initial billable hours. You okay with that?"

Zak sunk even farther into the chair. "I guess I don't qualify as a charity case," he thought. "Yeah, I can take it out of my savings account. I don't imagine I'm going to have time to do any lawyer shopping."

"Yes. Right. Okay, let's talk about this situation. I'm going to be honest with you, Zak. You're being railroaded. Robin told me what's been going on at the school, with tenure-line faculty being targeted around this union thing. It's clear that they want you gone. There's a sexual panic going on around Title IX issues these days and they've got a pretty big weapon to, excuse my French, fuck you up good."

Her use of the F-word eased Zak a bit even though it should have made him more worried. At least he could speak freely about how something went from relatively innocent to insanely fucked up in sixty seconds. So he laid out the chronology, starting from Kiko coming to his office all the way to him politely trying to let her down easy when she got a bit over attached to him.

"I have to say this very clearly. She's a consenting adult. I don't really feel like I did anything wrong here. I mean, what business is my love life to them?"

Nevada took off her librarian glasses and leaned back in her chair. "It's not about that, Zak. It's about two things. It's about the university wanting to trim tenure-line faculty from the budget, and this union thing gives them a perfect reason to do that with haste. And the second thing is that these people are career bureaucrats, and the way you get ahead in a bureaucracy is by identifying a problem that doesn't exist and then solving it."

"And I'm the problem," said Zak, resignation in his voice.

"Right. You're the problem. And they will destroy you to move a half rung up the ladder."

There was a weight hanging over his head. He could see it. It was the weight of the life he should be having with Claire and Caroline snatched away. It was the weight of not being able to regain his footing after their loss. It was the weight of not being able to shut down a student crush from the first second. It was the weight of selling his soul to the company store that was now coming to collect its debt. It looked like a giant grey concrete slab that was hanging from the ceiling by a frayed pink ribbon.

"I think you need to understand what we're up against, Zak. You are an all-powerful professor who has used your charismatic authority to lure a young girl into your sexual trap. She's not the aggressor, she is the victim."

"Wait a second, it's not like that at all. I told you, she pursued me. I've got emails that prove it." He was sweating now. Was this his life?

"It doesn't matter. They will use the fact that there is a power differential against you. For them, everything is black and white. You and I know that romantic and sexual relationships are a dance. I slept with a few professors in college because I wanted to. Lots of young women did, almost like a sport. There were no victims. But these women buy into this melodramatic version of feminism that believes all men are rapists and all women are victims. It's not feminism. It denies the agency of women. It's anti-feminist. But these HR bitches came of age in the seventies and that's the fucked up version of feminism they subscribed to. I've seen it a million times. So accept the fact that they want you to be a sexual predator. It fulfills an ideology they've committed themselves to. They're damaged women, damaged by society, and this is their victim feminism." She paused to hand Zak a bottle of water.

Zak took a deep breath. "This is not a black and white issue."

"It doesn't matter."

"She wanted to have sex with me a lot more than I wanted have sex with her."

"It doesn't matter."

"Jesus Christ. So is there any defense against this bullshit?"

"We need to do three things. We need to make a strong case that you are an asset to the university. And we need to scare them with a lawsuit and the threat of a wave of bad publicity. Lastly, we need to demonstrate that Kiko is acting this way because you broke up with her, not because you took advantage of her."

"Well, she's completely crazy, so…"

Nevada interrupted him. "Be careful here. I agree that she seems emotionally unstable, but they can say that you saw that as an opportunity to manipulate her. It could go either way."

"Fuck. People should have to wear signs that say whether or not they are crazy so you can decide before you get involved with them," said Zak.

"Agreed on that one. That would have saved me one very short marriage." A little peek into her back story. "You had no reason to know she was unstable when this started, but they are going to assume you did. Remember, you are a predator."

"Oh, right. I forgot. What about the publicity thing? I was hoping we could keep all this quiet. I really don't want this splashed across the local news." The slab of concrete seemed to be growing.

"There are stories like this all over the country. College professors are easy targets of this hysteria and it cripples the cases of actual sexual abuse. They are obligated to keep these proceedings confidential but you, my friend, are not. Look, this is your case not my cause, but if you want to threaten to drag the university's name through the mud we can quite easily. All we need is a rally of female students to come out in support of you and a few local reporters and they could end up looking really bad."

"Or I could," said Zak.

"Everything is a gamble in this business."

Kelly was in her office deciding on whether or not to read an email from her ex-husband or daydream a bit more about her Sunday with Walt that didn't end on the eighteenth green. A knock on her door brought her head back to campus. It was Abigail Williams.

"Hi, Kelly. Have a minute?"

"Oh, hi Abby. Yeah, come on in." Was Walt now sending his underlings to avoid any look of impropriety? She liked the impropriety.

Abigail Williams was a large woman with short hair and visceral loyalty to the bureaucracy that was invisible to the students of the university. She ran Woodbine's affairs with a stern ruthlessness. Managing the inner workings of the school made up for the absence of a personal life. Like Catholic nuns married to Jesus, she was married to Woodbine's administration.

"I wanted to pow-wow a little bit before this Crisp thing tomorrow. There's another wrinkle I think we can use to sanction him." She made air quotes with her fingers when she used the word *sanction*. "We've received a long letter from an inmate in Eastern Oregon who is his subject or something. It claims that Crisp brags about getting students drunk so he can sleep with them." Stan Stipich, you have perfect timing.

A smile spread across Kelly's face. "Holy God. I knew it! Can we use it at the hearing tomorrow?"

"Well, you can. I'm supposed to be impartial in this matter. I'm also bringing the faculty representative to the hearing. It's in the by-laws so it's gonna be Duncan Paone from Chemistry. He's firmly on our side and as disgusted by this little insurgency as Walt is. I'm sure Crisp will bring Robin Nielsen and probably a lawyer so we need a firewall."

"He's really disgusting, isn't he?" Kelly asked knowing the answer.

"He certainly is. For all the female students who he's done this to we need to get him out the door as quickly as possible."

And that was that. The die was cast.

Lenny dedicated Monday evening to getting Zak's head and heart out of the sling. He had spent the day meeting with The Falsies and their lawyer (Mollie's uncle) and going over the publishing agreement. Afterwards they wanted to go out for drinks on the promise of the advance that was coming their way when the paperwork cleared, but Lenny begged off saying he had previous plans. Then he pulled Mollie aside, telling her that he was meeting Zak at Jinks and she should stop by because the boy could probably use a pretty smiling face.

Zak didn't go to his office after his meeting with Nevada. He went home and opened a bottle of wine. Oregon pinot. Blood of damp Christ. When he got a text from Lenny to meet him at Jinks, he finished a deep glass with a few gulps. Why not drink tonight? Why the fuck not?

Needless to say, Zak got to Jinks before Lenny and saddled up to the bar, switching from wine to whiskey. Bessy Smith was singing "Muddy Water" and the mood seemed down. He felt like Frank Sinatra on the cover of the 1959 album *No One Cares*. His circle of friends had disappeared while he was in a coma. His colleagues had began to avoid him as soon was word was out that unionizers were becoming targets for a purge. The administrators that he had previously considered part of his university family wanted to rebrand him as a rapist. And there was a fake Japanese girl that was hellbent on destroying him for spurning her.

On the Facebook app on his phone he checked in to Jinks and wrote, "I feel like I'm in a bad version of *Fatal Attraction*." The rather cryptic post was a reference to the 1987 film in which Michael Douglas has an affair with Glenn Close. When he tries to break it off she goes completely mental and tries to wreck his life. In the end, his wife kills her in a scene that had a lot of men cheering in the Reagan era.

Then Lenny arrived, swinging the bar open like he was in an Old West saloon. Seeing Zak hunched over the bar he moved into the space next to him.

"Barkeep! A shot of Cazadores for my friend and I," he said with his arm around Zak's shoulder. Zak barely looked up but the bartender didn't seem amused and continued to fill a few more beer glasses before grabbing the tequila off the middle shelf.

"I have a feeling this night is going to end with my head in a toilet," muttered Zak.

"No, no, we're going to pick things up. Give me a very quick recap of your meeting with the hot lawyer lady and then we're going to do these shots, put some Stones on the jukebox and celebrate all the joy of life itself." A simple man with a simple plan.

"Right. Okay, basically I'm fucked. These women think I represent all that's wrong with men in the world and are ready to kick me to the curb. The end."

"Alright, we can work with that. More important, did she ask about me?"

"Who?"

"Hot lawyer lady!"

"How did this become about you, Lenny? No. But I told her that you met Kiko so you might have to provide an affidavit or something. It's not court so the rules are different."

"But you think she's gonna come on strong?"

"Who?" asked Zak, again.

"Hot lawyer lady!"

"Strong enough, I hope. Everything's a gamble in this business."

That's when Mollie came in. The bar was filling up with the happy hour crowd but there was still space at the bar by Zak and Lenny.

"Hiya, fellas. Watcha drinking?" She had cool dripping off of her.

"Excuse me! One more shot of tequila here," Lenny barked at the bartender. "Keep it cheery, old friend," he said quietly to Zak. "Why, we are about to enjoy these little glasses of Mexican liquid," he said to Mollie.

Salt. Shot. Lime. Suddenly the evening had completely different trajectory.

"Mollie's voice is coming to a TV set near you. The deal was signed today. We're gonna start working to place some songs this week," said Lenny.

"Sweet Jesus, I hope it's a commercial for a toilet bowl cleaner. That would make mama so proud," said Mollie, looking up at the ceiling like Jesus was looking down from the lights. Then she turned to Zak who was hoping the shot wasn't making his face any more discombobulated. "So, Lenny tells me you're old enough to remember when there was actual music on MTV. What was that like, old man?"

"Ah, those were the days," Zak pined. "I seem to remember a lot of funny haircuts."

"C'mon, there were some great songs then," Lenny interjected. "Don't tell me you still don't get a chubby when you hear 'Rock the Casbah' now."

"And then I lose it when I hear 'Wake Me Up Before You Go Go'," said Zak.

"Here, give me a dollar. I will find four totally awesome 80s songs on the jukebox, and we can explain to Miss Mollie here what the songs actually looked like." The move was an effort to let Mollie have a little one-on-one time with the sad professor while Lenny ordered a round of PBRs and made a beeline for the jukebox.

She leaned in and Zak focused on the spot where her neck met her right shoulder. It seemed like he was still high on pot because he felt himself linger there long enough to think it might be a nice place to move in to, at least on days when he didn't have to get up early the next morning.

"So how's it going? He told me you were going through some shit." Those words came out of that neck.

"Oh, just some work drama. Ain't no big thing." Zak was committed to not thinking about it tonight. "So are you excited about this deal? You guys are really good. You deserve to have a bigger audience. Advertising is the way to go these days."

"I guess it's better than going on *The Voice*, right? I mean, my heart broke when Carrie Brownstein started doing Old Navy commercials. But I guess it's pretty cool."

"It's really cool. How many people are listening to Feist or Band of Horses now because they heard them in a commercial. Big things, Mollie. I predict big things. I get a little thrill just sitting her next to you."

"That might be the tequila talking. So are we going to hang out again? I had a lot fun the other night," Mollie softly cooed.

"I think *that's* the tequila talking." Zak couldn't figure out what her deal was. He was so banged up. "But you know I'd like to."

"We should go out for karaoke," she said.

"No, just no to that. I, um, can't sing." Zak felt like sitting on the floor.

Before she could try to twist his arm. Lenny returned, beers in hand, to announce, "Get ready for some Duran Duran."

Zak felt his phone vibrate in his pocket. It was a text from Nevada Standish.

Got the hearing moved to Wednesday at 11 am. Sorry. Wish it was more time. Call tomorrow.

The news meant he could truly let go and not worry about making sure all his lame ducks were in row before he went to sleep. It also meant the execution would be only delayed by a day. Another day of his stomach burning, waiting for the bureaucrats to complete their pointless mission.

"Important news?" asked Lenny.

"Yeah, it's news that I can rock all night. Give me that beer."

And that's how the night went. The three talked rock shop and told Portland "back in the day" stories. All three were so drunk by ten o'clock that they had to Uber their way home. But before that Zak asked Mollie to go to a movie on Thursday. "Anything without spaceships," he said. She showed him some pictures on her Facebook page of when she was a little Riot Grrrl that Zak had already looked at (being careful not to "Like" them, as much as he wanted to).

Since Zak's house was the first stop, Lenny convinced Mollie to come in and crash there. Zak was too far gone by this point to way in. The wine/whiskey/beer mix moved him a few steps back towards his previous comatose state. He could only drool something that seemed like agreement. So they sent the Uber driver on her way and, after Mollie and Lenny poured Zak into his bed, they stayed up talking and playing Zak's records.

Zak was riding his bike into work. It wasn't something he did much anymore but it was a sunny day. He made a left turn from a side street onto a main road towards downtown and almost went over the handlebars. He had felt like he was racing along in a Tour de France and now his bike slowed to a stop and fell over.

The main road was under construction. They were laying a new layer of asphalt and nobody had thought to block the traffic off. Zak drove his bike right into it. His tires sank in the black gravel and he fell into on his right side and started to sink in. The asphalt burned his arm as it disappeared under the new street.

He screamed for help but his voice had suddenly become hoarse. Only a gasp came out. The machinery drowned out what sound he could make and the street pavers all had their back to him. He was stuck in the hot muck. All he could think was, "I'm gonna sue somebody."

Kiko hated the kind of mail that came to her apartment mailbox. It was mostly junk like advertisements for pizza delivery and vet clinics. Millions of trees mowed down on the outside chance that somebody might respond to an ad for another credit card. The trashcan next to the mailboxes in the foyer was full of them. But a letter had come from her mother that didn't go into the trashcan. It spent a couple of days on the kitchen counter.

She didn't feel like going to sleep so she thought she'd better open it. It was a connection to the world she denied but it might be important. Probably not. In fact she surely would regret reading it, but she really didn't have anything better to do, so she found a knife she could use to slice open this ancient artifact called an envelope.

Dear Jeong,

How are you? We have not heard from you in a while. Your sister is going to spend this summer in the Philippines and was hoping to have your room when she returned. We all hope you well and are completing your education in a timely manner.

I must ask you about the $3000 loan I gave you last year for your books and living expenses. You agreed to pay it back with earnings from your teaching job a month ago. Have you sent the check?

Your father is very concerned that you are not honoring the family with your time in Portland. It is very important to him that you pay your debts and finish your study with high marks. Do not forget where you are from.

dangsin-ui eomeoni

Kiko took a pen and outlined her left hand on the letter giving the one finger salute. Then she threw the letter in the trash.

There would be no check. That bridge was on fire. She cracked open her laptop and headed to white light of Reddit.

Lenny had a lot of jobs when he was young. He was a busboy and an assistant roof shingler (that's the guy who carries the heavy tar shingles up to the roofers) and, briefly, a telemarketer for a bogus veterans' charity. But this had to be the worst of all jobs. The smell alone made it a like a dream of death.

Every job has a hierarchy, a ranking with a top rung and most horridly, an absolute bottom. Somebody's gotta wipe down the tanning beds or clean the bathroom in the dive bar. In the mortuary field, anything might seem like the bottom, but if you were where Lenny was, you would trade your left nut to be the guy who swept out the crematorium. Lenny was the new kid on the block and his job was to clean the asses of the dead.

People regularly vacated their bowls at the moment of death but it is not uncommon for corpses to shit, pee and fart for days as the body lets go of the blood flow to the muscles that hold everything in. Since most people don't want a body that smells like a truck stop toilet on display at the funeral, somebody's gotta a wipe dat ass.

Lenny stood in front of a corpse of a dead white man, 47 years old and 350 pounds. There was a white blanket over the body as it lay motionless on the preparation table. The blanket didn't hide the sound of the wet flatulence as the last of the stomach contents turned to gas or the fact that this blob of a man had an erection. Undertakers call it "angel lust." Lenny stared at the job and tried to remember when he was a rock star.

He went to the counter to grab a stack of paper towels and saw that the towels were all folded up lyrics sheets of his songs. The sound of something hitting the floor pulled his gaze back the to table. The man's teeth were falling out his mouth, one by one. "Wait, that's not right," Lenny thought.

4

Zak woke up with his right arm under Mollie's neck. At first he was startled and then somewhat pleased and then concerned that he was stuck. He was still in his clothes as was she, so he shouldn't be too pleased, but he had to pee and didn't want to wake her for fear of an awkward conversation at five in the morning.

He gently rotated his shoulder away from her face and thought she mumbled something about "just friends" that made him feel like his dream life was becoming braided to his waking life in a way that blurred some important lines. But as far as he could tell he was in his house now on the way to his bathroom to release the various potions he had consumed. The world is a strange place at five am, quiet and barely illuminated. It's the perfect time to see ghosts.

After a long pee that made him think he was still high he popped open his laptop to see if he had any messages. None that were pressing. He made a brief to-do list for Wednesday's hearing that included explaining his important research and how his pregnant wife was crushed by a rock so don't expect him to be a fucking rational actor. Then he got half undressed and quietly climbed back into bed with Mollie.

Zak had read that these little breaks in a night's sleep were a doorway into lucid dreaming. The hardcore dreamers call it WILD, Wake Initiated Lucid Dreaming. This seemed like as good as time as any to find Claire and maybe right some wrongs, at least in another dimension. So he laid still in his bed with his "just friend" next to him as he tried to conjure her memory up.

As he slipped into the twilight between wake and sleep, he focused on her voice. "There's three of us now," he heard her say. There were streaks of light under his eyelids as a kaleidoscope of colors filtered in from either the dawn sunlight or the back of his brain, and then the blackness that was now as comfortable as home plate.

"C'mon man, why do you want to see her so bad?" asked a voice.

"What? Where is this?" responded Zak.

It was one of the police officers that had been living inside his head. Just one. He had curly brown hair and a square jaw.

"Oh, you know," he said.

"Shit, you guys are driving me insane. I'm supposed to be able to control these dreams," said Zak, exasperated that this whole lucid dreaming thing was more trouble than it was worth. Lenny had already given up on it, maybe he should, too.

"Sure, sure, you can. But why do you want to waste all this time on her? You could literally do anything you want." He sat down next to Zak on a bench that didn't appear to exist. "Why not take a break from your quest tonight. I know what you want right now."

"Music?" Zak said without hesitating.

"Exactly. That's who you are. What kind of music?"

"Very sad jazz."

"Jesus, man you're such a bummer. You could go to see Hendrix at the Monterey Pop Festival and you want downbeat."

Zak got defensive. "Hey, that's some good shit. And Portland had an amazing jazz scene back in the 40s. Look, I know what I want." It was time to take some agency in this mindscape.

"And you know how to get it but don't say I didn't warn you. Have fun, Professor Blue Note." And the cop faded.

It was a rainy night in Portland, like most nights, but Zak had lost his bearings. Nothing looked right. He was on a busy street corner with lots of black and white pedestrians in fine clothes right out of an old movie. The street sign said this was the intersection of Northeast Weidler and Northeast Williams, but that was where the I-5 overpass should be. There was no Interstate 5 let alone an overpass. There was no giant Moda Center, where the Trailblazers played. Not even a Memorial Coliseum, where The Beatles played in 1965. This was Portland before all that.

"Oh, hell yeah!" said Zak out loud, startling a young African-American man in a tan suit and a fedora.

The steamroller of progress had obliterated the heart of the Albina neighborhood. The African-American population, that had been pushed there from downtown in the early twentieth century and then pushed there from Vanport after the massive 1948 flood, was pushed out by all those urban development projects designed to make the area safe for white people. The drivers of thousands of cars that drive down I-5 everyday, passing along the east bank of Portland's Willamette River had no idea what was once overhead. The Williams and Weidler intersection was now a mass of concrete and green houses gasses, created by commuters either going north or south on the eternally clogged highway, or going east to west on the eternally clogged NE Weidler/NE Broadway corridor. And heaven help you if there is a Blazers game. People thought about the traffic, not jazz.

But that was now, this was then. Zak could smell the cigarettes and cigars and perfume and leaded gasoline. How many times had he wished he had a time machine to see this version of Portland, heavily segregated with a black beat that defied the white sensibilities of the pioneer town?

"Excuse me, is there any good jazz on tonight?" He asked a young black couple that looked at him like he dropped out of a flying saucer. "Sorry, I just got in from out of town."

"Why, yes sir, there is. Later on there's a session across the street at the Acme but we're going down to the Dude Ranch. Pic and Pat got a combo from New York in town called Jazz at the Philharmonic. It should be hep if that's what you are looking for, sir. It's just down the block."

Zak forgot about the deference to whites that came from generations of in-your-face racism. "Thank you, good sir. That sounds perfect. You two have a wonderful evening and maybe I'll see you there." He resisted the temptation to tag along and spent a little bit of time walking around North Williams Avenue, a stretch that was now as nondescript as any urban landscape on Earth. Tonight it was the exact opposite, filled with music, laughing people and amazing cars, none later than 1940s models. It felt like a dream because it was, but it also felt real. He stopped to check on all five of his senses as he touched the front door of the Madrona record store on the corner of Williams and Broadway.

Worried he would shake himself out of the dream he walked down the hill to the Dude Ranch, in a building that still stands and now houses a coffee shop and high tech offices across from the Rose Garden complex. It still had the brick walls with the rounded windows, but there were some crazy cats outside instead of bike messengers and people looking for a parking place for the Beyoncé concert. Zak moved right toward the door on the corner and a tall black man in a yellow suit ushered him in.

"Have a good time, Professor Crisp," he said in a Creole accent.

Inside the walls were adorned with paintings of cowboys. Men and women, black and white, were dancing in front of the small stage crowded with eight musicians blowing down the walls to the classic tune, "Stompin' at the Savoy." It was hard to believe that white-bread Portland ever swung like this. He moved past the clouds of cigar smoke and odd stares to get closer to the band.

Zak wasn't a huge jazz expert, but he knew enough to recognize a young Charlie Mingus on bass and none other than Coleman Hawkins shredding licks on tenor saxophone. This was jazz ground zero. It had been cold outside but the sweat was dripping inside and Zak put his hand on the bar to stay in the moment.

"They might not be much to look at but these coons sure can play," said a white man in a pinstriped suit.

"Excuse me? That's Coleman fucking Hawkins, one of the greatest musicians alive! What have you done?" Zak didn't need the distraction.

"Hey, bub, no need to get your dander up. I'm just enjoying this before the city shuts it down. No way they're gonna let these negroes get their hands on all the white women that come here. You know what I mean, right?" The guy was smug in a way that said he had the whole establishment propping him up. "The war is over. It's time to get things back to normal," he added before walking away.

Right on cue the drummer brought the tempo down and Hawkins took the microphone off the stand. "Right now were going to play one of our favorite ballads, 'Body and Soul'." The crowd cheered like it was a homecoming. "And to sing it we've got one of your own, a hometown girl named Miss Mollie Saldano. Please give her a nice welcome."

There she was. Both in the bed beside him and on stage at the Dude Ranch in 1945 with her hair pinned back like Jessica Rabbit in a dress that could have belonged to an Andrews sister. The singer that Zak had heard screaming at The Lonesome Pine was now cooing to the jazz standard, with patrons slow dancing in front of her. "My heart is sad and lonely, for you I cry…" Maybe there was room in his heart for her. For now he was going to listen and sway and try to not think about the present world or the race cops who were about to raid this one.

5

The buzzing of the phone on the bed stand awoke Zak and Mollie at the same time. He begged pardon to his guest and saw that it was Nevada calling.

"Hi, Zak? Am I waking you up? Sorry, but we've only got this day to prepare for your hearing tomorrow. We need to make the most of it."

"Hey, yeah, I've got my classes today but I can work on it after that." He had managed to put the whole thing out of his mind for a bit.

"That's not gonna work. You need to cancel your classes. I need you to get to work on that statement and get me a draft as soon as possible so I can go over it. In the meantime, I'm going to put the paperwork in to depose Kiko. That should prevent her from filing any criminal charges. So get up, okay?"

"Criminal charges?" He wished he hadn't said that out loud in front of Mollie. "Okay, let me see if I can get my TA to cover my classes. I'll let you know as soon as I have something."

"I emailed you some bullet points to be sure to hit. Alright, get to work. I'll be waiting."

"That work drama?" asked Mollie, looking starkly innocent in the morning sunlight against the dark backdrop of Zak's reality. "Don't worry, I can show myself out."

"Stop. No rush. Let's have coffee first. I need to start today on a positive note." Zak felt slightly human with her there, partially redeemed. Maybe there was light at the end of the tunnel for Frankenstein's monster.

So Zak put on a fresh pot and a Decemberists album and Lenny joined them in the living room. Zak gave Mollie the basics of the case against him so she knew what she was potentially getting into. She seemed more impressed than concerned.

"You think you're the first person to sleep with some obsessive nutjob?" she asked. "Maybe when you have a free week I can tell you about the baggage I still lug around." Zak's wasn't the only story in the world. Like most women, Mollie had learned to keep her problems locked up for fear of scaring off suitors. After thirty everybody's got baggage that's gotta be dealt with.

Mollie wasn't scared off but she did have a lunch meeting with her lawyer-uncle and told Zak she'd call later in the day. Lenny was up and then out to visit his father one more time before heading to back to Seattle. And Zak called Heather to ask if she could cover his classes so he could get some "research" written up before a looming deadline. She told him that there were some rumors going around campus and she hoped he was okay. That only made him feel worse.

Delia gave Kiko a job at the Devil's House. They were down an Asian stripper and she said she could start on Tuesday's lunch shift. So here she was in the dressing room before her big debut. She had bought one piece of lingerie to dance in with hope of more when she started making some tips. Sitting in front of the mirror it seemed to be all wrong, like a bad housewife dressing up for a bad husband. But she was more concerned that customers would focus on the razor stubble from her poorly done crotch shave. She let the humanity drain out of her fingertips and toes as she heard the DJ announce, "Coming up next our new girl from the Far East, Koneko!" Kitten.

She had brought a stack of J-pop CDs to dance to but the DJ said no way in hell, so Kiko took the stage, like a million strippers before her, to Guns N Roses' "Paradise City." She never had been much of a dancer and rejected most American style of dancing as "too black." Instead she blankly moved around the pole on the small stage, making eye contact with the half dozen customers in the dark bar. First it was contempt for them and then it was pleading. The DJ helped out by announcing it was her first time stripping which brought a few sympathy dollars on the rack around the stage. Let's see the scared girl take off her clothes for our pocket change.

As the dollar bills appeared, Kiko began to feel a powerful surge. She could use her hatred towards these men against them. They wanted to be punished. They wanted to give her their dirty money.

Lenny was standing in front of his father, his clothes in a pile on the floor. He wanted his father to see him naked. To see how the boy grew into a man. He sucked in his belly and tried to channel Michelangelo's David. He let the older man's eyes trace his form his forehead to his feet.

Then he laid face down on the bed. He could hear his father come out of the chair and move toward him. First his hands were on Lenny's back and then his breath was on his neck. His father's naked body was then softly on top of him, warming him. Lenny knew this was how to keep him close and not lose him again. His father anchored himself inside him and told him that he loved him.

The framed picture on the dresser of Lenny as a boy with his mother now included his father. But there was a gasp and image faded back to just the two.

The extra day didn't seem like much to Zak. He had a sent several versions of his chronology and statement to Nevada for editing. She had collected an affidavit from Lenny about meeting Kiko and the consensual nature of the their relationship (which led Lenny to send an excited text to Zak that just said, *Boing!*). There was long phone conversation with Robin, who had promised to be there but Nevada thought it would incite the union busting administrators. Matthew Brant, Zak's department chair begged off from coming to speak on Zak's behalf. He had gotten a copy of the allegations from the dean and was told that he was officially "management" in this matter and was "advised" not to come to the hearing. There was no time to fill in anyone else on the broad background story so Zak hoped his honest testimony would be enough.

He had his most professorial outfit picked out and a pot of coffee in his veins. What else could he do to prepare? He took a photo of Claire off the fridge and kissed it, tucking it into his jacket pocket. He remembered her saying how important his work was and how he should think of jumping off to a university that paid better.

The hearing was on the sixth floor of the administration building, back into the lion's den. Robin was in the lobby to wish him well. As the two professors and one lawyer chatted, President Woodbine walked by, with his head down. Later Zak would wish that he had grabbed him to make an appeal regarding his loyalty to the institution and the whole "high-minded values" thing. But he stood there frozen, like he was watching his hangman walking to the gallows.

At 10 am it was time to enter the room. Nevada was dressed smartly in a black jacket and pencil skirt with gold thread, her hair pulled back and her glasses on her head. Zak felt a bit of support having a female lawyer defend him against these accusations. He wasn't a "bro," trying to get away with some drunken indiscretion. He was still hopeful reason would win the day and everyone could get back to work, so he kept up a brave face.

Inside everyone was smiles and collegiality. There might even have been some talk about the weather. But make no mistake, the university frontline was intimidating. Seated on one side of the table was Kelly Claiborne, Dean Margolis, Abigail Williams, and Chemistry Professor Duncan Paone. The four horsemen of the apocalypse. All four, on a normal day, would have been seen as colleagues, sharing wine and cheese after President Woodbine's annual convocation. But today was not any day. It was the showdown, the beginning of the purge.

"Well, let's go ahead and get started. I don't want to keep us too long," said Williams, putting her reading glasses on. Zak immediately thought she looked like Mr. Potter, from *It's a Wonderful Life*. Maybe it was the constipated look on her face. Lionel Barrymore died in 1954 so it was possible, but Williams seemed too old to be the reincarnation of one of the best Ebenezer Scrooge's ever.

"We reserve the right to not call this hearing to a close until we feel all the evidence and statements have been presented," said Nevada, speaking for Zak which was fine because he was busy thinking about Lionel Barrymore.

"Very well. The first statement will come from Vice Provost Claiborne and then Professor Crisp will have the opportunity to respond." Williams was in place as the judge, jury and executioner.

Claiborne took over. She looked like the angel of death, too much make up and hair dyed flat black but failing to cover her grey roots. She kept her eyes on her report. "After an extensive investigation we have found that Professor Crisp violated the sacred relationship between teacher and student by sexually pursuing Kiko Matsugane…"

Zak groaned at the wording. It was the other way around but Claiborne was working a narrative that made Kiko the victim. Nevada put her hand on Zak's arm as if to say, patience, you'll have your turn.

"Yes, sexually pursuing Miss Matsugane. This relationship was of a romantic, amorous and sexual nature violating university policy about faculty-student relations. The sexual part of this relationship began after the consumption of alcohol and fits the university's definition of date rape." Zak looked at the ceiling. Wait your turn boy. "Furthermore, ample evidence demonstrates that Professor Crisp sent Miss Matsugane numerous sexually explicit emails, including several that could be viewed as bestiality and child pornography. Additionally, once the complaint was filed, Professor Crisp sent hostile texts to the victim in violation of the No Contact rule. Professor Crisp's actions do not reflect the high standards we hold at this university and it is our position that he be terminated from his faculty position immediately and all his privileges at the university be revoked." Short and sweet. Was this a dream? Zak felt a salty taste on the back of his tongue.

As much as he wanted to identify this hearing for what it was, he kept calm. Nevada put her hand on his back and Zak opened his prepared statement that had been word-smithed extensively over the last twenty-four hours.

He thanked the assembled for allowing him to defend himself against these bogus charges. He went through the chronology of how Kiko had been relentless in her pursuit of him, including initiating the first sexual contact, and how he tried to end the relationship when she appeared to show signs of obsessiveness. He discussed how they had drinks, like any typical dating situation and the sex didn't occur until much later, when the effects of the alcohol had disappeared. He then tried to explain the world of Japanese anime to the panel and how it would be understandable for Americans to, at first, view it as perverse. Nevada had prepared a small report on hentai anime, how popular it was across the globe and some examples of typical images that she handed to each of the representatives of the university. They acted shocked at that cartoon images and Nevada tried to read the faces of this jury.

Zak continued with a summary of contributions to the university, including his awards, the popularity of his classes and the fit of his important research with the university's mission statement. He explained how he had been on this path since his freshman year in college, building a career that would help to make the world a kinder place. He made a strong case that he was a feminist, morally opposed to sexual exploitation and that his research and coursework, especially his class on the medicalization of birth, were all designed with an eye to empower young women in a world where they are often taken advantage of. He read the last line of the statement very slowly. "I am an asset to this university not a liability based on unsubstantiated accusations of a former fling." Nevada wasn't sure about the word, "fling."

"They seem pretty substantiated to me," said Duncan Paone, who looked like he was about five seconds from retirement. ""Professor Crisp, are you aware that Miss Matsugane is now working as an exotic dancer?" Paone asked. Zak and Nevada looked at each other, both in shock of the depth they were going. "I spoke to her yesterday as part of our investigation and she told me that your abusive treatment of her created a mindset that this was the only work she could do. Stripping."

Zak was defensive. "I had no idea but that should speak to the evidence that's she's completely nuts. I didn't make her do anything, including become a stripper."

Kelly wanted to jump back in to the lynch mob. "Professor Crisp, who is Stan Stipich?"

What the fuck. "Um, he's an inmate who is a part of my research on inmate health behaviors. Why?"

"Did you ever tell him that you often take female students out to get them drunk and have sex with them?"

What the cluster fuck. Well, here's why Stipich had gone silent. Zak thought he was over his little tantrum, but instead he had mounted a character assassination campaign against him. "Absolutely not! It's not true and I never said that. This guy is completely psychotic!"

"It seems like everyone who has something bad to say about you is crazy, Professor," said Paone, making air quotes. "Let's be clear, we are going to remove you from this university for the sake of all involved."

"No, you don't understand. He's actually psychotic. You can call the prison and ask. He's on several anti-psychotic medications. I have letters that prove it." He hoped that Heather had held on to those rambling letters.

Finally, Nevada stepped in. "I find it quite shocking that the university is not defending Professor Crisp against these flimsy accusations instead of using them to railroad him. This man has built a respectable career here and may have made some poor choices, but nothing that actually violates university policy as I understand it. He is still grieving from the loss of his pregnant wife and was taken advantage of by an opportunistic woman. Not a girl, but a woman. I think you realize that none of this so-called evidence would ever stand up in a court of law."

Williams stepped in. "I assure you, Ms. Standish, nobody is being railroaded here. We are just trying to establish the facts of this case."

"One might think the judgement has already been rendered based on the presentation of these questionable facts. I move that any statements from this inmate whom I have not had the opportunity to interview be stricken from the record." Her red hair gave her face a certain fire that Zak hoped would shut them down.

"This is not a criminal court. The evidence will remain in the file. If you would like contact information for Mr. Stipich, we can provide it to you," said Williams.

"Thank you." So much for the fire.

Zak had one more chance to clarify all his points and at some point decided it would be wise to fall on his sword and beg forgiveness for his transgressions. When Williams agreed that Kiko appeared unstable he felt a breeze of hope. But then he realized that she was of the mind that Zak knew she was unstable from the get-go and was preying on emotionally troubled "girls."

Nevada provided a closing statement, full of solid bullet points that stated repeatedly that this was a relationship among consenting adults that began after Kiko was a student in his class, not during. She asked Williams to review Zak's extensive curriculum vitae to see his numerous accomplishments as a representative of the university. Then she paused before launching this mortar shell.

"It must be said that this questionable persecution of my client is happening against the backdrop of the campaign by faculty to unionize for a fair contract. There are those who would view this case as a clear example of malicious prosecution that has nothing to do with his consensual relationship with a student and everything to do with his efforts on behalf of the union. I'm quite sure that this theory would have a lot of legs outside of this room." Drop the mike.

"Again," said Williams, "this is not a court of law, just a hearing to to establish the facts. But I would request that all parties respect the need to keep these proceedings confidential. Does anybody else have any questions.?"

The dean had remained silent for the entire hearing. She had a sad look on her face that Zak couldn't interpret. Did it mean, "Lord all the bad things that have happened to this guy. Maybe we should cut him a break." Or did it mean, "I can't believe this disgusting rapist has lived among us, undetected until now."

After everyone had been dismissed, Zak and Nevada met in a coffee shop across the street from the administration building for a confab. Robin was there wanting an update, but Nevada sent her away so she could have a private conversation with her client.

"Boy, that was about as close to a kangaroo court as you get. I half expected a baby joey to pop out of the dean's pouch," she said, untying her hair.

"That bad, huh?"

"Yeah, that was a show. They're required by your guidelines to do it. They've already made their decision. Let me tell you about what just happened. Obviously, they have something they think they can use to scare the other faculty. You're the sacrificial lamb, letting them demonstrate their absolute power. It makes sense to take down someone with tenure first. It show's that nobody is safe. But there's something else going on there that was so clear to me."

"What do you mean?" asked Zak, hoping it provided hope.

"That you're a man. You are there representing all men. These women in their fifties or sixties see you dating a woman in her twenties and it kills them. If you're a woman that age and single and all the men your age are dating younger women, who is there left for you? Some guy in his eighties? As they get older, their looks go away and the only power they have is in their jobs. As a woman, I know this feeling. But it's also why HR departments are loaded with older women who want to bust every man in sight. They think they're being good feminists, but they're denying there are plenty of young women who like dating older men. Younger men are idiots. Believe me. So these women see you as representing every man who thinks they're invisible but who will fall over himself for any young trollop."

"Trollops, huh? Wow. I did get the feeling that they really hated me. You think that's Abigail Williams, too?" Zak thought Nevada might have minored in psychology.

"No, she's a lesbian."

"Huh?

"Yeah, I'd know that haircut and belly fat anywhere. She hates you too but for different reasons. She probably spent most of her life in the closet so she resents everybody who has been out hooking up while she stayed home, watching episodes of *Cagney and Lacey*. It's super sad but a common tale. And that hatchet face of hers only adds to her hatred of the world."

Seemed harsh. "Okay, what does all this mean?"

"Oh, you're fucked. But we can still hope the threat of going public will scare them off. But just in case, we need to prepare to file a lawsuit against them. We should send a tort notice tomorrow. I need to interview your friend Lenny and anybody that talked to you the night you and Kiko went to go see that band." That sounded like more billable hours and dragging Mollie into it. "And I'm going to have to depose Kiko. It's going to be a race to get it done before Williams submits her recommendation to the president. So take a break and then come to my office at two. Don't worry. I still have a few tricks up my sleeve."

Kiko was trying to get up a hill that turned into a small tunnel, so she had to crawl on her belly. Finally, she had no room to move and began to get claustrophobic. Her fears were calmed when she realized she was laying on Zak's chest. He was sleeping or unconscious, but she felt safe and strong, like her muscles were being infused with his life force. Staying in the cave for a while seemed like a good idea. Protected.

Suddenly she saw her laptop, her precious laptop, fly over her shoulder and smash against the cave wall. She looked back behind her and there was her mother coming toward her holding a larger mirror, about three feet tall. She raised the mirror up above her head and brought it down on Kiko repeatedly. Each time she slammed the mirror down on her daughter, Kiko saw her own bloody face, defeated. There was really no point in resisting.

"When I live my dream, please be there to meet me." (David Bowie)

Chapter 9:
Need Your Love

1

Zak headed straight home and made himself a drink. He didn't want music. He didn't want legal briefings. He just wanted his life back. A whiskey and Coke seemed like the quickest route. The floor seemed to be dropping out and every possible move was wrong. His queen was exposed and he had no moves left unless his lawyer knew magic.

He crashed on to the couch with his drink and his laptop. Time to lose himself to some online contests. Maybe a kitchen remodel or a trip to Las Vegas. You can't win if you don't enter. But before he got to the contest website he saw that a Facebook message had pinged in from Mollie.

I know you've got a rough day today so I made a little playlist for you. It's a soundtrack for fighters. And no, I didn't put "Eye of the Tiger" on it (as much as I wanted to).

There was a link to a Spotify playlist called "Everything Works if You Let It" that contained these twenty songs:

The Ramones - "Blitzkrieg Bop"
Chumbawumba - "Tubthumping"
Isaac Hayes - "Theme from Shaft"
Britney Spears - "Stronger"
Patti Smith Group - "Pissing in the River"
Eminem - "Lose Yourself"
The Stooges - "Search & Destroy"
MC5 - "Kick Out the Jams"
Judas Priest - "You've Got Another Thing Coming"
Rolling Stones - "Rip This Joint"

The Beatles - "I've Got a Feeling"
Public Enemy - "Fight the Power"
L7 - "Till the Wheels Fall Off"
Motorhead - "Ace of Spades"
The Cult - "Love Removal Machine"
Crime Mob - "Stilettos"
Pink - "Funhouse"
Gang of Four - "I Found That Essence Rare"
Husker Du - "Divide and Conquer"
Billy Squire - "Everybody Wants You"

He clicked on *play* and let the sound of punk rock from a thousand years ago feed into his blood system. Better than the sound was the fact that she had spent the time to craft a set of songs to move him forward. It reminded him of all the mix tapes he made before his musical world had become digitized. So he gave himself a little time to enjoy it and mindlessly bop around on the internet before getting ready for the next last ditch meeting with Nevada.

He didn't get halfway through the Chumbawumba song when there was a knock on the door. Looking out the front window he saw it was a Portland police officer. What was next in this cavalcade of shit?

"Zachary Crisp?"

He nodded and hesitantly said, "Yes?"

"I'm Officer Overstreet. I'm here to serve a restraining order to you with regard to a Ms. Kiko Matsugane. From this point until the order is revoked you are not allowed to contact her or be within one hundred feet of her at anytime. If you do it will be considered harassment and will be reported to us. You will be arrested. Do you understand this?"

Zak was stunned. Where had this insanity gone to now? "No, I don't understand. Do you know anything about this?" He needed some context.

The officer seemed like he had delivered this bad news before. "Not much, sir. Apparently you made a threat to kill her on Twitter. I'm going to give you a contact number with the order that you can call for more information. Often these things are big misunderstandings and can be cleared up by a judge." It didn't seem like he was going to throw Zak to the ground just yet. "You do understand the order. No contact, one hundred feet."

"I understand. Thank you for your service."

The police officer gave Zak a confused smile and returned to his cruiser. Zak sat down on his front steps and wondered what the neighbors must think. Then he called the number on the top of the form.

After a frustrating Portland Police phone menu he got to an actual person, a woman, who took the case number. Apparently, Kiko had seen his Facebook post from Monday stating that he felt like he was in a version of *Fatal Attraction* and took it as some kind of veiled threat that he planned to kill her.

"Yeah, I posted that but it wasn't a threat. I haven't even seen that film but doesn't the wife, not Michael Douglas, kill Glenn Close ?"

"Yeah, Ann Archer shoots her in the chest. I've seen it ten times," said the woman. "Look, the sooner you appeal this, the better. You got a lawyer?"

His next call was to Nevada to give her the bad news and her response was simple, "We're gonna need a bigger boat." She urged him to consider adding a criminal defense lawyer to his team to stop any possible indictment. They could discuss it during their meeting. Either way he was going to have free up another two or three grand to pay for his defense. He asked if they could put off talking for a day and she told him to take a quick nap instead.

He couldn't do that, so he walked to the corner store and bought cheese crackers and a Powerball ticket. On the way home he fantasized about taking his millions and buying a small plane; a small plane that he could fly into the side of the administration building.

After two cheese and pickle sandwiches, half a bag of stale tortilla chips and three gulps of whiskey he went to Caroline's nursery to lay on the floor. Closing his eyes he tried to summon Claire. He needed her to take him back in time and escape this madness. The beautiful, smooth child of their love had been replaced with a hideous cancerous omnivore, consuming everything in its path. His life was infected with a virus that was rapidly destroying its host.

When Zak got to Nevada's office, Lenny was sitting at her desk with a shit-eating grin. He seemed to be oblivious to the fact that the Titanic had broken in half and was making its last circle around the drain. "Hello, old sport," was all he said.

"Hi, Zak. I was getting Lenny's recollection of meeting Kiko and the night she, um, stayed over at your house. I thought it was best to get this part done, now that things have escalated." Nevada's hair was down and Zak felt like he had walked in on something extra-legal.

"Sure. Why not? Let's get everybody involved. Maybe we could even sponsor a screening of *Fatal Attraction* for everyone."

"I fuckin' love that movie!" said Lenny.

"Okay, guys. Let's get to work. I want you to go over this tort claim so we can serve them as soon as possible." Nevada handed him a two page document that said he was seeking potential damages due to the university's "adverse employment actions," based on claims of breach of employment contract, invasion of privacy, defamation, slander, "intentional infliction of emotional distress," and violation of constitutional freedoms, including the freedom of association. It was a sledgehammer to bash Woodbine's screwdriver.

"Wow." Zak tried to imagine the look on the administrators' faces when this was handed to them. "Why not throw the kitchen sink at them, too?"

"Well, that's part two," said Nevada, looking like she was now fully in the zone. "I was hoping that the two of you could help me come up with a list of people in the local media who would be friendly to the cause of faculty or labor struggles. We need to line up supportive students and faculty who are part of the union thing, especially others that have been targeted. We're going to let it leak out that we're going to mount a massive media campaign to clear your name and show them as the aggressors. I'm sure their board of regents is not going to like publicity that shows that the university is this hostile to its faculty."

"What about Kiko?" asked Zak.

"She's a disturbed woman who was manipulated by the administrators to target a union organizer." Plain and simple.

"My Zak in the middle of his own sex scandal!" cheered Lenny.

It didn't sound so exciting to Zak.

Nevada tried to calm things. "Everything hinges on what Williams' decision is. Maybe they're ready to back off. But if not, we've got to be ready to go to the media, get this tort claim filed and file a grievance with the university. That last part would be a lot better if your union was up and operational."

"If we ever get a union," Zak said with a sigh.

"You very well may have one. They're counting the votes now," she said.

Zak had completely missed the card collecting. It would be ironic if the union vote fell short because he had been wrapped up in his drama and escaping to dreamland instead of beating the bushes for faculty support.

Nevada continued. "The problem is that if they decide your case before the vote tally is publicized, the union protection is lost on you. You'll be left to dangle."

Suddenly the clock was ticking and Zak had flashes of Florida in the year 2000.

"Hey, pretty lady. How did it go today?" It was Walt checking in for a postmortem. His normal jolliness seemed tempered.

"Hi." She resisted the urge to say, "Hi, honey." Appearances. "Well, we hit him with a pretty big wall of evidence. He seemed kind of stunned. I think he's gone." Kelly saw it as a win.

"Sort of hate to do it to him. He seemed like a good guy. I guess we'll find out if it was all worthwhile when they finish their little count. A little bird told me they are planning a press conference tomorrow, so we might have some media attention. This is not the part of academics that I enjoy. Hopefully it will blow over soon." Walt put his hands on his belly and struck a Buddha-like pose.

It was exactly the part of academics that Kelly enjoyed; a horse race where she could jockey her way to the front. Just dig the spurs in a little deeper.

"Yeah, speaking of, I don't know if Abby mentioned this but Crisp's lawyer dropped a hint that they might go to the media with this story. Something about malicious prosecution to intimidate faculty. Should we be concerned about any blowback?" There was always the possibility that their little love affair could become fodder for some news rag.

Walt pushed his glasses back up his nose and smiled. "Oh, that's lawyer talk. I wouldn't be too worried. Abigail is going to have her judgement out soon and I think it will be all over. He'll have to pack up his office and move on with his life."

With Lenny headed back to Seattle, Zak went home to watch the clock. The waiting game had begun. Waiting for a verdict from Williams. Waiting for Nevada to put the full response together and appeal the restraining order. Waiting for faculty volunteers to count a bunch of cards. There was still whiskey in the jar.

He left his laptop closed and let NPR take his attention to the middle east and the plight of families trying to get their kids away from dropping bombs and religious extremists. Then a text popped in from Lenny:

Hubba hubba I think I'm in lubba

And don't worry. We all have your back

Before Zak could answer a text blooped in from Mollie

Rough weeks suck. Let me take you out Friday - my treat.

If he could just get to Friday.

Why would he be in New York again? Why did his dreams always bring him there? He knew it was a dream because he had no idea how he got there. He was just there, sitting in the open space downtown that was the 9/11 Memorial. In front of him were the twin fountains where the twin towers once stood. Behind them One World Trade Center, the 107 floor modernist behemoth meant to send a message to the terrorists that you will not cut off our giant phalluses. And it was 1776 feet tall to bring that point home to the historical trivia obsessed Taliban.

Zak looked down into the dark fountain, a stark void to honor the lives that ceased to exist there on that Tuesday. The water calmly cascaded down the walls into a dark hole at the center. He couldn't tell if it was real or some symbolic dream affectation. The border was wrung with all the names of those in the tower and the on the planes that struck it. He slowly walked around the edge until he reached one name.

Sylvia San Pio Resta and her unborn child

He noticed that several of the names were of women and their unborn children and he sat down on the pavement and began to sob. He needed her love and she never knew it. She was taken away before she knew she was needed. Zak squeezed his head between his knees and just wanted this melancholia to end. Let him be reborn into a new lifestream and try to get this one right without killing his family.

"Zak?"

He looked up to see white leather shoes and white pant legs. Looking up farther he saw it was one of the dream cops, the blonde.

"Oh, it's you. What do you want?" He wiped the tears off his cheek.

The man crouched down next to Zak. "Zak, what is it that you really want?"

"I want to see my daughter. I want to see what she was like. Can you do that? I never got to see her face. I want to see it so I can remember it." It was all he really wanted.

"Okay, I think you've earned that much. But it's not a cheap little trick. You need to stay calm and when it's time to go you gotta go. Got it?" He stood up and helped Zak to his feet.

"Yeah, yeah, of course!" The excitement shook his body, which trembled at the thought that he was finally going to meet his daughter.

"Zachary, what's rule number one?"

"Right, stay calm. Okay, where is she?"

The cop pointed to the west, to a tree with a small fence around it. There was woman with a baby in a push stroller next to it. It was her. It was them.

"Over there by the Survivor Tree. Go ahead, my friend." And he walked away.

Zak quickly walked across the park, trying to hide his limp. He saw Claire as she turned around to stand up and then he saw Caroline's face, her perfectly formed face with big eyes and a tiny nose. When she saw Zak she reached out her tiny arms and gurgled happily. There was his family alive and well.

"Hi, honey. Did you get them?" asked Claire. She had a red t-shirt on and green shorts with her hair pulled back in a headband. The tree was in bloom. It smelled like spring.

"Um, get what? Hi. God, you look beautiful." He was torn between taking his wife in and melting all over his baby.

"The tickets, silly. For the museum?" She didn't notice his face was slightly different.

"Oh, no, not yet. I will. I just need to look at the baby."

He sunk to his knees and began crying again. She was perfection. She looked like a perfect mix of her two parents. She had her mother's mouth but his eyes. Her little hands reached out to her daddy and he felt the strong urge to eat her entirely before she faded from his view so he could keep her safe inside him.

"Aw, she wants you to pick her up. You okay?" It was an emotional place after all. "Are you thinking about when Lenny and Cozy were here?"

Zak unbuckled the baby from the stroller and lifted her up, holding her tight. She was real. Caroline buried her face into her father's neck and he could feel the drool run down his collarbone. This is what he wanted. This moment. He didn't bother to answer. He looked up at the blue sky and listened to the baby talk in his ear.

"Oh, sorry. I was reading some the names over there and some were pregnant women and their unborn children are listed, too. It really got to me."

"Good lord. I can't even imagine. It's so horrible. How have their families been able to move on? It feels like it just happened."

"I really wish I knew the answer to that." He looked into Caroline's smiling face and kissed her cheek. Then he kissed it again. "I love you, little one. I love you so much. I'm so happy I got to see you today."

"Are you sure you're okay? We don't have to do this today. We can save it for another visit." She rubbed her hand on his back. He had forgotten that that was a thing she did and it felt better than he remembered. Another part of her that his memory had dismissed.

Then he looked across the plaza at the crowd lined up to visit the 9/11 memorial museum. He almost missed him in the throng. It was him. His doppelgänger in this parallel universe. There were two Zak Crisps. He was told he would know when it was time to go. This must be it. He hoped Zak 2 (or was he Zak 2?) would veer off, giving him a few more precious seconds but no such luck. He was headed towards the Survivor Tree and his family.

"Claire, take the baby. I'll be right back." And again he had to say goodbye with his eyes only.

"You sure are acting weird. Okay, don't be long. I need to nurse the baby soon."

He handed the baby to his parallel world wife and it twisted the bones in his arms. He felt like the phalanges in his fingers were pulling away from his hands as he let her go. Then he quickly stepped away and faded into crowd. He thought he might be choking as he saw himself falling into the black box at the center of the fountain, the foamy water covering his view of the blue New York sky.

When Zak woke up, he fumbled for the dream journal next to his bed and wrote: *I am bewitched by my own dreams. I must return to my family.*

Feeling invigorated that he had finally had the dream he wanted and needing to burn off the headache that came from polishing off the whiskey, he got up and made a fresh pot of coffee. The good beans this time, the dark espresso roast. There was a certain meditativeness of watching the water drip through the ground beans that had, through a complex maze of globalization, made their way to Portland from the hills of Ethiopia, and then fall into the pot, charged with the optimism of a new day.

He had seen his daughter! He held her and kissed her and was drooled on by her! Whatever happens he knew that they were there in a world where they were safe. That's where he needed to be. He felt his jaw balance as he connected to the person he was before. What a face she had! What would that face look like at sweet sixteen, or thoughtful thirty? What kind of personality would his not dead daughter have? Would she love the arts or be a gaming nerd? Would she be gay or straight or otherwise inclined? And what would she think of her professor father? The thought of the potential of her sent beams of light through Zak's eyes and filled up the room that existed in a world where she did not.

With a steaming cup in front of him he mustered the courage to pry open his laptop and check his inbox. It was 8 am, and like a police siren in a rearview window, glaring from the very top of the unread messages was an email from Abigail Williams.

Concerning the disposition of Professor Zachary Crisp

Christ. What would happen if he just deleted it? Would it all go away? Obviously she busted her ass to get it out before the faculty announcement about the union, so that meant bad news. Or maybe she was an early bird and wanted to dismiss the charges so Zak could get on teaching his Thursday classes without the cloud over his head. Exonerated!

The email could wait. He took his coffee back into his bedroom and climbed back between his sheets. When he was a kid he would hide from the monsters under his covers. It always worked. He pulled the covers over his head and thought of seeing

Claire and Caroline there on the plaza in New York. He was sure he would see them again away from his dream twin. Somehow. He had made it this far.

Claire looked so sexy in her casual gear. Another thing he had started to forget about. She didn't need any make-up to look hot. The curve of her lips, the sway of her breasts under a t-shirt. It was enough for him to develop tunnel vision whenever she came into the frame of his dreams. He slunk farther under the covers and decided to masturbate. But the faces of Abigail Williams and Kelly Claiborne kept getting in the way, haggard and pinched, preventing him from getting an erection.

"Fuck it," he said and threw the sheets off his head.

He took the kind of loud slurp from his coffee that would've annoyed the hell out Claire and read the email. He tried to blur his eyes so the words would be unclear and perhaps misread the news. But they were clear enough. Williams wanted him out the door *toute suite*, citing "overwhelming evidence" from Kiko and Stan Stipich, which was no real evidence at all. It was as if she had ignored every thing he had said and presented. The hearing was pointless. The goal was to remove him as quickly as possible. Now it would be up to the lawyers.

He set the coffee down on the table next to the laptop and tried to wake himself up. There was a glycerin feeling to the air that made him think this may not be occurring in a wakened state. But he could trace all his actions right up to that point. He tried to fly off the couch, right up to the ceiling, but he went nowhere.

After refreshing his browser he saw an email from Nevada. She had received a copy of the email and was ready to launch her three pronged response, waiting for Zak's authorization to turn the key. With shaking hands, he typed his response.

Bury them

2

He couldn't remember the last time he smoked a cigar, but Lenny had one hanging out of his mouth and it tasted like paste. He was at a wedding reception at the snack table but most of the

guests were boxy metallic robots, the kind from *The Jetsons*.
"Who got married?" he wondered. At the end of the table he saw
Julia Louis Dreyfus taking careful notes on a tomato she had
taken from a salad. Edith Bunker, from a 1970s episode of *All In
The Family*, asked him if he had a banana. A life-size Raggedy
Ann doll took the cigar from his mouth and walked out the door.

　　"Wait a minute. This is a dream!" said Lenny. Julia Louis-
Dreyfus wrote that down. He thought about what to do next.

　　He turned around and Cozy was standing there in a sleek
black party dress.

　　"Hey, Lenny. You wanted to talk to me?" She handed him
a cocktail that felt cold in his hand.

　　"Hi, Coze. Um, yeah. I've been thinking about how much
I miss Daniel and I was wondering if we could work something
out where he could spend next summer with me in Seattle. I can
get some time off work and maybe we could do a road trip or
something."

　　She made that "I'm impressed" face and smiled. "Wow,
this is a bit of turnaround for you. What happened?"

　　"I guess it's Zak. Seeing him so sad all the time about the
kid he never got to meet. I don't want to waste any more time
with Daniel. It's not like you guys are on a different planet." His
posture seemed to improve as he said it, even though he thought
she might be on another planet.

　　"I think I like *this* Lenny. Yeah, I'll ask him but I'm sure
he'd be up for it. Promise that you won't have a girl over at your
place every night. I'm trying to teach him to respect women."

　　"Promise."

　　Lenny looked out the window and saw the Raggedy Ann
doll leaning against a tree, smoking the cigar. She gave him a
thumbs up.

　　Lenny awoke to his phone buzzing on the coffee table next
to the couch. Naps were essential to his lifestyle. It was Zak.

　　"Hey, Professor. Any word?"

　　"Do you think your dad knows how to have an inmate
killed?"

　　"What? I don't doubt that he does. What's going on?"

Zak was quiet for a second. "They're firing me. I think it was that inmate that gave them the final nail in my coffin. He needs to die a painful death." He was steaming. He should know about the stages of grief by now.

"Have you talked to Nevada? I know she has a plan." Lenny tried to create an air of calm.

"Yeah, she's going after them. I'm not sure what good it will do. I won't be the first person to file a lawsuit against this university. They've got a ton of lawyers and other people's money to pay them with."

Lenny didn't know much about this legal field but Nevada seemed to know her shit.

Zak's frustration was clear. "Anyway, I think I'm going to hit myself on the head with a hammer and sleep for a while." Pause. "So, I got to hold Caroline." Pause.

"What? In a dream, right?"

The dagger of the email faded as Zak told of seeing Claire and Caroline at the 9/11 Memorial and how he wanted to eat his perfect child with a spoon. Then how the meeting was cut short when he saw himself coming through the crowd with no limp.

"That's the guy you need to kill," said Lenny.

Kiko called it the "I hate you" dance. It seemed her stares of contempt were starting to pay off. She made forty-two dollars at the lunch shift and another dancer who got her period asked her to cover her evening shift, six to eleven, allowing her to pay her stage fee for the week. There were even more men in need of her loathing as the night wore on. They might be there for the bean burgers, but she was going to give them the look anyway and slowly grind her hips in their direction. She was half iron magnet, half black widow. There was no room for mercy in this game.

She would tune out the AC/DC, Lil Wayne, or Def Leppard crap the DJ played. "Pour some sugar on me." Focus on the pathetic libido that would bring them into a dank place like this, willing to lay the money down. The angrier she got the more they coughed up; mindless ATMs who knew they needed a good kick in the crotch. This is what she had done to him and now she was the one making the money, not him. He was shit out of luck.

On her break, sitting at the bar and ignoring men, she watched the local news on the TV above the bar. The chyron said the faculty at her school had successfully voted to form a union. It was video of a press conference earlier in the day. She scanned the attendants, looking for her professor. The one that made her do this. "Probably off with some bimbo," she thought.

There was a cute older guy at the end of the bar giving her the eye. Short grey hair and vintage eyeglasses. Cute but whatever. Here's a guy she could fuck with for sport. Her anger at Zak was easily transferable to any man in her radius. She slid down the bar in his direction and batted her eyes, her make-up highlighting her as the Asian other. She was the exotic prize, Tokyo Rose lowering your defenses.

"Koneko, that's your name?" He asked, motioning to the bartender to get the dancer a drink. He didn't sound anything like Zak.

"It is to you," she replied.

"What part of Japan are you from?"

"Saigon," she said with a tired grin.

"Are you on a break? Wanna go outside and have a smoke?"

He seemed safe enough and maybe she could talk some money out of him with a sob story. He gave off the sugar daddy vibe so it was worth a try.

"Sure." She gulped her drink, grabbed her phone and headed to the rear exit of the Devil's House.

The rain was holding off at this particular moment of the evening and the pair found a spot under the floodlight where the man lit up a smoke.

"I'll give you a cigarette if you give me a blow job," he said.

"I don't smoke," said Kiko, feeling like she was worth more than one cigarette.

He laughed in a way that was not funny. "Then why did you come out here?"

"I don't know. I thought you might be interested in sponsoring me." She had no spiel worked up yet.

"What, for your promising career as a stripper? I don't think you understand how this works, honey." Suddenly he didn't look so cute.

"Sorry," she said and started to walk back into the club.

But he grabbed her arm, pulling her into the dark, the very dark dark. Then he pulled her top off and clutched her sweaty breast.

Kiko tried to fight him but was worried she would drop her phone so he managed to spin her around and push her face against the wall. When she heard his pants unzip she let out a scream that was lost among the roar of the trucks on the adjacent highway.

"Fuck it," he said. "You smell like shit" He shoved her to the ground and walked into the parking lot.

Kiko sat slumped against the wall and began to cry. Was this going to be her life now? Was she destined to go down on old men in parking lots for spare cigarettes? What had happened to her grand plan? And that's when the rain returned. Before she could pick herself up her phone beeped with a text. It was from her mother.

You are not who you are.

She wiped the rain off the screen and headed back inside for her next dance.

"Inmate! Wake up! You had a call!"

The guard was banging on Stan's metal door as he drifted in and out of sleep, the only real activity when you are in the shoe.

"What?" he said not deeming it worthy to raise his voice above a whisper.

"A lawyer called from Portland. She wants to interview you tomorrow regarding a professor you have been corresponding with. Do you consent to being interviewed? If so you will be delivered to a visitation room tomorrow for two hours."

Anything to get out of this box, he thought. "Sure. Why not?" Maybe he'd learn how deep his spear had impaled its target.

Zak did his best to put himself to sleep, but the coffee had a hammerlock on him. He could feel it pushing his heart around. He needed the twilight so he could find the portal back to Caroline and Claire. He put on Bowie's *Station To Station* album and opened up a folder of pictures from the baby shower. There was so much promise that day in the backyard. Little words of wisdom from friends and colleagues.

One of Claire's friends from the prison, who was almost unrecognizable out of her guard uniform, kept saying, "It goes by so fast. Remember every second. Smell your baby every chance you get." She kept telling them to smell the baby. And he finally did there in the plaza in New York.

Bowie chugged through the house, telling him to keep searching. It was too late to be late again. "I won't let the day pass without her," he said to the stars.

The Portland sky was filling up with rain. There's some liquid state between mist and downpour, like standing next to a open carwash with five hundred cars going through, one after another. If you live in Portland, you get used to it, but visitors think it's something to hide from. Or at least open umbrellas for.

He was standing outside his house staring at the front porch. It seemed identical to his home. Rose Jackson had put a sign in her yard that read, "Stop the demolition of Portland homes." There it was. There was the garbage can that he had recently hosed out. But there was a jogging stroller on the porch locked to the banister. This was not his house. At least not the one he lived in.

He looked up at the overcast sky. It all felt so right. But he noticed the rain had a slightly oily taste. Okay, close enough.

Zak contemplated waking in the front door and reclaiming his life. Bunny hop over the accident and the last year and pretend the whole thing had been a bad dream. He put his hand on the metal gate and felt it sway against the clasp.

That's when he came out. His other self. The one that hadn't been put through the greatest hell imaginable. The one who did not know what it was like to lose everything. That Zak didn't have stalker students and psychotic inmates biting his ass and constant reminders that his wife and child were dead. He had the life that was supposed to be Sad Zak's.

Happy Zak was carrying a bag of garbage. How domestic. But he stopped when he saw the sad version of himself standing at his gate and dropped the white bag. He looked back into the doorway like he was going to retreat into the house but then pulled the door closed behind him and walked toward the street.

Sad Zak froze. Would they explode if they shook hands, like matter meeting anti-matter?

Happy Zak was stoic and spoke calmly. "I know you. You've been in my dreams."

This surprised Sad Zak. Was he in somebody else's dream now?

"Oh, okay. Do you know who I am?" he asked.

"You're some twisted version of me, like a malformed clone."

"Gee, thanks. I was in a really horrible car crash, alright? I wasn't always like this." He stopped himself from saying that his pregnant Claire had been killed.

"Sorry, man. What do you want?" He fidgeted, looking back at the house.

"I want to know what it's like. What is being Caroline's dad like?"

Happy Zak perked up. "It's wonderful. Every day it's something new. Today she crawled out of the room by herself. Off on an adventure. It goes so fast. I try to take it all in. The cloud is about to fall down from all the pictures I take of her. Want to see some?"

"Zak? What are you doing?" Both men looked up to see two of the dream police on the sidewalk. One put his hand on Sad Zak's back. "I know what you're thinking but it's a bad idea. You don't want to upset the balance of the universe do you?"

What was he thinking? Oh, right, that there can only be one Zak Crisp in this world and it should be him.

"C'mon, buddy. Come with us." He pulled Sad Zak away from the gate. "Sorry about that," the cop said to Happy Zak, who seemed even more confused.

"That's hardly fair," said Sad Zak as his street faded to black.

The garbage truck smacking the plastic cans against the street woke Zak up. Fridays are usually a chance to sleep in anyway, and since there were no messages on his phone so he closed his eyes and went back to sleep.

He quickly fell into a dream about being on a huge escalator that was moving in the wrong direction. His legs would not move to race up it as it continued to carry him downward. They were like jelly legs. Nevada Standish appeared out of nowhere and handed him a Mason jar of blood which he poured over his white dress shirt. The blood gave him the power to float to the top of the escalator. At the top were lovely green hills and three of the four Teletubbies.

The phone vibrating off the nightstand took him away from his green pastures under the baby sun. Reality. That damn thing. It was getting annoying. Nevada.

"Zak. Get up. We've got some movement. I've got some good news for once." It sounded like they had been friends for years.

He looked at his phone and saw it was a little after ten. Who gets this kind of work done before ten, besides lawyers in the Army? He grunted.

"I've been on the phone with them all morning. I think the threat of going to the media scared them. I called your chair pretending that I was a reporter from OPB wanting a comment on the allegations and five minutes later I got a call from the school's lawyer!"

Zak was impressed by her creativity. It sounded like something Veronica Mars would do. "So what's the story?" he asked.

"I think they are going to agree to a limited sanction. They'll dock your pay for a quarter and you have to agree to never date any student in the university. Can you live with that?" She seemed eager to push the deal through.

Zak still had insurance money from the crash tucked away in his savings account that he hadn't really touched, so he could handle a skinny paycheck for three months. The not dating a student thing was a no-brainer. Never again. He was a fool not to see the red flags this time around.

"Yeah, that sounds okay. And then that's it? It will be over?" It sounded too good to be true.

"Yep. They'll probably want to put a Non-Disclosure Agreement in there so you can't discuss the terms of the deal. It's possible that they'll want to include an agreement that you are not going to sue them. Let me hammer out the details and I'll email you the draft. I was supposed to interview Stipich today, but this takes precedence. Maybe I can get out there tomorrow."

Zak was confused. "If we wrap this up today, why do you need to talk to him?"

"Well, this should be it, but there's still that chance that Kiko might try to press criminal charges. Better to get all the testimony now."

"Lord," Zak thought. "Will this nightmare ever truly be over?"

Kelly, Walt and Provost Sanders were having lunch at Bentley's, the upscale restaurant next to campus that was out of the faculty price range. It was a strategy session but Kelly had a dual agenda.

"I'd like this whole matter to be done by this afternoon. I don't want to be thinking about it this weekend," said Walt, once his beer arrived.

"I don't understand why we would let that man stay on campus," said Kelly, incredulous that all her hard work to take Zak down would be all for naught.

"I think faculty got the message," said Sanders. "Besides, they're getting their union. It might be better to cozy up to them now since we are going to 'collectively bargain' their next contract. We don't want to push them towards a strike. Now is the time to reel them back in. One big happy family, right Walt?"

"Right. Like I said, I think Crisp is a nice guy. He lost his wife. He doesn't need to lose his job, too."

"Well, I know a young girl that might disagree with that." Kelly was not ready to give up the crusade. "It's possible that she might charge him with rape. You're worried about media attention, but think about what it will look like if we knew he had a rapist professor and only slapped him on the wrist. The media is gonna love that."

The provost titled her head. "She has a good point, Walt. Maybe we should walk this offer back."

"We've looked at this very carefully. It doesn't really look like she has any case. They had a few drinks over dinner. The emails are pretty clear that she was sexually interested in him. I don't think the DA would touch it with a ten foot pole." Woodbine did have a law degree after all.

"Those emails were disgusting." As soon as Kelly said that she realized she might sound like a prude to her new paramour. "I don't understand the Japanese race."

"Okay, I need to run back to the office to see if anything has changed," said Provost Sanders, getting up from her half-eaten Cobb salad. "I'll let you know."

As she walked away, Walt put his hand on Kelly's lap. "Hey, how about we go have a drink tonight to celebrate?"

Kiko spent the afternoon writing a blog post. It was another one of her fictional tales about her life in the city. In this episode she had rescued a girl from being sexually assaulted by an old man. She wrote that she had seen a girl being dragged into a car on Market Street. After screaming at him to stop she slammed his car door shut on his leg and the girl escaped when the man fell to the ground. After she made sure the girl was safe she snapped a picture of the man as he yelled at her and sent it to the police. Apparently he was arrested within the hour and was a registered sex offender with a long history of offenses.

Within one hour of posting it, one reader commented below the piece, "Show us the picture you took! We want to see him!" For more than a second she considered posting a pic of her former professor.

"Man, be glad this thing will be all over soon," said Lenny through the FaceTime box on Zak's laptop. "I thought they were gonna wipe you off the map. I saw you standing on a corner with a sign. Will lecture for food."

"Yeah, I'd probably have to sell the house. I certainly couldn't afford this house in this neighborhood now. But I'd be screwed on the job market. Not a lot of openings for professors who have been fired in a sex scandal." Zak seemed resigned to signing whatever deal was put in front of him.

"Hey, you could finally open that record store you've always talked about. Vinyl is back, baby! Zak's Stacks. You can specialize in mopey music." It wasn't a bad idea. "Besides, you've got Miss Mollie. She's really into you for some weird reason. Go out with her and celebrate being done with this chapter. Besides, I have some cool news for you."

"Did you have a dream about being backstage at a Stones concert?"

"No, even cooler. I had a lucid dream about talking to Cozy about Daniel. I told her that I wanted him to spend the summer with me. Then I wake up and the phone is ringing, right? Get this. It's Cozy saying that she thinks Daniel should spend the summer in Seattle. Like, how did that happen? I told her in my dream what I wanted and then it was like real!"

"Or it's just a coincidence." Scientist Zak.

"No, she's never even mentioned it before. There was some weird link between the dream world and the waking world."

Zak wanted to believe this was possible even more now. "Well, anyway, I think that's great. You need to spend as much time with that kid as possible. Bring him down to Portland. You guys can visit me in my cardboard box under the Burnside Bridge."

"Shut up. Sign the deal with the devil and go back to work. It's that simple. You beat them, old man."

"I'm not even sure they're the enemy anymore. I think I'm my own worst enemy. It's like I don't have the basic skills to live in this world. It's gotten too complicated," said Zak in a moment of truth. "I would have made a good eighteenth century farmer. This world sucks. The trolls can have it."

Lenny had seen this vector before. "Back that ass up, Professor. Remember when I lost that job for posting that a co-worker was retarded? We are all pieces of shit. It's just the world has changed and the vultures are on your shit even before you've taken it. You know what I mean. You're less of a piece of shit than most people. You do important stuff. Get through this tunnel and it will all make a good story someday."

But Zak was already thinking of an escape plan.

In the end, after several versions of agreement zipped around, Zak signed the one that Nevada thought was the best possible deal. He agreed not to sue the university, not have a "romantic, amorous or sexual" relationship with any student at the university and to keep the details of the agreement confidential. If he violated any part of the contract he would be immediately removed from his position and banned from the campus. After signing it he scanned it and prepared to send the PDF to Nevada. But there was something on his shoulder urging him to not do it. He was signing away his autonomy. It didn't feel like a victory. It felt like a prison. It felt dirty.

Then he thought of his students and his research and the need to get back to work. To get back to something approaching normality. Maybe a new phase of his life could start. So he hit the send button and turned control over to them.

3

"I hope you're feeling a little more relaxed." Mollie and Zak had made a big night of it. She took him to her favorite Thai restaurant where they talked feverishly about seventies female singers and eighties films set in Portland. Then she took him to see her favorite DJ at the Failing Street Parlor. As the DJ mixed classic ska and African music with jazz fusion records they retired to a back room and made out. Zak's face finally felt even and whole as he pressed his cheek to hers.

"Let's go grab a nightcap," he said.

"The Sandy Shack?" The bar had been upgraded recently with a remodel and more top shelf liquor. The well-stocked jukebox had been replaced by one of those internet jukeboxes, devoid of personality, but there was still a no-tell motel across the street for drunken lovers equally unable to give consent.

There at The Sandy Shack bar the two enjoyed shots of whiskey and future dreams: a Falsies tour, a journal article about homeless ex-cons, a road trip to Vancouver, BC. Zak began to see that his grief might have a finish line.

"I gotta make some dough first. My student loan is about to bite me on my ass," Mollie said.

"When is it due?" Strangely they hadn't discussed her education. It was a topic Zak cared little about these days.

"I've been delaying it by taking online classes but I'm almost done. One more quarter and then I gotta pay the piper." It was the plague of a generation. Student loan debt was the great destroyer of dreams. The majority of students were paying more to banks than universities for their education, starting adulthood in a deep, dark hole.

"Hopefully your publishing deal will help out. Where are you taking classes?" Zak asked.

Mollie set down her drink. "You're school, Doctor. I thought I told you. Just some science classes I needed. God, I hate online classes. Half the time I get someone else to do my assignments. Don't tell the dean, okay?" she said with a wink.

Zak felt like his head had slammed against the bar, like he had passed out right there. But he was wide awake. "Jenny from the Block" was playing. Someone standing outside the door was vaping. The bartender had a CBGB's shirt on that was probably bought at Hot Topic. Mollie had a cross around her neck on a silver chain. His right hand tingled.

"You're a student at my school."

"Yeah, well, online at least. I've never even been on the campus. You should give me a tour sometime," she said with a smile as Zak's chest constricted.

As if in a dream, Zak saw a dark figure at the other end of the bar. He had to squint to see in the dim light, but then her face got the illumination of a PBR sign at just the right moment and it had to be her. Kelly Claiborne. Of all the gin joints in all the towns in all the world, she walks into this one. Zak didn't even think she drank, but there she was, cozy with some black man having a gay old time. Was she still spying on him?

"What are you looking at?" asked Mollie, seeing his focus had moved down the bar.

"One of the administrators who has been making my life hell getting shitfaced at the end of the bar."

Mollie turned to look, past all the shitfaced faces at the bar to the very end. "Her? Yuck. Who's that guy she's with?"

Zak put his hand over his face for fear of being recognized with a woman who was now off limits, according to the university sex police. He peered through his fingers and saw her with an arm around a large black man, kissing him on the cheek. When he turned to set his cocktail back on the bar Zak saw his profile. This had to be a scene from a movie.

"Holy shit. I don't believe it. That's Walt Woodbine, the president of the university!"

Mollie laughed. "Ten bucks says they are headed across the street to the motel. She's all over him!"

Zak put his hand down and resigned himself to the absurdity of the situation. "Lenny once told me, why go off half cocked when you can cock all the way?"

"Huh?"

"Excuse me, bartender? Will you send that couple at the end of the bar a round of drinks and tell them it's from me?"

Zak sat back and watched the drinks get delivered to Walt and Kelly. It was all worth it for the look on Kelly's face. Walt smiled and waved but Kelly turned ghost white. So much for "power dynamics" and "improper relationships." Zak was probably the last person she expected to see and her tryst had now diminished what victory she could claim. While Walt played friendly she simply nodded and pushed the free drink to the side.

"Oh, you're good," chuckled Mollie. "Here's my phone. Quick take a picture of me with them in the background. It might come in handy later."

"She's quick," he thought. Zak took her phone and snapped a pic of Mollie with a huge grin on her face, Walt and Kelly dimly lit in the background. It offset the fact that Kelly would be likely be reporting that he was already violating his agreement. The ink wasn't even dry on his signature and he was already dragging another coed into his alcohol driven sexual obsession. At least he had the weekend.

"Let's get out of here." Zak put a twenty on the bar and he and Mollie headed toward her car. They went to Zak's house and stayed up late listening to Roxy Music records. Zak told her how much he missed the daughter he never had but had held her in his dream. She told him he would have another chance to have children. Then when the last Side Two ended, they spent the rest of the night becoming romantic, amorous and sexual.

Stan waited for the transfer to the interview room that seemed to be delayed. He was so tired of being dicked around. A vehicle for other people's agendas. He needed to get out of that cell and tell his story to whomever. His story mattered. He mattered. If not to this lawyer then maybe a reporter. He needed to tell it before this isolation drove him completely mad.

Finally the electronic lock on his door clicked and it opened slightly. There would probably only be one guard to walk him over to the central wing where the interview rooms were as he wasn't known as a violent trouble maker. If he was a gang banger or head case he'd have no less than three guards, but he was a cell solider. On the other side of his door, he went with the flow.

It wasn't a CO that came to collect him. The CO surely unlocked the door, but it was Derek Stemphill and some other faceless skinhead that entered the cell. Before Stan had a chance to stand up, Stemphill shoved him into his bed and pushed a pillow against his face.

"You think you can hide from the Syndicate down here in the hole, fat boy? You've got no friends left in this joint."

Stemphill's voice was hushed and Stan knew what was coming next. The other skinhead held his legs down and Stemphill pulled his arm away from Stan's neck long enough to grab something from his pocket. The next sensation was both cold and warm. He could feel a bent piece of metal pierce his gut and turn sideways. Then a similar jab penetrated his thigh. And then the whole thing happened again and again. He was being stabbed with two shivs made from bed springs, the Aryan weapon of choice.

Stan didn't hear much after that, just the repeated thud of each jab and the squirting of his blood, the last thing he could claim as his own. He thought about his mother who had turned her back on him. He thought about the cold nights on the streets of Seattle. He thought about all the times he had thought that he wouldn't get out of this prison alive. Then he thought the blueish white lights were coming to protect him from any more pain. That it was about to end soon, the nightmare of his life. Maybe the next one would be better and he would die an old man in a feather bed next to a beautiful wife.

This life had been a waste and its closure was a welcome relief.

Mollie's face seemed so restful. Zak wished he could sleep like that. She had everything ahead of her. He had more drama. Claiborne would make sure of it. But if he was going to lose his career over a woman, at least it was one he actually had feelings for. The phone bleeped with a new text. He reached over Mollie to get it. It was from Robin.

I heard you signed a deal. Call me?

Zak was anxious for closure from all angles so he slipped out of bed and stepped into the nursery to call Robin and give her as much context as he could.

"Hey, yeah. It's done. Well, I think it's done. I can't do anything else."

"What did you agree to?" she asked.

The desire to tell the whole story was strong. "They made me sign a confidentiality agreement on the terms, which should tell you that they knew they were in the wrong. We were going to file a lawsuit and go to the media and I think they caved. They were ready to take everything away from me to make a point. To destroy a career that I'd like to think made a little bit of difference in the world. I'm not sure I'll ever be able to forgive them for that."

"To be honest, I think the admins focusing on you gave us the space to get the union vote through. Plus it pissed off a lot of faculty. So we owe you. You'll have a union to back you up now."

Zak didn't think it mattered much since the violation of his agreement was asleep in his bed. And his anger at the people who created this situation was still roiling his head. "So get this. I was out last night having drinks with a friend and who is in the bar but Kelly Claiborne."

"That lush!"

"And guess who she was there with. Walt Woodbine."

"No way! Were they drunk? I would have love to seen that. Probably planning on the next faculty member to target," said Robin, still in a defensive position.

"No, get this. She was all over him. It was some kind of romantic rendezvous. When she saw me, she about shit in her Depends." Kelly was no more than ten years older than Zak but in his mind she was a hundred.

Robin gasped at the news. "Okay, besides the fact that I just threw up in my mouth I'm about to laugh my ass off. Woodbine is banging some chick in Financial Aid who is like 22. It's not a huge secret. He's probably got plenty of action across campus. Too bad you didn't know that before your hearing. You could have dropped it right in her lap. Fucking hypocrites."

"Yeah, I'd like to have a time machine and go back a week and give her a lecture on inappropriate relationships in the workplace." Zak would replay his rewrite of the hearing over in his head many times.

"Well, that little tidbit might not help you, but I hope you don't mind if I tuck it into my back pocket." Robin's tone got more sympathetic. "Listen, I'm really sorry you had to go through this. You were the sacrificial lamb. You and a few other profs they went after. It was ugly but we're gonna have rights now we never had. And from this point on, their free reign of power is gonna be boxed in."

"If they don't replace us all with websites first. The provost wants to turn the whole place into the University of Phoenix." Zak was resigned to the fate that Provost Sanders had already proclaimed; that the university as we know it would be gone in fifty years.

"One battle at a time, my friend. I wanted to call and give you my support. I'll shoot you an email about our next meeting."

Zak didn't think he would be going to any union meetings any time soon.

Zak and Mollie spent the Saturday doing things young lovers do. They went for coffee in a café that doubled as a motorcycle shop. They went to All Day Music and looked at record albums from prog-rock bands and Zak tried to convince her of the importance of 10cc. Mollie said she would give them a try if he would listen to Perfect Pussy. Zak couldn't bring himself to tell her that every wonderful second they spent together inched him closer to the demolition of his life.

They went to Laurelhurst Park to watch the kids chase the ducks and Zak stepped away to take a call from Lenny.

"Hey, Professor. Just checking in on you. How did it go last night?"

"Well, we're at the park looking at ducks if that tells you anything." Zak wasn't one to kiss and tell but let's celebrate something positive for a change.

"Nicely done. Hey, I just got off the phone with Danny. We talked for an hour about outer space. He's really into it. Did you know they think there is life on one of the moons of Jupiter? Anyway, I'm going to make him a Bowie mix today. Maybe get him into a little space rock." Lenny seemed energized.

"That's great, Lenny. Long overdue. Glad you guys are reconnecting. He seems like a sweet kid." Zak said that without a pang of hurt for his own lost child. It was sincere. "I bet he loves talking to you about what he's into."

"And get this. Nevada is coming up to Seattle today. I think she likes me. She asked if I was free and said she was thinking of coming up and I said, 'Right on!' You don't mind, do you? I like the cut of her jib."

Zak laughed. "She is my lawyer not my girlfriend, Len. I don't mind. I think it would do you good to hang out with a classy broad like that. Maybe she could take you shopping."

"Hey, what's wrong with my style? If I can wear a t-shirt until it falls off, that's one less t-shirt kids in Bangladesh have to make. But I'll be cool. I don't want to wreck things when they seem to be finally going right. Maybe this is the dream. One long weird dream that we will wake up from someday." Lenny and his theories.

"I'm not sure if this is the dream I would choose if I was lucid. Anyway, I should get back to Mollie. It looks like she's being harassed by a drake." He saw a large duck following her like she had a pocket full of corn.

"I think the dream chooses you. Okay, tell Mollie I have a call with a pharmaceutical company on Monday that's looking for something 'punk' for their next ad campaign. And be happy it's all over. Later, skater!"

"Keep the dream alive, Lenny." Was it all over? Everything seemed like a gamble. All of it. The most basic happiness was a gamble.

Kiko didn't get the Saturday night shift like she hoped, which meant she was done by six. The Devil's House was in an industrial district, so she tried to change into her most nondescript street clothes before catching the bus home. A young woman dressed in stripper clothes standing in front of a strip club on a busy street clogged with long haul truckers was an invitation to harassment. The cops would eye her and the bros would throw shit. Even if she kept her head down at the bus stop someone would say something. "Hey, honey! How much for a hummer?"

So it helped to take some of those dirty tip dollars and get a large kicker of coffee to hide her face behind. There was a French Brothers Coffee kiosk across the street. Apparently it used to be one of those bikini barista stands but they had to close it down because all the eighteen-wheelers pulling in for their eyeful and caffeine blocked traffic on the usually busy street.

Since there was a VW Jetta at the window, Kiko had to stand behind the car and wait her turn, sucking up the exhaust fumes. Once she had her jug of coffee, she headed back towards the bus stop. The next bus would get her home in time to decide which of the guys who had slid her their number she might text tonight. More on her mind was working on her blog. She really wanted to turn it into a stripper blog, which was sure to send her mother into hysterics.

She took a big draw of coffee and was thinking about a new name for her blog, like *Just the Tip* or *Skin in the Game*, when a Peterbilt semi slammed on it's brakes ten feet from her. She was easy to miss, small, dressed in black, her hood up, and walking against the light. She didn't have much time to respond before the 50,000 pound truck slammed into her, first throwing her forward and then dragging her under the giant rig, snapping her neck like a piece of uncooked spaghetti.

She wasn't the first pedestrian struck and killed by a truck on that street but there never was much will to do anything about the problem. Maybe it was the class of people that were being mowed down. If they were West Hills types, they'd at least put in speed bumps. But Kiko was just another stripper with a hard luck story, so nobody much noticed.

Kelly didn't socialize with the people she worked with, other than Walt. But some of the women from the Human Resources department were having a "girls night out" at the Applebee's by the mall and she sort of invited herself along. She thought after a couple of rounds of watermelon margaritas or Sex on the Beaches tongues would loosen and she could get the gossip on faculty sex lives. And maybe any hint that her affair with President Woodbine was floating around water coolers. Not that that would be a bad thing.

She certainly got plenty of rumor mongering, but not what she hoped for. Apparently the president's dalliance wasn't just in the Admin building. When the story about Walt and the young woman in Financial Aid popped up, after much laughter, other stories about the good president emerged. "He grabbed my ass last week," said one woman. "What was I gonna do? He's a hunk. I'd give him a ride!" More laughter. Kelly got very quiet and then excused herself from the little party.

The drive home felt like it was in slow motion. The rain on her windshield was viscous, as if the windshield wipers were too weak to wipe it away. She wept at her folly. "All men are exactly alike," she repeated to herself. She could feel the skin on her upper arms sag as she tried to steer. By the time she got to her front door, dripping wet and fumbling for keys, she vowed to never give another man the time of day. Work then home, work then home to her sanctuary.

When she opened the door, her house was warm and there was likely something soothing on TV. A glass of wine, a throw pillow to clutch and her cats would help wall her off from the corrosive assault of the man's world. She threw her keys on the table and was happy to see one of her cats approach. But this one, the fluffy tabby hissed at her like she was an intruder. Two other cats came around the corner from the kitchen and hissed as well. What was going on? Suddenly a half dozen cats were surrounding her in her foyer, hissing wildly.

"What's going on guys? Are you hungry? Sorry I'm home late."

The tabby leaped at her, claws out, and struck Kelly's chest with the force of a tiger, knocking her backwards. She tripped on a another cat and fell to the floor. Like an organized hunting pack, all the cats began clawing and biting her, her ankles and neck. She screamed and tried to push them off, but they kept coming at her, sinking their teeth into her bloody hands. She looked up at the sign next to her coat rack that said, *God made cats so you could pet a tiger*. Maybe God made tigers so cats could shred people to bits. The last thing she saw was her dear tabby pull the jugular vein from her neck.

4

He was standing back in front of the house again, the one with the stroller on the porch. No rain today. The sky was blue with puffy clouds, the sky most people know from the beginning of *The Simpsons*, the TV show created by Portlander Matt Groening. When Zak first moved to Portland, he said, "Oh, the sky looks like *The Simpsons*." He was in the right place. Local hipsters were heading up to Alberta to get overpriced ice cream and shrug at how much the neighborhood had changed.

"Why don't you go inside and kiss that pretty wife?" Rose Jackson was weeding her flower bed.

"Hi, Rose. I think I will." He had no plan whatsoever. But then he saw Happy Zak on the side of the house in yard work clothes, washing out the kitchen compost bucket. He quietly opened the gate headed straight for him.

"You again! What do you want? What are you doing here?" Happy Zak seemed shocked to a standstill, seeing his limping double coming toward him.

"Keep your voice down. We need to talk. Come back here." Sad Zak grabbed Happy Zak by the shoulder and pulled him into the backyard. It was a much more manicured version of his backyard, with freshly planted flowers and an empty kiddie pool. Like Sad Zak, Happy Zak kept his garden tools in the corner of the back porch.

"I know what you want. You're here to take Claire and the baby away. I dreamt about it. But that's not going to happen," said Happy Zak, backing towards the porch.

"What are you talking about?" asked Sad Zak.

"I keep having a dream that I'm driving with them in the car and then they're gone. Just an empty carseat. And my face is fucked up like yours. Either I'm having a psychotic episode or you're here to try and take them from me."

Things started to come into focus for Sad Zak. This was it, the magic moment he prayed for but the toll would not be cheap. He reached for a shovel and used it to push Happy Zak to the ground. "I don't think this is a psychotic episode, my friend and I'm really sorry about that." And as his mirror image, who probably had all the exact same DNA he did, tried to get back up Sad Zak hit him in the neck as hard as he could, remembering to follow through on the swing.

Happy Zak wasn't ready to let go. He had too much to fight for; a life that was finally fully realized. He had his beautiful daughter inside the house. But he didn't know he was up against the version of himself that was losing that and more. And when you know what you've already lost and have one chance to get it back, there's no amount of resistance that can stop the momentum. So Sad Zak struck him again and again. He was killing himself and his hatred of every mistake he had made. A blow for driving under the falling boulder. A blow for letting Kiko into his life. A blow for trusting the administrators of his university. And the hardest blow for the hatred of himself, for surviving, each strike making him feel both heavier and lighter. With that last strike blood started pouring out of his twin's ear and the body grew limp. Before Happy Zak surrendered his consciousness he looked at his attacker for a moment, as if to say, "Take care of them."

When Zak realized his violent mission was complete, he fell to his knees on his back porch next to the clump that was the happy version of himself. What had he done? He was a teacher, not a homicidal maniac! But in that moment he saw a way to get his family back and acted without thinking. He needed a third Zak to tell him what the best option should have been. Now there he was dead in front of himself. How could this possibly work?

"Zachary, Zachary, my, my. Aren't you the violent little nightmare." It was the blonde dream cop with the other three standing behind him. "You've really made a mess of this."

"I told you he couldn't handle real dream travel," said the boyish-faced cop.

"I'm sorry. I acted on impulse. He has my life. Can you help me get rid of the body?" Zak asked, coming to his feet.

"You want us to become accomplices to your little dream crime?" said the blonde.

"Let's arrest him and sentence him to an eternity of Josh Groban music!" said the cop with the curly hair.

The four police huddled in the backyard and discussed their discretion in the matter. The blonde seemed to be in charge.

"Okay, Professor, we'll take care of the body." Two of the cops picked up dead Happy Zak and then faded into nothingness. Zak noticed he was now wearing the corpse's clothes, dirty jeans and a grey sweatshirt.

The blonde continued. "You can have his life and everything that comes with it, but here's the deal." He paused as Zak began to smile. "You live here now. You can't go back. And you are forever banned from any and all dreams. We can't risk another incident. So I hope this world is everything you want."

"Not a problem. Thank you, thank you. No more dreams." Zak thought it seemed like a fair trade.

Then the bizarre scene was shattered by a loud scream from the house. It was Claire. Had she seen what had happened?

"Alright, here's where you new life starts. Get in there, Zachary."

"And don't fuck it up," said the cop with the boyish-face. Then they were gone.

"Zak get in here!" Claire screamed.

The back door was the same but the steps up to the kitchen had been painted and there were baby toys on the floor. Sweet baby toys. Claire was in the kitchen in similar yard work clothes, jumping up and down like her hair was on fire. In her frenzy, she still looked radiant to Zak. He felt like he was doing a shot of heroin when he saw her but he was taking over this life in the middle of some serious crisis. Step in to your new reality, Zak.

"Claire! Good God, what's happening?" He remembered that he now had a child. "Where's Caroline?"

"She's in her crib. I probably woke her up." She tried to hold herself down. Her hand was shaking as she held a small piece of paper. "Baby, we got five numbers on last night's Megabucks ticket! I just checked! That's over three thousand dollars! One more number and it would have been nine million!" She was almost hyperventilating.

What better way to begin his new existence. Sorry, Happy Zak, there's a new Happy Zak in town. "Three thousand is a nice little payday," he said. "We should go out and celebrate tonight. I'm going to check on the baby." He gave his wife a hug. Over the last year he and his broken heart had fallen apart. Now that was playing in reverse and all the pieces were reassembling. "I love you more than you will ever know," he said to her.

"If I woke Caroline up we can go now and celebrate," she said as Zak made his way through his new baby-proofed house. "I'll look and see how much the pay out is. Of course Cosby will have to have his cut."

What? Okay. Small detail.

The nursery was not the collection of half-packed boxes stacked on a tear-stained rug. It was bright and cheerful, full of stuffed animals and cloth diapers. Caroline had pulled herself up in the crib and reached out to her daddy. She looked to be about nine-months old, which would make this world directly parallel to Zak's, except that he had missed a year of events. But he was here now and he lifted Caroline up into his arms.

"Hello, daughter. God, you're a beautiful little creature. I'm here now. I'm gonna give you everything. And your mama won a bunch of money!" Caroline cooed and gurgled and touched Zak's face and he marveled at how soft her hand was.

At that moment Zak heard a rumble and the house trembled. His first thought that he was being shook out of this dreamworld and all this was going to be ripped away again as punishment for the backyard murder. But when it stopped he thought it might have been a small earthquake. Not uncommon in the Northwest. Zak's house had a crack in the foundation from the big 1993 "spring break quake." Occasional tremors were a better deal than the endless tornadoes back in the South.

"Did you feel that?" asked Claire, coming into the room. "Second one today. So it's $3,190! We can go down to Salem tomorrow and pick it up!"

Zak was in the nursery with Claire and Caroline and he was not going to wake up. He was on top of the world and wanted to let it soak in. Lenny must've been right. Somehow he transported to a parallel world through a dream door. He was here. Now it was time to act like he had never not been here. As he was about to speak, he realized his right side was not aching. His face seemed balanced. Here there had never been the accident, which meant he never had been in the coma and suffered from the brain injury. He was as he was meant to be.

"That's a lot. Why don't we get dressed and go down to the Pearl District for dinner? The three of us," he said.

"Or we could get a babysitter and go to the Pearl and get wasted at a swanky bar. I'm calling in sick tomorrow."

That's what they used to do; occasionally get drunk in bars they had no business being in and then she would call in sick and he would teach hungover. But Zak had literally killed to be here. He wanted to soak his family in tonight.

"Can we do that after we get the check? I just want to be with you and the baby tonight. It's been sort of a hard week for me. Please?" He knew he could never tell her how he got there.

"Okay, baby. That sounds fine. Are you alright? You seem off. It's a good thing, I promise. We can pay off a few bills and maybe take a little trip. But I'm getting dressed up tonight, so you better take a shower. You're looking a little rough."

Zak spent the next hour walking from his/their bedroom to the bathroom to the nursery and finally the shower. Everything seemed like what it should look like back in his reality if the accident hadn't happened. Claire's toiletries were on the sink, her clothes on the floor and baby supplies that Zak didn't even recognize filled the nursery: wipes and diaper genies and such. While he stood in the shower he stared at his wife's shampoo bottle in sheer disbelief. He was here and he could care less what was going on in the other Portland. Maybe they thought he was taken in the hipster Rapture. Finally he toweled off and walked into the bedroom that was back to being "theirs."

"That was a long shower. Doing some deep cleaning?"

Zak would have remembered that Claire was a stickler for water conservation but he was stopped cold by the sight of his wife breastfeeding his daughter. Like the Da Vinci of Mary nursing Jesus the pair radiated life and tranquility. It was sensual without being sexual and Zak had to resist the overwhelming need to fall to his knees and thank the dream gods for bringing him to this spot of transcendence. Even if it existed inside some great snow globe that would be dropped on a concrete floor in ten minutes, it was all worth it for this communion.

"Well, don't just stare, doctor, get dressed. Don't worry, I'm having drinks tonight so you can have your feeding when we get home," she said with a wink.

Zak sat down next to her on the bed and kissed her cheek then cupped his hand around Caroline's head as she drank from her mother's breast. "I am so happy right now. You have no idea."

"We're pretty lucky," said Claire. "I'm pretty lucky. This love is pretty amazing."

"And this love came back to me," added Zak.

"Okay, Taylor Swift. Now if you stay wrapped in that towel much longer, we are not going to leave this house tonight."

Zak couldn't take his eyes off of Caroline's face. She seemed like such a content baby. He'd missed all the sleepless nights he had been warned about by his friends with kids. He missed the birth and all the firsts that come with a newborn, but he had this moment. He hoped the other Zak had been a doting father because he sure planned to be.

Quick plans were made to go to a Peruvian restaurant in the Pearl District. Caroline reminded him that she hadn't been across the river since the shooting at the school, making the occasion even more significant. By the time the family got out of the front door, dusk was creeping in and the blue sky to the east was turning purple. Zak was confused because there was no VW in the driveway or his Acura. He had grabbed a set of keys off his dresser that had his house and office key on the ring and pressed the button on the fob. Of course the beep that beeped was in a minivan. A Toyota Sienna was parked on the street in front of the house. Not exactly cool but who the fuck cares. He had a baby carrier with his child in his right hand, so everything else was a gift. Unfortunately he had never actually put a baby in a car before.

"Hey Claire, will you do me a favor? Will you put Caroline in the car? I forgot my wallet."

He ran back in the house. He had a wallet and promised to inspect its contents later. He needed a moment. He ran to the bathroom and looked at himself in the mirror. His face was his but totally unaffected by the accident which, in this timeline, had never happened. He moved his jaw around and then touched the mirror. Then he hesitantly tried, one last time, to push his fingers through the palm of his hand. Everything was solid. Solid. Solid.

As they headed into the city, the radio was aflutter with talk about the small earthquake and its epicenter south of the city. As was the ritual the jabber was about the "big one" and how Portland was overdue for a huge quake. One of the commentators said, "Portland is like a woman in the eight-and-a-half month of her pregnancy and that baby is already morbidly obese."

"Lord, Zak can we listen to some music?" Claire looked stunning in a red and black dress, her faux pearls and her brown hair down around her shoulders.

Zak fumbled with this new car radio and managed to make it to the "new rock" channel as Soundgarden's "Black Hole Sun" came on, happy to hear a familiar song. He looked in the rearview mirror to peek at his baby's face. Caroline's carseat faced the back of the car so there was a mirror in front of her that reflected into the rearview mirror. It made her seem like she was in another dimension. A reflection of a reflection of his daughter. He trusted that she was actually there and not another phantom in his dislodged mind.

As they came down the hill towards the Broadway Bridge into the city, Claire reached over to turn up the song and then put her left hand on Zak's thigh. He suddenly had a dejá vu feeling that shook the surface of his skin, from head to toe.

At that moment, he noticed that the cars ahead of him on the red iron bridge were hitting their brakes and skidding. It was another tremor. The tires of the minivan absorbed it at first but then the car began to buck.

"Whoa! This is a big one!" said Zak. "Hold on!"

Claire had a panicked look on her face. She tried to look back at the baby but the mirror in front of her face had swung away.

"Black hole sun, won't you come."

They were trapped on the bridge. People were honking and trying to get out of their cars. Zak, looked to his left and saw a cyclist bounce over the railing into the water. Farther down the Willamette River he saw the Steel Bridge that was over a hundred years old start to come apart. The Tri-Met train that crossed it was off its tracks, pushing cars into the river. The rumbling kept getting stronger.

"Zak!" screamed Caroline. "We've got to get out of here! The baby!!!'

Zak held the steering wheel and said nothing. He looked ahead at downtown Portland, so beautiful in the sunset. The whole skyline seemed to be swaying. He could see some of the big houses in the West Hills sliding off their moorings and crashing downward. The Bank Tower was swinging from side to side like a fir tree in a hurricane. The ancient clock tower at Union Station crumbled on to the train station below. This was how Portland's story ended.

There was a strange sense of calmness in Zak's heart. He got the cosmic joke. He was getting the chance he didn't get before. Caroline's mirror swung around giving him a quick glimpse of her face. She was smiling like she was being swung around by her daddy in the backyard. "Would you like to go to heaven tonight?" he thought as he saw her face in the mirrors.

"Hang my head, drown my fear."

The Broadway Bridge began to pull apart and half dozen cars ahead of them plunged into the river.

"Zak! Help us! We're going to die!" Claire undid her seatbelt and tried to climb back to release the baby but the shaking threw her forward. He knew their fate and he accepted it without any need to fight.

Zak felt a rolling sensation and then the floor of the bridge dropped a few feet. He noticed everything was moving in slow motion, like this planet was encased in molasses instead of oxygen. There were two young women in the car facing them clutching each other. A jogger with a stroller was trying in vain to get her child off the bridge when the railing fell away and all the cyclists and pedestrians went over the edge. There were huge explosions on both sides of the river. The Memorial Coliseum behind him caved in and the top deck of the Fremont Bridge to his left pancaked into the lower level and then crashed into the river. Ahead of him, construction cranes toppled in clouds of dust. So much for the new Portland.

"Black hole sun, won't you come."

He turned to look at Claire. Even in hysterics she was lovely. They weren't going to make it to dinner tonight, but at least he had this afternoon. He couldn't see Caroline but he had already said goodbye. A bag of baby toys spilled into the front seat as the deck of the Broadway Bridge began to tilt down and Zak could see the moving current of the Willamette in front of him, a rubber duck on the dashboard. There was a snap as Caroline's carseat broke loose and fell forward. Claire grabbed it before it broke through the windshield. She looked at sweet Caroline who was now softly crying and turned the seat toward her husband.

She was so beautiful. I'm glad I got to meet you my little wonder.

The half dozen cars that were on that part of the bridge simultaneously began to slide forward and a fall into the river. Let his family's death not be too painful, he hoped. The baby was in her carseat held tightly by Claire, mother and child.

The blackness of the water put an end to the horrible sights around him. The water was warmer than expected. "It must be summer," he thought.

"Whenever I want you, all I have to do is dream." (Everly Brothers)

Coda

"Hi Mr. and Mrs. Crisp. It's nice to see you again. I wish it wasn't for this." Cozy had moved back to Portland a month ago to bring her son closer to his father. It was nice to be back on the rain planet, but the twin hammer of autumn's growing darkness and the driving precip from a record-breaking Pineapple Express would bow even the hardiest Oregonian's back.

"I'm glad you've been here for him through this," said Mrs. Crisp. She was wearing a black dress even though it wasn't necessary. "I'm sure he's known it."

"I can't believe it's been a year." And that's all Mr. Crisp said.

Cozy took Zak's hand in hers and gave it a gentle stroke. He seemed ready.

The doctor came into the hospital room with the last forms to be signed and Zak's mother took the clipboard.

"I really appreciate you all coming across the country for this. I know it's difficult, but I think it means a lot that you're here," she said. It was one of the less common rituals in the medical field but there was still bedside manner even for the undead.

"Doctor, is there really no chance he can ever come out of this?" Mrs. Crisp asked. Zak was barely recognizable. Between the breathing apparatus and monitors and the frightening weight loss, he looked more like an alien than Lazarus.

"I'm afraid once a patient is declared brain dead, all hope of recovery is gone. We haven't had any brain activity in the last month. Once you switch off the breathing machine we can harvest his organs and hopefully save the lives of some very desperate people," she said. It wasn't an easy transition but it seemed to bring peace to families to be in the room when the plug was pulled.

Zak's parents were calm but Cozy burst into tears. Zak's father tried to pat her back but she moved back to Zak's side again. This should be a moment between him and his parents. But Cozy needed a chance for a last goodbye to an old friend. She sat on the bed and sang to him one last time. One last aria for the man who loved all music.

She chose "When I Am Laid In Earth," the seventeenth century Baroque piece by Henry Purcell. It was a simple send-off after a long year of holding a hopeful vigil that Zak would somehow survive the crash that took his wife and unborn daughter. The rain on the window sounded a soft ancient drumming for the rite of passage into the dark, as our beloved slip the surely bonds of this world.

When I am laid, am laid in earth, may my wrongs create
no trouble, no trouble in, in thy breast.
Remember me, but ah,
forget my fate.